CRYPTO SHRUGGED

BitPats Book One

J. LEE PORTER

ED TEJA

Nomadic Giant

Published by Nomadic Giant, LLC.
www.nomadicgiant.com

ISBN: 978-1-949063-00-4

The cover was designed by Elizabeth Mackey
www.elizabethmackeygraphics.com
And uses an illustration by Kira Poole

The interior design is by Domini Dragoone
www.dominidragoone.com

"Under the gold standard, a free banking system stands as the protector of an economy's stability and balanced growth. . . . The abandonment of the gold standard made it possible for the welfare statists to use the banking system as a means to an unlimited expansion of credit. . . . In the absence of the gold standard, there is no way to protect savings from confiscation through inflation."

—ALAN GREENSPAN
CHAIRMAN OF THE FEDERAL RESERVE OF THE
UNITED STATES (1987-2006)

FOREWORD

The book you are about to read and thoroughly enjoy is guaranteed to meet Orwell's criteria to be among "the best books." I suppose it's not a difficult hurdle to clear. Tell us what we already know and we'll call your book the best. So what is it about telling us what we already know that is so powerful? It is to illuminate that which we are afraid to face up to fully.

There is plenty of great literature out there that composes the list of classic books we want our kids to read before leaving high school because they illuminate some of the basics of the human experience. They have easy, obvious morals like, "always be honest," "don't judge others," "family comes first." But rarely do books like this stand out and make history. The books that drive movements must deal with issues much more pressing and difficult to tease out.

This book has the power to drive movement because of the uniquely relevant truths it illuminates: Cryptocurrency has the power to take down governments. Dark forces are actively working to control it. As always, people are willing to kill when large sums of money are at stake. It still pays to do the right thing most of the time.

I hope that this book succeeds—and not just because I have the honor of writing the foreword! I want this book to succeed because many people are only barely aware of these truths and having confidence in them inspires us to commit to their implications. As for those

barely aware of these truths, even someone with a cursory understanding of cryptos and governments has to know that there are vast
sums of money involved and cryptos are a fundamental threat to the
government money racket.

In this book, J. Lee Porter and Ed Teja masterfully paint the
picture of the forces behind the manipulation in a sinister, yet easily
believable way. Their expertise on the technical and political aspects
of launching a government-backed cryptocurrency gave me a much
more specific backdrop on which to play out the various possibilities
of where we are headed with cryptos.

This kind of storytelling gives me confidence in the conclusions
I had come to for myself when it comes to cryptos. The implications
are huge. I've been a Bitcoin user and enthusiast since 2012. I wish I
had been a more serious investor, but I spent all my $10 Bitcoins on
The Silk Road!

At the heart of this story is a bundle of truths wrapped up around
freedom, realized and affirmed in action by the protagonist, Wyatt
Osgood. Escape wage slavery if you want to be happy. You should
take risks and get what you want out of life. Do the right thing, even
if it seems risky. Do the right thing, especially when it seems risky. Be
open to new experiences. You can change the world. I want the world
to be shown these truths that we all fundamentally know already.

The technologies necessary to move humanity to a voluntary
society are already here. All that is missing is sufficient, deliberate
engagement with the new systems so as they render the old ones
laughably obsolete. This book promises to be a powerful inspiration
for such engagement, and I hope it inspires you to better live by these
truths, as it has inspired me.

—Adam Kokesh, 4/22/18
Ash Fork, AZ

Adam is a pragmatic Libertarian running for
President of the United States in 2020 with the goal of
peacefully, responsibly dissolving the federal government.
adam@thefreedomline.com

PART ONE

CREATING WEALTH,
DECREASING DEBT

"Bitcoin is an attempt to replace fiat currency and evade regulation and government intervention. I don't think that's going to be a success."

—BEN SHALOM BERNANKE
CHAIRMAN OF THE FEDERAL RESERVE FROM 2006 TO 2014

CHAPTER 1

A CURRENCY SOLUTION

"Bitcoin has made more institutions obsolete, in more
rapid fashion, than any invention in human history."

— ANDY HOFFMAN
PROPRIETOR OF CRYPTOGOLDCENTRAL.COM

OFFICE OF THE DEPUTY MINISTER OF FINANCE
MINISTRY OF FINANCE
DAR ES SALAAM, TANZANIA

Mitch Childer strode purposefully down the wide, marbled hallway, stopping at the end, just outside the carved wooden door to the office. There was a mirror there, hanging over a small marble table. It was a good one and he looked into it. He was checking the knot of his Turnbull & Asser silk tie and his attitude that showed on his face. After the flight from Zurich and the usual problems with the airline, both were somewhat askew.

That wouldn't do at all. Mitch Childer had an image to maintain. It worked well for him. He was known for being neat and tidy. If you were to try and capture Mitch Childer in a single word, you couldn't do any better than the word "precise."

His effectiveness in his job was certainly partly due to being good at what he did, but also from the way he instilled confidence, sometimes fear in the people he worked with. He was always perfectly congruent—his appearance and demeanor projected the exact same message, whatever that message might be.

Satisfied that he'd corrected both his appearance and attitude, brought them into powerful alignment, he was ready to go to work. In a few short moments, he would begin a process that promised to influence the entire world and Mitch Childer would accomplish that while making a man in power think that he, Mitch Childer, was agreeing to do him a favor.

The idea pleased him.

A glance at the Tank Louis Cartier watch his mentor had given him when he rose to his current position reassured him. The simple, yet elegant timepiece wasn't the most expensive watch in the world, not even $20,000 new, but this one had been owned by President John F. Kennedy and been gifted to his mentor. Now it was his. It was a wonderful piece of Swiss craftsmanship, and it was unfailingly accurate. With a single glance he was able to open the door to the room and step into the office confident that he was exactly three minutes late for his meeting. That was just late enough to show he was in command without being so late as to be obviously rude. It was a fine balance, and his command of it was as impeccable as his dress.

"Good morning, Deputy Minister Dola," he said. He kept his face businesslike, almost serene so that he masked his personal reactions to his surroundings. It was never helpful to let his distaste for an office like this one, or it's inhabitant, be apparent.

And both were distasteful to Mitch Childer in the extreme. The office was, at best, gauche. He understood the attempt, the intention, if not the result. This ornate office, and its furnishings, was intended to instill confidence, or intimidate supplicants, just as Mitch Childer used his appearance and demeanor. Unfortunately, the execution failed horribly. It was far too ostentatious to be either comfortable or awe-inspiring.

As for the man . . . the portly bureaucrat who sat behind the mahogany desk—Deputy Finance Minister Haki Dola—well, he was very much like his office. The congruency was ironic and amusing. Childer was certain that the decor pleased Deputy Finance Minister Dola and felt it suited him. Childer agreed with that.

Although they'd met only twice, Mitch Childer knew everything worth knowing about Haki Dola. Not that he cared about the man, but Deputy Finance Minister Dola was a necessary tool to accomplish his own goals—the group's goals. To do that, Mitch Childer could be polite and even respectful. If it hadn't been for that, he would never even talk to a man like Dola. Childer's analysis was that, as a person, Haki Dola was a waste of time and space.

From a professional point of view, it pleased him that he knew Dola far better than the man would've liked anyone to know him. His personal staff in Zurich, not the staff in Washington who served him in his official role, had compiled a thick, mostly dull, dossier on the man. They'd been thorough. After sifting through tons of information, some of which might prove useful levers if needed, they had boiled everything down into a rather sad summary: Deputy Finance Minister Haki Dola had a third-rate mind and he was a second-rate thief, but he had first-rate connections. That's how he had secured his current lofty position. That, in itself, was useful information.

"This is my assistant, Andwele Kassain," Dola said, indicating a trim and relatively dapper young black man who had been sitting in the chair across from him.

Mitch Childer knew far less about Kassain. He was an economist with a background in public policy. . . . and he was ambitious. Those things made him promising as an asset, and Childer's staff was collecting data on him now.

As Kassain stood and offered his hand, Mitch Childer noted that the man had decent manners. That was another point in his favor—a big point. When he took the man's hand and shook it, he was pleased by the sincere smile and firm handshake. Those things were superficial; they meant nothing of substance, but in his experience, paying attention to just such superficial things often decided success or failure in the world of finance and politics.

Haki Dola waved Childer into an uncomfortable leather chair. "Please be seated. We are delighted to have you here. Your insights into the good and bad of creating our own currency will be much appreciated."

Childer sat, noting that Kassain waited until he was seated before retaking his own chair. "You mean creating your own cryptocurrency," he said curtly.

Dola gave him an odd look. "I beg your pardon."

"You wanted to talk about crypto. You have a currency in circulation—the shilingi. It was introduced when your country abandoned the East African shilling in 1966."

"Yes, of course. Crypto. That's exactly what I meant," Dola said.

That Dola didn't bother getting terms right annoyed Childer. Finance, in his opinion, had to be dealt with precisely, the terminology correct. Sloppiness resulted in failure. "I just wanted to be clear," Childer said.

He studied the man's face, noting the pinched look. The minister didn't like being corrected. That was how bureaucrats were, but here and now, given that Mitch Childer was there on behalf of the International Monetary Fund, he held his anger in check. "Of course."

"And what will creating your own currency get you?" Childer asked. "Why bother?"

Dola looked shocked. "What will it get us? Why Tanzania is a poor country. Thirty-four percent of our people live in poverty, and youth unemployment is abysmal. Despite our booming economy, compared with other countries, the poor stay poor."

"That is, in part, due to poor and inadequate education. The UN report was rather clear. The students pass whether or not they do the work—you are not training a workforce for the future."

"Yes, yes. But, you see, we lack the funds. Instead of having the money to improve schools, we spend too much on financial transactions . . . wasting money on paying interest on old debt. And getting foreign investment, even with a growing economy, is difficult."

Even Dola knew that debt relief wasn't in the cards, not now. Childer directed the conversation on track. "Tell me how introducing crypto will reduce the financial costs. What are your biggest problems, the large obstacles to turning things around?" Childer asked. He already knew the answers—he was curious if the minister did.

The man looked nervous, clearly out of his depth. "Andwele, you speak this man's language—explain that to me."

Childer saw the young man draw himself up. Another good sign. He was prepared and confident. "One factor is the poor receipt of tax monies," Andwele said. "Currently there is a great deal of waste . . . of corruption."

"Andwele!" the deputy minister said, his voice harsh with anger.

"I apologize for being so blunt, but we gain nothing by sugar-coating the truth, Minister. We have a serious problem with corruption that the new system, the platform can resolve."

Dola's face was even darker. "Go on."

Kassain nodded. "You see the paper system is inefficient and it invites corruption. Businesses don't report sales. In a cash economy, there are no checks and balances. Even large businesses can get away with blatantly cheating."

"So business is part of the problem."

"It is. When the government sold off the state-owned businesses that the old socialist-style government mistakenly created, many went into the hands of powerful people. Because these men and women have friends in high places, it is hard to convince the tax authorities to audit them." A subtle nod of his head toward Dola made his point. "It can be hazardous to one's career to even suggest that they are doing anything wrong. So they don't report all the taxes they should pay. Naturally, the poorer people follow their example. Thus, the government is deprived of that revenue. It's the same for income tax. Companies hire workers and pay them with cash. That saves them payroll taxes, and the people don't even file, much less pay any tax. If, however, transactions are conducted through a blockchain that is properly implemented, we have the opportunity to collect the taxes at the instant they are due. The tax money streams in constantly, which means we have the use of it for longer as well."

"Why?" Childer asked. He wanted to see how firm a grasp the young man had of it.

"Consider this. We implement our digital currency, then a sale takes place in a small shop. Payment is made using a cell phone. If we use a well-designed blockchain to execute the exchange, not only does the shopkeeper get the payment instantly, but the sales tax is collected immediately as well. The shopkeeper is freed from the responsibility of reporting it as it is paid as part of the transaction—it goes directly into the government coffers. There is no opportunity to steal or accidentally miscount. Collections increase and so does the government's cash flow."

"That sounds well thought out."

Kassain looked pleased. "And that is just the start."

"It certainly is just the start," Childer thought. "Implementing the use of the blockchain will also prevent embarrassing incidents like the one in 2005 when an audit of the external arrears account found that the Bank of Tanzania lost 133 billion shilingi in dubious payments."

"That little mishap cost Mr. Ballali, the bank's governor, his job," Dola said.

"So it provides important safeguards," Childer said. "But it does take control away from the enterprises. Do you think your banks and businesses will adopt it willingly and not discourage its use?" Childer directed his question to Kassain. He liked the man's careful, organized thinking.

"I know they will. We've talked to them. It's a matter of offering some incentives," Kassain said. "First, if a business brings its transactions to our platform, then they will be offered a lower tax rate that reflects the savings to the government. If a bank works with us in getting their clients to adopt the platform, then they will be acting as full nodes."

"They get to mine the currency," Childer said.

"Exactly. The government and the banks will create new currency at a rate of 5 percent, so they share in that. Furthermore, that will become the only way to transact business with the government. All new government loans, for instance, will be made in the new currency and loan payments will be made through the platform."

"So they join or they can't play in the game?" Childer asked.

Kassain nodded. "Basically. And there are many other advantages to implementing e-Shilingi, which is the proposed name for the currency. We can go into them if you wish. Ultimately, the intention is to eliminate cash entirely."

Childer smiled. You bet your ass there are other advantages. And Kassain was clever enough to leave those out of this brief discussion. There was no sense getting too deep and confusing his boss. "You and I should have that discussion later, Mr. Kassain," he said.

"Then you approve?" Dola asked.

"Deputy Minister Dola, I will confess that I am impressed. You and your team seem to have thought this project through carefully."

"We do our best to serve the people," Dola said, nodding his head in a pretense of humility.

"From what I've heard so far, I think the International Monetary Fund will be delighted to support this project. The IMF can would begin work under the auspices of our existing Policy Support Instrument, the PSI. I recommend that my people work directly with Mr. Kassain and his team, as I'm sure you won't wish to get bogged down in the details."

The man rubbed his hands together. "The only remaining question . . ."

"Money?"

He nodded. "Is it possible that this support you mentioned could include funding?" Dola asked. His face was rigid as he tried to hide his anxiety.

Childer smiled. They'd finally gotten to the bottom line—the reason Dola was even at this meeting; the reason he'd asked Childer to come. As a sovereign state, Tanzania didn't need his permission to create a national cryptocurrency—but they did need his money. The country was deeply in debt.

Dola had been right about them spending too much on servicing debt. The IMF Policy Support Instrument intended to provide advice and consultation that would help the country figure out how to get back on its feet. It wasn't a way to give them money. But there were always ways. "I don't see why we can't convince the executive board that this deserves funding under the poverty reduction and growth facility. I'm sure I can convince those people to cooperate. Especially if my office was working closely with you, of course."

"Of course." Dola sat calmly now. The offer had been made, but he was a clever enough politician to wait to hear what strings were attached to the funding before he let himself get enthusiastic about his victory. "Can you tell me what that would entail? So I can report to the finance minister."

"I recommend that you consider bringing in outside financial tech people with experience in the payment system tech and other financial technology, as well as blockchain."

"We have good people," Kassain said. Childer could see he'd hurt the man's pride. That was another useful thing to know about him. "We have some who helped develop the Kenyan BitPesa system."

"I'm sure you do, and they will be key to this. Bringing in a consultancy like Hoenig Fintech gives you the knowledge of international banking technology. That will make things go easier and faster. And the IMF would be happier to share the costs if someone we knew approved of the overall plan." He grinned. "If you can accommodate this request, then I'm sure the executive board will be delighted to make use of the Rapid Credit Facility to get things started. We can forgive the debt when the project meets its first milestones."

Dola nodded. He understood that this was not optional. "Then that is what we shall do. How do we proceed?"

"I can call them for you, give them the benefit of our input," Childer said. "I can arrange for Claude Hoenig to personally call Mr. Kassain and discuss how to proceed." He gave Kassain a reassuring look. "Perhaps we can arrange a meeting where I can sit down with you and his team."

Dola rubbed his hands together. "Excellent. I do like things to be easier and faster," he said. "Time is of the essence."

Childer smiled. Elections were on the horizon. The government needed to show some dramatic progress. Dola looked at his assistant. "Kassain, this is good. You know as well as I that there is never any damage done by listening to an informed outside opinion."

Childer smiled at the way Dola managed to make it seem as if the consultant was his own idea. Let him. Kassain didn't seem as thrilled and Childer understood. Outsiders stepping in meant he had less control. Well, he'd come to appreciate what those outsiders would actually provide. For now, his objections didn't matter. Childer had taken away that choice.

"Yes, Deputy Minister," Kassain said.

So now it was done. The deal was signed, sealed, and delivered. Childer could hear Stevie Wonder singing the words. Despite his desire for a predictable and ordered world, soul music, the raucous, gorgeous music that came out of Motown, was Childer's vice. Well, one of his vices—the one he let people know about. Everyone had to have one, and it was foolish not to let one be obvious.

Dola beamed. "Well, then, I think, Mr. Childer, that everything seems settled. Kassain will work with you on developing the strategy, Mr. Childer. Andwele, I'll need a white paper on this to present to my boss, the minister of finance. He will want to report to the cabinet as soon as possible." Deputy Minister Dola stood up. "This has been an exceptional meeting, gentlemen."

"Yes it has been," Childer said.

As Dola waddled out of the room, he looked over Andwele Kassain, sizing him up. The man was revealing himself slowly. Childer saw that he would need to play to his pride of country. He needed to introduce a few suggestions on tools, parts of the platform that would make the new system better. Let him see how they, together, could help a people who, despite an annualized 4 percent improvement in economic conditions, couldn't drag themselves out of poverty. Although that wasn't the sum total of Childer's goals, if Tanzania succeeded that would be useful. If nothing else, it would please the IMF and cause other countries to use their system as a template and that would be . . . deliciously perfect.

"Mr. Childer," Kassain called. "I wanted to make you aware that my colleagues and I have already mapped out a fairly decent blueprint for implementation of the blockchain. It truly covers everything."

"That's a good starting point then."

"Starting point?"

"My concern is that you haven't considered all the angles, foreseen all the potential complications. When we get Hoenig's people involved, they will help with that."

His smile faded. He'd tried to preempt outsiders and failed. "How soon can we begin working?"

Childer put a hand on the younger man's shoulder. "Andwele, may I call you that?" The man nodded. "I'm of the school that says there is no time like the present. If you can recommend a decent restaurant, I'd like to buy you lunch and hear a summary of this blueprint. And if you have a copy sent to my hotel room, this evening I'll contact Hoenig's people so that we can get some valuable feedback on the work you've done. You will find them wonderful to work with. They will be happy to use every idea of yours that works."

"Excellent." A sudden resurgence of eagerness shone in the young man's eyes. Good. He was out to prove himself. That in itself would be useful.

"I've heard good things about the Serena Hotel," Andwele said. Their Serengeti Restaurant is famous for international and locally inspired cuisine. The best in Dar es Salaam."

Childer smiled. Locally inspired was hotel code for 'palatable for tourists.' "Excellent. If you can have someone get us a reservation and arrange a car . . ." Childer said. With the hardest task accomplished, he was feeling hungry.

"The deputy minister has a table there," Kassain said. "He'd want you to use it."

Childer smiled. "Excellent." He was certain the deputy minister would be happy to share other local resources as well. After lunch, he would see that Dola got a private message telling him exactly the sort of welcome he would like to find in his room. Tanzania had some beautiful women.

He sighed. All in all, it was turning into a very good day. The other members of his group, including the stupid nationalistic bastards that he had to deal with on the executive board of the IMF, would be pleased.

CHAPTER 2
AN INSIGHTFUL VIDEO

"Every society honors its live conformists and its dead troublemakers."

—MARSHALL MCLUHAN
FUTURIST WHO PREDICTED THE WORLD WIDE WEB
ALMOST THIRTY YEARS BEFORE IT WAS INVENTED.

CRYSTAL TOWERS APARTMENTS
CRYSTAL CITY, VIRGINIA, USA

Wyatt Osgood got up early. That was normal for him. Not that he was some early bird who wanted to catch more worms, just that he hated being rushed. He preferred to go at his own pace—especially in the morning. It was easier to get up early to give himself time to be lazy. All too soon he'd have to get in his car and head to the little tech park where he worked. Having this time for himself felt good. It was a self-indulgence.

The early morning habit had driven his girlfriend Janet nuts. Her routine was to shower the night before, lay everything out, sleep in until the last instant, dress hurriedly, and grab a coffee from a drive-through on the way to the office.

He got up, showered, and then put on his robe and went into the kitchen. While the coffee perked, he fried some eggs for his breakfast. As he often did, Wyatt took his breakfast and wandered into to his living room and turned on the computer. As it booted, he turned on the Bluetooth speakers carefully positioned in the corners of the room. As soon as the large flat screen came to life, he clicked on his browser, going to his favorite bookmark, opening the "Sindilux" video channel. If Sindi was on schedule, today she'd have a new video.

There it was—posted just a few hours before. He hit play and was treated to a shot of Sindi. She wore a bikini and was sitting at a table by a swimming pool.

"Hey guys, it's Sindi," the bright-eyed, petite black woman said. Her trademark Brazilian samba theme music played as the camera panned around a rather opulent pool area. "Today finds comfort-seeking Sindi in the old Tanzanian capital of Dar es Salaam. I'm here being pampered. How come you're sitting on your ass at home?" Then came her laugh and Wyatt thought it flowed like a waterfall.

The blue pool water sparkled amazingly. Beautiful dark-skinned waitresses carrying drinks circulated among mostly pale tourists in lounge chairs, but Wyatt waited to see Sindi again. Something about her intrigued him. He had no idea what it was. The things she liked made him think they had nothing in common at all. After all, she always stayed in high-end places, expensive, five-star hotels that had no appeal for him at all. Most of her video spouted the same pro-tourism propaganda that all these young travel bloggers dumped out. Total bullshit. Or mostly. She was often talking about the fancy and expensive food the places offered and things like that, which was . . . okay, a lot of them did that. Still, Wyatt was addicted to watching her videos. He chuckled. The truth was that he was addicted to Sindi.

Ironically, it had been his girlfriend Janet who got him to watch the videos in the first place. Beautiful, arrogant, recently departed from his life, Janet had been a fan. She'd liked the upmarket locales, the all-inclusive resorts, and the elegance Sindi displayed and promoted. Janet was always commenting, with a touch of jealousy, on the name brand clothes Sindi wore, or how lucky she was.

For Wyatt, well, he liked her videos despite those things.

Janet and Sindi had more in common than he did with either woman. So the breakup with Janet had been one of life's inevitabilities. It was no one's fault, and it was a long time coming. He accepted that. When he told Janet that he'd turned down the job offer from the Treasury Department, she exploded. She couldn't believe it.

"You turned down a plum job like that?"

He had. He didn't see it as a plum job at all. Who wanted to spend their lives reviewing technical regulations concerning cryptocurrency for the Federal Reserve?

PORTER & TEJA **//** 13

Janet thought he should, and his refusal had pushed their relationship right off the cliff.

"You don't have any interest in succeeding," she said as if that was
somehow a vile failing worthy of some great torment. "You aren't
even trying to get ahead in the world."

"Why bother?" he'd asked. That seemed to end any hope of further discussion. She thought he was putting her down when he was
just asking.

The thing was, when you got down to basics, Janet was right about
him. He didn't really want to get ahead any more than he wanted to fall
behind. In fact, those concepts seldom occurred to him, so he hadn't
seen his life in those terms until she exploded at him. Her accusation
dazed him at first, and he'd been defensive. It was, however, both accurate and true. Every syllable of it. He'd seldom done anything to get
ahead. The things he did were to enjoy life and part of that meant protecting his privacy. The job he'd been offered involved (among many
other tasks) doing things that would eliminate privacy, especially
that of financial transactions. Worse, a federal job meant agreeing to
extensive background checks and authorizing the government to pry
into his life. Not that he had much to hide—Wyatt considered himself
a pretty boring guy. He was a programmer, after all. A nerd.

More to the point, without ever giving it a great deal of thought,
Wyatt found himself drifting toward considering himself a libertarian. But he wasn't that political, so maybe he was more of a nerd with
a serious anti-authority ax to grind. Whatever it was, regulating
things that couldn't and shouldn't (in his opinion) be regulated was
not his idea of fun. Neither was a government job. And if it wasn't fun,
why do it?

Janet didn't think jobs should be fun. Or careers. They were
serious shit, dude. The fight made that rift between them all too
apparent. Luckily, the end came fast. Now both Janet and the job
offer were history.

He thought it ironic that what had brought him (and Janet) to this
fork in his life had all been because of a stupid little white paper he'd
written and published online. It wasn't a particularly insightful paper,
just one that addressed a way to solve a problem that people like
Wyatt, financial techs, or fintechs, as they were being called, dealt

with. No big deal. He'd come up with a clever (not at all brilliant) little piece of code he called "the benign regulator." In his mind, it solved all sorts of small headaches.

From the little they told him, the Treasury Department seemed to want to militarize it. Actually, they wanted him to do it for them. At least that's how it seemed to him. That's how he'd seen the job offer and that's why he walked away.

He had no intention of doing that, even if it was possible. No matter what it cost. Almost immediately, he was asked to pay the price for his ethics or politics or whatever it was—Janet left.

He turned his attention back to the video. She was done doing a slow motion panorama of the pool and Sindi herself came back into view. She flashed her wonderful smile and it went to his core. It seemed to be just for him. That was mind-game bullshit.. Sindi was an accomplished on-camera personality, but there was no doubt that even knowing it was bullshit, her smile turned him on. She was a hot little piece. Of course, since Janet moved out . . . well, Wyatt was feeling pretty randy.

That Sindi was perky and incredibly sexy was part of her draw—that's what got her the huge following, which is what got her free rooms at these lavish places. But he knew there was something to her appeal, more to the attraction of watching her videos. Sometimes he wondered if he watched them in the hope that he'd figure out just what it was.

On his screen, Sindi raised a tall glass with an umbrella in it and saluted her audience. She saluted him. "Folks, this is my view from a comfortable seat at the Island Trader Bar on the pool terrace. I'm at the Dar es Salaam Serena Hotel and this is what I see every single afternoon. I'm sitting here with a delicious mojito, fresh from this elegant bar." The camera panned to a scrumptious looking meal. "What you see here are some Tanzanian dishes from the hotel's fabulous Jahazi Seafood Restaurant. I'm lunching on nyama choma, which is a barbecued meat, along with wali wa nazi, a coconut rice. They also have mishkake, which is barbecued beef kabobs. For dinner tonight I'm tempted to try their duckling Dar es Salaam—it's a Tanzanian delicacy made from duckling cooked with tomatoes, red peppers, and onions." She took a sip of her drink. "Now that's my idea of sampling a culture."

She tasted her meal, taking delicate bites, and then smiled. "I'm definitely enjoying the food here, as well as the atmosphere. And if you think the hotel is nothing but a nice pool, good drinks, and great food, wait until I post my next video. I'm going to show you the crazy-assed room I've got here with a view of the city."

Wyatt was certain he would like to see her room—if she was in it. If they were alone in it. He sighed and forced his mind off of the idea of undressing the woman and grabbing that cute ass. He'd never get to work on time if he let his mind wander down that trail. He switched off the computer and shook his head. Something about that woman awakened a number of longings in him, and some of them had little or nothing to do with sex. Not that he knew what they were exactly. That was the trouble with longings. It was hard to pin down what the longing was for—precisely.

Taking the dishes into the kitchen, he put them in the dishwasher, then poured a second cup of coffee to sip while he got dressed. Not that it was a big deal, this dressing business—it didn't take much to put on jeans, a sweatshirt, socks, and shoes. The problem was that once he was dressed, it was time to go to the office.

That damn office. He was dying in that fucking hole.

It was time to go to work. Hoenig expected him to finish his project today. But then, Claude Hoenig wanted everything immediately. Wyatt sighed, knowing the scowl his news would earn him. Today he would have to disappoint Claude. That was never fun, so he promised himself he'd do it right away, before the office settled into its routine.

Sure he would.

CHAPTER 3
A PLIABLE ALLEGIANCE

"It is easier to forgive an enemy than to forgive a friend."

—WILLIAM BLAKE
ENGLISH POET, PAINTER, AND PRINTMAKER IN THE EIGHTEEN HUNDREDS

TERRACE BAR
THE DOLDER GRAND HOTEL
ZURICH, SWITZERLAND

At three in the afternoon, Greenwich Mean Time (GMT), which has been improved in some mystical way to Coordinated Universal Time (UTC), Peggy Anne Dory was smiling with pleasure. She felt like a million bucks. On top of the world. It was a damn good feeling, and she fully intended to wallow in it. It had been a long time coming and was worth savoring.

She sat on the lounge terrace of the bar at the Dolder Grand Hotel, looking out over Zurich, Switzerland, in amazement. She was absorbing a variety of firsts. It was her first trip to Europe. It was her first time in a five-star hotel and for the first time in her life, she felt that she was on the cusp of getting her due.

And she was waiting. Normally she hated waiting, but no . . . she was waiting for a meeting that would change her life.

The sight from the terrace pleased her, but not as much as the old-world elegance of the hotel. Not as much as the fact that she was here, staying in a goddamn hotel suite and traveling in the firstest of first class. "I could get used to this," she said. "You sure could," she agreed with herself. "I would thoroughly enjoy being among the muckiest of mucky mucks."

Sinking back in the plush leather seat of the booth, Peggy was pleased with the knowledge that this was the beginning. She was finally finding the fucking beginning of Peggy Anne Dory's rise to prominence. If she played her cards right, she'd be able to enjoy this kind of luxury more often. Hell, she'd make it the norm. The trick, the thing she had to do was, as always, decide on the best way to play the cards she'd been dealt. She'd finally found her way to the table, which was more than most people managed to do. Now she needed to step up her game.

And enjoy the process.

She watched the slim waiter who had taken her order walk smoothly to her table and carefully place the drink she'd ordered on a napkin in front of her—just so. The man had surprisingly rough hands for a waiter. Strong hands. She looked up at him, checking him out. He was in his twenties and not bad at all.

"*Hier sind sie, Fräulein,*" he said, then he caught himself and spoke again, this time in flawless, slightly accented English. "Here you are, miss. I hope you enjoy our saffron mojito . . . it's a signature drink of the hotel." She smiled at him, rather liking his thin face and even the scar on his cheek, near his ear. It made him look sexy.

"Thank you," she said, "Franz." His name was on a name tag. "I believe in trying new things." She let the words carry whatever meaning he wanted to read into them, and she pouted slightly as spoke. Then she took the straw between her fingers and poked it into the drink. He didn't rush off, but watched her, his eyes on her lips. She realized she had licked them. "Do you like them? These mojitos."

He smiled but said nothing. She looked into his eyes, letting him know she expected an answer. He blinked. "You see, I prefer Schnapps, or bourbon, myself. I'm not a cocktail drinker."

"I do see. You like a man's drink." He smiled and nodded. "So you haven't tried them?"

"No."

This was good. He was strong, but she was in control. Peggy liked strong men and she liked dominating them even more. She found something delicious in controlling a macho guy, even if the actual sex was the same. This waiter was lean but powerful, and, she estimated, educated. He didn't seem all that smart, but then if he was smart, he wouldn't be a fucking waiter. If he was smart and ambitious, even working in a five-star hotel would seem dreary. That much she was certain of. So Franz had possibilities. What she did with those possibilities would depend on how her meeting went. She had no real idea of what these people expected. She didn't even have a name. So she stayed fluid, prepared to keep her options open.

She held up a finger and he cocked his head. Certain he was watching her, she put her lips to the straw and took a long, sensual sip, then lifted her face, licking her lips. "It's good. Very flavorful. I find it a bit sweet, however."

"Such is the nature of those drinks," he said. "Can I bring you anything else?"

"Not now," she said, letting her blue eyes smile at him. If nothing else, she wanted to keep the man intrigued. Just in case. "I'm meeting someone shortly. Perhaps later." He nodded and backed away, heading toward other customers who had drifted in. She watched his ass as he walked away, delighted that the hotel had their waiters wear such tight pants.

If she hadn't been waiting for someone important . . . well, under the circumstances she would wait and see how things went. She was committed to making this meeting work, but if things didn't go well, or the man was unappealing . . .well, she was prepared to pursue her options. She could definitely see hanging around the bar for a while. Say, until the waiter got off duty.

She glanced at her phone, which sat next to her on the table. It was still a few minutes before they'd agreed to meet—she was impatient. The stakes were high.

Moments later the man she was waiting for walked into the bar. She'd never met him, but he looked exactly like the photo he'd sent—a short, dapper man in a goatee. He saw her and walked confidently, importantly, toward her table. Her sharp eyes took in the expensive suit and silk tie, the Italian leather shoes. They looked natural on him, not affected. Combined with his walk, these were good signs. Power and affluence were important to her, to the outcome of this meeting.

"Ms. Dory," he said as he slipped into the curved booth opposite her. She caught his gaze taking her in quickly, analyzing, measuring her just as carefully as she had measured him. Unconsciously, she pulled her shoulders back, emphasizing her ample breasts. In her experience, short men were especially fond of big breasts. Not that it made any sense, but it sure seemed that way. Not that this man was terribly short. Having seen him walk past the waiter on the way into the bar, she put him at five foot seven, maybe eight. The waiter had to be six feet.

A flicker in his eyes told her that this short man had noticed her breasts. For her purposes, that was good. It meant he probably wasn't gay. She liked gay men; her best friend in college had been a gay man, and maybe still was her best friend. But she was playing in the big leagues now, and in these games, she had no leverage with gay men. There was no way to work the sexual tension, implied (or real) seduction. It worked better with other women than it did with gay men.

Those were the facts of life. You had to roll with the punches.

"I trust your suite is satisfactory?" he asked.

That was an incredible understatement. "It's lovely."

"Excellent. And Mr. Hoenig . . ."

"My employer thinks I'm enjoying myself at an all-inclusive resort in Cancun," she said. "As we discussed."

"Excellent. Form matters." He put an envelope on the table.

"What is this?"

"Receipts from your trip to Mexico. I suggest you put some in the desk drawers in your office and leave some in your apartment."

"Why?"

"Corroboration."

"You think Claude would . . ."

"He is former CIA," the man said. "He is an exceptional man; however, I don't think trust is one of his strengths."

The thought startled her. She'd wondered about her boss being an ex-spook, but oddly enough, the idea that he'd spy on her hadn't occurred to her. Now it made her mouth dry. She raised a hand and caught the waiter's eye. "You should have a drink." He pursed his lips. She was sure he was about to tell her it was too early in the day. "Form matters and we are in a bar."

"Just so," he said. She heard approval.

As the waiter walked up, he looked at her companion and gave her a puzzled look. "What can I get you, sir? The lady is enjoying our saffron mojito."

The man looked at Peggy's mojito. "Certainly not something as gauche as that. How about a glass of your best brandy?"

"Excellent choice, sir."

"I'll have the same," Peggy said, pushing the mojito away.

When the waiter left, the man reached into the inside pocket of his jacket and pulled out an envelope. "These are the initial requirements for the modifications I require to the project." He put it on the table and pushed it over to her.

She looked at it, thinking it was smaller than she expected, and telling herself to be studied, not rushed.

"Can you tell me why all the secrecy? And why contact me? I'm sure Claude, my boss, would be happy to accommodate requests from the IMF."

"For my own reasons, I'd rather he didn't know, just as I set this meeting up so that he won't know about it."

She nodded. She was aware that this man, Mitch Childer, was a top official in the IMF. She'd thought he was proposing a side project for the IMF. Suddenly, she wasn't so sure. "So he knows about your involvement through the IMF—"

"And nothing more. That is why I'm offering a great deal of money—to ensure that he doesn't. That should be enough explanation to satisfy you."

She nodded. "Of course."

"Do this well, and I promise you many other projects of this type."

"What can you tell me about these requirements?"

He tipped his head. "I'm not a programmer. I'm barely technical, but these are some additions, adjustments you will make to the side-chain you'll develop. They are the core. We can't know what other changes will be needed until we have the complete specification and the work starts."

"Adding things, changing things later in a project is always more difficult and harder to conceal."

He nodded. "Just so. Which is why we are paying you a substantial amount of money. We intend to keep changes to the minimum; however, we must anticipate events or situations that will force us to adapt. Your job, your paycheck, depends on you accommodating those things."

"If it was easy, anyone could do it, right?"

He scowled. "I'm not sure . . ."

"It's just a saying. You obviously don't spend enough time in your office in America."

His face twisted into a sneer. "Washington DC is not my favorite place. I have a comfortable life here in Zurich, where it is civilized."

She took the envelope from the table, slipping it into her purse, which sat on the seat beside her. She'd examine it later. "I'll take care of it."

"You seem confident."

She smiled. She was quite sure the man knew that she'd been a serious hacker. He wouldn't have come to her without thinking she could work covertly and well. He sure wouldn't be paying her such a large amount—and in lovely Bitcoin that could never be traced to her. "I am. Claude, like you, doesn't get into project details—he has people like me to do that. If the code works, he wouldn't think to ask what else it might do."

"That sounds like the voice of experience."

The question caught her by surprise and made her wonder if he knew about some of the back doors she'd put into Hoenig's recent projects. Then she decided he didn't. "I know he doesn't spend time going over the code and wouldn't know if I'd changed things. So unless there is something incredibly large or a high volume of changes that delay things . . ."

"Nothing of the sort," he said. "We aren't interested in altering the project goals. We simply wish to add some subtle things that will enable us to monitor things and ensure that things go . . . smoothly."

With the discussion shifting into technology, Peggy was pleased to find herself able to go toe-to-toe with the man. He was clever and possibly dangerous. He didn't need to spell things out and didn't care too. That would make him a formidable ally or enemy. It was good to be on his side. He'd take her places.

As a man, however, she was disappointed in him. Although he had the regal bearing of a power broker, there wasn't any real life force in him. No personal juice or zest for life. That he was calculating and cold might make him great at his job, but he wasn't her cup of tea. And she could tell that his interest in her was limited to the role she'd play in his game.

He wouldn't want to fuck her. She'd expected more of a man's man. Not this machine.

Now she saw him studying her, analyzing her responses. She knew she needed to make him see that she understood what was going on, that she was a bigger, smarter player than he thought. "Look, clearly you intend to use Wyatt Osgood's benign regulator to make this happen," she said smiling. "That's why you want to use Hoenig's company."

The man sat up, alert now. "Is it that obvious?"

The waiter appeared with the brandy. He put the snifter in front of the man and watched curiously while he lifted it, swirled it around, and then inhaled the bouquet. The man looked at the waiter. "I suppose this is a reasonable brandy for everyday consumption," he said.

"I'll inform management of your displeasure," the waiter said.

As the waiter put one in front of her, she saw that his words pleased the man, and when the waiter left, he almost smiled. "It's true that Mr. Osgood's work is part of the equation," he said. "There is no one better to make the modifications. In addition, Hoenig Fintech has the credentials that will keep eyebrows from being raised when it's announced they've gotten the consulting contract. The final piece is your involvement—assuming, of course, that you really can run the project and control both Hoenig and Osgood."

"I'll run the project. But why do you need Wyatt? He already published his results. I have his code."

"I don't need Wyatt Osgood, but you might. As I understand it, his white paper describes a form of his benign regulator—a pathway for providing central control over an otherwise decentralized sidechain. However, he obviously hasn't considered all its possibilities, the things it can be modified to do."

"Those things wouldn't occur to him. He wouldn't want to do them."

The man sipped his brandy, then cupped the snifter in his hands. "When you see our requirements, you will see that he is needed to design and implement the modifications we have spelled out."

"That's easy enough. I have a handle on Wyatt." Her mind was racing. She was lying. Wyatt was unpredictable—a bit of a wildcard when it came to his attitude about the project. She'd have to fragment the tasks and somehow spoon-feed him problems to solve and keep him in the dark about the overall project. Then she'd have to incorporate the solutions into the overall framework and make it seamless. That would be a lot of work, but the rewards were incredible. She had plans that the man sitting across from her couldn't even imagine. Working for him was only an entrée, not the answer to her prayers. Once she got rolling, this first-class flight to Zurich, this hotel room. . . . were chump change. This was just the start.

The man stared. "My one concern in using this Mr. Osgood is that for all his talent, based on considerable research into his background, I'm convinced that it would be unfortunate if he were to understand what we are doing."

She smiled, picturing his outrage. "To put it mildly, he would object strenuously."

"And?"

"Don't worry. I'll see that he doesn't get the big picture."

"That will be an important part of what we are paying you for," he said.

"I'll handle him. And Hoenig will want him on the project too. I'll make certain Hoenig knows we will need Wyatt's help."

"He can't be on site, however."

"No?"

"He isn't an idiot and you can't watch him all the time. He'd talk to other people. Therefore, the contract is set up so that you are the only US programmer on the job. The work will be done by local staff who are competent but not interested in understanding the full project. We will take advantage of that indifference."

"It's easier to work with the team I know."

"And it would be harder to keep them in the dark." The man pursed his lips. "I want to be clear about something. While I'm certain the rewards of taking this job have been carefully spelled out for you, you also need to know the cost of failure. And failure comes if the project doesn't work properly or if these extra functions are made public."

She put her hands in her lap and focused on him. "I'm listening."

"In the unlikely case that these efforts are discovered, all tracks will have to be eliminated. There can be no links back to . . . the source of the modifications."

"Surely the IMF or World Bank . . ."

"Don't think so narrowly. There are forces involved that make the role the IMF is playing insignificant."

She nodded and swallowed. Suddenly, the man had raised the ante. Clearly, he represented the bigger forces he mentioned. For the first time, she wondered if she wasn't in over her head. He hadn't actually said anything concrete, but she knew more than a paycheck was at stake—her life had been threatened. The way he'd said it was more chilling than if he actually threatened to kill her. He probably knew that. He damn well knew it. That was the real reason he'd insisted on a face-to-face meeting. The rest could've been done over a secure telephone, but this little man, this confident fucking elf, as dried up as he was, wanted to impress her with the carrots he offered. Then he'd show her the big fucking stick he'd hit her with if she balked.

And she had to admit that it was damn effective. She might've been tempted to walk away but damn those carrots were yummy looking and Peggy Anne Dory was hungry. Besides, the project had gotten exciting. The adrenaline hit was wild. And erotic.

He dawdled briefly, watching her reaction. The threats and promises were real, tangible. Peggy Anne Dory was on the edge of a cliff and the idea made her catch her breath. Yet, Peggy made her decision long before she had this offer. She'd vowed that when a chance came up, when she saw an opening that would let her leapfrog up the social ladder, she would take it. No matter what.

Taking the job with Hoenig, going legit, or appearing to, had been a stopgap, a breather. Knowing who she was, he'd tracked her down and offered her serious money. Because of his connections, his background, the idea seemed exciting. It hadn't been. The work was routine. Sure, he'd demanded a lot from her and paid her well. But it was too fucking dull. As scary as it was, this was the best opportunity she'd ever seen. It could make her richer than Hoenig ever thought of being and would let her feel the rush of the extralegal, if not outright illegal.

The man took another sip of the brandy and scowled. "This swill really doesn't improve with warming. At least the waiter was polite about my complaint, even if he was lying." He stood. "I think we understand each other well, Ms. Dory. The hotel bill is paid and there is a reasonable amount of credit established for your meals. I recommend taking an hour to enjoy a massage at the Grand Spa. The masseuses are excellent. I'll pay for the drinks on my way out. Have a pleasant trip home. I'll expect to see you again soon, but when we meet, you won't know me. The next time we meet it will be the first time you've ever seen me."

"Understood," she said.

As he walked away, Peggy thought through things and felt her heart pound. It was really fucking happening. She was about to become a minor player in some very big plan and sensed that, even if they didn't exactly introduce themselves, she was working with some of the biggest players in the fucking world. That was so hot. So fucking hot. It deserved a celebration.

"Anything else, fräulein?" the waiter asked. She saw that her glass was empty. She didn't remember drinking it.

"My name's Peggy, Franz," she said.

"And was that truly Mitch Childer you were drinking with?"

She caught her breath.

He grinned. "He paid by credit card. And I know the name of the head of the International Monetary Fund. And I know he lives in Zurich."

"Is that who he is?" She liked playing ignorant, especially knowing that it made the meeting sound secret.

"You actually know him?" He looked impressed.

"We had some business to conduct." She was pleased to see that knowing the man had raised her in Franz's esteem. "You know what? I want another drink. This brandy isn't right for me either. And since you mentioned it, I'd like to try a Schnapps. Is there one you recommend?"

He smiled. "Kräuterlikör, Peggy. It is herbal, not fruit based."

"Then I'll try that."

"You'll like it." He lingered and she felt confident. "Some people sweeten it."

She saw that he didn't approve. "I'll try it straight."

"Excellent."

"I'd like something else as well." She let him see the question in her eyes.

"Something I can get you? Peanuts, perhaps."

"Something more personal." She looked at his crotch.

He smiled. "If it is something that can wait, I'd be happy to discuss it. My shift ends in an hour?"

"Oh, it can wait that long."

He smiled. "It's sad to see a woman sitting all alone."

"Sad?"

"Yes. If you were to go to your room now, I'd be happy to bring a bottle of Kräuterlikör up to you when my shift ends. Then you can explain what the something else you want is."

"What a gentleman."

He gave her a wicked smile. "Not really."

"I'm glad to hear that," she said. She wrote her room number on a napkin and handed it to him.

"That's one of the nicest suites in the hotel," he said.

"And even the nicest suite can be improved with the right company . . . and Schnapps."

In the elevator to her room, Peggy Anne Dory felt a rush that was due in part from the anticipation of a sexual adventure and partly from inhaling the heady scent of victory. The world was suddenly much more beautiful than she'd ever hoped it could be.

And who deserved it more than she did? Who was better equipped to fly so high?

CHAPTER 4

THE QUITTER

"Strategic quitting is the secret of successful organizations."

—SETH GODIN
AMERICAN AUTHOR AND FORMER DOT COM BUSINESS EXECUTIVE

FINTECH INDUSTRIAL PARK
CRYSTAL CITY, VIRGINIA, USA

Wyatt stared at his terminal, rubbed his beard, then stared at the gray fabric on the wall of his cubicle and let out a soft, gentle sigh. There wasn't an iota of contentment in that sigh. It was heavy with despair. Every time he tried to look at the code on his terminal his brain drifted off of it. He just couldn't focus. He was bored, unmotivated.

The neutral color of that divider seemed to sum up his entire existence in a single emotion—blah. He'd thought the damn fabric was ugly and depressing the first time he saw it, the day they installed the partitions that divided up the bullpen into pseudo offices. He'd hated it then and time hadn't mellowed his attitude or improved the way it looked. Even the tranquil picture of a sunset over a beach in Mexico that he'd stuck to it didn't offset the dullness or relieve the monotony. He tried to picture himself on that beach. What was it Sindi always said: "Today I'm on a beach in Mexico. How come you're sitting on your ass at home?"

He shook off the feeling of ennui and looked at the code on his screen again, trying to focus, angry with himself. Whatever he was missing would inevitably be blindingly obvious when he found it. All he had to do was follow the logic, pay attention. His brain refused to cooperate. He reached for his cola can but it was empty. He paused, rubbing his beard, trying to think and regroup. The fucking inoffensive gray wall stared back at him. He stared at his picture, tried to imagine the salt air on his face, but it eluded him. The dark mood, the web of frustration he was in had him trapped.

Also, he wanted a drink. Wyatt stared at the empty cola can on his desk. That wasn't what he wanted. It was one in the afternoon and he wanted a nice double shot of Maker's Mark bourbon. He wanted a drink in his hand—hard liquor; Kentucky Bourbon. He wanted to be sitting on that damn beach, not trying to imagine doing it.

In truth, he wanted to be anywhere but stuck in that damn cubicle with its neutral gray view of nothing.

He looked up, letting his eyes wander through the opening that passed for a door to his space. Across the room, he could see Claude Hoenig shuffling papers in his office. Claude owned the company—he was its founder and a he'd proven himself a successful businessman. An ex-CIA employee (in what capacity, Wyatt had no idea) and former honcho at some private intelligence firm, he was well connected . . . So he rated a corner office with real windows and a real door if he wanted it. Granted, the view was of the parking lot and the door was usually open, but Wyatt was still jealous. The door could be closed and he had a view.

Claude looked busy, but then he usually did. He was a whirlwind of activity, always hopping into DC for meetings. Wyatt wasn't sure what he did, but it brought in business with big name companies and government contractors. Claude was approachable, but employees had trouble getting meetings. If you wanted to talk to him, you had to grab the man when you saw him. At that moment, with Claude hovering at his desk, a hummingbird about to dart to the next feeder, Wyatt knew that if he didn't talk to him right now, he was going to blow a gasket.

Part of him also didn't want to talk to him. Chatting with Claude always gave him an opportunity to ask you to do something. There was always something he wanted from you that he hadn't mentioned before. Just one more thing for your to-do list. But he had to do it. He had to get off his ass and make change happen in his life.

After a long, anxious minute, Wyatt stood up. He walked across the narrow aisle and into the office. Claude looked up. "Hey Ozzie, what's happening? Have you finished with that routine already?" He sounded practically cheerful.

The question caught him off guard. It shouldn't have. "Done with the code? Not yet."

"How soon can we have it?"

Wyatt laughed. That was Claude's management style. Ask for an estimate then pretend to be incredibly hurt and disappointed if you didn't meet it as if it was a deadline. "I can't even guess. You know that. I'm chasing a bug and it's tedious shit. It takes as long as it takes. And the deadline is . . ."

"Screw the deadlines if I can have it now." Seeing the look Wyatt gave him, Claude shrugged. "I just thought I'd ask. It never hurts to ask, right? And you don't normally walk in here to shoot the shit so I thought you had some news."

"I do have some news, but not about the code. I came in to tell you that I'm quitting."

Claude's smile faded. "Quitting? Whoa there. I hate that word. Is it something I said? Did the work finally lose its luster? Did you get tired of playing with all those ones and zeros?"

"Nothing like that."

Claude twisted his head and then grinned. "You got another offer, right? I heard you got a call from some people at the Treasury Department." That surprised Wyatt. How did he know? "And here I thought it was just that you were cheating on your taxes, like everyone else."

"Nope. I didn't take another job, and you didn't insult me any more than usual. And, for the record, I still like coding." He was thinking as he talked, figuring out how to explain it. If Janet had been around, he would've talked it out with her, gotten to the core of it, but now it was coming to him as he explained it. "It's this office. I'm climbing the walls in that fucking cubicle."

"That's no problem."

"No?"

"You can have my office," Claude said. "I don't use it that much."

Wyatt watched his face, waiting for him to laugh at his own joke. The laugh didn't come. "You're serious?"

"When it comes to doing the work, you are more important than I am. I do my best work over lunch or on the phone. I don't need an office for that. I can work out of my car."

Wyatt toyed with the idea, looking around, imagining himself working in there. "I appreciate the offer. It's nicer, but basically it's still the same office. The same daily commute. The same office stink."

"Hmm. Let's work on that."

Wyatt reeled. Claude was a manipulator but he never expected this sort of sincere concern for his well-being. "I don't think the problem can be fixed by rearranging the furniture. I'm in a rut. My entire life sucks."

"Can't help you with that part. I'm told there's no app for that."

"You could fire me." He smiled. "Then I'd get unemployment."

"Fire you? Then what?" He waved an arm. "You think these other people want to do all your coding? What do you think I underpay you for?"

Wyatt thought for a moment, realizing for the first time that this hatred of the office had been smoldering for years. The excitement of the work, especially as they did cutting-edge stuff, was still there. The thought of actually being cut off from it made him shudder. It was going to the office—the routines, the rituals, the banality of being an office drone. "I need to get out of here."

Claude turned to face him squarely, then sank into his leather chair. "Maybe we can do that."

"What?"

"You still want to work, right? You need a purpose."

He knew Claude was a Christian—a conservative with a strong work ethic. That was one of the few commonalities, one of the things that let them get along. "You know I do. Even if I didn't want to work, I have to. You know I can't just sit around. Don't play stupid."

"Who's playing? I am stupid. If I were smart I would've learned to do coding myself. Think of the money I'd save." He touched his cheek. "But let's put our heads together and think this through . . . the outcome you want . . . you just want to be out of here . . . this place, not the company."

"Yeah," Wyatt said. "That pretty much sums it up."

"I might have an idea."

Wyatt's heart pounded. The man was serious about this. "How?"

"Two possibilities. What would you think about moving to Belarus?"

Wyatt laughed, then realized the man was serious. "I have no idea. First, I'd have to find it on the map."

"It's a country—in Eastern Europe. I'm opening an office there. It will be our new HQ."

"Why?"

He ticked his answers off on his fingers. "One, because they've legalized cryptocurrency; two, they are offering a five-year tax break on income earned in crypto and on the tax on capital gains from investing in it." He grinned. "And I hear they have really nice beaches."

"That sounds perfect. I imagine that for the two months a year it isn't frozen solid it would be a paradise."

"Okay, that was a long shot. I know an office there would still be an office. So what if you worked for me freelance?"

"You mean, I wouldn't be an employee?"

"Nope. You'd be an independent contractor." He picked up a pen and tapped his cheek with it, thinking. "Let's brainstorm, see how that would work . . . I'd have you use an encrypted laptop to do the work on." Claude gave him a meaningful look. "We need to think about security."

That made sense. Their clients had proprietary data, and they had to ensure the code was secure. "You'd have to use our encrypted platform for any communications using the laptop—and it remains company property."

"Right."

"And I'd pay you a little less and you would work at home."

The way things had gone, money wasn't an issue. The work would be wonderful, and some cash flow would be good. The important thing was the lifestyle. He had to be out of the office.

Wyatt let himself picture it, saw himself at home on his couch with his beach picture showing on his television set instead of the gray wall. It was a major improvement. Except for one thing. "I'm sick of living here too. I'm tired of this city."

"You said . . ."

"That I want to work at home. I know. I just realized that I'm also sick of my apartment."

Claude shrugged. "Then you can move somewhere else. You don't need to come in but every now and then for meetings. So I don't care where you live as long as you write the code I need and get it in on time."

Wyatt felt his pulse race. He hoped Claude was serious. "How about Italy? That okay?"

He snorted. "Fine. Send me a pizza now and then and don't go entirely off our grid. I don't care about anyone else's grid."

"I can do that."

"To fund that . . . well, there is a project that would make this all possible. It could take us to the next level, which would be good for you and me. But I need your help."

"Shit, Claude." He sighed. "What?"

"I'm pitching some big, really big new business. It's pretty much in the bag."

"Government?"

"Working on a project for another government."

"Does this involve your spook pals? I don't need that."

"Not them. This is something we'd be doing to make our bones with the International Monetary Fund."

Wyatt considered it. He had mixed feelings about the one-world organizations. "They are just another form of the CIA."

"Except, as I understand things, they don't usually kill people."

Wyatt broke out laughing. "Fair point."

"This paper you wrote that got the Treasury folks trying to recruit you apparently has worked up some people at the IMF. Peggy is working on the specs for our pitch and putting together our quote."

"Peggy?"

Claude Hoenig looked at Wyatt steadily. "Unless you want to run a project. . . ."

"No way."

"Then she'll run the team. But we need you for support. I need you to go with us, Peggy and I, to a meeting with the principals."

"To lunch?"

"Dinner, probably. The thing is it's in Zurich."

"Switzerland?"

"Christ, are there others? I sure hope they meant Switzerland. I assumed they meant that one."

"Don't worry. I think that's the only one. But why Zurich? This isn't a project for the Swiss government, is it?"

"No. Zurich is just where the project definition meeting is being held. I'm told it's more convenient for us all, including the IMF guy, to meet there than in Dar es Salaam. That's a city in Tanzania. In Africa, in case you were wondering."

Wyatt turned over what he knew about Africa. There wasn't much substance to any of it. He'd read Beryl Markham and other stuff and seen movies. "I'm not really keen on the idea of going to Africa right now."

"You only need to go to Zurich and show that the project will be blessed with your presence. Peggy will be there too. We meet the principles, plan the project with a broad brush and, when Peggy tells you what to start on, you go home. Or Italy. Or wherever. That's up to you."

"You expect me to play nice with the IMF? Me?"

"Yup. That's the deal," Claude said. "You go to this meeting, be nice, and promise to write the code Peggy needs. In return, I'll pay to fly you anywhere in the world. Close up shop here and go right from Zurich. I'll pop for first-class tickets."

Wyatt juggled ideas, conflicting emotions. His impulse was to head to a beach in Mexico. Even if that didn't work out, that was the fantasy. Why not start there? "So I go to this meeting and help sell us. Then I get an assignment, some code to write, and go wherever I want on your dime?"

"On many, many of my dimes. And wherever you are, you write the code."

"Why do I need to go to this meeting? You've never included me before."

Claude looked at him. "You know, the urge to bullshit you on this point is incredibly strong right now, but here's the story. We would be in the running for this anyway, but the paper you published convinced some powerful, not necessarily smart, people that you have the chops to pull this off. They think having you consulting on the project is safer than having other people do it. I managed to reinforce that idea. It's our edge. And this gig will finance your ability to work wherever you like."

"So am I your trained innovator?"

"Not too innovative. Real innovation might scare the shit out of them. I need you to be the clever, but cautious, guy who will be their salvation. All they want is to use your idea in their project. With your help."

"And after the meeting I work where I want?"

"That's the deal. You've got a few days to get ready. Got a passport?"

"Yup. Can you give Charlie the task of finishing my routine? I'll use the time to jot down some new thoughts on my clever code that you are selling and wrap things up here."

Claude smiled. "You've always hated Charlie."

Wyatt happily pictured Charlie's fat face when he heard he was getting loaded with extra work. "Damn right."

"Fine."

"I do need to think about it."

Claude stared. "What's to think about?"

"The whole thing. I'm still wondering if maybe I'd be better off quitting. If I quit, I can go where I want—not get dragged to some boring meeting in Zurich."

Claude grinned. "Except that you are dying to find out what this project is all about. I intend to leave next Wednesday. I'll have human resources do the paperwork and send it to your place for you to sign."

"And Peggy's running the project?"

"Right. I'll have her get you the travel information—where to be and when."

"Some information on the project might be nice too. If I'm supposed to sound like I know what I'm doing at this meeting, some idea of what kind of code I'll be writing would be helpful."

Claude held out his hand. "Peggy will give you a complete briefing on the flight over. We will all be crammed in that little tin tube for a long time; we might as well make the hours productive."

Wyatt sighed. He preferred looking at the specs, coming to his own ideas honestly, but he wasn't going to win this one. He took Claude's hand and shook it. "Fine. We probably have a deal. Possibly."

Claude grinned. "I love it when two reasonable men can get together and work things out." He patted Wyatt's shoulder. "Seriously, this idea will work out brilliantly for us both. You keep the code coming, and I'll keep the money coming."

"Sent directly to my account?"

"Sent directly to the North Pole if that's what you want. What do I care where the money goes as long as you are happy?"

Wyatt let himself get cranked up. The truth was, he was excited. "I'm pretty sure I'll take you up on this, but I do need to think about it. I need time away from your salesmanship."

"Then let's do this. Here and now, I'm going to fire you. Then I'll offer you this contract. When the contract arrives at your place tomorrow, you read it. As soon as you've read it, call me and tell me what you've decided. The details will be negotiable, but not the substance. Either I replace you, my employee, with you as my new contractor, or I'll need to hire some pimply kid fresh out of MIT to do the work."

Wyatt grinned. He didn't like a lot about Claude, and given his background, the fact that he'd been a spy for a lot of years, and who knew what else, made it hard to trust him entirely, but for some crazy reason, he liked the man. Claude Hoenig didn't agree with him, but he always respected what he said, and, from what he could tell, the man was true to his principles. "Deal. I'll go clean out my cubicle."

Claude laughed. "Really? Then you better set aside at least ten minutes for that project. All you've ever put in it is that picture of the beach."

"That will take a considerable amount time. It has to be folded very carefully."

"If this works, you can take your own fucking beach photo."

Wyatt smiled. That was true. He would definitely take his own pictures. Then, as he headed out the door, he was suddenly overwhelmed by a giant rush of suspicion. "You had this planned, didn't you?"

Claude laughed. "I've seen you mooning at the picture. And honestly, your focus has been off lately. I've seen it before. Once a guy like you gets fidgety, he's gonna leave. This way, I get you working for me longer. For a time, at least, I figure you will love the new deal and write code even faster, even if it's just so you have more time for whatever it is you want to do."

"I have no idea what I want to do. Or where I want to do it. I just need out of this damn office."

"Then get out of my sight. After this meeting, when you are in the wind, I'll expect you to log in regularly."

Wyatt's stomach knotted. "And tell you where I am?"

He laughed. "I don't care where you go. I want to know you are thinking of me and measuring your love for me in lines of code."

"That's my kind of boss."

"I'm not your boss. You are an unemployed freelance bum taking advantage of my Christian charity." He stepped to the door of his office and caught the attention of a passing woman. "Karen, I have a job for you."

She frowned. "You think I have nothing to do?"

"I just fired Ozballs, here. Make it official."

She poked her head in the door. "Congratulations, Wyatt. How did you do that? What can I do to get myself fired?"

"You're the human resources person," Wyatt said.

She grinned. "Awful, isn't it? I set a terrible example."

Claude snorted. "Just do the paperwork to fire him. Then do the goddamn paperwork that puts him under contract as a freelancer. Don't give him any benefits. He'll tell you where to send his base salary."

"I suppose you think that's a priority job," the chubby woman shouted back.

"Damn right. I want it, so it's priority."

"That figures."

"This is my company, Karen. I'm the boss."

"So you keep telling me," she snorted. "I'm not always sure."

Wyatt was still taking it in, wondering if it was really happening. He'd walked into the office and asked for something. . . . and gotten it. Business people were strange and Claude was among the strangest. He saw the man looking at him. "I'm going to miss you," Wyatt said.

"Not if you don't leave. You can't miss anyone if you don't leave."

"Why so eager to get rid of me?"

"Why drag it out? If I let you hang around here, some of the others are gonna want the same thing. Better they think I fired you and that's the end of it. Just don't make it the end of things. Call me tomorrow when you read the contract and tell me that I'm far too kind and you want to work for me forever."

"We'll see. I'll go clean out my desk."

"Take the damn desk with you if you want it. Or I can ship it to you."

"No, I just want the paper clips I've stolen over the years. I intend to travel light."

He held up his hands. "Don't tell me any more than that. I don't want to know where you are going or who you are doing. It's better if I don't know."

"Why?"

"Because if I knew you were out of the country, on a beach, for example, it might complicate my deals and make clients wonder if I have control over you. So I'm happy to be misled and to think you are squirreled away just down the street in that sleazy apartment of yours, busily cranking out code."

"It isn't so sleazy, Claude. It isn't even particularly cheap. It's just. . . . nothing at all. A convenient box to exist in, like my cubicle."

"So go find a nicer box. A box in a nicer place. This town stinks of the Pentagon next door and that annoys you."

Wyatt felt a weight lifted off his shoulders. "You are right. I think I'll do exactly that." As he walked out of his office, he thought about the things in his desk. There was a coffee mug with 'Don't tread on me' emblazoned across it in a godawful comic font, an ancient thermos, a notebook with indecipherable notes in it, and not much else except some batteries for a watch that broke last year. Or were they from an old camera? He couldn't remember.

He carefully took down the beach picture. It was one he'd ripped out of a travel magazine. The beach was lovely and there were pretty girls in skimpy bikinis and thongs walking all over the place. It was a pretty beach with lovely girls. Even if the girls were models, it looked like a far better place to be this coming winter than here in Virginia. A guy could code on a beach like that. He could have a drink when he wanted one. He would be free.

CHAPTER 5
DOUBTS AND MISGIVINGS

"Nobody ever launched an attack without having misgivings beforehand, You ought to have misgivings before; but when the moment of action is come, the hour of misgivings is passed. It is often not possible to go backward from a course which has been adopted in war. A man must answer Aye or No to the great questions which are put, and by that decision he must be bound."

—WINSTON CHURCHILL

CERCLE DE LORRAINE
BRUSSELS, BELGIUM

Mitch Childer sat uncomfortably in a leather chair. On the other side of a large mahogany table, a man with piercing green eyes stared levelly at him.

"You insisted I come to Brussels. Here I am. Is there a problem?" Childer asked.

The man sneered. "Perhaps. You tell me."

"None that I know of."

"I'm less sure. And others of the group share my concern. We have been trying to get our heads around the fact that you invited a fucking US intelligence agent to work with you on our project."

Childer nodded. "Yes."

The green eyes and the dark face around them were expressionless. "I invited you to sit down and explain to me face-to-face why you have done this. Are you out of your mind? How does that even begin to make sense?"

Although he'd come here sure of himself, of his plan, Childer felt himself shiver a bit under the withering gaze directed at him. "I was told to do what was necessary to get this done," he said.

"What was necessary. Not what was suicidal. As soon as we heard that you enlisted Hoenig Fintech in the project, I felt it necessary to summon you here to explain. The others want to know as well—what in the world possessed you to include Claude Hoenig in this project? You are fully aware of his association with the CIA and more than one private corporate intelligence agency. Are you trying to expose our efforts?"

"The simple answer is that the project requires the skills of a particular programmer who works for Hoenig."

"And no one else can do the work? Christ, man. Why would you start a project that lives or dies on one man that you don't even have on your own payroll? Why not hire him away? It isn't like that would be a problem."

"Other programmers could do the work," Childer said, forcing himself to be calm. "It isn't anything incredibly innovative, although this person understands the ins and outs better than most."

The green eyes didn't flicker. Childer knew he needed to sound confident—he needed to be confident. This man, people like him, could smell blood in the water and would go for the kill. Hell, comparing this man to a shark would offend sharks. This man enjoyed crucifying anyone who wilted under his interrogation. "Hiring him away would mean getting the IMF or the Tanzanian government to hire him. He just refused a job with the US Department of the Treasury. My sources tell me that he is less than enthusiastic about any government or trans-governmental agency."

"Then why would he work on the project?"

"We've set it up so that his needs are met. He doesn't understand what is going on."

"What if he realizes. . . ."

"In that case, he is replaceable."

"Then why do you need Hoenig?"

"For the sake of elegance and simplicity. Naturally, there are other ways to do this, and I gave this considerable thought before I even approached Hoenig. As I explored the options, two factors, several actually, evolved that make this choice not just acceptable but an excellent idea."

"Let me hear them." The man sat back in the plush leather chair. Childer took him in, weighing how his sometimes mercurial temperament was shifting. For the moment, he was analyzing. He would listen. The implication was that he'd better agree with Childer's reasoning.

"First, despite his firm's involvement, only two people will be directly involved and only one, a person who is on my payroll, has any idea of our involvement. Even then, she thinks this is an IMF project."

The man nodded. "Go on."

"And involving Hoenig has a tremendous upside. We totally destroy any suspicion that we, any of us, are doing anything not entirely transparent. Hoenig will feel he is at the table, that he knows what is going on. Since he is unaware that his right-hand person is on my payroll, he will continue to believe he is fully informed. He is greedy and thinks this will give him an inside track. And that works well for us. Think about it—even you asked who in their right mind would invite US intelligence operatives to the table if they intended anything nefarious? By this maneuver, we co-opt any question, any suspicion that we might be manipulating the Tanzanian government."

"And your other factors?"

"The key programmer in question is the best possible person to make this happen quickly. He developed the technique we will rely on. If something happened, he is replaceable; it would just slow the project. I believe that is a reasonable risk and one we'd bear no matter who we chose."

"So you are relying mostly on the local staff to do the work?"

"That's right. The government gets kudos for making it a local project, not something imposed. They are training their staff."

"I still worry about Hoenig himself. If things go bad, you might have to cover your tracks."

Childer folded his hands on the table. "Sir, I have considered that. If that happened, and I see no reason to think it will, there are three people involved in this project who would be considered loose ends—the two employees Hoenig had involved in it and the Tanzanian who has been our liaison to the Ministry of Finance. We can either discredit or bribe the Tanzanian without difficulty. The key programmer will only know what happened—that the project failed. He won't be on site and so won't be privy to who did what. That leaves only my person in Hoenig's company, and I've already made contingency plans. If it became necessary to abort the project, I've established protocols that ensure she will have a fatal accident. But, as I've said, those are only precautionary plans. The likelihood is that the project will be successful."

The man stared unflinchingly at Childer. He knew the man was absorbing what he had told him, taking it in, turning it over and looking for flaws. He was a common man, and clever, in terms of what they called street smarts. He had no class, no manners, other than threatening manners. It was unfortunate that they needed him and people like him. In some ways, it had been so much better when the group wielded power through politics, connections. Influence had been their leverage. Now they needed data—information about things and trends, not the dirt on some official, although that could be useful at times. The change was unfortunate in the sense that data was classless. Even people like this one could use it, turning it over to technicians to process, to spot trends, to define new stratagems. The battle had grown crude.

But Childer was a realist and had adapted. Still, that didn't mean he had to like it.

The man let out a breath. He was about to pronounce his verdict. "Your reasons seem sound. We work with strange people these days." He shook his head. "It's a new world and this is a new approach. You have to expect doubt and misgivings, especially from the older heads."

Childer nodded. He knew exactly who the man meant.

"I'll placate them, tell them it appears you know what you are doing." Then a wicked smile crossed his face. "If it works, then the part about using Hoenig will be delicious."

Childer allowed himself a satisfied smile. "It most certainly will. He thinks he is getting on the gravy train, as Americans call it, when he is being led down a primrose path."

The man stood. "Very well. Keep the damn man firmly on that path."

And then he left. Childer saw that he had been dismissed and it rankled.

CHAPTER 6

CALL HOME

"As long as our government is administered for the good
of the people, and is regulated by their will; as long as it
secures to us the rights of persons and of property, liberty of
conscience, and of the press, it will be worth defending."

—ANDREW JACKSON
SEVENTH PRESIDENT OF THE UNITED STATES
FIRST INAUGURAL ADDRESS (4 MARCH 1829)

CRYSTAL TOWERS APARTMENTS
CRYSTAL CITY, VIRGINIA, USA

When Wyatt got back to the quiet of his apartment, walked into it at an unusually early time with no reason to feel guilty about missing work, the enormity of the changes that had been put into motion hit him hard. They staggered him. After working for other people for ten years, with almost no break, suddenly he was free. Free and disconnected. He was in free fall. Floating.

Suddenly, after years of his life remaining a deadly constant, now he had no office, no boss, and no ties to his old world. With that came the realization that it was a world that he'd never cared for. The work had been fine, but his life? The most powerful emotion rippling through him came in the form of a question: Why didn't I do this before?

There was no answer. He was at a crossroads and had chosen a fork. He still had the option of continuing to work, but on his own terms. It was a new world—his future was beautiful and frightening.

He went into the living room and found a bottle of bourbon he'd been given at the last office Christmas party. It was cheap stuff, but he was out of the good stuff, and it would do. He poured a glass of the amber liquid, took a sip, and slumped in his chair. He needed to think about the options.

Taking the freelance gig would give him the ability to work anywhere, keep any hours he wanted. It would only last as long as Claude needed him and was happy with the arrangement. But then, that was true of his tenure as an employee. Besides, his goal was to live simply, in cheap places, and he had plenty of money to do that. If the gig ended and he didn't want to touch his Bitcoin principle, well, he always had other people asking him to do other work. It wasn't usually as interesting as the stuff he did for Claude, but he could do it easily. He didn't want to touch the crypto unless he had to. It was a safety net. That made the idea of taking Claude's offer attractive. The man needed him for now, and it funded Wyatt's search for a better lifestyle. As things changed, he'd adjust.

The thoughts, the realization that he'd already made his decision, made the cheap bourbon taste fantastic. A load had been lifted from his shoulders. Even second-guessing himself, he couldn't think of any downside to signing the contract. It was for one project, not indefinite. That he didn't like the project didn't even matter. It would go on with or without him. Hoenig would use his code and so would the US Treasury. He'd put it out there and it was free for them all to use. That made him regret the impulse to share it. He'd never even considered the idea that governments would be combing the forums and coder sites for exactly such things.

So that was water under the bridge. Taking the work would help him launch his new, disconnected, nomadic existence. If Sindi was an elegant gypsy, what was he? A nomad without an adjective? At any rate, the deed was done. Now he just had to untangle himself from his life here. If he was going to cut the cord, he intended to do it completely. He would get his ass out, away from home.

"I'm coming, Sindi. Save some room at the beach."

He didn't have that much stuff. The apartment was a rental, and unless he gave thirty days' notice and waited around, he'd have to forfeit his deposit, but he didn't care. He'd turn off the utilities. His neighbor, Karl, worked for the Gospel Mission. Although Wyatt wasn't religious, he admired the work they did. Karl's outfit fed and clothed people in need and provided hot meals. They didn't skim. He'd give all of his stuff to Karl. They could sell anything that had any value in their second-hand store and give away or trash the rest. He'd give them his car too. He wouldn't need it, didn't want it, and couldn't be bothered with selling it.

"And that, friends, sums up Wyatt Osgood's total connections to this town," he said out loud to his empty apartment. Hearing himself say it, it sure as hell didn't seem like much. The good news was that it made leaving easier.

The timing was good, in a macabre way. His social life had been Janet. Now she was gone. No one else in town was more than a casual friend. In fact, with Janet out of his life, there was only one person in the entire world that mattered to him. She was also the only person he could trust as a sounding board for his plan. She'd help him make a last-minute sanity check. Besides, she needed to know what he was up to.

Wyatt took his drink and went into the bedroom. He sat on the bed, put his glass down, hung over the side, and pulled a laptop out from under his bed. Then he sat up, took a sip of the bourbon, and turned the computer on. When it came to life, he logged on and clicked an app called "contact Ellen." The software loaded, telling him to wait.

While he waited, he plugged the cord from a small box into a USB port. When the computer beeped a few minutes later, he put his right index finger into a hole in the box and felt the press of the sensors. "Wyatt confirmed," displayed on the screen. "Contacting Ellen." After a few minutes, it flashed: "Ellen confirmed." He pressed a button the button that made the connection and there she was, on screen in real time—his kid sister.

"Hey there, Wy. How are the ones and zeros doing?" she asked.

"About the same. They keep me going and pay the bills. How's the farming doing?"

Ellen grinned. "Which farm?"

He grinned. His sister had an organic farm in Colorado. She also grew medical marijuana. Both were totally legal. Government regulations made organic farming an unprofitable nightmare for a small grower, and it was the marijuana that kept her in business.

That business model faced one serious difficulty—the conflict between state legalization and federal criminalization made it difficult to get banks to do business with a marijuana grower. Wyatt had solved that. He'd set her up so the commercial marijuana buyers, mostly legal dispensaries, paid her in Bitcoin. The Bitcoin was converted to shares in an offshore hedge fund that somehow managed to lose large amounts of money every year. An import/export company registered in the Cayman Islands regularly purchased large amounts of organic produce from her that existed only on shipping invoices.

At the end of the day, Ellen's organic farm was one of the most profitable in the country. She paid taxes on every cent she earned. If anyone ever unraveled the mess, the only crime she could ever be found guilty of was making the accounting too complex.

Ellen's entire operation was off the grid—totally. She had installed a solar and wind power system, and she had a sophisticated computer-controlled drip irrigation system with environmental monitoring that even monitored the soil.

"And how's my farm doing?" he asked her.

"You think I spend my days babysitting your noisy toys?" she asked. "I gave you basement space and provide electricity. Our deal doesn't involve maintenance, although I'd water them for you if you want."

He laughed. They were talking about his computers that ran twenty-four hours a day mining cryptocurrencies in the basement of one of her hothouses.

"I still don't quite get what those beasts are doing down there," she said.

He laughed. "They are mining. They update the blockchain each time a transaction is made. They earn money by ensuring the authenticity of information. They let the blockchain work."

"If you say so," she said.

"Okay, then what they do is generate heat to keep your crops at the right temperature. I wouldn't ask you to water them. They don't need to be green."

"They do need to be fed, however. I'm going to add a row of solar panels to the west field."

"How much?"

"Ten grand."

"Take it from the loan account." Some of Ellen's Bitcoin money went into an escrow account that was built on a blockchain. It was a new service that let her borrow against the Bitcoin in his wallet using smart contracts. If the Bitcoin did well, the appreciation more than made up for the interest he'd pay. Another set of smart contracts allowed his mining operation to automatically repay the loan.

"It isn't just for you," she said. "Cough up half and we can call it even."

"Take it all from the account. Call it an investment instead. The account earns money enough to afford it."

"So big brother is buying my affections again?"

"Trying to. So sue me."

"Funny. By the way, some woman called for you a couple of days ago," Ellen said.

"She called you?"

"She didn't know who I was. I think she called every Osgood in every directory she could find looking for you. At least it seemed like she was going through a list. She took my word for it that I'd never heard of you."

"Any idea . . ."

"Something about a paper you wrote. She said you published it online. Really?"

"Yeah. That was a mistake, apparently. Was her name Janet?"

"Like your girlfriend?"

"Another Janet. I was thinking it might be the official-sounding Janet from the official fucking Treasury Department looking for some angle."

"An angle?" Ellen asked.

"They wanted me to work for them. I said no. And the other Janet is an ex-girlfriend anyway."

"I don't think that was the name. I think it was more like a last name. Of course, she might've lied to me. Horrible and shocking as the idea that people might lie is. I guessed she was either selling something or a tech reporter for one of those sites you read. Bustfeed, right?"

"BuzzFeed." That puzzled him. If it wasn't the woman from the Treasury Department who had wanted to hire him, he had no idea who it could be. He couldn't imagine why anyone would want to contact him so badly, unless it was had to do with his white paper. But the paper spoke for itself. "Well, keep on not knowing who and where I am."

"Who are you again?"

"Good girl. Otherwise, things there are . . . ?"

"Things are good. Very good. Now tell me the real reason you called. I know you love me, but you don't chit-chat. You don't even chit . . . on a good day, you text or email."

"I think I might be disappearing for a time. I'm pretty sure I am, and I'm just weighing the how. I didn't want you to worry if I fell off the radar. And I wanted to make sure everything was going along well before I took off."

"So they finally caught up with you for that bank job in Tulsa?"

He laughed. "I know this is a secure line and all, but please don't make those sorts of jokes. Anyone who does manage to hear this conversation is likely a shoot first and verify later sort of person."

"That's okay. I have no idea who you are, remember? So what's the disappearing act for? Surely Janet isn't a threat."

He sighed. "Being a boring nerd is finally getting to me, sis. I've decided I need a little beach time. Hoenig is going to let me freelance—I'll be mobile and I want to take advantage of that. I need to get away from . . . everything."

"Why do you want to keep working for Claude Hoenig? You sure as hell don't need the money."

"I like the work and . . . I don't know. Claude and I have a history. As much as we are opposites politically, he's always been looking out for me. When I was poor, he was trying to get me to invest in silver and gold."

Ellen laughed. "Stodgy stuff for a high flier like you."

"Yeah. It was right about the time I discovered Bitcoin—in 2010. The company did IT systems back then. Claude and I used to go out for a beer after work and talk about investing . . . about finance and economics in general."

"Your good Christian boss drinks beer?"

"Only to excess, like any red-blooded American. Anyway, he was really into precious metals. He made all the classic arguments about intrinsic value. He actually listened to my counter arguments, and as I shot them down, he saw the logic, the potential in cryptocurrencies. Finally, he decided to give it a shot. He made a million bucks riding it up, and that's when he decided to shift the company into fintech and out of dealing with irate users who wanted to connect their iPhone to the cloud server and work from home."

"So that's why he's grateful to you. Why your loyalty to him?"

Wyatt laughed. "I have no idea. We bonded. We are good old boys or some shit. Now he's really launching the company into the latest and greatest stuff. The work will be exciting, and he needs me. So I'll work. I will be cutting back and working from the beach, though."

"That's going to be an adjustment," she said. "Good for you for doing it. You bury yourself far too much in your work. Always have. You need to stick your head up from time to time."

"So you say."

"Go to some nice place and drink mojitos or your god awful bourbon. Find yourself a sweet, willing beach bunny and fuck yourself blind."

"Speaking of which . . ."

"Harold is fine and usually pretty damn randy, thank you very much. That's as much detail as you get. Let it be known far and wide that he and I are getting along well."

"Then I won't worry about you."

"Good. Worry about finding beach bunnies. Now I have to get to work. My boss is a bitch."

"I know her and I have to agree. Try having her for a sister."

"I meant Mother Nature, dumbass." She snorted. "You always were a bit of an asshole, big brother."

"I know. I hear that all the time. It's a curse."

"Maybe some beach time with the right bunnies will help you let that out."

"You never know."

"Send a postcard."

"Sure."

"It can be of any beach. If you want to be disappeared, then it doesn't have to be the right one. I'll stick it up on the fridge and pretend I know where you are—but never who. And it will be terrific if someone comes looking for you and sees it there."

"That's a thought."

"Should I expect anyone?"

"Not that I know of."

"Then put on your invisible cloak and vanish."

"Seems that I have to make a trip to Zurich first."

"Poor baby. You suffer so for whatever it is you live for."

"Go dig potatoes or some shit, wench."

"Bye, Wy."

And she hung up. Wyatt loved his sister. He didn't understand her affection for things in the dirt any more than she understood why smart contracts were even remotely interesting. So there it was. Life was like that.

"Beach bunnies," he said out loud and smiled. He hadn't even thought that far ahead but fuck yeah. Tanned, lithe beach bunnies.

CHAPTER 7

PROJECT MEETING

"So in many ways, virtual currencies might just give existing currencies
and monetary policy a run for their money. The best response by
central bankers is to continue running effective monetary policy, while
being open to fresh ideas and new demands, as economies evolve."

—CHRISTINE LAGARDE
INTERNATIONAL MONETARY FUND (IMF) CHIEF

DOLDER GRAND HOTEL
ZURICH, SWITZERLAND

As far as Wyatt was concerned, in terms of creature comforts, the
flight to Zurich was an absolute delight. He hadn't realized the difference between the quality of service, the food . . . of everything in first
class as opposed to cattle class. Traveling that way was outrageously
expensive, but it sure as hell made flying fun. It was almost worth
wanting to be rich to be able to travel so pleasantly.

The Dolder Grand Hotel, where they stayed, was another matter.
It didn't suit him at all. He smiled, imagining Sindi doing a video here.
Telling people to get off their asses and come to Zurich. He wondered
if she had done one. This was the kind of place she often picked, so it
was entirely plausible. When he had a chance, it would be fun to look
it up. If she had, he could compare his impressions with hers. That
would be fun.

For his tastes, the place was uncomfortable. The place had a
starched feel to it, as if it was in its finest clothes. Every room he'd
been in made him feel stiff and formal. It wasn't that his room was

awful—it was elegant. But he felt awkward in it and doubted any of the 173 rooms in the hotel would be better.

And the meeting . . . From a practical standpoint, it was a waste of his time. They didn't cover anything that couldn't have been easily discussed in a video conference. On a personal level, meeting Rashmi Patel and Andwele Kassain was interesting. Rashmi was very slim and beautiful. He could see that she was of mixed race, with soft, brown skin. "My father was from Mumbai," she said. "He was a Sindhi. My mother was Tanzanian—a Sunni Muslim."

Wyatt nodded. Obviously, she'd benefited from best that the blending of those races had to offer. She made Wyatt's head spin.

"That's quite a mix."

She was smart as a whip too. The Tanzanian government had given her a scholarship to the London School of Economics. "After I got my programming degree," she said. "In return, I agreed to come home and work for the government for five years." She sounded almost apologetic. "Two years ago, after I graduated, I came back. I went to work in the Ministry of Finance. And that's when I met Andwele."

From his perspective, the epic tragedy in her story was that she was engaged. He rather liked Andwele but thought it amusing that the man had announced their engagement when introductions were made. He couldn't blame Andwele for wanting to get that little tidbit on the table right away. The man was claiming his turf and making it clear to one and all that she was there to talk to, not flirt with.

The question was always how serious they were. But testing those waters required time and there was little he could do in two days of meetings. So Wyatt focused on the business at hand. He could get this over with and head out to his beach.

Peggy had briefed him on the project during the flight. The modifications that he needed to implement the system in the proposal were fairly obvious to him, if not simple. From a technical perspective, the project was straightforward. They would copy the code for the Bitcoin blockchain and create a sidechain that worked much the same way, but they would also create some routed payment channels and other code that would make it do some new tricks.

Given what they intended to use it for, in his opinion, he would destroy its intrinsic value. But that was what they wanted and what they'd get, one way or another. What he could do was see that it was at least done right. So he walked them through his ideas and showed them how his benign regulator would solve several problems in implementing a national currency. That part was great. What he hated was that it wasn't free—it would be government owned and controlled.

"It doesn't care what you use to value the tokens at all," he said. "You can tie it to a fiat currency, or gold, or a stock index, or let it float free."

"So it's versatile," Andwele said.

"No," Rashmi said. "He means that its functionality has nothing to do with the underlying valuation. It only addresses the way transactions are processed. What the transaction might be, money, cars, drugs, doesn't matter. The country could switch from dollars to pesos and it would work the same way."

"Exactly," Wyatt said.

"Why a benign regulator?" Andwele asked.

Wyatt shifted in his seat. He felt a little defensive. "Because it regulates the transactions in the sense of verifying that everything is valid, but that's all it does. It doesn't have access to information about the participates or the nature of the transaction."

"But that same regulation process. or approach to handling the validation, could be used to do those things, right?" Andwele asked.

"Not the way I wrote it," Wyatt explained. The issue made him uncomfortable. He'd come up with the idea to provide benefits in a limited application. But what everyone, from the US Department of the Treasury to the government of Tanzania, was making him see was that his idea could be used to control anything. He didn't want to focus on that. "You'd have to centralize everything. You'd need to undermine the decentralization."

"But isn't that what your code does?" Andwele shook his head. "You are evaluating transactions within the system."

"Outside of the blockchain." Wyatt saw he didn't get it. Their inability to see what he was talking about, to understand his white paper, was maddening. "My code is a form of a lightning network—it simply accelerates transactions within a framework that is outside of the blockchain. It combines a series of similar or related transactions and makes sure they meet the criteria of a contract, then sends a single transaction to be processed by the blockchain. It's really a clever, in my opinion, approach to using a specific set of check/sequence/ verify operations. It isn't the way the transactions are recorded or validated. It isn't the system."

"But that would work as well, right?" Andwele insisted.

Wyatt took a long breath. "The point of my regulator is to provide a set of controls over the transactions as they accumulate. It doesn't make them. That would actually centralize them and would defeat the major advantage of using a blockchain."

Peggy reached over and touched his hand. "That's probably as deep as we should go into this now," she said. "They'll get a clearer picture as we go along." She smiled at the two. "So, Rashmi, I understand that your role is to write some transaction simulations and use those to test the system before we bring it online?"

"That and more. Rigorous testing is important to ensure it works like we promise the banks and the people it will work. My job is to ensure that when this system is running it will be totally compliant with international banking regulations and, almost as important, conventions. I'll take your specs and run the code through the wringer."

Claude smiled. "Then you will be working closely with Peggy. She'll be running the project for us on site."

"And you, Wyatt?" Rashmi asked.

Claude laughed. "Wyatt wants us to believe he has no idea where he'll be, but I think that's just to upset me. What matters is that he'll be doing his code."

That seemed to surprise her. "A project of this importance and you won't be on site?"

Claude nodded. "Ask Andwele about that."

Wyatt saw she was really surprised. "I convinced Deputy Minister Dola that our programmers need the experience of working on the project. And that keeps the salaries in the department."

"So the contract only lets us have a project manager on site with your people doing the work."

Rashmi looked at Wyatt. "So you will be in the US office?"

He laughed. "Not even. I agreed to work closely with the project, not to be in some soulless office."

Claude grinned." Never fear. Wyatt has agreed to make it happen. Wherever he is physically, he will be busily modifying the modules he designed to execute the tasks you need, inserting the regulatory and supervisory functions while keeping the distributed nature of the blockchain. We have his word."

Rashmi made a face. "That seems so . . ."

"The word you're looking for is 'wrong'," Wyatt said. "And I agree. Not about me working off-site being wrong, but using a blockchain this way definitely is wrong."

She looked at him in surprise. "But you wrote the code."

"As I said, my intention was to find a way to regulate some specific functions within a transaction database. Using it to centralize control of the blockchain takes a giant step in a direction that never occurred to me."

Claude clapped his hands. "You didn't intend that, and yet, for everyone else, it appears to be the perfect solution to the needs of a national cryptocurrency."

"So it seems," Wyatt said.

"I have to wonder who is correct. I suspect we will learn the truth and, if it works, we will be using it in many more implementations." He winked at Peggy. "You need to make that happen, lady."

"The IMF will be monitoring this closely," Andwele said.

"Of course," Claude laughed. "After all, it's their money that is paying for it, isn't it? They are happy to fund you doing research into things they don't understand and don't even particularly like, but can't figure out how to stop. That way, if a project fails it isn't their failure—just a bad investment. And if it works, why they can shout to the world how they managed to fund innovation while assisting a highly indebted country. You have to admit it's diabolically clever."

"That's called being a diplomat," a voice said. They turned to see a dapper man standing there.

"Mr. Childer," Andwele said, hopping up. "This is Mr. Mitch Childer, head of. . . . Some part of the IMF."

"It changes frequently," Childer said. "I'm currently going back and forth between a couple of special projects—this is just one that we are involved in." He held out a hand to Claude. "Mr. Hoenig, I presume."

"The voice on the phone," Claude said. "It's good to meet you. This is Peggy Dory, our project lead, and Wyatt Osgood, a senior programmer."

"The man who invented the benign regulator," Childer said. "The

IMF is grateful to you for publishing that little bit of insight into solving some . . . difficulties."

When Wyatt shook the man's hand, he made an amazing discovery. Until that moment, touching him, he hadn't thought it would be possible to like the man any less than he did. His opinion had been based on his reputation, but now it was tangible and personal. He remembered an ancient Roman poem called *No te amo*:

> *"I do not like thee, Dr. Fell,*
> *The reason why, I cannot tell;*
> *But this alone I know full well,*
> *I do not like thee, Dr. Fell."*

Knowing that he decided to lay his cards on the table. He looked Childer in the eye. "If I'd known everyone, meaning people like you, would see it as a way of circumventing distributed systems, I wouldn't have even let anyone know about it," Wyatt said. "Just so you understand."

He nodded. "I do know about you, sir, and I know you aren't a fan of the IMF. Therefore, I am extremely grateful that the possibility of our application didn't occur to you. I'm also glad that you are working on this project with us."

Wyatt sighed. The man didn't even mind being disliked, which made his dislike for Childer even stronger. "I'm here in the hope that I can keep you bastards from fucking up some sweet code."

Childer smiled. "An excellent reason, sir. I will expect you to do exactly that."

Then he turned and nodded at Peggy. "Ms. Dory, it's indeed a pleasure to meet you. I'll be interested in seeing how you implement this platform. Even though there are other sovereign nations with cryptocurrencies, because of our involvement the entire world will be very interested in seeing how it works."

"But there's absolutely no pressure on you at all, Peggy," Claude laughed. "Besides having the world watching."

"Mr. Childer, I'd like you to meet Rashmi Patel," Andwele said. "She is both my colleague and fiancé."

He smiled. "Charmed, Ms. Patel. I've read your resume, and the thesis you wrote at the London School of Economics."

"I don't believe that," she said.

"It's unusual to have a student there take a positive view of Georgism."

"Georgism?" Andwele asked.

"You should read her paper," Childer said. "The Georgist paradigm tries to solve social and ecological problems using the principles of land rights and public finance."

"I'm impressed," Rashmi said. "But my thesis falls short because of some naive understanding of the way public finance actually functions."

Childer licked his lips. "Perhaps. I'd enjoy discussing this with you in detail someday."

"Well, pull up a seat," Claude said.

Childer seemed to catch himself. "No thank you, Herr Hoenig. I have no desire to interrupt your meeting. I merely stopped by to welcome you to Zurich and let you know that I am available if you think I can be of any help."

Wyatt waved a hand. "You aren't interrupting, Herr Childer. I, for one, have grown weary of talking about the mystical properties of code and public policy. It's time for drinks and I think the IMF should buy the first and every round."

"I have an engagement, I'm afraid," Childer said. He waved to a waiter who came toward them. "In terms of the time . . ." he glanced at his watch. Out of the corner of his eye, he saw Claude giving the ornate timepiece what could only be described in biblical terms—a covetous look. "I do apologize for not joining you, and as compensation, I have arranged for a round of drinks. They will be charged to the IMF as our way of welcoming you to this project."

"Hurrah for the IMF," Peggy said.

Mitch Childer nodded at Claude Hoenig. "Would you have a few moments for a word or two in private?"

Hoenig looked up at him, then shrugged. Wyatt was certain that shrug was for them, making the group think he'd rather be there with them. "Certainly. We can chat in the bar."

"Fine."

As the two men left, Wyatt found himself sulking. He shouldn't have said so much to Childer, but the man pissed him off. Childer was pretty much the poster boy for everything he thought was wrong with the world. He was one of the elites who thought they should control people; they were fascists who thought democracy meant everyone surrendering their independence for the greater good as defined by that elite.

The entire trip wasn't his idea of a good time. First, he learned that they were using his code, co-opting his ideas, for a project he disliked; then he met the sexy Rashmi and found out she was engaged; now he had this IMF fuck walk in, get chummy with Claude, and rub his face in his misery. It was almost as if the man was testing him, trying to see if he could make him stomp off in a huff, like some ten-year-old. Why he might do that was an unanswerable question, but it felt that way and so, like that ten-year-old, Wyatt refused to give him the satisfaction.

Andwele leaned over to him. "That," he said, "is a very important man."

Wyatt was stunned. "Are you talking about that asshole Childer?"

Andwele sat up straight. "Of course. He is way up in the IMF and involved with so many governments."

"More to the point, Childer is a self-involved fuck," Wyatt said.

Andwele looked shocked for a moment, then shrugged. "Perhaps he is that too. But why do you care?"

It was a valid question and Wyatt had no answer. He hated not having answers. So, when the young, prototypically blonde German, or possibly Swiss, waiter looked at him, Wyatt ordered a bourbon. "Maker's Mark. A double," he said. "Make it neat."

Peggy ordered a Schnapps he'd never heard of. Well, why shouldn't she go exotic? It was on the tab of the vultures of the global government.

And then came an odd moment. Wyatt sat back anticipating the taste of bourbon on his tongue and saw the waiter turn to go to the bar. As he passed Peggy, he brushed against her. He stopped and apologized, then went on. But in the moment of contact Wyatt could've sworn he saw her slip a piece of paper, a napkin, into the man's pocket.

Curious. It was none of his business, of course, but easily the most interesting development on the trip. How did Peggy know the waiter?

"When do you leave Zurich?" Rashmi asked him.

Her smile, that she was interested, sent a warmth through him. "The day after tomorrow. I'm assuming we'll have finished thrashing the system out by then."

"I'm certain of it. But why won't you tell us where you are going?"

He was flattered by her attention, at the fact that she actually seemed interested in his plans. There was no reason not to tell any-one where he was going. It wasn't like he was going into hiding. Part of him wanted to tell her and see her response. "And make all of you jealous, or worse run the risk of you sending me Christmas cards? No way. Besides, I promised myself I'd be flexible, so even if I told you where I'm headed this week, I can't say how long I'd be there. It could be days or weeks, maybe months."

She clapped her hands. "That sounds delightful."

She was delightful. Andwele was not so happy, although what was bothering him wasn't clear.

Wyatt shrugged it off. In two days he'd be on an Air Portugal flight to Lisbon, and from there to Miami. He'd be flying first class and he wouldn't even have to listen to Peggy tell him about the project.

When the waiter came back with their drinks, Wyatt watched him. The man definitely paid Peggy more attention, and she had trouble keeping her eyes off him.

He was happy to see that she had such a human streak. "May you get well laid," he thought. For his part, it didn't seem likely he would. Not now. Not until he got to the beach he'd picked out as his first des-tination. But once he got there, getting laid was high up on his to-do list. There might be more important things to do, but the way he was feeling now, they could damn well wait.

CHAPTER 8
A SIDEBAR

"For what shall it profit a man, if he shall gain the whole world, and lose his own soul?"

—MARK 8:36 THE BIBLE (KING JAMES VERSION)

HOTEL BAR
DOLDER GRAND
ZURICH, SWITZERLAND

Claude Hoenig followed Mitch Childer's purposeful step as the small man strode briskly out of the conference room, down a long carpeted hall, through large carved double doors, and into the plush hotel bar. By habit, as much as design, Claude trailed a few steps behind the man. Keeping this distance had nothing to do with respect; it was a holdover from his past, from more uncertain days working in intelligence, both with the Agency and in private work. It was a survival instinct.

Claude had no illusions about the limits of his own patriotism, and he'd never seen the percentage in being a bodyguard or deliberately taking a bullet for anyone else. Even worse would be getting hit by a stray bullet. Keeping your distance from anyone important enough to be a target, just sufficient space to avoid getting hit in the frenzy of an attack, was smart. A strategy like that kept you alive.

The habit hadn't saved his own life, but he knew it had worked for others; some of his colleagues who didn't acquire it weren't around anymore. Now, even though he was ostensibly out of that business, and when he caught himself doing it, he smiled. There were some reflexes he saw no reason to lose. Just because he was in the world of finance now, just because he wasn't expecting a hit, didn't mean the people, the important ones like Mitch Childer, didn't have deadly enemies. These might be less dangerous times in terms of physical danger, but maybe not. There was no reason to assume things like that.

With that distance also came some valuable perspective, even insight. A person looked different from the back. There were no facial expressions, no cues of that sort to use in evaluating the man. It also meant they couldn't use them to fool you. From this vantage point, his stride, the way he carried himself, offered a lot of information if you knew what to look for. Fortunately, Claude Hoenig was skilled in such matters.

In this case, he didn't glean much that he didn't know already, and that made him grouchy. From Claude Hoenig's point of view, he didn't know nearly enough about this man. He could never know too much about him. He wanted to understand him, fathom what drove him. Because he did business with people, he wanted to know those things. Here, he seemed to be tying his near-term future to that man's star and to those of his mysterious colleagues. To an intelligence operative, the unknown was dangerous. The group Childer belonged to was definitely dangerous and powerful.

It would've been useful even to know where Mitch Childer fit in the organization—whether he was a top dog or just a key operative. He ran his section of the IMF, but that wasn't the group Hoenig cared about. The IMF was a functional group. A visible and reasonably transparent entity. But they weren't the ones who pulled the strings, who pushed the world in a direction that suited them. The group that did that was the one he wanted to know about and to collaborate with. They were the ones that offered the big payday and made the big decisions.

They weren't invisible, but the group was subtle. Most people didn't know it existed. From the outside, working with the IMF and the World Bank meant you'd arrived. For Claude, it was simply a way of meeting the people who counted, of getting a foot in the door. The people who paid attention to how the world worked, those with intelligence assets, at least, knew that some of their people were among that mysterious group. His research was inconclusive, but Hoenig was fairly sure that Childer ranked among the unmentioned elite—the ones seldom in the news beyond making boring speeches at the UN or releasing statements that said little. Faces in the news, but never personalities.

Claude had gotten this job because he'd worked for Childer once before. He'd only been a small contractor then, hired to do a specific task. His firm had written some transaction code in a complex project. He'd never even been privy to what the system actually did. Still, it had been good money and something to add to his portfolio. During the project, Hoenig had sucked up to Childer; he made sure he knew Claude Hoenig was competent and could be trusted—to do his work and be invisible. Now that effort was paying dividends.

This time, for this high-profile project, his firm would carry the load and be visible. The world would know that his firm had been selected, by Childer personally, to act as the lead contractor in this IMF sanctioned effort. That held both promise and danger. But Hoenig was, at heart, a risk taker—at least up to a point, and only when he couldn't manage the risks.

The project wasn't anything that difficult. The trick would be managing the relationship with Mitch Childer, proving his firm's worth. Publicly, Childer was all business and totally pragmatic. Some of the work he'd done was impressive, on paper at least. But then, he was the public face of those projects. Who knew who actually did the work? The information he had on the man himself was thin—he was a workaholic with an apartment in Washington, where the IMF office was, and another in Zurich. He had many colleagues and no visible friends or social life outside his work.

Based on what he knew, what he saw, Claude didn't like the man. While he appreciated elegance, he found that Childer could be prissy and a snob. Working with him, he could be a pain in the ass. And as a devout fundamentalist Christian, it grated on Hoenig that Childer, like the majority of the members of this mystery group that he and his friends had identified, were Jewish. A religious bias for power groups wasn't unusual. Like the so-called Mormon Mafia in Salt Lake City, the generations of Catholic secret societies, including the Freemasons, the Japanese yakuza, Cosa Nostra, and the liberal Jewish intellectuals, people within the groups supported each other against outside forces.

Unlike the others, this one had grown into a potent contemporary force—pushing toward its goal of a one-world super government.

Hoenig and his intelligence colleagues knew that much. They knew some things and suspected a lot more, but the group was a powerful and tightly-knit clique, which meant that more hard information, actual specifics, was hard to come by. The members associated with their own, and connections were based on commonalities among them—shared culture and heritage. That made them hard, if not impossible, to infiltrate.

Despite being part of the power elite in the US, and wielding great power, despite dining with presidents and kings, Hoenig was on the outside. None of his group were invited to that dance as anything more than a heavily chaperoned guest.

Hoenig was intent on changing that. After walking the corridors of power in the US, he was hungry to move beyond them. The work of Childer's mysterious group went well beyond the charters of the World Bank, IMF, and International Court. He was sure they were up to far more than their liberal agenda admitted. The question was how much? And he wanted in.

So Mitch Childer had been on his radar for a long time. He'd cultivated him. He asked his advice when he started the company. As distant as the man was, as inhuman as he acted at times, Childer seemed to respect what he was doing—converting his experience in intelligence and applying it to financial technology. While never warm, Childer had been supportive. That brought him that first job, and now they were in Zurich, sharing a drink and talking one-on-one.

They settled into a booth and ordered drinks. "You needed a sidebar conversation?" Hoenig asked. "Is there something the group shouldn't know?"

"There's a great deal the group shouldn't know. But this chat is because I want some assurances," Childer said. "Can I assume that your team is ready to go?"

Hoenig snorted. "They were born ready."

"What a very American way of expressing your confidence," Childer said with a sneer.

Hoenig winced. Knowing Childer was a snob didn't take away the sting of the barb. It was a reminder that Mitch Childer had the aristocratic European view of Americans—that they were crude, violent, and sometimes useful, but they had no place at the table with the civilized adults. That attitude made his task seem a huge challenge. But, as always, he shook it off and struck back. He would be loyal and efficient, but not a whipping boy. When dealing with men like Childer, Claude made a point of using Americanisms extensively. It irritated them and that gave him an advantage. Their snobbery made it impossible to keep from underestimating him. It offset their knowledge of his background and made him seem less threatening. They saw him as a pawn who could be used, and it seemed a good idea to encourage that attitude. "I'm a very American man, Mr. Childer."

"Indeed."

"At any rate, yes, the team has its mission and is well prepared. We understand what the IMF wants out of this project."

Childer raised an eyebrow. "You do? Beyond helping an indebted country get on its feet, what do you think that would be?"

The man's condescending attitude rankled. It made Claude want to smack him one. In the old days, he might have done just that, but over the years he'd learned better ways to deal with men like this. He'd had to. While you could be an effective agent and leave a certain number of bodies lying around, moving up the ladder in intelligence required different tactics and a lot of restraint. For instance, at that moment Claude wanted to tell Childer that he knew he had gone behind his back and was making side deals with Peggy Dory. He wanted to see the look on his face when he told him that he knew he'd flown her to Zurich—first class on KLM. He wished he could tell him that he knew this wasn't Peggy's first stay at the Dolder Hotel.

That she'd snuck around and was feathering her own nest didn't surprise him at all. It certainly didn't disappoint him. He'd hired the bitch because she was an incredible hacker and an innovative thinker. Unfortunately, the very things that made her good at that, the skills she'd developed, meant her morals and allegiance were questionable. Despite the large salary he paid her, she enjoyed working on the darker side. She couldn't resist. Childer must've determined that as well.

As a good Christian, he hated the need to mistrust and spy on his own people. Yet, as a businessman, people like Peggy, untrustworthy people, were pure gold—if they were properly managed. And he was a skilled manager of rogue agents. Dealing with someone like that, someone valuable but not loyal, was where his background in covert intelligence operations paid dividends. He'd dealt with hundreds like her—people recruited in the field, people of dubious allegiance. To extract maximum value, you had to give them free rein, but then watch them without them knowing. You needed to make them feel they were trusted, no matter how you felt about them.

None of that was particularly Christian and that often made Hoenig wonder about himself. Still, when all was said and done, the things he did were for the good of the world. Through his work, he helped maintain order and prosperity and prevented chaos. So it was necessary. If he had to break some commandments to ensure the world was safe for God's children, then he was willing to bear that burden. He'd done it for his country, after all.

This work, to be effective, required other operatives as well. He needed team members that Childer would never know about—eyes and ears in thousands of places. And he had them. Despite leaving the intelligence business, Claude Hoenig never let his connections, his network, lapse. He had a small band of loyal, trained, ruthless operatives and each of them had assets. Because he couldn't pay them directly without raising eyebrows, they were technically employed by the intelligence firm he'd started in conjunction with some ex-CIA friends. Technically, he'd sold out to them when he started this business but he was on the board of directors and they shared intel and resources. It was a cozy relationship.

One reason for the eyes and ears was simply keeping track of the really good people—where they went and who they met with. People like Peggy and Wyatt didn't tend to play by the rules. They didn't even recognize the rules. For instance, because it was unreasonable to take Peggy Anne Dory's word for anything, when she'd asked for time off for a vacation in Mexico, he had her followed. His people learned that she'd bought a ticket for Switzerland and he put a tail on her. They'd followed her here, to this very hotel, where she'd met with Mitch Childer.

Those things were, in Claude's world, not issues of trust but basic craft. He didn't expect loyalty but rewarded it when he found it. He didn't know what he'd offered her to do this little job and he didn't care. What was important was knowing that Childer had an agenda that he was leaving Hoenig Fintech out of—officially. That wasn't betrayal so much as good business. The question was whose agenda was it? If it was IMF business, then coming straight to him would have made more sense. Claude was a pragmatic person and he understood when the funding organization had an agenda that they didn't want the client to know about. And certainly Childer knew that Claude could be discrete. That was his profession. That meant it wasn't IMF business. It was bigger. And, for him, it was an opening, a crack in the wall the elite raised to protect them from the common herd.

He wasn't sure what was going on yet, but he'd track that. Information was leverage. Using that leverage effectively, exerting pressure, gave you power. With that power in your hands, you didn't need armies to get what you wanted. Not anymore. Today, important battles were won far away from the battlefield.

For now, he would say nothing. Not to Peggy and not to Childer. As far as Peggy was concerned, he still trusted her to produce the code. Whatever she was doing for Childer wouldn't compromise that. That being the case, what it was, the technical issues, or even the functional aspect, didn't matter. No, what mattered was knowing they were up to something. He'd decide how to deal with her later. Maybe he'd promote her. It all depended on how this went down. He'd watch how things evolved and, in doing so, he'd learn everything he needed to know about her true reliability and usefulness, or even the risk of leaving her running free.

In the meantime, he had no intention of telling Childer that he knew. While he knew it would shock the man, seeing his startled expression wouldn't do anything more than make Hoenig feel good for a fleeting moment; this information, his intel, wasn't something he was willing to squander on the sin of pride. The Good Book told him where that path led. Pride was the greatest of sins; it was the summit of self-love and directly opposed to submission to God.

Hoenig loved God. God forgave him for his sins, even murder. The crimes were, after all, in his name, for his country, his people.

Knowing that Childer was running a game that seemed outside the scope of his role with the IMF was exactly what he'd hoped for. In some ways, Peggy deserved a raise for leading him to this gold. It was something for the end game. In Iceland, in 1972, the American whiz kid Bobby Fischer defeated the defending world chess champion, the Russian Boris Spassky, primarily through his spectacular end game. There was a lesson in that. Claude would let this smiling Jewish bastard enjoy his feeling of superiority—for now. "I had my people go through your job requirements and noticed a couple of things that aren't in the spec that we got from Andwele Kassain. That led me to assume that you, the IMF, had some minor items on your agenda that aren't on the Tanzanian government's radar."

Childer shifted in his seat. Clearly, he didn't like seeing a man put the cards on the table face up. It was abrupt. Crude. Probably too open, too American, for his taste. "Not at all," he said. He said it quickly and then paused to think over his answer. "It's true that we added some features that will give us feedback. It's important to be able to learn from the system and optimize the approach for other countries. If your people do their jobs well, you'll be working on those as well. It's in your interest to make sure they work effectively."

There it was—the carrot he'd expected the man to pull out. The message was simple: play along and we might let you stay on board for the entire ride. Hoenig decided to push the man a little. "What sort of feedback are you talking about?"

Childer tipped his head. "Well, given that there are four national banks, plus the Bank of Tanzania, the central bank, involved in this, we'd like to know how they actually react—if they adopt it and use it as it's intended."

"But your plan will effectively usurp the only job the Bank of Tanzania has had since the Bank of Tanzania Act of 1995. Why would they be excited about helping?"

"It's true that it undercuts them," Childer said. "And yes, the government initiated this act because the bank had too many responsibilities; they used the act to reduce them to nothing but setting monetary policy."

"So I can't imagine the bank is supportive."

Mitch Childer's lips twisted. "They are petty bureaucrats who do what they are told in something as major as this. Being involved is their only chance of hanging onto any power at all. And the other banks are actual banks; I will be interested in their reactions. I want to see if they fully support the crypto. Implementing the project has given us access to their computers so we can get the data feed in real time for analysis. We've added a module that will let us see what other transactions they process—those that have nothing to do with the crypto." He gave Hoenig a conspiratorial glance." Naturally, we won't do anything but collect some raw data. We'd never interfere with private transactions."

"Of course." As if collecting data on private transactions was nothing. As if it weren't beyond illegal. "I assume, however, that you would prefer that we be discreet about the existence of those functions? It is surveillance, after all."

Childer waved his hand, dismissing an invisible fly. "I don't really care. It isn't anything secret, but some of their banking people have rather parochial views on privacy issues. If they didn't know about it, that would be more convenient. They'd be less inclined to raise troublesome objections."

Hoenig nodded. You'd think the man would just spell it out. They were on the same side, after all, at least up to a point. He sipped his drink and said nothing. Fine. Let him think the dumb American Christian barbarian couldn't be expected to appreciate the nuances of politics. Well, there would be a lot of business to come from dealing with this man and his friends at the World Bank if he let them think he was just a minion. More importantly, he would gain their trust, even if only because they thought he was stupid. That would mean he got to hear about changes in international policy before they happened. That meant money in his pocket and probably a lot of work for his associates. As a bonus, it gave him intel to feed his old colleagues. When you danced with people in this crowd, it never hurt to have some powerful people on your side. People who profited from the information you fed them on a regular basis.

Long ago, back when he watched his friends at the private military company, Xe Services, makeover the company, turning it into Academi and rebooting a tarnished image, Hoenig had seen the shift already taking place. Political intelligence was well and good, but he'd seen the future. It was in finance. He'd left behind military and industry, to a large extent. Getting into finance, into fintech, had been his way of getting himself a stake, a foothold in this new world. And damn if it wasn't paying off. Even if he hadn't bought Bitcoin when it was cheap and made millions, he was building the platform for a new age intelligence agency. An agency that was tapped into what was happening globally and, more importantly, how it was financed.

Childer, as unlikeable as he was, provided an amazing opportunity; he was holding a door open for Hoenig to enter that world. Wide open. Claude Hoenig took a deep breath and stepped through.

"I think my team can accommodate anything the IMF needs to have incorporated into the project without altering the specifications or the workflow significantly."

"Excellent," Childer said. The man knew he'd been understood. Still, he didn't volunteer information about the job he'd asked Peggy to do. That was telling.

Hoenig nodded. "I'm glad to work closely with you. As you said, this job lays the groundwork for the future."

"In so many ways," Childer said. He sipped his cognac. "We are the future, my friend."

Sometimes, like this moment, Claude Hoenig thought that the old days had been somehow cleaner. You disrupted a political party, perhaps. Maybe ruined a candidate, framing him or her for something. And you eliminated the ones that needed that. After all, the stakes were global.

Now, however, it was countries that were blackmailed and destroyed financially. And the stakes were the same. You had to wonder if that constituted progress.

"I might have some minor requests in the future," Childer said. "But now, I do have another appointment."

The audience was over and as Childer left, Hoenig sat there finishing his drink and imagining the dapper little shit lying in a dank, dark alley bleeding to death. The vision made him feel more peaceful. Then it was time to rejoin the crew for dinner.

With Childer gone, he suddenly had an appetite.

CHAPTER 9

GROUP DINNER

> "Technology imposes its economic reality on the world. Gold replaced seashells as money irrespective of seashell holders' feelings."
>
> —SAIFEDEAN AMMOUS
> AUTHOR OF THE BITCOIN STANDARD

THE DOLDER GRAND HOTEL
ZURICH, SWITZERLAND

Rashmi Patel was pleased to see that when Claude Hoenig left to talk to Mitch Childer, and the drinks arrived, the conversation moved away from business. People began asking questions, wanting to get to know each other and talking about their various interests. She was interested in this diverse selection of people and had to wonder how the personalities would interact over the course of the project. She learned that Peggy was a big movie buff, for instance, and seemed to share her fascination with some of the old classics—the movies starring Bogart and Bacall were a passion of hers.

When Claude returned to join them, he was smiling broadly.

"Everything good?" Wyatt asked.

"God blesses this project," he said. "And Washington DC approves too. What could be better?" Then Claude picked up the thread of the conversation that he'd interrupted, surprising Rashmi by animatedly expressing a love of London. "I adore Cambridge," he said as they shared some of their favorite places in that city. "I was based in London for a year and used to spend a lot of my time off there."

"I wish I could've stayed there, in London," Rashmi admitted.

"Why didn't you? I'm sure you could've found a high-paying job in the city."

She smiled. "Because I had to come home to fulfill my obligation."

"Oh yes, the government paid for your schooling."

"I intended to leave after that, but then I met Andwele."

She reached over and linked her arm in Andwele's and he smiled at her. The gesture had been sincere, but reflexive. Now she felt a twinge of guilt, of concern. Their relationship wasn't developing the way she had expected, as she had hoped. At first, as with most relationships, they were caught up in each other's charms. But as they got to know each other, she became aware of too many things that unsettled her.

Deputy Minister Haki Dola had happily put Andwele in charge of the project, reporting to him. That was a huge step up the ladder for her future husband. Pulling this off would guarantee his future in government. He wanted that very much.

And that was precisely the problem. While Andwele had taken up the political swirl eagerly, it wearied her. The more successful he was, the more his job seemed to be little more than politics. Rashmi had seen her dreams vanquished by the personal agendas that corrupted government projects. Her thesis had been based on the premise that good governance was a real thing, that some good people were working for the good of the country and its people. But after two years, her cheerful hopefulness had evaporated. All that seemed to matter was the appearance of things, and in her small role, at best, she could implement poorly thought out policies well.

It wasn't a game she was willing to play, yet Andwele was thriving. That he was coming into his own in a world that she increasingly disliked pulled them in different directions. And now, that gave her an unexpected bond with Wyatt who obviously was unhappy with the project goals.

She'd pressed him on his objections, curious. "Obviously you think this entire project is wrongheaded. Yet you work in the field and developed this code that will make it possible. How is that?"

He'd been curt. "I object on two levels. The first is philosophical—giving a small group of people control over the rest never works out well. What's the point of replacing the fiat currency with crypto beyond doing the same things faster?"

"And cheaper," Andwele said.

Wyatt sneered. "So it's a cost-savings effort. You aren't really creating a crypto or a blockchain."

"Of course we are."

"Andreas Antonopoulos called bullshit on that idea a while back."

"Who?" Andwele asked.

"He is an expert on the internet of money—that's what he talks about."

"And he doesn't think our national currency will be a cryptocurrency? Even if we base it on the Bitcoin blockchain?"

"Nope. At the Blockchain Africa Conference in 2017, he pointed out that if a blockchain is centralized, if a payment system depends on users trusting the same banks and government that give perceived value to regular currencies, it's just a database. You aren't creating anything new. All you are doing is reducing transaction costs."

"I was at that conference," Rashmi said. "I remember his talk. He's an excellent speaker and I was impressed, although his talk was fairly general."

"Get him to critique your proposal and I can guarantee he will get specific fast," Wyatt said grinning.

"You said you object on two levels," Rashmi said. "What's the second one?"

"Well, since the first was philosophical, for balance, this one is pragmatic. It's based on basic engineering principles. A system is only as robust as its weakest link." She smiled. He even said it like a tech. "If you take a distributed system, and force it to operate through any centralized mechanism, you actually create a point of failure. You've diminished the value the system can offer." He snorted. "Not that those arguments will influence anyone who believes that the people are not to be trusted."

"Yet the average person needs help and needs protection," Claude said. "That's why governments exist. Consider the literacy rate in Tanzania. Think about that and then explain to me how those people can possibly make use of a technological system on their own. If it weren't for developers providing sophisticated user interfaces, they wouldn't be able to use their cell phones."

Wyatt stared at the man for a moment. "Actually, Claude, you just made my point. Obviously, this system isn't intended to be for the people or we'd leave it centralized and the work the IMF wanted us to do would be to develop user interfaces for the applications. We could do it at the same level as the childlike point-of-sale terminals in fast-food restaurants if necessary. They do limit what the user can do with a system, but not in a supervisory way. That wouldn't require centralization."

Rashmi smiled. In Wyatt, she saw a refreshing and different sort of person. Of course, he didn't fit in . . . not with the project staff or the hotel they were in. Not at all. He didn't want to be at the meeting and was ill at ease. It was obviously a command performance. His suit didn't fit him well . . . it was probably an old one he'd dug out of a closet for this trip. His attitude, making it clear that despite his distaste for the project, he was going to insist that the implementation was the best it could be . . . that pleased her. She hadn't encountered his type before, except in movies. Not that Wyatt was someone she was entirely comfortable with. He challenged people, which she found unsettling. But even that was refreshing in its way.

From the conversation she'd heard, and because of the focus of Mitch Childer's abrupt and brief appearance, Rashmi suspected that Wyatt was present for only one reason—he'd been forced to. Claude Hoenig had made him come to Zurich to demonstrate to the IMF that he could produce the man behind the pivotal piece of code. By implication, he could make it walk and talk and dance on the water.

There were other reasons Childer might have for insisting Hoenig's company be involved. Childer and Hoenig seemed to have some connections. From what Andwele had told her, it was Childer who required that these particular Americans were part of the team. Wyatt's knowledge and insight, but mostly his ability to look at things from every angle, would be pivotal to making the project flow.

Peggy Dory seemed competent and knowledgeable, but she didn't strike Rashmi as the kind of person who could come up with truly innovative workarounds when the inevitable problems arose. Undoubtedly, she'd be able to ramrod the team and be a good leader, but she'd have to turn to Wyatt for the important things.

That was her take.

Now, with that dynamic in mind, she watched the interaction between Wyatt and his boss with even more interest. How far would the men go in their duel?

Disappointingly, Claude decided to play his trump card. "Regardless of what we might think or what we would do in their place, the IMF and the government of Tanzania have determined what they want us to create," Claude said. "We are here to make it happen." He looked around at the group. "I suggest we finish our drinks and adjourn to the restaurant for dinner."

It was, Rashmi thought, a clever way to shift the subject of conversation from dangerous territory. Wyatt was getting a little worked up.

The restaurant, like everything in the hotel, was elegant to the point of being almost overdone. Through the meal, Rashmi shifted uncomfortably in her chair. She'd been excited about making the trip. She hadn't been outside of Tanzania since she'd returned from London to fulfill her contract with the government. This trip, then, was an unexpected treat.

Or she'd thought it would be, but it wasn't turning out the way she'd expected. The stilted conversation, overly rich food . . . those were things she'd expected. What she hadn't anticipated was her growing malaise. There were things, undercurrents swirling around her, that made it hard to relax.

None of them were on their home turf, and it was mildly amusing to see Claude Hoenig and Andwele vying to play the role of host, guiding the conversation. Both of them seemed in their element, although the older Hoenig had the confidence of experience to draw on. Andwele held his own, however, and it surprised her to see the continuous shifting of his personality. He'd always been a charmer, but now, without intending to, he was showing her his ambition.

She'd sensed that Andwele had taken an instant dislike to Wyatt, almost as if he was jealous. That made her wonder if she'd missed the moment when Andwele had seen Wyatt make an admiring glance at her. More likely, it was simply that Wyatt was so self-confident and assured in his own strange way—a way that Andwele wouldn't understand. Andwele achieved his goals by promoting those of his bosses, whereas Wyatt was proudly a rebel.

She often found that men could be competitive that way, with pride arising from their differences, each sure of the validity of his view. That made the way Claude Hoenig and Wyatt seemed to get on so well even more amazing. They argued and sniped at each other, yet despite their incredibly divergent views, there was an obvious level of respect between them. Their barbs were political, economic, and even aimed at the other's affections or lifestyle, yet they would laugh about their differences. That spoke volumes about Wyatt's competence. She couldn't imagine any other reason a man like Hoenig would even tolerate the sloppy, outspoken, anarchist Wyatt seemed to be. On Wyatt's side, it seemed more that he didn't really put any importance on others agreeing with him as long as they let him air his views—which Hoenig did.

Bored, restless, and mostly left out of the conversation, Rashmi watched the others, listened, and thought about the key players she'd be working with on the project. After their brief introduction, she knew that she didn't care for Mitch Childer. He struck her as cold and distant—undoubtedly a manipulator. Thankfully, he wouldn't be around all the time and would be more Andwele's problem than hers.

Despite Wyatt's tolerance for the man, she hadn't warmed to Claude Hoenig either. She respected his accomplishments and was certain he knew what he was doing, but he had an air of self-importance, of being the guiding light and voice of truth, that put her off. He was often brusque and dismissive. It was hard to tell if he knew he came across that way. Perhaps he didn't care that his manner was. . . . rude. If that was the case, she definitely didn't care for him.

She'd be able to get along with Peggy. Unless they clashed about something, both of them would be focused on getting the job done quickly and properly. Or so it seemed. Like Rashmi, Peggy spent much of the conversations sitting back, studying the people. One difference was that while she stayed out of the discussions that wandered into what ought to be, when they turned to what was needed to make the system work, Peggy was quick to speak up.

Yes, it was likely they would work well together.

Ironically, one of her biggest concerns was Andwele. With his new-found confidence, he didn't seem to take her concerns, her questions seriously. She was beginning to see that underneath the modern African man she admired lurked a more traditional person, one who didn't think wives, even future wives, were serious players. Unconsciously, perhaps, he dismissed women. Peggy was an American and a senior team member, so he treated her differently . . . much as he'd treated Rashmi when she was a rising star in the Ministry of Finance before she'd started letting her pessimism about the way the department worked chill her enthusiasm.

The changes in him needed some careful consideration. When he'd first proposed, she hadn't wanted a long engagement; now it seemed the one they had might not be long enough for her to determine if Andwele was the man she wanted to spend her life with.

Lately, along with her reluctant admission of the failures of the established system, she began to question the entire idea of marriage itself. Basically, for someone who wasn't religious, like herself, it was an economic contract and nothing else. You could claim it was a pronouncement of love, but she didn't think love needed pronouncing. And if it did, certainly there were better ways to celebrate finding happiness with someone—ways that didn't involve the government.

As they finished the meal, the group began to break up. "I've got to do some work," Claude said. "When you are defining a new project, the old ones still need attention." He nodded at Wyatt. "Since you'll be leaving early the day after tomorrow, and tomorrow will be busy, could you come to my room and talk over some ideas on the point-of-sale app that Charles has been working on?"

Wyatt stood up. "Get a bottle of Maker's Mark bourbon sent up and you have a deal."

Claude nodded and called the waiter over. He handed the man a bill and gave him instructions. "Quickly, please. I don't want my colleague to die of thirst." Smiling, the waiter moved away and the men headed for the room. Peggy stood up. "I'm making it an early night," she told Rashmi and Andwele. "Probably watch half of a movie before I fall asleep."

Rashmi noted that Peggy glanced around the room as if she expected someone to challenge her statement. Then she grabbed her purse and left.

Finally, she was left alone with Andwele. He held her chair for her as she got up. When he put his hand on her arm, she smiled at him. "Andwele, we need to talk."

"Your room or mine?" he said.

The wink and smile he flashed her told her he was expecting sex more than talk. They'd been sleeping together regularly. Only the propriety of his position, his desire to move up the ladder, had kept him from moving in with her. Now, she was glad. And for the first time, she was pleased that they had booked separate rooms. Andwele had pointed out that the ethics team would be reviewing their expenses when they returned and they would be expected to keep up decorum. Now she found that worked well for her—it would make things easier. "Your room," she said. If he got upset, it would be easier to walk out of his room than to get him to leave hers.

He held up his room pass card. "Then off we go."

CHAPTER 10

POSTPONING THE FUTURE

"There is a huge risk from virtual currency use, so we hope
fintech providers won't engage [in the business]."

—DEPUTY GOVERNOR SUGENG
CENTRAL BANK OF INDONESIA
DECEMBER 8, 2017

THE DOLDER GRAND HOTEL
ZURICH, SWITZERLAND

As they walked to his room in the hotel, Andwele put his arm around
Rashmi, pulling her against him. The sudden nearness of his body made
her tense. That surprised her. For the first time since she'd met him, she
didn't want to be near him, have his arm around her. Having him hug
her, the very intimacy of it, put her on edge. Being close to him right
then, with her head buzzing with unanswered questions, felt suffocating.

No matter what else happened, she would have to resolve her
questions.

"These are exciting times," he said.

"You mean this project?"

"Oh it's far more than that." He was beaming, overflowing. "We
are on the edge of breaking into the upper ranks. We are half in, half
out already."

"Because our government sent us to another country? Because
Mitch Childer knows your name?" That seemed pathetic to her.

"This is the beginning of the dream. I'm thinking of the future, of
all the things this project will lead to."

"You see all that?" The idea saddened her.

He was oblivious to the concern in her voice. "The natural progression from here is obvious, isn't it? When the project is in place it will be celebrated, used as a model by the IMF. We will be celebrated. That will lay the groundwork for the next changes."

"What sort of changes?"

"Far too many to contemplate." He was happy. That made it harder to say what she intended to tell him. Still, it had to be done. She would wait for the right moment and then spit it out. "That sounds chaotic to me. Why do you get so much pleasure from that?"

"It won't be chaotic at all. The control will be in my hands and the changes will all flow in one direction—upward. With the completion of this project, the banks will be more willing to follow the finance minister's directions and directives. They will be part of the new system more completely than mere regulations could manage. With the tax monies a continuous incoming stream, the government will have more money to solve the country's problems. And we will all rise on the tide of success."

"We?"

"Haki Dola is well connected and growing in power. He is likely to become our next finance minister. I've worked to support his new power, to enhance it. In return, he has promised to create a new job for me. I will run the Finance Technology Department. I will be in charge and will take over all IT functions related to the Ministry of Finance."

"I see."

Not even noticing her lack of enthusiasm, Andwele let her go and walked to the minibar. "A drink?"

"Is there whiskey?"

"If not, then we will order a bottle from room service. Mr. Childer will pay for it."

Suddenly she recognized what she heard in his voice. It was greed, lust . . . the sheer delight in having access to the good life. "Whatever is in there will do," she told him. "Anything strong. I don't want you to call room service." Somehow charging their drinks to Childer seemed like taking a bribe. It wasn't, of course. It was common practice. And yet . . .

She watched him as he opened two small bottles and emptied them into glasses, handing her one. She thought about how she had seen him when they first met. He'd seemed dashing compared to the other men she knew. He had reminded her of London, in a strange way . . . possibly only because he was exciting and full of life, not a drone. But now . . .

"A toast," he said, raising his glass. "To our project."

A strange trembling made her hand shake as she touched her glass to his. "May the work we do make things better for the people," she said.

He gave her an odd look. "Yes, of course, the people." She knew that the people were not on his mind at all. Then they drank and he gave her a measured look. "The changes . . ." he started. "They require some sacrifice."

"We will be working hard on the project—long hours. We've done that before."

"What I mean is that before we go further, we should discuss a couple of things. About our future."

She sighed her relief. He had moved the conversation in the direction she needed it to go. "Of course. There are always personal things to talk about. And facing a large-scale project. . . ."

"Exactly." He nodded and gave her a serious look that was almost a scowl. "So I have been thinking. I've looked at possible timetables for this project. It appears the peak workload will be right when our wedding is scheduled."

She stared at him, stunned. That was exactly the point she wanted to raise. "I was thinking that too, Andwele. It's a concern."

"Good. Then I'm sure you'll agree that we need to postpone our wedding."

The wedding was a concern to her, but she was certain his issue and his reasons were quite different from hers. This was going to be interesting. "And why is that?"

"Because of your role in the project. You are vital to its success but your biggest effort would come toward the end, when we are testing the code. Your main job is to verify that the code, the system, meets the specifications. You'll need to interface with the banks and it will be important for you to be there to supervise any fixes to problems and design new tests. Your staff doesn't have the thorough understanding that you do."

The reasoning was curious. "That's true enough, but why wouldn't I be there? Where would I be?"

Andwele took another sip of his drink. "At home, of course. We'd be married."

"We'd be married, but why would I be at home?"

Now it was Andwele's turn to show surprise. "Because we'll be married."

Rashmi shook her head. "You aren't making sense. I won't be coming down with the plague. I'll just be your wife. Why does that mean I'll be at home?"

Andwele stood there looking shocked. "Because a man in my position can't have his wife working."

"A man in your position?"

"Yes. So, of course, when we are married, you'll stay at home."

"Impossible. That's nonsense."

"A man of means, of position, can't allow his wife to work. It would look like I had no real income, no influence. No, I couldn't allow that."

She laughed. "Allow? You think you could stop me from working."

"Of course. The husband is the master of the house."

She sipped her drink, giving herself time to think. Suddenly it tasted sour. "I thought I knew you."

"You do. Of course, you do. No one knows me better."

"I thought you were a modern man, a man adopting the ways of the industrialized world."

"Without sacrificing what is good from our culture."

"And do you think that I will see a man making decisions for me as a good thing? Any man?"

"I will be your husband. That will be my right."

She saw him shifting his feet nervously. He'd made assumptions. So had she, and now that he was stating them and she was pushing back, it unsettled him. His plans, his vision of the future, were clear— and unfettered by reality. He thought he could map it all out and other people would fall in line. "You're right? Are you telling me that all this time you thought that I would be willing to be your slave? After knowing me, how independent I am, do you really think that I would allow any man to control me?"

"But that's you as a single woman. After we are married, you'd be my wife, part of my household, part of my life."

"And give up my dreams?"

"You've already agreed to give up things for our future. You said that marrying me was important. Even if it meant you would stay in Tanzania, despite your foolish desire to return to London, you would do it."

"Foolish?" That hurt and showed he didn't understand her. "Do you honestly think I would give up my career when I've worked so long to achieve the little bit of success I have? Andwele, I was willing to give up my dream of going back to London, but that doesn't mean I was ready to turn off my brain. I hoped we would work together to improve this country. And now, I learn that isn't true."

"It is true."

"No. Sadly, it isn't. I thought it was, but now it seems that your dedication to the work is a fraud."

"That's absurd. You know I work long hours."

"Mostly sucking up to Deputy Minister Dola. You don't do much real work."

"I. . . ."

"You have become obsessed with the trajectory of your career in government, not with doing good things, innovative things. And your affection for me turns out to be with the idea that once the ceremony was complete you would own me, be able to have me remain home— become a docile housewife who has a drink waiting for you at the end of your busy day of meetings with important people."

"And what is wrong with that? The higher my position in government, the more good I can do. And why shouldn't a man want his wife at home? I hate the way other men look at you in those provocative Western clothes."

She sat the empty glass down and walked to the window. The lights of Zurich were on, providing a colorful, vibrant display. It was gorgeous. Andwele stood stiffly, waiting for her to answer his questions. She heard the thud of the door to the minibar and the sound of him refilling his glass. He didn't ask if she wanted another one.

Everything was changing so fast. The revelations were sudden and painful. Her work wasn't what she wanted it to be, but when her contract ended she could change jobs. There weren't many openings in Tanzania, but there were in other places. Perhaps even Childer would give her a reference.

"You are right, Andwele."

"Of course, I am."

"We need to postpone the wedding."

"Yes. I will tell my mother. What date do you think we should pick? The project might last a year, after all."

"Well then, perhaps we can base the date on events."

"Certainly." He sounded relieved. "We could say we will have the ceremony three months after the project launches. That would give her time to prepare things."

"I have a better milestone."

"And that is?"

"I think we should wait until three months after hell freezes over."

Then she turned and walked to the door, almost enjoying the sight of him standing wide-eyed and immobile.

The heavy hotel room door swished shut behind her, and she headed toward her own room with determined strides.

"Damn that man! Damn the entire culture."

PART TWO

A WORK IN PROGRESS

`1010101010101010101010101010101010101010101`

"Bitcoin is better than currency in that you don't have to
be physically in the same place and, of course, for large
transactions, currency can get pretty inconvenient."

—BILL GATES
AN INTERVIEW WITH ERIK SCHATZKER ON BLOOMBERG
TV's SMART STREET SHOW, MARCH 3, 2014

CHAPTER 11
THE ATTENTION OF THE WORLD

"Privacy is necessary for an open society in the electronic
age. Privacy is not secrecy. A private matter is something one
doesn't want the whole world to know, but a secret matter
is something one doesn't want anybody to know. Privacy
is the power to selectively reveal oneself to the world."

—ERIC HUGHES
"A CYPHERPUNK'S MANIFESTO" 1993

A PRIVATE VILLA
PRASLIN ISLAND
THE REPUBLIC OF THE SEYCHELLES

Approximately one thousand miles east of Mozambique lies the island
of Mahé, home to Victoria, the capital city of the archipelago of the
Seychelles, officially the Republic of Seychelles. The country consists
of 115 islands. A further twenty-seven miles northeast, lies the island
of Praslin. It was named Isle de Palmes by the explorer Lazare Picault
in 1744. In 1768, it was renamed Praslin in honor of César Gabriel de
Choiseul, duc de Praslin.

A small, distinguished group gathered in a private villa. They'd
flown in from their headquarters around the world, flying into
Victoria airport on Mahé, then boarding Air Seychelles flights to
Praslin Island Airport. They were all corporate and government leaders and all of them had been summoned for a meeting of the group's
inner circle. It was not a summons to be ignored.

Now they gathered in a private villa on this gorgeous island,
famed for coco-de-mer and vanilla orchids, as well as the Seychelles

black parrot. None of those things, nor the tropical beauty of the islands, warranted a single thought. Each of the group was focused on one thing and one thing only.

"Tell us more about the project, Mr. Childer," an ancient man said. "I fear it puts our efforts at great risk."

Mitch Childer looked at him. The old man owned the villa. He had called this meeting and now he held court. He sat at the head of the long, mahogany table, wearing a dull regimental tie and an archaic black suit that had probably once been perfectly tailored— before his body had withered. Despite his advanced years, his voice carried the same authority it had during his prime, when he'd been among the top echelon at MI6.

"I could've answered this question easily by telephone or video conference without adding the inconvenience and risk of bringing us all together," he said, watching the old man's face.

Besides Childer and the old man, nine other people sat around the table in the room, but for Mitch Childer's purposes, only three of them mattered. The old man was one. The conference room was in his office and he'd called the meeting. The group met erratically, so as to not draw attention to themselves. They met secretly, and names were never used. Childer doubted anyone would dare record their meetings, but the old man had established that rule when he was a much younger, up and coming agent. And now it was sacrosanct.

"You are letting things go to shit," the old man said. "There are aspects to this that are out of control."

"That's not a reasonable summary of the situation at all," Childer said calmly.

"You are too young to realize," the old man said. "This group was formed when I was just a lad . . . but the point is that our charter, our mission, is to use our political influence to move the world to a safer path. To protect it from war and chaos. This artificial, invisible currency shit undermines what we do. Why aren't you stopping it instead of involving us in a pilot project to make it viable?"

Childer nodded. "There is a risk in doing anything, of course, and even a risk in doing nothing. The evolution of cryptocurrencies is inevitable at this point. If there was a chance to stop it, then we missed it. And, after all, you've invested in cryptocurrencies yourself, sir."

The man scowled. "The fact that I've taken opportunities presented to me to make a personal profit has little or nothing to do with our goals as a group. But promoting, or at least not halting, the spread of cryptocurrencies controlled by nations doesn't seem in line with what we are doing. I understand that our goals aren't threatened by the use of digital money, but we need to worry about decentralized control. While we need to ensure that government currencies remain viable for the time being and that the technology develops more, we can't have people turning to sovereign digital currencies, or worse, Bitcoin, and dropping the Euro. That undoes much of our work. And now, with this project it seems that the IMF endorses the thing we fear," the man said, shaking his head. "And if it's learned we are involved . . ."

Childer snorted. He wanted to show his derision. "In this case, any risk of our plan being discovered is minimal; furthermore, the upside potential far more than justifies more risk than we incur."

"Will you please explain, in simple terms, this potential, this upside you see." This command, and there was no doubt that's what it was, came from a tall, dark-haired woman with a stern, unpleasant expression that always seemed to dominate her face. Mitch thought she looked as if she'd eaten something distasteful twenty years before and never gotten it out of her mouth. The truth was that she was just an unpleasant bitch. She was also the second of the three people that mattered. She was used to being obeyed.

Mitch Childer looked around the room, taking in the faces of the people surrounding him, unconsciously evaluating them, categorizing them. Most were junior members still coming into their own. Putting that in context, one woman was the head of the fraud division at Interpol. In a normal group, she would be a potent force. Here, she was still clawing her way up.

Another was a personal assistant, sent by his boss, who was in the hospital. That man had been eager to step into his boss's shoes. There was a slim blonde who looked more like a secretary than a power broker. Childer thought she would've been gorgeous except for her constant look of intense concentration. She was the old man's assistant and increasingly his right hand. He'd been bringing her to meetings regularly. Mitch always made a point of including her when he made eye contact or addressed the group. There was no point in making enemies who might be on their way up.

And finally, there was the dark-faced man with piercing green eyes who had come from Brussels. A quiet man who tended to say little and was the third of this group of powerful people who wielded true power. He represented a vast criminal enterprise, not that many governments weren't also vast criminal enterprises. Why they had been included in what was a political group was a mystery. The green eyes were intimidating and he had been intimidating people within the group for years before Childer was brought into the circle.

He knew better than to ask or challenge the place of the three senior to him on the council.

And now he'd been called on to justify his actions, as he'd known he would be. "The upside I see, the upside that I explained when we discussed this before I engaged in it, is what we will learn from this project."

"Assuming it succeeds," the old man said.

"It will."

"You've brought in outsiders. That brings another interest group into what is already a complex and tricky project. Even you will have to admit there's a fifty-fifty chance of this going tits up."

Out of the corner of his eye, he saw the dark-haired woman flinch at the vulgarity, which was exactly why the old man had used it.

"I don't admit that at all. Bringing in an outside party gives us additional resources."

"Resources owned by our enemies," the woman said.

Childer shook his head. They seemed like children sometimes. "Involving a group that's connected to US intelligence operations gives us someone to blame for anything that might go wrong. If it blows up, then it's because the CIA wanted it to. And they can't claim plausible deniability, not with Hoenig's obvious connections."

The old man grunted. "So we'd cover our asses. But the project could go down in smoke because your little sham turns out to be true. What if Hoenig bid on the project to sabotage it?"

"He wants it to succeed. He wants to get in our good graces."

The woman stood up. "Are you telling me he knows about this group? That he is doing it to work for us and not the IMF?"

"Precisely. While much about this group is secret, its existence isn't. Anyone with Wikipedia can read up on the Bilderberg Group. They know what we are up to, at least generally."

"They did, or thought they did," the old man said. "Of course, that's exactly why we split the vital functions of our operation off into the Retinger Oculistica. Let them track the Bilderberg Group all they want. It operates fairly openly while we do the work the founders intended."

"Naturally, the international intelligence community figured that ploy out. As you know better than anyone, they can deduce our existence from the influence we wield. My membership in an organization of this sort would be obvious to them. This co-opts having them plant people. We open our arms to them."

The old man made a face and bit his lip. "Yes, yes, but there is no good to come from bringing them into our projects."

"I disagree. As I said, they provide resources and are excellent scapegoats," Childer said. He couldn't let any hint of doubt stand. "And before you worry about failure, you must define it precisely. An effective Tanzanian cryptocurrency might be the ostensible goal for the government and the IMF, but it's hardly an issue for us. We all agree that this mania for every country to have its own cryptocurrency isn't sustainable, yet it is almost a fad. They all want it for different reasons, whether it's to avoid international sanctions, be able to attract foreign investment, or simply control their own economies, but it introduces a new chaos. Even the World Bank has been issuing warnings along those lines. I had to argue that the IMF involvement would help keep things manageable. And it will."

"But ultimately this project, this cryptocurrency and others like it, is going to impede our work," the dark-haired woman said. "I don't understand why on earth you are leveraging the power of the IMF to make it happen?"

"It won't impede us if we stick to our plan. Fiat currency is going to die. This is a phase of that death—its death throes. Regional and country digital currencies are a short-term thing, and we need to use it. This project will serve as a test bed, a proving ground for our ideas and technologies. We can't stop the mania; there is no way to convince the governments not to use it to their advantage, but we can use it by working with them. Whether this experiment fails or thrives, the IMF will be able to say it did its part. For our purposes, the data we collect and what we learn about how that data can function, how it can be used, is invaluable. It will find application in the next project. I expect this won't be our last foray into creating national cryptocurrencies, and if this one fails, then we will improve things for the next attempt."

"And what does this get us?" the green-eyed man asked, "besides the attention of the world, the notoriety of trying to get indebted nations to waste money and effort on this foolish cryptocurrency?"

Childer suppressed a smile at the dismissive comment. According to his sources, the old man had already made hundreds of millions in the new digital financial world. Not only had he put money into Litecoin, he'd backed an initial coin offering, an ICO, that made him a bundle. It had been a scam and was worthless now, but he'd gotten out at the peak. Perhaps he honestly thought all of it was a scam. Over time, he'd see his error. "What we get from this is primarily data and technology," Mitch Childer said. "Financial technology is new. Before it establishes itself, expect to see many grand successes and failures. With each one we are involved with, we will become more entrenched, better positioned to move our agenda forward. We need to grasp the reins now, early, if we are going to use a technology that is as inevitable as the Internet to accomplish our goals. We can help people, but only if we have the appropriate tools."

The blonde smiled. "I see that smile. Do you have something to contribute?" the dark-haired woman asked her. Obviously, she saw the woman as Childer did and had decided that a little respect now might go a long way later.

She nodded. "I was thinking of a quote. '"Our Age of Anxiety is, in great part, the result of trying to do today's jobs with yesterday's tools!'"

"That's perfect," Childer said. "Who said that?"

"Marshall McLuhan."

"Old, but amazingly appropriate," the dark-haired woman said.

The blonde almost smiled.

Childer couldn't believe his luck. Her little comment, her quote, made his point perfectly. "Agreed. Obtaining and developing tools—that's precisely the point. With this project, with the tactics we've developed for this and future projects, we intend to ensure that we, and only we, have tomorrow's tools and can do tomorrow's jobs," Childer said.

"The tactics you've developed and sold us, you mean," the old man said. "Half the time I don't know what the hell you are talking about with blockchains, distributed ledgers, master nodes, and proof-of-stake, and all that."

"What matters is that I, and my staff, do know what we are talking about. And those tactics, sir, are designed specifically to implement your strategy—the group's strategy, which will ensure we accomplish our mission. We will help the people of the world. When we control the global economy, then we will be able to protect them and guarantee them a decent life."

The dark-haired woman slapped her hands on the table. "Then you must keep us informed of your progress or of any setbacks. Other than that, it appears we are already committed to this project and we all understand the situation now. There doesn't seem to be anything left to discuss."

"Except the amount of money he needs to execute this game of his," the old man said.

"You could pay that much out of your slush funds," she said, sneering. "It's unimportant."

The old man gasped. "Hundreds of millions of dollars is unimportant?"

"Keep things in perspective," Childer said. "First of all, it's only few million Euros. And we are starting the final economic phase. This takes us quickly into the end game." He paused for effect. "With the global economy estimated at over 70 trillion dollars, yes, I'd say even a few hundreds of millions is unimportant . . . a small investment."

There was quiet around the table.

The dark-haired woman sighed. "Fine then. You have pushed your authority in this matter beyond the limits, but I'm inclined to think it will work out."

"It will."

She leveled a cold glare at him. "For your sake more than mine, I hope so. It's been a long day. What does a person have to do to get a drink in this place?"

The blonde smiled. "I've alerted the servants to prepare. Why don't we adjourn to a more comfortable room where they can get you your drinks? And dinner will be ready in an hour."

"Now that I find satisfactory," the old man said.

"As she pointed out," he said, indicating the dark-haired woman, "we are not all thrilled with this course. It's on your head."

Childer felt a chill. He was being threatened or warned. In this case, it was clear that those two things weren't much different. His fate was tied to the project's success or failure; he had been shown the carrot and the stick. "Of course," he said.

"Walk with me," the dark-haired woman said, coming to his side and putting her arm in his. "I'm trying to decide if you are insightful, almost prophetic in your vision of the future, or an incredibly naive adventurer."

"It seems clear to me," he said. "The future has momentum that is easy to see."

"As I said, incredibly clever or stupid, and it's so hard to tell the difference sometimes. But we will all get to find out which it is soon enough. Won't that be fun?"

Her sudden smile almost shocked Mitch Childer. He'd never seen her smile before. It was an omen, or portent. But of what?

CHAPTER 12

THE PURSUIT OF HAPPINESS

"We hold these truths to be self-evident, that all men are created equal, that they are endowed by their Creator with certain unalienable Rights, that among these are Life, Liberty and the pursuit of Happiness. —That to secure these rights, Governments are instituted among Men, deriving their just powers from the consent of the governed—, —That whenever any Form of Government becomes destructive of these ends, it is the Right of the People to alter or to abolish it, and to institute new Government, laying its foundation on such principles and organizing its powers in such form, as to them shall seem most likely to effect their Safety and Happiness."

THE DECLARATION OF INDEPENDENCE
THE WANT, WILL, AND HOPES OF THE PEOPLE

ZURICH, SWITZERLAND TO
PRINCESS MUNDO IMPERIAL HOTEL
ACAPULCO, MEXICO

Wyatt thought he might burst with joy—at least he assumed it was joy. Whatever it was, it had him filled to the brim. He felt more alive than he had in his life. He was supercharged. Delirious.

Despite the long and arduous flights, two things made his trip, and therefore his attitude, magical. The first was the simple fact of traveling first class—he found he was enjoying comfortable VIP lounges with free food and drink, even hot showers. That was a bonus in addition to the extra space and comfort of the first-class section on the aircraft. The other factor, the more important one, was knowing that he was heading off to something brand new—a new life, a new way of living. No one would know him there, or be waiting for him. He hadn't even known where he was going until that last morning in Zurich.

While sitting through the meetings, his mind raced ahead to where he'd go, what he'd do once this tedious crap was finished. With so many incredible options out there, places he knew little or nothing about to choose from, he'd decided he would go to the airport and take the first plane headed in the direction of a tropical beach. If he was going to throw caution to the wind, why not let his fate choose him?

Before he left Zurich, before he'd decided where he would begin his search for his tropical paradise, he got an email from Ellen. "Start your new life here," it said. "Hang with your people and see where it leads." Attached to the email was a confirmed reservation for the Anarchapulco conference, run by The Dollar Vigilante. It was starting in a few days. He looked at the site. "Make anarchy great again," was the sell line. The program included several days of talks about government, freedom, and cryptocurrency. She'd also reserved him a room at the conference hotel—the Princess Mundo Imperial.

"Brat," he wrote back. "Giving me a gift I can't refuse is dirty pool."

"This looked like a start in the right direction to me, Wyatt. It sounds like your kind of thing. So go and enjoy yourself."

"There's no chance in hell I won't," he said. "I can't ever remember getting a present that surprised or pleased me more."

She laughed. "As I recall, you seemed to like the camping and fishing trip Dad took you on when you guys went into wilderness areas in Wyoming."

"Yeah, but I was twelve then."

"You thought it was cool. And I was jealous."

"I did enjoy it. And it was cool. But this. . . . my little sister sure knows me well."

"Yeah. Your tough luck."

The timing seemed perfect, almost as if they planned it for him. He already could feel how change, this earth-shaking total upset of his life that he'd initiated, was invigorating him. Going with the flow showed him a side of himself he'd never explored before and he was finding that he relished going into free fall—who would've thought that was inside him? There was something exhilarating not having to be anywhere, knowing that no one expected him to be in any particular place on the planet for any reason. That made it easier to breathe. He was nowhere and everywhere.

And what a trip it was. From Zurich, he had flown Air Portugal to Miami, by way of Lisbon. During the long layover in Miami, before boarding an Aeromexico flight to Mexico City, he went online and studied the program, seeing the names of people he had followed for years, watching their videos and learning about new ideas.

A push in the right direction from Ellen. Damn. He was going to be an explorer of new ideas as well as new places. God, how he would explore.

After a short Aeromexico flight to Acapulco, Wyatt got out of a taxi and stepped into brilliant tropical sunshine—he had arrived in a wild and warm new world. His heavy jacket, pants, and shoes, the clothes he'd put on before leaving for the airport in Zurich, were laughably inappropriate. Around him were people in shorts, tank tops, and tee shirts. This, he decided, was going to be good.

The hotel was open to the elements and the lobby in a breezeway. His room was on the seventh floor of the newest building, number three. "An ocean view" it had said, and indeed, he had a balcony overlooking a gorgeous beach that was being pounded by Pacific rollers. The hillsides were dotted with buildings, all trying to capture that view.

He managed to arrive just in time for the conference, which started the next morning. He showered, changed, and went downstairs for dinner at the Beach Club Restaurant. Then exhaustion caught up with him. He signed for the check and went back to his room, collapsing in his bed and sleeping until morning.

Breakfast at the poolside Chula Vista Restaurant was a buffet of Mexican and American food, although he saw a tray of sushi as well. Then he made his way to the main salon where the talks were held. He got his badge from a desk and then wandered to the lobby, nodding to people and wondering how the hell he might start a conversation.

"First time here?"

He turned to see a slim woman in her late twenties with ash-blonde hair that hung down to her shoulders. She had bright, vibrant eyes that sparkled with curiosity. She wore a red tee shirt that said

'Socialism sucks' and was tight enough to show that she didn't wear a bra. Her shorts gave a lovely view of long, tanned legs. "Does my newness show that much? Hayseed Billy Bob goes to New York?"

"Not that bad, but it shows," she said, smiling. "But even if I was guessing. . . . I've been here every year and the conference is growing so fast that most people are new. I had good odds of being right."

He held out a hand. "Wyatt Osgood," he said.

"Rebecca," she said. "Where are you from?"

"That's to be determined," he said.

"Like some of the speeches," she said. "The government apparently prevented some of the speakers from coming to the conference. They grabbed them at the airport and sent them home. So a few of the talks won't be the ones that were intended."

"That's a shame. What are they afraid of?"

Her laughter was music. "The wrong things, of course. And mostly, the wrong people. They think that having these people singing to the choir is a threat of some sort, but that's because they don't understand at all."

"So who should they be afraid of?"

She smiled. "Me, for one," she said flatly. "And perhaps you, Wyatt Osgood."

"Me?"

She shrugged. "That remains to be seen, but I'd rate it as rather likely."

"Did someone tell you that I find enigmatic women sexy, or are you always like this?"

"Always. Why would anyone tell me about you?"

"Why would governments care about anarchists talking to each other?"

"Touché." She touched his arm and it sent a spark running through him. "Wyatt Osgood, I think we are going to be friends."

That idea was appealing. Very appealing. "Where are you from?"

She tossed her head. "Why. . . . the same place you are."

"What a coincidence."

"Indeed," she said.

Staff standing by the doors opened them and people began flowing into the conference hall. "Shall we?" he said.

"We should."

Rebecca stayed with him, introducing him to people, many of them speakers, all of them interesting.

At lunch time they went back to the poolside restaurant. As they ate, he noticed two women next to the pool. It was a distance, but he could see that one of them, an Asian woman, held a video camera. The other, facing the camera, was a petite black woman in a bikini. "Isn't that Sindi?" he said, trying not to point.

"Who is Sindi?" Rebecca asked.

"An online travel blogger."

Rebecca shook her head. "Not one I know. But this is a five-star resort. . . . that's perfect fodder for a travel blogger, I'd guess. I don't normally stay in places like this."

That made sense. "I suppose it makes sense. Yet, there is a certain element of coincidence."

"Coincidence?"

"The thing is, she did a segment on a fancy hotel in Dar es Salaam just before the company I work for took on a job there."

"That seems unreasonable to you? Isn't that what she does?"

"Now she's here. It's the timing of it that makes it seem like an uncomfortably coincidental set of circumstances."

"Is it?" She reached over and touched his hand. It could be some-thing else, you know."

"Besides actual coincidence?"

"Besides that. Maybe you are just stepping into a new river of possi-bilities. What you're feeling is the flow of the right working of things."

He stared at her. "What does that mean?"

"Be gracious enough to let me be enigmatic. You'll get it but you need to absorb more before it will make sense. I just meant that maybe your awareness is changing."

He thought there was some truth in that. "That made you sound like some of the new age anarchists."

"Oh, there is little new about my ideas, Wyatt."

He turned and watched Sindi, certain now that it was her. Her movements, the body. . . .

"She's cute," Rebecca said. "Is she on your to-do list?"

He choked on a laugh that forced its way out. "My to-do list?"

"Most people know of celebrities that they fantasize about having sex with. Is she one of yours?"

The idea of doing Sindi was more than just appealing, and it had occurred to him, but it wasn't a real desire. "I'm a fan of hers. So maybe it would be fair to say that she's someone on my fantasy list, although I've never thought about her that way," he said. That, at least, was honest. "I have no expectation of it being more than that, but I'd never deny that I loved to check out beautiful women, or that I'd turn down someone like Sindi if she showed a flicker of interest in me."

"I like that you don't deny being attracted to her," Rebecca said. "Honesty is good."

The idea seemed to amuse her more than annoy her and that pleased him. She seemed to like him without feeling a need to compete with other women. Suddenly it occurred to him that one of the things that drew him to this woman was her joyous self- confidence. Even without knowing how she felt about him, other than she seemed to enjoy his company, he found it unusual that she didn't feel at all slighted when his attention was drawn to another woman. That was refreshing and attractive. "Tell me about you. You come every year? What do you do?"

She laughed again as if his naiveté and interest delighted her. "I'm a crypto investor and a rampant bitpat."

"A bitpat?"

She chuckled. "Yeah."

"Is that something like an expat?"

"Sort of; generally speaking it is. You know about digital nomads, right?"

"People who travel around making their living online?"

She nodded. "More or less. So, think of us this way—bitpats are a group of digital nomads, a subset, who work together. It's almost as incongruous as this conference since none of us are actually joiners. We are mostly independent cusses that band together for specific projects."

"Projects?"

"Projects of passion or to make money. Really high-level stuff where we think we can make a difference."

"So you work for governments?"

She looked away. "Hardly. That's what you do."

"How do you. . . .?"

"I read your paper. Then I looked you up. So when I saw you here, my curiosity was, shall we say, multileveled, multifaceted."

"My paper?"

"You are a programmer and an insightful one. How do you fit in here with these anarchists, Wyatt Osgood?"

Wyatt looked at the couple at the next table. They were young. He had a stubble of a beard, a shaved head, and wore an olive drab tank top and shorts. She was too thin, had green hair, and lots of piercings, which made him wonder where else she might have them. They were both tattooed and sucking on tubes, vaping. He caught a whiff of cannabis mixed with something fruity. A chubby girl dressed in black who was walking by their table dangled a lit cigarette from her fingers. Obviously, if there were any rules against smoking in the resort, the overworked staff seemed to have given up on any idea of enforcing them.

At another table an older man in a bowtie sat with a blonde woman, both looking elegantly out of place in a poolside bar.

Wyatt looked into Rebecca's limpid blue eyes and sighed. "I think I fit in the same way everyone else around us does—by not fitting in at all."

The comment got a deep laugh. "All right. And what do you gain from coming here?"

"Perspective." She folded her hands, waiting. Without asking, she was probing for details, and he suddenly wanted to share. So he told her about his decision back in Virginia, how his universe was changing. He talked about his deal with Hoenig and Ellen's gift. "I have no idea where it's taking me," he said, "but it all feels right."

"That's simply lovely," she said. "It can be unsettling, but we should all turn our worlds upside down every now and then."

"We should?"

"It's really the only way to get some clarity."

"Good word, clarity."

"It's a tangible way to be an objectivist, to truly check your premises."

"Ayn Rand," he said.

"Right."

"Although from watching the people at this conference, the only thing that is clear is that there are so many different factions; people are moving in every direction at once."

"True, but they are open to moving in other directions, some of them. Truth seeking can seem chaotic at times. Is truth what you want?"

"That's a fair question," he said. "I think so."

She leaned forward, resting her elbows on the table. He couldn't resist looking at her breasts. "And what else are you interested in finding out?"

He swallowed, hesitating before deciding to come straight out with it. "I'm interested in finding out if you would like to have sex with me."

She smiled. "Direct. . . . I like that approach and I'll admit I'm interested. Whether I'd actually like having sex with you is a rather empirical question, don't you think?"

"I suppose it is."

"And, given that there won't be much special in the afternoon talks, why don't we go to your room and see if we can't determine an answer to that pressing question?"

"Yes," he said, calling for the waitress.

As he paid the bill, he saw Rebecca looking him over and he started to realize that the question did have some very pressing dimensions.

CHAPTER 13
CONSIDERING ALLEGIANCES

"When I was young I thought that money was the most important thing in life; now that I am old I know that it is."

—OSCAR WILDE
IRISH POET AND PLAYWRIGHT

GOLDEN TULIP DAR ES SALAAM CITY CENTER HOTEL
CITY PLAZA, JAMHURI STREET
DAR ES SALAAM, TANZANIA

Peggy took a morning Swiss International Air Lines flight from Zurich to Nairobi, had a one hour layover in the VIP lounge at the airport, then left for Dar es Salaam. The total trip was around twelve hours, and it left her frazzled and disoriented. Fortunately, the Tanzanian Government had everything arranged on their end. A smiling man in a black suit was holding up a sign with her name on it as she came out of the baggage claim. He took her bags and led her to a waiting limo that drove her to the Golden Tulip Hotel in downtown Dar es Salaam.

She smiled, remembering how people compared the Bitcoin boom to the tulip mania that spread across Europe in the 1600s. There was a certain unintended irony in the choice of hotels. At least she hoped it was unintended. Inside, the staff was waiting for her.

"Welcome to Dar es Salaam," a smiling man with the darkest skin she'd ever seen said as he handed her the keys. A smiling younger man in a uniform took her bags and took her to her room.

If everyone was like these first two people, Peggy worried that she might be smiled to death. This city had to be whatever the exact opposite of New York City was. Smiles instead of frowns. Pleasantries instead of rudeness. So far, at least.

The hotel itself was an upmarket place. Part of a chain and obviously targeting business people. Andwele had told her they would put her conveniently close to the office where she would be working—with him and Rashmi, and a handful of coders who worked for him.

When the bellhop left, she looked around. At first, the ordinariness of the Golden Tulip disappointed her. After the Dolder Grand, it was a letdown, but that was an unfair comparison. The place was clean and attractive and had everything she really needed. Elegance didn't matter much now. She wouldn't be spending much time there anyway. She had work to do, work that excited her—she had an opportunity to change her own world for the better. Given all that, knowing it was a temporary haven until she set herself free, it was fine. More than fine.

And it was nice, as such places go. She had a view of the city from a lovely balcony. Her room had all the modern conveniences, including a wet bar. Andwele even had the management leave her a bottle of cognac. It was a nice, welcoming gesture. Certainly better than flowers, and she sipped a snifter of the smooth liquor as she unpacked her bags.

She laid everything out on the bed . . . all of her clothes, her things, before putting them away. She'd brought all her business clothing and some nice dresses for fancy occasions. You couldn't know how much pomp and ceremony you'd encounter working on a government job—maybe none at all.

She looked at it and sighed. Everything she owned, beyond some furniture in an apartment back in Virginia, lay on that king-sized bed. It didn't amount to much. Her vagabond life hadn't lent itself to accumulating much. She bought computers and software, but those things were consumables. Once this was complete, once the cash was flowing into the accounts she had carefully set up through shelf corporations she'd bought on the dark web, then she would treat herself . . . to nice clothes, lavish resorts, hot sex . . . whatever she wanted. So yes, the hotel, her clothes, her entire present existence, would do for now.

And, with a well-equipped business center, pool, and gym, the hotel lacked nothing important. In truth, the Dolder Grand in Zurich had only one amenity she truly missed—a certain waiter. The memory of nights with Franz sent a pleasant shiver rippling through her.

The encounters with him had been pure sex. He said almost nothing to her and she didn't ask about him. He could be married or a wanted criminal. All that had mattered was that he had stripped her naked and devoured her. What made her tingle was his strong, masculine body and that he'd been a barbarian between the sheets. She'd had affairs before, but never anything that intense, that purely physical, and never with a man who took control of her and made her body dance. Each night that he came to her, he stayed the entire night, repeatedly waking her to fuck her again. By morning, when he'd wordlessly get up and dress to return to whatever place he'd sprung from, he left her weak and satisfied.

She had no doubt that bedding female guests was a regular thing for him. She didn't give a damn. She'd wanted him and he'd fucked her better than anyone ever had. And when she'd found herself returning to the hotel so soon, it almost seemed as if he'd been waiting for her to arrive. He'd taken the note with her room number so smoothly, and she felt wicked doing it right there under Claude's self-righteous, Christian nose. The damn prig.

That night in Zurich, right after dinner, she'd gone to her room. Franz appeared moments later, to undress her, spread her out on that huge bed, and he'd fucked her. No one had ever made her come so many times, so hard. He was incredible. She let herself fantasize. Perhaps, when she was rich . . .

But now she was here. She had to put him out of her mind and get the work done. If she did it well, she'd be able to find lots of men like Franz. They would be drawn to her, be at her beck and call. The very thought made her shiver.

She turned her mind back to the project. Being in charge of such an important project was a heady experience and she alternated between being excited and nervous. The scope of the project was daunting. No one had ever created a system like the one she was about to implement. The opportunity to improve the economic fate of an entire country was in her hands.

If it went well, then no one would even know about some of the best parts of it. That was a bittersweet thought. Another way to see it was that the best parts, the trickiest pieces, the cleverest innovations would be for her benefit alone.

But it had to work. From her perspective, she had to overcome a couple of obstacles. One of those was Childer's insistence that she implement the new system, meet the deadline, and somehow manage to keep the resident nerds, as well as Wyatt, from puzzling out all of the things it did, especially the 'features' he requested. Being in charge helped. She could tell the coders to mind their own business and to work on modules. Hell, they were government employees and they'd do what they were told—slowly, perhaps incompetently, but she could deal with that.

Rashmi Patel was a bigger danger. It was Rashmi's job to understand the system and then make sure it did what she was told it was supposed to do. It was Peggy's job to make sure it did a few things that Rashmi never knew about. In a sense, that worked in her favor. As long as she was hiding things, it was no big deal to hide the additional functions that even that fuck Childer wouldn't know about. Her own additions were the reason she'd taken the job. She'd seen the future was in financial systems. She'd courted Hoenig, while making him think he was after her, because it was easier to hack from the inside than the outside. She'd pushed to get this project and it was a gamble. Failure would mean she'd have trouble finding work again. So doing it for a salary would have been a nonstarter. No, if she was going to gamble her career, she wanted more as a reward than what he'd put on the table.

"Some call it greed; I call it a guarantee of job satisfaction," she told the attractive, half-naked woman in her bedroom mirror. "Satisfaction is important," she said, then she looked around the room. She had a momentary tactile memory of Franz coming into her room, of hiking her dress up, pulling her panties down, and forcing himself into her. Damn, but that was sweet.

She sighed and refocused. Getting the job done would mean getting some allies. Peggy got along with coders and she'd find some among the locals she could gain the loyalty of. Some would nurse a vague hope that she'd be impressed with them and either offer them a job in the US or a blowjob. Statistically, the odds were that 90 percent would be young guys, after all. She'd let them get their hopes up on either count if that helped her cause.

That would let her hide the funny business and still get the work done, but she needed a buffer at the top. She needed help in giving

Rashmi some misleading information and, more importantly, someone who would know, tip her off, if she smelled a rat. Her best bet
there was Andwele Kassain. He might be engaged, but he was a man.
And he was ambitious. If she was lucky, he had a weak will and a
streak of greed. That would make him perfect for her needs.

With part of the day to kill, and work starting the next day,
she grabbed the moment. She picked up her phone and called him.
"Peggy," he said. He sounded pleased that she'd called. "Are you settling in okay?"

"Pretty well. I was wondering about getting to the office tomorrow . . ."

"A car will pick you up at nine. The driver will be in the lobby waiting."

"Excellent. I was wondering . . ."

"What?"

"I feel a little disoriented and, well . . . I'm all alone. I'm not an
experienced traveler and I'm overwhelmed. I was wondering if it was
possible for us to have dinner together tonight. It would give us a
chance to get to know each other better. We really need to hit the
ground running if we are going to make our milestones and that's
easier if we develop a relationship."

"I'd be delighted," he said. "Unfortunately, Rashmi is not feeling well."

"Poor thing," Peggy said, feeling like she was on a roll. "I understand if you need to be with her."

He laughed. "The last thing that woman wants is me hovering over
her when she is feeling poorly. All my well-intentioned suggestions
drive her mad. She is so independent. Almost like an American woman."

"And that bothers you?"

"No," he said. She could hear his breath. She knew he was forcing
himself to be calm. "Not at all."

He was already excited. She licked her lips. "Then can you come
to the hotel?"

"Did you want to eat there?"

"We are on your turf, Andwele. You pick a place."

Again she heard him inhale. "Then I will be there in, say, an hour?"

"Make it two," she said. Giving him time to anticipate the dinner
would unnerve him more. He was responding nicely. She began to feel
like things were going to move along smoothly.

CHAPTER 14

A NEW DESTINATION

*"The more people you have to ask for permission,
the more dangerous a project gets."*

—ALAIN DE BOTTON
THE ARCHITECTURE OF HAPPINESS

PRINCESS MUNDO IMPERIAL HOTEL
ACAPULCO, MEXICO

With the bright morning light of southern Mexico pouring in through the glass doors that led from his balcony, Wyatt woke alone. A note was sitting on the nightstand. "See you at breakfast," it said. "Text me before you head down."

He smiled, recalling the night he'd spent with Rebecca. They had clicked together in the best of all possible ways. He found her an incredibly sensual, exciting woman. She was stimulating sexually and mentally.

As he showered and dressed, he thought back to his life before. It was almost amusing to think about it—it seemed decades ago now, and he must have been a different person entirely. It didn't seem possible that he ever thought the lukewarm passion he'd shared with Janet was significant. Sex with her had been fun and a release, not love, and it certainly never reached the heights he'd experienced with Rebecca in his arms.

The question was whether this was a passing moment in his life, a wild awakening, or the beginning of something. He didn't know. He doubted she did either and he refused to let himself expect too much, think too far ahead. He was just beginning to live in the here and now and worrying about what might happen would ruin it for them both.

Hell, he didn't even know where he was going when the conference ended. He laughed. That was a week away. A lifetime. He wanted to celebrate the now. After sending her a quick text to meet him at the Chula Vista, he poured a tall glass of Jack Daniels and headed down the elevator thinking about the breakfast buffet.

He asked for a table for two. "*Café*" the waiter asked as he sat him at a table at the edge of the restaurant. Black birds with striking yellow eyes, birds that looked like small ravens, danced on the umbrellas, made mad dashes inside to steal bread from plates. "Would you care for orange juice, or *jugo verde*?"

He held up his glass. "Bourbon before breakfast suits me just fine," he said.

A chuckle from the next table made him turn to see a man in a crisp blue suit and bowtie shaking his head. "Can I help you somehow? Do you find my drinking in the morning amusing?"

"Not as such," the man said.

"We are at an anarchist conference, after all . . ."

"Oh, yes, amusing, but in a good way, I just thought the way you said it, making the pronouncement to the waiter, was for my benefit."

Wyatt laughed. "Your benefit? How does that work? I'm the one drinking."

"Good morning, Wyatt," Rebecca said, flowing to the table. She wore a light summer dress that accented her figure. "I see you've met Jeffrey."

"Jeffrey?" It surprised him that she knew this man.

"Good morning, Rebecca," he said. "Yes, my name is Jeffrey. I'm Jeffrey A. Tucker," the man said.

The name sounded familiar. "And?"

"And I wasn't judging your drinking. But when I heard you say you preferred bourbon before breakfast, I assumed you knew who I was."

"I don't get it."

"That's the title of a book I wrote almost a decade ago."

It came to him then. He even remembered the book. "Didn't you just write up something on the Venezuelan crypto debacle? I saw it online. You trashed the Petro. That was great."

He smiled and nodded. "I'm glad you enjoyed it."

"My God, what idiots they must've had planning that shitshow." Wyatt held out a hand. "I am pleased to meet you; the name is Wyatt Osgood."

They shook. "In that case, I hope to see you at my talk today. It's good to have fans in the audience."

"We will be there," Rebecca said.

Jeffrey Tucker stood. "Now I'll leave you to your bourbon and I'll offer my congratulations on your ability to live outside the statist quo. Keep on."

"I'll try," Wyatt said, thinking that 'living outside the statist quo' had a lovely ring to it.

"When we go over to the conference again, I'll introduce you to Jeff Berwick," she said. "I want you two to meet."

"Do you know everyone here?"

She gave him a conspiratorial wink. "I know the ones that matter. People like you."

Again the idea that she regarded him as special unsettled Wyatt. It wasn't that he wasn't flattered, but the sense that she had known who he was before he got there rattled him. Okay, she'd read his paper, but once she connected with him, it almost seemed like she'd come there to meet him.

That was absurd, of course.

"Where are you going from here?" he asked her, mostly just stalling while he thought.

"Here and there," she said. "I have some cleanup work to do on a couple of programs. A smart contract doesn't seem to be living up to its reputation and is being rather stupid; I've been asked to take a peek. How about you?"

"A beach," he said.

"Well, that narrows things a lot."

"The truth is, I hadn't decided yet."

"I see."

"Any ideas or recommendations you'd care to make?"

She licked her lips. "I don't normally like to make recommendations. People's tastes vary too much."

"I'm looking for a quiet place, most of the time, where I can live simply and do my work."

She made a face. "For this government job?"

"I promised. It's how I break free."

"Says you."

"I do."

"And I know you believe it. Well, in my experience, one such place that isn't even that far away is in the Yucatán. Progreso is a beach town not too far from the city of Mérida. If you need anything, it's handy to have a city nearby. And who knows? Maybe the allure of the beach will fade."

"That's pure sacrilege, Rebecca."

"Not that the beach becomes old so much, but think of cruise ships and Canadian snowbirds. They can intrude on a regular basis. At any rate, if the idea appeals to you, I can even suggest you talk to Charlie and Maya. They own the Milk Bar and have two apartments upstairs that are reasonable and have the best beach view on the malecón— that's the main beach."

"Really?"

"I certainly enjoyed my time there."

"That sounds ideal. How do I. . . ."

"I'll call him and see what he's got. It's low season coming up, so he might have something."

"That would be great." Mixed feelings flooded through him. Obviously, they'd be going their separate ways after the conference and that was a slightly bitter pill. Here and now, he reminded himself. Enjoy the time together.

"I might even drop by one day and see how you are getting on," she said. "Assuming you'd want company."

Wyatt's heart jumped. "That would be great."

She looked out at the pool, over toward where several women were playing with a group of noisy children who seemed to find the pool a wonderland. "It all depends on my workload, of course. I've given my word to some people myself so I can't make promises. . . . I won't make any I can't keep. Quite often my time isn't my own."

"I understand."

She touched his arm again. "No, you don't; there's no way you could, not yet."

"Yet?"

"You are trying very hard to work it all out and I think you will. So you get points." She waved to get the waiter's attention. "Now I need coffee and breakfast before we go listen to Jeffrey's talk." She took out a program and scanned it. "It seems, however, that the talks after his aren't of a lot of interest to me personally. Unless there is one you really need to hear, maybe we could find a way to entertain ourselves for a time after his talk."

Wyatt found his mouth dry. "I think that would be great," he said, hating how trivial the word 'great' made his feelings sound.

She stood up. "Then I'm going to see if they've got some nice breakfast tortillas on the buffet."

Wyatt got up, suddenly feeling hungry. After all, if things went well, he was going to need his strength. As he made his way toward the buffet, he glanced out across the lush grounds of the hotel and wondered if Sindi was still making videos. He'd have to remember to watch for the one from this hotel. It would be weird to watch one that was made while he was right there.

There was an eerie strangeness to this conference, to meeting Rebecca, seeing Sindi. . . . to everything that was happening to him. Strange and wonderful.

As he watched Rebecca lift the stainless steel lid on the rice and spoon it onto her plate, his gaze traced the lines of her body, thinking how remarkable it was to meet someone who seemed so congruent, whose body and mind were in such beautiful harmony. And yet, he was sure that this delicious package contained secrets. She'd alluded to them. He hoped he'd have the chance to find out what they were.

CHAPTER 15
INTERPOL AND POLICY

"They who can give up essential liberty to obtain a little temporary safety deserve neither liberty nor safety."

—BENJAMIN FRANKLIN
MEMOIRS OF THE LIFE & WRITINGS OF BENJAMIN FRANKLIN

HAKI DOLA'S OFFICE
MINISTRY OF FINANCE
DAR ES SALAAM, TANZANIA

Mitch Childer sat down in an expensive, new, elegant, yet amazingly uncomfortable, leather chair and folded his hands in his lap. Then he smiled at Deputy Finance Minister Haki Dola, who sat behind his desk before turning his head, just the slightest amount, to acknowledge the presence of Andwele Kassain.

"Mr. Childer, it is truly excellent to see you again . . . so soon. You are looking well."

Childer nodded. "And you, Deputy Minister. I would like to thank you for agreeing to this meeting."

"And this lovely lady is . . ."

"She is the point of the meeting. I asked for this meeting to introduce you to Osk Barstad," he said, indicating the large, blonde, and pale woman who sat next to him. "She is with the computer bank fraud group at Interpol—she runs that division." She was thirty-one, a career woman with a steady and calm demeanor and a ready smile. Childer knew that exterior hid an aggressive and hard interior. The woman had nerves of steel.

Deputy Minister Dola managed a smile. "And what do we owe the pleasure of your visit, Ms. Barstad?" he asked.

"I'm here to examine the ramifications of your new financial transaction project. Your project has attracted our attention. Because you are turning to distributed transactions, cryptocurrency, and because your banks are linked to international banks, we are very interested in tracking what you are doing. You are exposing international banking to some new, possibly disruptive, technology and I am here to review it."

Haki Dola's face grew tense. "It's a sovereign matter."

Osk shook her head. "The Sustainable Banking Network (SBN) would disagree with that assessment. And the International Banking Research Network is already asking for information as well. Furthermore, several of the banks involved are branches of international banks headquartered in European Union (EU) countries and subject to EU regulations. As a matter of expediency, they've agreed to let my group monitor the situation. Of course, if you wish to disconnect your banks from the international community, to have them isolated, then it would totally be a sovereign matter. You are perfectly free to tell them all to go to hell."

"No, that isn't what I meant at all," Dola said.

Childer put out a calming hand. "No need to panic. In any case, I'd expect you to embrace the input and interest from Interpol, Deputy Minister," Childer pointed out. "The IMF is supporting this project to ensure that it is compliant with strategies that will foster world financial markets. Ms. Barstad wishes to see that your approaches can't be easily compromised, that there are safeguards in place."

"Our approaches?" Childer smiled, seeing the man's hackles rise. "Much of the design of the system, its very inspiration, comes directly from you at the IMF and the contractors you have recommended."

"While that is entirely true, don't underestimate the need to bend over backward to demonstrate our openness about what we are doing. Oversight from Interpol will see that we all get what we want. Think of the insurance factor."

"I don't understand," Dola said.

"If you open up your records to Ms. Barstad, let her see the inner workings, talk to the banks and other involved parties, then if anything were to go wrong, no one could ever blame you or your government. You will have gone to great lengths to use internal and external audits, combining the efforts of Ms. Patel, the IMF, and Interpol, to guarantee that everything is transparent."

Suddenly, Mitch Childer saw the slump in Dola's shoulders that told him he'd made his point. He'd been certain that Dola was working on some scam with the help of friends in the financial markets. Denying Barstad access would be tantamount to admitting that he was hatching some scheme to benefit directly from the new system. Now the opportunity was being taken from him. "I suppose that is all true enough," he said. "It's just that it gives the impression we are being controlled by foreign agencies."

"You are," Osk said happily. "The price of playing in international finance, of borrowing money from the World Bank, of letting the IMF help you, is that they become stakeholders in your country. That's how it is."

"It's politics," Childer added.

Andwele coughed. "The real problem I see . . ."

They all turned to him and he hesitated. "Go on," Childer said. This was good. They could browbeat Dola, but he wanted Andwele on board voluntarily. "Adding yet another layer to the project is going to slow down the progress. You've given us rather ambitious deadlines to meet already." He glanced at Dola. "The requirement of using only one outside programmer to run the project has taxed our resources." He shook his head. "Things seem to be constantly added to the work."

"What sorts of things are being added?" Osk asked. "I was under the impression that everything was all clearly specified at the outset. Adding new functions . . ."

Andwele Kassain rubbed his nose. "I don't mean new functions, Ms. Barstad. I'm talking about things we've found that are needed to make the system do what we've promised it will do. The functionality is more comprehensive than we initially understood it to be and our infrastructure, less so."

"How can that be?" she asked.

"Until we started work, we didn't know that the banks hadn't fully integrated some aspects of the financial system. They were being run almost as separate efforts. For example, our system uses smart contracts to escrow various transactions, eliminating the time and expense, and potential for error or corruption that comes from human interaction. But we discovered that the credit rating system was something the local banks had been doing with a totally separate database—an entirely separate department, with its own computer system, evaluates the credit risk factors and then generate a simple credit score. They pass the score along, but the data is kept on their computers. For our purposes, the credit rating must be an integral part of the distributed system so the contracts will securely execute without the possibility of someone altering a score or any other factor. That has meant building new databases with all the borrower and lender personal data into our system. We hadn't counted on the need for that effort."

"It's obviously a large task," Osk said. "But your brief explanation is exactly the sort of thing I'm looking at. I have no intention of digging into the details of how you do it, but knowing that you are doing that to preserve the integrity of the system is useful to us at Interpol. I won't be harassing your techs."

Childer saw the relief on Andwele's face and decided he wasn't hiding anything. He had no issues with transparency. "You see, we can all work together."

"But how will you learn these things without going over the code or having the programmers explain every little thing?" Andwele asked.

Osk looked at Dola. "He thinks like a fintech person," she said, then turned back to Andwele, "And that's how you should think. What you don't see, and I'm sure Mr. Dola does, is that I'm more interested in the theory of operation and the contributions of the various financial institutions. So, with Deputy Minister Dola's permission, I will require the bankers to explain how they interface with the system, the nature of the information they provide access to . . . In this case, if I understand correctly, it seems that once this system is up and running, the banks won't need individual databases on the customers. Is that correct?"

Andwele nodded. "Exactly. The system will run future credit scores and the bank will simply inquire based on a person's identification number and learn that they could loan them a certain amount and a certain risk level—they translate that into an interest rate."

"So the banks will no longer require all this information themselves and the system will ensure privacy. That, in turn, protects the international system," Osk said.

Childer loved the spin she put on the facts. It all sounded safe and cozy, even to him.

Osk smiled at Andwele. "So I say well done. That is a step forward. No longer will multiple banks, loan companies, and brokerages be allowed to store personal data. They are too easily hacked."

"That's very true," Andwele said.

"You see, that is how I will work. Mostly I just need to learn how the financial functions will be changing so I can assure my people, the banking industry, and the European Union's regulators, that adequate precautions are being made. That means asking questions like this one . . . enough for me to find out how you are handling things, but nothing more. From the perspective of your daily work, the work your programmers are doing, I'll simply be a fly on the wall."

Childer saw that Andwele was still uncertain, but he'd adjust. "Then I am delighted you are here," Andwele said. Childer noted that Dola, on the other hand, looked worried. He was obviously thinking about ways to cover his tracks. It was a sucker bet to go against the idea that as soon as they left his office, he'd be on the phone to whomever he was working a scam with within the banking or finance sector.

"We should let you gentlemen get back to work," Childer said, standing. "I'll show Ms. Barstad around, introduce her to people. So, Deputy Minister, if you'd just make a few calls and let the key people know that she will be dropping in on them and that your office is asking them to cooperate fully . . ."

"Of course, of course," Dola said. "We are delighted to have Interpol's blessing on the project."

"That went well," Osk said as they left the meeting.

Mitch Childer smiled his agreement. "It did. I told you that alerting them wouldn't make things smoother. This way it is a fait accompli before Dola has a chance to put up a defense. Now, of course, he'll hide the evidence of whatever he was doing."

"He doesn't seem all that clever. What do you want me to do if I do find he was up to something?"

Childer smiled. "When you do, get some clear-cut evidence and hold onto it in case we need something from him later. It will be much more useful if he manages to move up in the government."

She shook her head. "That seems unlikely. A man like that . . ."

"Bureaucrats can amaze you with their ability to slither up the food chain despite a total lack of qualifications," Childer told her. "It astounds me and I've simply learned to accept it."

"Until we make them obsolete," she said.

"Until then."

He led her to the elevators and to the basement where Peggy Anne Dory worked with her programmers. It was a cluttered, chaotic office space, where the programmers worked at terminals in cubicles. The two far corners were glassed-in offices—one was a conference room with whiteboards covered with code and comments. The other was Peggy's office.

"Mr. Childer," Peggy said when they walked in.

Once again enjoying the advantage he gained from the element of surprise, Childer beamed as he made the introductions. "Ms. Barstad works closely with the IMF," he said. "She's fully briefed on our additions to the project."

"Andwele wasn't thrilled about the credit score integration," Peggy said. "And not being able to tell him why it was critical made it a hard sell."

"He obviously bought into the scenario you fed him," Osk said. "He just read it back to us rather nicely, as if he believed it."

"And doing that is why you are getting well paid," Childer said. It was an important point and needed reinforcing. It bothered him that Peggy didn't seem as grateful about the addition to her salary as he expected. That made it seem unimportant to her and put her loyalty in question. He didn't trust people he'd bought who were too confident. But this wasn't the time or place to probe. Besides, having Osk on site would limit Peggy's ability to do anything he didn't like. She needed to know he had eyes on her.

"It's hard," Peggy repeated.

"Well, Osk, Ms. Barstad will make that part easier. If anyone questions a feature or a change, tell them it's at Interpol's request, as a means of combating fraud, but that we only see a piece of it and aren't cleared to know exactly how it works."

Peggy grinned. "You know, I like that. That has legs."

"Legs?" Childer asked.

"An American expression," Osk said. "She means it will do nicely."

Childer looked at Peggy and saw her nod. "Yup." Another expression for him to detest Americans for, if there weren't more than enough reasons already. One day . . . "Good. I'm glad to see that you two will work well together."

Peggy was thinking, calculating, he saw it in her eyes. "Yes, I think that Osk and I will work well together." She raised a finger. "I'm surprised that Interpol and the IMF would work so closely."

Osk touched her arm. "Many alliances in this world function more smoothly if they aren't examined too closely, my dear. This one might be one of those."

Childer allowed himself a thin smile. Osk was, as always, able to tell the truth without giving much away. That's why the board of directors valued her, that's why they had approved him bringing her in on this. On the downside, her loyalty wasn't directly to him. Osk had her own supporters on the board and her own power base in and outside of Interpol. She was a force. In this case, a useful one.

He couldn't quite read Peggy's face. She had clearly understood the value to her of Osk being there, of the leverage the woman gave her. But there was something else. He felt it in his gut—like Dola, she had her own agenda. Unlike Dola, she saw Osk Barstad as a means to her own end.

That bore watching.

CHAPTER 16

ARRIVAL IN PARADISE

"For more and more of us, home has really less to do with a
piece of soil, than you could say, with a piece of soul."

—Pico Iyer

Malecón de Progreso
Yucatán, Mexico

After a 45 minute ride from the airport, the cab dropped Wyatt
Osgood off on a sun-drenched street. The early afternoon heat was
intense. He sat in the taxi getting his bearings. Above street level, a
sign said, "Milk Bar."

"Progreso," the driver said. "My home town. You stay long?"

"I have no idea."

The man handed back a card with the name Raul and a phone
number. "You need things, I help."

For a price, Wyatt thought. "Thanks, man. I'll hang onto this."

"I show you the best places," he said.

"Well, I'll start with this one," Wyatt said staring out the window.
This was the place Rebecca had liked, had recommended. She'd said
the rooms were upstairs and he glanced up at the second floor. There
was a strange, interestingly curved balcony that reminded him of the
curve of a piano's lid.

He sat in the taxi for a moment taking it all in. He was overwhelmed but he knew that he'd instantly fallen in love with the place.
He paid the driver the fare they'd agreed on and a small tip, then got
out with his duffle. The driver waved, and as the taxi pulled away,

Wyatt turned toward the door of the hotel. Next to it, he saw a small store, a tienda—one of those small stores that sold a little of all the everyday things a person needed for daily life. It had a tall, glass-fronted cooler filled with frosty cans and bottles of beer. Lovely. That was just what the doctor ordered and an auspicious welcoming to a new home.

A dark-skinned lady with a bright smile rattled something at him in Spanish as she sold him a bottle of Corona Extra for some of the pesos he'd changed at the airport during his layover in Mexico City on his way to Acapulco. At the resort, everything had gone on his credit card and he hadn't spent more than the 500 pesos for taxis to and from the airport. He opened the beer and took a sip. The uneven lip of the bottle was rough against his lips and he tasted rust—the bottle was recycled but not with any particular care it seemed. But the beer tasted like the best thing he'd ever had and he drank it down.

Across the street was the wide expanse of white beach, calling to him. Hot and tired, but no longer parched, it was time to find his room. Before he went in, he bought another beer, a can this time, and a bottle of tequila (he was in Mexico, after all) and took it into the hotel. A man looked up when he came in, a gringo, he was sure.

"Are you Charlie?"

"If you're the guy Rebecca said to expect, then I will be," he said, grinning. "Otherwise, do I need to run?"

The welcome, the feel of the place, made Wyatt comfortable. "I'm the guy, Charlie; I understand you have a room with a nice view of the beach?" he asked.

"Best views you can find. Both of our places have fantastic views—it's the same view, as a matter of fact," he laughed. "Rebecca thought you'd want the bigger one."

"She did?"

"Well, I hope she got that right, considering it's the one that's available," the man said, sounding pleased with himself. "The other isn't occupied but it is rented."

"I'd like to see it before I say yes," Wyatt said.

"Now that's reasonable."

When Charlie led him around to the stairs at the side of the building and onto the balcony, he saw that the rooms were actually apartments and they shared the balcony. Charlie opened the sliding glass door and led him inside. The sound of the ocean was faint, but a steady onshore breeze made everything seem fresh. The kitchen was tiny but fine for times when he wanted to eat in, assuming that happened.

"I'll try it for a month, if that's okay," he said.

Charlie held out a hand. "Fine with me. If you want it for a longer period of time, there could be a discount for that, and another small one if you pay in Bitcoin."

"Really?"

"Hey, amigo, you are visiting an ancient, yet advanced civilization; the Milk Bar is often home to cutting-edge expats passing through." He tipped his head. "And some that are not so cutting edge as well." He handed Wyatt the keys. He turned to walk out, then stopped and turned back. "There is a kitchen in this place but I like to mention that we have an excellent restaurant downstairs, and you can run a tab up to a reasonable amount. It's open six days a week, three meals a day."

"That's convenient."

Charlie laughed. "Isn't it though? And convenience suckers folks into spending more money with us, which is a good thing."

"Smart business."

"In a place like this, you need all the leverage you can get. As you settle in, if you need anything, you tell me," he said.

"Like what?"

The man shrugged. "You're new in town and might need things. How do I know? But Maya, my wife, and I can be a resource."

"Thanks," Wyatt said. "I'm pretty beat after the trip." And that was true. Tiredness was beginning to weigh on him heavily.

"Take a nap and come down for dinner," the man said. "For a friend of Rebecca, the first meal is on the house. You pay for your liquor, though."

"Fair enough."

Charlie grinned and left. With him gone, Wyatt sat and listened to the sea breeze coming in through the door and a few sounds from the street below. He sure wasn't at the Dolder Grand anymore. For better and worse, he was living in a beachfront apartment—a totally different kind of elegance. He grabbed his duffle and took it into the bedroom where he tossed it on the bed. My place, he thought.

The day was warm and the door stood open. He poured a drink, walked to the railing, and looked out over his domain. Below him was a street; across the street were the thatched-roof *palapas* where the restaurants set up tables for patrons to eat on the beach. Beyond them, the blue Caribbean Sea lapped gently at the white sand like a scene from a travel documentary. And it was his view.

All the place lacked was Rebecca. He tried not to hope too hard that she'd come and see him. Even if she did, he had no idea how long it would be.

"Don't stop living and don't wait for anyone," she'd said when they parted. "Go ahead with following your dream, figuring it out as you go. Never expect anything from other people."

He began shedding his Hawaiian shirt and then his shorts; the sensual caress of the sea breeze was wonderful on his naked body. He left his clothes scattered on the floor. My place, he said, thinking how odd that he could manage to feel a sense of true ownership on a short-term rental.

He picked up the tequila bottle and went to sit on the couch to enjoy the cool sea breeze coming through the open doors. He poured a large shot of the amber liquid into a glass and drank it down while staring out over the nearly empty beach. In the distance, a cruise ship headed out to sea; it had a small plume of smoke coming from its fin-shaped stack, looking like a big blue and red bird heading off into the horizon.

Reality was slow in coming to him. The transitions from the stuffy meetings in a five-star hotel in Zurich to a passionate affair in Acapulco at yet another resort, to being alone in a laid-back beach town had been abrupt. Mind-boggling. But now, Wyatt felt himself relaxing . . . tension seemed to seep out of him.

As his mind calmed, he began taking stock of his surroundings. Ironically, he decided that there wasn't anything special about this place. It was a nice apartment with a grand view. What was special was that this situation was exactly what he'd dreamed of. This place, this feeling, was exactly the kind of feeling he'd been looking for. That didn't excite him. Instead of being excited about these first steps into a new and unknown world, he felt content for the first time in a long time. Rebecca's admonitions about enjoying the moments, about letting the future unfold, provided the rock, the base for everything.

Yes, Wyatt Osgood had arrived.

He let out a long sigh, let the last uncertainties about what he was doing, the last doubt that he'd make it here, sink out of sight. He poured a second shot, and it felt self-indulgent to sip it slowly while watching the cruise ship disappear over the horizon. It grew smaller and smaller, and finally disappeared off the edge of the flat earth, taking with it the uncertainties and doubts his sigh had sent in the same direction. They all left together to be eaten by ravenous monsters of the deep.

Then he stretched out on the couch and drifted into a deep and peaceful sleep.

He woke refreshed. The sun was going down when he sat up and looked out over the Caribbean Sea. His stomach growled, reminding him that he hadn't eaten, so he dressed and went downstairs where he found that the beachfront was starting to come to life . . . the night crowd was waking.

He was heading for the restaurant, but right near the bottom of the stairs from his apartment, he found a place selling delicious smelling tacos. Why walk further?

A chubby woman with a beautiful smile walked up to him. "Welcome," she said, pointing to a plastic chair at a table. "You sit and eat."

So he sat and ate a delicious meal that she brought him. As he finished, feeling more energetic than full, he wondered about the possibilities for adventure. What would be an interesting way to spend his first evening in paradise?

"Hey, amigo." He turned and saw Raul, the taxi driver who'd brought him from the airport, coming toward him. "You like my town, amigo?"

"So far so good," he said. "All I've done so far is sleep."

Unsure of protocol, he ordered them each a beer. Raul nodded and they clinked bottles. "Is a nice town, Progreso." He winked. "There are many pretty chicas here who know how to please a man."

"Is that so? I wouldn't know yet. I just stepped out the door."

"Well, you need a chica. Maybe I find you a lovely little chica to help you enjoy your stay," he said. "You don't need to be bothered by the girls of the street."

The hustle amused Wyatt and he admired that man's salesmanship. The truth was, he was feeling a little lonely and more than a little randy. That amazed him. Rebecca's absence seemed to have left a void that demanded to be filled. Yet, that made him feel guilty.

"I don't want some old woman, Raul."

Raul laughed a waved a hand. A young woman came toward them. She wore shorts, a tight tee shirt, sandals, and an uncertain smile. Wyatt took in her soft and curvaceous body, and when she sat down, he decided he liked her eyes. He wouldn't call her beautiful, but she was attractive. "I Maria. I no speak English good," she told him, pulling her shoulders back to make sure he noticed her breasts. He could see her nipples through the thin, damp cotton of her tee shirt.

Raul sipped his beer and Maria pulled up a chair beside Wyatt. "Maria just came from the country, from a poor family. She needs to make money. She is new in town . . . fresh, not like some of the *putas* who work the beach. She is special."

"I'm not sure," Wyatt told him. This was a first for him. He'd never been with a prostitute, so although he had nothing against sex workers, he wasn't sure if it was a game he wanted to play. Then, too, he still had Rebecca lurking in the recesses of his brain and it felt like she might be watching, that she'd know what he did.

"You get a better price this early in the evening," Raul said. "And because this is the slow season."

On cue, Maria put her hand in Wyatt's lap. It felt wonderful and got him hard. "You like Maria," she said, stating the obvious. "I be very nice."

"Don't wait for anyone," Rebecca said again in his head. He figured he was rationalizing his lust, but he'd stopped caring that much.

He looked into Maria's soft brown eyes; her face was still unmarked from seeing too much of the bad that life could deal out. Yet, she wasn't a child. He guessed she was at least in her mid twenties. As he looked at her, she smiled seductively, then she began to lick her lips slowly, suggestively.

"Maria, you might not speak English, but you do know how to close a deal."

Raul stood up. "You talk with her, see if you like to fuck her. Only 2000 pesos for the night." Then he picked up his beer and wandered off as if he didn't care what happened next. He didn't want to distract Wyatt's attention from the girl and what she was doing to him.

For a moment, Wyatt struggled with the challenge of converting pesos to dollars in his head. It would have been easy, but not with Maria rubbing his crotch and giving him that enticing smile. *"Por favor,"* she said. "I will make you happy. Okay? You like me?"

He sighed. "I like you."

"Then we go fuck," she said as if that was all that needed saying.

Wyatt laughed—at himself. To hell with the conversion rate. He had a hunch that whatever it came out to be, screwing Maria would be worth it.

He stood up and held out a hand. She grinned and took it and pressed her warm body against his as he led her inside and up the stairs to his room and to whatever adventure came next.

CHAPTER 17

CHAPTER 17
KEEPING PRYING NOSES OUT

"Bitcoin has made more institutions obsolete, in more
rapid fashion, than any invention in human history."

—ANDY HOFFMAN
PROPRIETOR OF CRYPTOGOLDCENTRAL.COM

IT DEPARTMENT
MINISTRY OF FINANCE
DAR ES SALAAM, TANZANIA

Once she started work in the IT department of the Ministry of
Finance in Dar es Salaam, Peggy settled in quickly. She had a cubicle
and a computer that were no different than they'd be anywhere else.
That made it easy to establish a productive routine. Her days were
mostly spent in the office at her terminal, unless she was in meetings.
After a long day working alone, or giving instructions to the local
programmers assigned to her, she went back to the hotel.

Morning and night a van shuttled her between the two locations.
It was dull. One evening she tried to involve herself more with the
crew. She went out for a beer with her team after work. They were
pleasant enough, but she felt the distance between them. She was an
American, their boss, and a woman, not one of them. She promised
herself she wouldn't force herself on them again. It was just too fucking awkward.

She wondered if she'd ever even see anything of the city before
she left. She hadn't come to sightsee and the schedule they had to
meet didn't leave much time for doing anything but work, but since

she was there, part of her wanted to look around. But there wasn't much chance. The work was more stressful and she was more on her own than she had expected. She learned quickly that the programmers that worked for the government weren't the most highly motivated. They were there to do what they were told and collect a paycheck. When she did manage to generate some enthusiasm among them, she found their solutions to problems uninspired and often far too complicated.

"What is it with you guys?" she asked one of the more open of her crew. "Where is your creativity?"

He grinned. "Creativity? Hey, the fellas that know how to do clever things are gonna be working for the hackers and scam places," he told her, surprising her with his candid analysis. "This place doesn't pay so good, and programmers don't get promoted."

"What about Andwele?" she asked.

The man snorted. "He doesn't know programming. Mr. Kassain is a self-important college boy who gets to hire programmers to do the work. He is a politician."

She reported all that to Hoenig, who told her not to use it as an excuse. So she bit her tongue when Childer or Andwele complained that progress was sluggish. They were right. In her time at Hoenig, Peggy had gotten used to working with smart, clever, and often outrageous people . . . people like Wyatt. Even the dullards back in the Virginia office tended to show more enthusiasm than this bunch. She'd expected to be riding herd over some knowledgeable programmers. Instead, she had to show a reluctant group of surprisingly unsophisticated young men how to solve problems.

Part of the difficulty was they hadn't worked with blockchains or done much with any new technology. They had zero experience with Solidity coding, the high-level language for implementing smart contracts on Ethereum, for example, and they didn't even understand the basics of lightning networks. They were decent at writing programs for accounting and traditional banking, but distributed ledger technology was all new to them.

It didn't help that she knew she should have seen that possibility, but she hadn't. All she'd seen was the opportunity to insert her code into this project and make her future glow bright. If it was more work than she'd planned for, she would have to deal with it. Unfortunately, that meant doing the bulk of the work, the creative work herself— mapping out the logic and then ensuring that the code monkeys implemented it.

That took longer than she had anticipated and she almost missed the old days. It was so much easier to analyze someone else's code, find the weak spots, the holes, and write routines to exploit them. Due to her hacker background, she tended to think in terms of routines. A short bit of code to do this or that. She was good at that. Making a system work in harmony was something else. The timing of modules that passed data back and forth had to be synchronized or things went south. Accounting software, financial transaction software, was the worst, the pickiest, because it also had to conform to banking protocols that sometimes made no sense.

She'd taken the job with Hoenig to learn about these systems and she'd learned a lot. But her goal, her focus, had been learning their weaknesses, not building them. She was interested in how she would access them surreptitiously once she was independent again. For once, she understood how smart programmers could write programs that were easy to hack. She had to think of every damn thing.

Wyatt was another pain in the ass. Unfortunately, she needed him. He was her best coding resource and his code always worked. But he also harassed her, wanting to know more details, more about how the system modules interacted.

"The code you are sending works great," she told him. "It does everything it's supposed to."

"But it is crude, brute force shit," he said. "If you'd show me what the other modules do, how they do it, then I could streamline everything. It would run faster, be easier to maintain . . ."

"It's fine. We need functional now. We can optimize it later, Wyatt."

She knew the man was a fucking perfectionist and totally paranoid that his code would be less than the best. That morning he'd emailed her a classic bitch that cut far too close to the bone: "What the fuck are you using an onion router for?" he'd emailed.

"Damn," she said, letting out a long breath and trying to think clearly.

The onion router he mentioned was what they called a series of anonymous links in the communication protocol stack that were layered like an onion. That was where the name came from and Wyatt was right to question its usefulness. Peggy had only installed it for one reason—to pass transaction fees she'd added along to her own private wallet and make the transfers impossible to track.

She could only do so much to hide her code. That part had to be integral to the system, so Wyatt finding it so quickly was a serious problem. It was a clue that would lead him to her additions and he'd find out that she planned to have the system extract money, taking tiny amounts from every single transaction and send it to her.

It was unfortunate that he seemed to be catching onto her own code and not the shit she'd put in for the IMF. If he was closing in on their antics, she'd just tell Childer or have Osk Barstad get on his ass. She couldn't very well tell them that Wyatt was discovering her scheme. If she got them after Wyatt and he explained what he'd found, life could get difficult. She'd have to come up with something. In the meantime, she didn't want him to chase this any further.

Experience had taught her that when she was caught with her hand in the cookie jar, the best thing for her to do was tough it out. So, she replied in her usual fashion. "Fuck you, Wyatt. We are using an onion router because that was what was called for in the spec. Deal with it. Get working on why the credit card transfers are so slow."

He wouldn't be pleased, but being the project manager had to count for something. Wyatt would probably bitch to Hoenig; she needed to figure out some story for him, and giving Wyatt a task would distract him. For a while.

Rashmi was another headache. Although she was just trying to do her job, which was to ensure that the system would function properly when they launched it, the damn woman kept digging for more details too. Peggy didn't dare give her everything she wanted and couldn't allow her to see the complete set of flow charts, not at a granular level. Hell, even forgetting about what Peggy was adding, which was tiny, if she got a peek at the complete specs, the woman was clever enough to see exactly what the IMF was having her do for them.

Mitch Childer had been very clear about the need to prevent that from happening. "Rashmi, to name just one person, might object to some of the political and social aspects of the data we are collecting and the way we are using it. I don't want her starting a public confrontation over side issues," he'd said. "You need to make sure she thinks the system only does what we've told her it does."

Peggy agreed with that, although she didn't give a rat's ass what the IMF was doing with the data herself. "Then I'll have to baffle her with bullshit," she said.

"You do whatever you need to do to keep her in the dark about our improvements," Childer said stiffly. "If you suspect that she, or anyone else, is suspicious or learns anything, let me know immediately." He frowned. "I hope it doesn't become necessary for me to take action, but this is vital and I will."

That didn't sound good for whoever discovered the truth, or for Peggy herself, so she worked as hard covering her tracks as she did on the project.

Rashmi, however, was just as determined to learn everything. "The bitch must be descended from a fucking pit bull," she told herself.

After a number of heated discussions in the office with Rashmi that bordered on confrontations, Peggy decided to take a more conciliatory tack. "Why don't you and I go out for dinner?"

"Dinner?" Rashmi seemed astonished.

"Look, we are two women in a world of men—it's truly their world. And here we are fighting each other. That makes no sense. We are the smartest people in the office."

"Andwele is smart," Rashmi ventured.

"Not as smart as he thinks," Peggy said. "It isn't that I think we can or should become best girlfriends, but dinner in a nice place would give us a chance to talk a bit. I'd like to sort out our conflicts away from this sterile place. And I haven't seen much of anything of Dar es Salaam. Even if I had the time and energy to get out and look around, all the men tell me I'm not supposed to go out on the town by myself."

She saw that the idea appealed to Rashmi. "That might be a good idea. I haven't been out for quite a while myself."

"Then let's have a girls' night out. You pick the place and I'll pay," Peggy told her.

Rashmi agreed and the next night they went to a small restaurant in an old part of town. Finally, she saw a place that offered traditional Tanzanian fare. It was much like the hotel food, but the atmosphere was less corporate. "It's nice to be eating in a different place and with some company," she said.

Rashmi looked at her with surprise. "You know, I was jealous of you living here and not having to worry about doing laundry or cleaning. I hadn't thought about the fact that you have to eat alone in a restaurant every day. I can't imagine that is much fun."

"It wears you down after a time. And here . . ."

"You don't like the city or the country?"

"I just hadn't realized how strongly the men here dislike seeing a woman out alone in public. It's uncomfortable at times, but I'll be damned if I'm going to eat in my room every night just because there's no man around."

Rashmi smiled. "That was certainly one of the things I enjoyed about living in London. The freedom. The only reason I could accept staying here was because I was expecting to be married soon."

"You were expecting it? Has something changed?"

Rashmi's smile was thin and forced. "Things are on hold. I'm not certain yet if that is a pause in the engagement or if it's over."

"I'm sorry to hear that," Peggy said. "Did you two have an argument?"

She smiled wistfully. "You are supposed to get along by talking through things, right? That's what they say. So, in Zurich, with the project ramping up, we talked about postponing the wedding. Our date was going to be rather inconvenient. Once we opened that can of worms, I learned for the first time that Andwele is of the old-fashioned opinion that wives do not work. Especially the wives of important men; especially his wife. I also learned that he has his heart set on being an important man. That goal might be more important to him than marrying me. As surprising as those things were for me, I saw that he was just as shocked by my assumption that I would continue to work. So we decided we needed time to come to an understanding. He seems to think I'll come around."

"And you . . ."

"I think we might wind up agreeing to disagree."

"That's rough. Are you okay?"

"Okay? I'm shaken by it all, I suppose, but I prefer knowing all that now. The breakup isn't as much of a shock as the fact that I didn't know Andwele at all, it seems."

Peggy's mind raced with the possibilities. The words of condolence she'd uttered were just what you said to someone. She didn't care whether they married or not. She didn't care if they were happy. Neither of them was of any consequence outside their role in the project. But the news itself was interesting and potentially useful. It explained why Andwele had been distant lately. She'd thought maybe he was avoiding her, that he might be a man who didn't like working with women. But apparently, he was staying away from the work site for his own reasons. Whether he was taking some time away from Rashmi, or she had told him to stay away, that suited her purpose. It meant that they were both distracted, and it was easier to hide her code.

Now she understood why Andwele had been absent, except when he needed updates so he could make his progress reports to the ministry. That made her job easier and had given her a chance to work more closely with the programmers than she would've had if he'd been acting as a go-between. That had been good, but this could prove to be even better. A man like that, one who had lost his woman, was much easier to manipulate—especially a man who didn't rate women highly. Ironically, a strong woman could take advantage of his stupidity.

"So you bury yourself in your work?" she asked.

Rashmi nodded. "Something like that. It strikes me as better than drinking."

"That depends on who you are drinking with, doesn't it?"

Rashmi grinned. "And where. In London, it's more viable for a woman than here. More pleasant."

Peggy nodded. "I wouldn't like staying here for a long time, I don't think. I'd never get used to that. But, for the sake of this project."

"Which you and I seem to collide on a great deal. I'm curious why you resist sharing information with me? I've never run into that before. I've encountered project managers who didn't have the information, but why not let me see all the documents?"

Peggy had decided on an approach that involved an intelligent partial truth. Rashmi's estrangement from Andwele helped with that. "Both the IMF and the Ministry of Finance review the work we're doing on a regular basis. Both of them feed us a stream of required changes or alterations. They seem to be infuriated by the fact that we aren't mind readers."

Rashmi smiled. "They can be that way."

"Andwele has his own takes on things." Peggy held out her hands. "I can't ask you to write tests for functions that are in flux," Peggy said. "Some of what we've done is just stubs of things. Unfortunately, I don't think we will have a final spec that is accurate until both of those groups come to see that the timetable they demand means they have to stop demanding changes. It's driving my boss nuts. He's already screaming at Mitch Childer about the cost overruns that he's creating with all the minor tweaks."

"That's coding as usual, isn't it?" Rashmi asked. "I could still write test functions and simulators for the way you write them and change them as we go."

"But the point of what you do is to find flaws. I don't have enough hours in my day to accommodate the things they are throwing at me without fixing functions that they are going to change anyway."

Rashmi studied Peggy's face. She wished she could figure her out and decide what she was actually on. All she saw was a mask, the look of a dedicated project leader frustrated with bureaucracy. "I can understand."

"I remember what you said about being disillusioned when you learned how public policy really works. I'm feeling the same way. I had high hopes for a simple system that would reduce the transaction costs of fiscal policies. But every time I find a way to do that, a bank or a government bean counter, or the IMF, tells me I can't do it that way. I think they stay up nights inventing new protocols."

"It's because of fear," Rashmi said.

"Fear? What are they afraid of?"

"Failing. They don't understand what you are doing, and because they don't understand, they have to view everything through the lens of the old ways. It doesn't make sense, so they implement new controls that make them feel better, literally more in control of what they are doing."

"And I wind up with a bloated digital money system that's of little benefit."

"You sound something like Wyatt now," Rashmi laughed.

Peggy joined her. It was true. "The man is smart. His complaint is that we are destroying what he sees as the good in blockchain; he thinks we are just doing it because we can. He isn't pragmatic like we are."

"Is that what we are?" Rashmi asked. "I'd like to think we are pragmatic, but sometimes I wonder. Playing along makes sense until it doesn't. I'd hate to suddenly realize we've been following a blind piper toward a cliff."

"It doesn't pay to think that way," Peggy said. "Look, I'm going to give you all the information I can. You come in the office tomorrow and I'll give you what I think are the final specs on a big block of the bank to bank transfer functions and the module that collects tax revenue from shop and store sales. We are still struggling with defining the business-to-business revenues since they tend to be wholesale transactions and need a completely different tax table."

"That would be great. I could get my teeth into that."

Their meal came and the food was good. Peggy chewed carefully and listened as Rashmi went on about the kinds of testing she envisioned. Peggy was glad she'd taken the time to isolate large code chunks that were exactly what she'd told Rashmi they were. There was little to hide in that code and obviously providing a rigorous testing would keep the woman busy and off her back.

"This is a marvelous restaurant," Peggy told her.

"I'm delighted you think so, and I'm glad we did this," Rashmi said. "It's better to work together."

Or at least create the illusion of working together, Peggy thought. All in all, the dinner had gone well, and she hadn't been lying about enjoying eating in a new place and with someone.

Tomorrow was the beginning of a new phase of her work and she'd found her passion again.

CHAPTER 18

SOMETHING AMISS

"The man who can smile when things go wrong has
thought of someone else he can blame it on."

—ROBERT BLOCH
AUTHOR OF PSYCHO: A NOVEL

IT DEPARTMENT
MINISTRY OF FINANCE
DAR ES SALAAM, TANZANIA

As the office cleared out in the evening with the hourly staff heading home, Rashmi stretched her arms and then walked into the break room to get another cup of tea. She had a long night ahead of her, and if she didn't have a clear head, she would just be wasting her time.

She sent a secretary out for some sandwiches that would serve as dinner. This was supposed to be a night when she was having dinner with Andwele. They'd agreed that they needed to talk about the issues that divided them and see if there was a future for them. The more she thought about their differences, the less hope she had that they could work things out. His unexpectedly traditional, patriarchal beliefs had caught her by surprise . . . her modern, more progressive views had surprised him. Unless one of them changed their thinking, she couldn't imagine a path that would let them reconcile.

For her part, Rashmi had no interest in becoming a traditional wife, of giving up her life, the career she'd started on. The culture and law still allowed men to have multiple wives. Granted, that required the permission of the first wife, but it still showed a pro-male bias.

When Andwele called and told her that he was meeting with the deputy minister for dinner, to give him a status report, and he couldn't make the dinner, Rashmi was relieved. She didn't see what there was to talk about, and she had no stomach for an argument with him. Artifacts of the past, tribal customs, were hardly something she wanted dictating the course of her life. She was an innovator, a creative person. She couldn't accept having her universe limited because of some primordial belief system about the superiority of men—or anything else.

Due to those thoughts, she felt quite certain that the relationship was finished entirely; it struck Rashmi as curious that she felt a new optimism. Now she could complete her contract with the government and then move on to another place, maybe back to England, or possibly somewhere else in Europe. She felt more at home there and the opportunities were fantastic, even for a woman. In some cases, especially for a woman with her skills. Some of the high-profile trans-national organizations, such as the World Bank, were promoting women as part of their mandate. And, with a project that included the IMF on her resume, she had a future of her own again, not just one tied to a throwback of a man. It felt good.

In the meantime, she was struggling with developing a test suite for the project. With the evening freed up, it was a perfect time to review the information she had and the work she and her people had done. Writing code to simulate transactions to test the program meant first learning how the system worked. Although the general guidelines were spelled out in the system specs, there were always changes or modifications. Sometimes things didn't work the way you thought they would during the design phase; sometimes coders found simpler or more elegant ways to implement a process that changed the way things happened.

As a result, Rashmi and her team were always in a position of playing catch up. They had to wait until the code was written, debugged, and at least roughly documented before they could begin writing the test code. Typically, they would be given completed modules—sections of code that performed functions—so that they could establish that it worked correctly . . . for instance, a tax collection module had to use the right tax tables and apply them correctly. That wasn't always a trivial thing.

The trickier part, the real challenge, was putting it all together to prove that the total system functioned as specified. Given that projects always came in late, there was always a mad rush to meet deadlines.

To reduce the pressure, Rashmi normally worked closely with the developers. She would start with an overall concept of what the system had to do and evolve her understanding of how it would do it, keeping abreast of changes. That made it possible to have her people begin writing test procedures and creating dummy data to use for tests and simulations. That helped her work with the developers. This time, however, everyone seemed to want to keep her in the dark.

When she got back to her desk, she looked at the flowcharts she'd put together on her own. They pictorially described the way the system operated—a view of the entire system. But there were a number of blocks that baffled her. They didn't seem to fit within the structure of a payment or transaction system. But then, this system was supposed to break some new ground, according to both Mitch Childer and Osk Barstad. Even if they wouldn't elaborate, it was easy to make some guesses—and she found it impossible not to speculate.

One confusing section of the system was the one that provided potential lenders with credit scores. The intention was to move those from individual banks, where there was no standardization or government oversight, to this new system, where it would be automated to produce credit scores. This had nothing directly to do with the new cryptocurrency, or the financial transactions, but was an IMF pilot project. And, in theory, it made sense. They were using distributed applications based on Ethereum—what were called *trustless arbiters.* If a module met certain conditions that granted authority, they could read, add, modify, and read the data without anyone granting other permission. This eliminated corruption. It wouldn't be possible to hack the data because it was stored in a secure blockchain, and you couldn't pay a person to get it for you because people, human beings, didn't have direct access to the data. It was integrated into the system for the benefit of the system. Using certain protocols, the information could be read but not modified. That kept everything safe but still convenient and usable.

The flaw in that was that some modules might be written to provide the data. The hacks would be built into the system. She had little doubt that part of the IMF and Interpol involvement in development was to ensure those hacks were in place.

The information stored was critical. To meet the increasing international demand to prevent money laundering and to control cash flow to illegal and terrorist organizations, the banking system had implemented increasingly complex "know your customer" (KYC) requirements that meant banks had to collect detailed information on the identities of all account holders. Most companies and organizations operating globally had accounts in different banks in multiple countries, which meant this private information was stored in multiple places, increasing the possibility of a hacker gaining access to it. Furthermore, it meant opening new accounts; re-entering the data in a new database was time-consuming and wasteful. The IMF, apparently, in conjunction with the World Bank, wanted to make that unnecessary. Banks would be freed from the onus of collecting and storing the information. Anyone authorized by the system could open an account and transact business.

"This is the first step in a global account registry," Mitch Childer had said. "And before you argue against it or celebrate its evolution, we need to test its feasibility." If it worked, it would make Tanzania a poster child for international banking. Naturally, the government was all for it.

Not only was the publicity a good thing, but as Rashmi reviewed what she knew about the system, a chill ran through her. Suddenly she saw what it would mean—the government would have centralized control of that information. There didn't seem to be any serious safeguards against a party in power using the system to track the expenditures of an opposing party. If she understood the system, the data wasn't only accessible through the loan application routines or other routine banking procedures—it was available in various ways through other modules. It wouldn't take a very clever person to figure out how to extract that information.

That, she decided, was why Interpol was so interested in the project. They didn't care what the system did to prevent fraud as much as they were interested in learning how they could gain access to that kind of information.

Wyatt was right. They were perverting the very concept of the security offered by distributed systems. Once upon a time, Rashmi believed that good people could use their abilities to help and protect people. Increasingly, she wondered if that was true. Even with good intentions, they necessarily took away their freedom to ensure their safety. It was "for the good of all" and therefore, it seemed, for the good of none.

"A desire for privacy, when not satisfied, leads to a need for secrecy," Wyatt had told her. At the time, she'd thought it was a flip comment from a cynic. But what she was staring at was a blueprint for eliminating privacy on a global scale. And, if that was known, it would push a lot of people into trying to find ways to pervert it, to bring the system down. Tyranny inevitably made revolutionaries of good people.

The idea of this as a force of tyranny worried her. She had no idea if that was the intention, but it seemed like it to her. The worst thing was that she was committed to helping make it real. She'd given her word that she would make this project successful.

As she thought about the system, the need for international banking systems and the demands they imposed, when she considered the way the world was going, this system, or one like it, a larger, more comprehensive version of it, seemed inevitable. It also seemed dark . . . very dark indeed.

CHAPTER 19

DREAMS IN PARADISE

"It is better to have your head in the clouds, and know
where you are. . . . than to breathe the clearer atmosphere
below them, and think that you are in paradise."

—HENRY DAVID THOREAU

MALECÓN DE PROGRESO
YUCATÁN, MEXICO

At times, Wyatt had trouble believing his luck. During the weeks he'd been in paradise, he found that his new life seemed to be playing out along the lines of his wildest fantasies. Sure, he hadn't imagined how humid it could be at times or that he'd have to deal with bugs, but they were such minor things when you considered that he didn't have to deal with owning a car and all that was involved with it. He could choose from a variety of transportation modes and they were all cheap. He had a decent room and, if he decided to stay on the beach for any length of time, Charlie would give him a better rate.

He resisted taking that step only because once he decided he would stay, well, it was easy to start accumulating things. It evolved and got more complicated. You bought a few items for the kitchen so you could fix your favorite meal, or you got a better television . . . but he didn't need any of that. So he avoided making a commitment, although sooner or later he'd have to make a decision. For now, he enjoyed keeping it simple. Breakfast on the beach, working on his balcony, or sitting under a *palapa* having a beer.

And in the evenings he could walk the beach, go to a bar, or call Maria. She was an eager and rather charming girl. His Spanish was improving and so was her English. They had nothing in common except the commerce, but he was happy to be a steady client and she seemed to enjoy herself. Some evenings he even took her to dinner.

One evening he found himself in a thoughtful, melancholic mood. It was one that demanded examination. He filled a glass with whiskey and went for a walk on the beach. It was a quiet night and there were no tourists, so he was alone. Many of the vendors had taken the night off.

He walked barefoot in the damp sand, then into the water, letting it wash his legs. Thoughts tumbled. He was doing the work that Peggy sent and it should've been challenging. There were a few aspects that could've been truly excellent, but without more information, information she wouldn't give him, he had to do a basic, minimal, unsatisfying job. There was a disconnect that he hadn't anticipated and it was frustrating his dream.

The dream wasn't clear, or even consistent. There was a mismatch between Wyatt Osgood, freethinking beach bum, and the man who was helping Tanzania implement a pseudo cryptocurrency. That was a mouthful, he thought. But it was accurate. It pained him to be co-opting cryptocurrency with a government-control digital payment system.

So he loved the programming and detested the project with all of his being. The things that were being done, that he was doing, to control the payment system instead of freeing it were wrong. He had known that when he accepted Claude Hoenig's deal. Attending Anarchapulco had made the problem clearer. The talks with people, and the lectures, had helped fuel his passion for freedom, and not just his own freedom. He ached for the people his work would enslave.

And Rebecca had pointed out to him that he wasn't always choosing to live by his own values in other ways. "Although," she told him, "I think running away is a good start. And you'll learn. Living that way, you won't be able to avoid learning the truth."

She'd never tell him what that 'truth' was. "Mine is not yours," she told him. That didn't help.

He knew she was leading to a path, hinting at some horizon he should be looking toward or some larger idea or ideal that he hadn't quite accepted, or at least not realized. And that left him walking alone on a beach with the watery horizon highlighted by a sliver of silvery moon.

The moon was the ideal—a thin, papery slip that represented some distant reality. And Rebecca hinted that he knew it already, but he hadn't committed to it. Yet, without knowing what that ideal was, he had no idea what committing to the idea would mean, or how it would resolve his dilemma. The work that fed him came from large corporations and governments. The real juice was found in large-scale national or international projects. If he didn't work for them, what did he do?

And yet, as long as he chose to live in the margins, on a tropical beach, he'd never be integral to any of those projects. Most project managers wanted face time, a chance to look over your work and control the flow of information. Peggy might be extreme in her control but she wasn't unique. When he did other projects, he faced the same situation. The workers on site seldom got along with those in the home office. A worker on a tropical beach couldn't expect to communicate and get along better.

Wyatt shook sand off his foot and accepted that he faced what seemed to be an unsolvable problem. Without walking away from his life's work as he already had in his previous day-to-day existence, the dichotomy couldn't go away. With the nagging, almost chronic angst he suffered, he wondered if it would eventually break him.

"Fuck no," he told the sea. The sea didn't reply. It was leaving it up to him to find a way to keep going.

When his thoughts played out without producing new insights or answers, and his glass was empty, he turned to walk back to his apartment.

The lights were off downstairs. It was the one night a week that the restaurant was closed and whoever had rented the apartment next door hadn't shown up yet. Walking up the stairs, he had a growing sense that things were slightly off. Something was different, but he couldn't place it.

Crossing the balcony, he went into the apartment and refilled his glass. Something moved on the balcony. It was his hammock. He walked back out. Light from the streetlights illuminated a lean, naked, very female body lying in it. "Hey, sailor, new in town?"

He couldn't speak. It was Rebecca. "What? When did you. . . ."

"I just got here a while ago. I didn't want to interrupt anything but I saw you were alone walking on the beach."

"You saw me?"

"From my apartment." She grinned. "I'm your neighbor. Howdy, neighbor."

Then she slipped out of the hammock. He stared at her for a moment before rushing to her, kissing her, and taking her in his arms. "I didn't know if you'd come."

"I didn't either," she said. "But doesn't that make the fact that I'm here now even more special?"

It did.

CHAPTER 20
WHEN THINGS GO WRONG

"Security and safety were the reward of dullness."

—Hanif Kureishi
British playwright, screenwriter, filmmaker, and novelist

IT Department
Ministry of Finance
Dar es Salaam, Tanzania

Mitch Childer was scowling. Although she seldom saw the man looking happy, Peggy had never seen his face darken like this. It looked unhealthy and ominous. Not that she could blame him.

"The fucking thing isn't working," Andwele said. He stood behind Childer looking stone-faced.

"That is stating the bloody obvious," Childer said sullenly.

Peggy turned her attention back to the flat screen and stared in disbelief. Glancing down at her notes and then the screen again didn't do a thing. The damn system was running but the transactions were backing up. And something else was terribly wrong. "The numbers are wrong."

Rashmi ran her finger down a column of figures. "The benchmarks and the results are both off. Nothing like what we should be getting," she said calmly.

Peggy's heart raced. This was just a test, but there was no reason for it not to be working right. She'd seeded the program with a set of values to simulate a set of conditions and then they'd run the program to see how it worked. Nothing was processing. Transfer requests just stacked up, apparently, unless the money was going to the wrong places.

"I can help you troubleshoot it," Rashmi said.

That was the last thing Peggy needed. "I'll find the problem myself, otherwise I won't really understand how it went wrong. If I troubleshoot it, it will be easier to fix it."

Childer adjusted the knot of his tie. "We don't have a lot of time. If Ms. Patel wants to help . . ."

"I know. We're in a rush, but I need to be methodical, not have extra hands messing with it."

"If you're sure that's best," Childer said. "Finding the solution is on you."

Rashmi picked up her tea mug. "That's fine with me." Peggy could see that the woman wasn't buying the explanation. She didn't blame her—it was pretty thin.

"I appreciate the offer. If I can't sort it out myself, I'll ask for help."

"I'll be in my office. Call me if you change your mind."

"I'll find the bug," Peggy said.

Rashmi laughed. "It's not a bug, Peggy. That's not the way to look at what's going on."

"What do you mean?" Childer asked.

Rashmi sighed. "A bug is an error in the code. This is more fundamental. From what I see, the modules aren't interacting the way they should."

"Explain," Childer said.

"Each module provides a function. Some are simple, some complex. The smart contracts, for instance, rely on several modules to operate during three phases, maybe even more."

Childer seemed confused. "Phases?"

"Yes. First, the contract has to be written and approved, then the system continuously tests to see if the conditions of the contract are met. Once it verifies that they have been, it executes the contract. That part alone can be multiple operations."

"I understand that much," Childer said.

"That isn't happening here," Rashmi said. "We are creating contracts, but when we enter dummy variables for the contract, we don't see it execute properly. That should force it to execute but that isn't happening."

"A number of things can cause that," Peggy said.

Rashmi nodded. "At this point, we don't know if the contract is being constructed properly in the first place, or if the system recognizes that its conditions are met. Until you get into the innards of the thing, we don't know what is going on."

"We've tested every damn one of the modules," Peggy said, hating that she sounded so defensive. The truth was that when it came to the overall operation of the system, she was out of her depth.

Rashmi was still nodding. "I know. They all perform correctly according to the specs you gave me. That's why I said that it must be a system logic or structure problem. It could be something as simple as a disagreement over which register is being used to pass data."

"Disagreement?" Andwele asked. "Can't you agree?"

"She doesn't mean us," Peggy said. "She means we might have used one register for one module and another one for the module it is working with. That can happen when different programmers write the various modules."

"And when the total spec isn't available for all to see," Rashmi said pointedly.

"Well, I'll go over everything again and figure it out."

"It's a strange problem to have," Rashmi said.

"Why is that?" Childer asked.

"I didn't expect a problem with this section—the smart contracts. And it's just for payment transactions too. The contracts for escrow work fine."

Childer looked puzzled. "Why is that odd, Ms. Patel?"

"Because we just copied a lot of it. A great deal of the code was taken wholesale from other digital payment systems. They all work. That suggests some of our modifications are at fault." Peggy didn't like the way the woman was looking at her when she said that.

Childer paced the floor. "We need this fixed immediately. Are you certain you can do it, Ms. Dory?"

"Nothing is certain, Childer, but I should be able to get it running."

Rashmi stared at the monitor. "If I'm right, when the problem is found, the fix won't take long to implement. It shouldn't involve much more than rewriting a few lines of code. Of course, the trick is in knowing which lines to rewrite so something else doesn't get messed up. It's a complex beast, this system."

"You seem fairly knowledgeable, Ms. Patel. What if I insisted that Ms. Dory let you help her?"

"My offer was sincere, but Peggy is probably right. I'm making a lot of general statements. I'm not up to speed on the system flow . . ." she glared at Peggy. " . . . and I have little experience with blockchain or sidechain coding."

"What about that other coder?" Childer asked. "The one who developed the basic idea."

Peggy didn't like where this was going. Childer had never shown a lot of faith in her, and now he was talking in ways that might upset her plans entirely. "Wyatt? I understand that he is sitting on a beach somewhere writing modules."

"Wouldn't he be the logical person to sort this out?" Childer wasn't really asking them. "He should have a clear picture of how it should work, which is more than anyone here seems to have."

"That does make sense," Rashmi said. "Certainly Wyatt would have better ideas about where to start looking for problems than we do. He's got the experience."

Peggy felt a rage building inside. The situation had been so sweet and she'd somehow fucked it up. Having Wyatt there, able to look at the code, could ruin everything. "His contract with the company says he gets to work off-site." She nodded in Andwele's direction. "And, as I understand it, the government here doesn't want other programmers, more foreigners, on site. They insisted on it being done by local programmers."

Childer touched his chin. "If it's necessary to accomplish our goals, the government will bend the rules. What's wrong with that?"

"Can we have a private word?" she asked him.

"I need more tea anyway," Rashmi said turning to leave.

Andwele hesitated, looking at Childer nervously for a long moment, obviously concerned that he was being left out of the loop. Then he turned and followed Rashmi out of the office.

After they left, Peggy sat, listening to the hum of cooling fans and knowing that Childer waited patiently for her to speak. She wanted him to wonder, but he didn't seem the least bit nervous. "Why on earth would you bring Wyatt Osgood here?"

"He is apparently the best person to find the problems."

"He's also a troublemaker. You told me you don't want him to know about your code, the functions we've introduced. If he's on site, if you ask him to troubleshoot the code, then he'll damn well have to be told about the modules you had me add or he'll find them himself."

"That is your problem and I'm trusting that your ingenuity can manage it," Childer said. "We need the system working smoothly and soon. If you aren't able to prevent him from seeing all the functions, then once the system is working, we can do damage control."

The words *damage control* took on a rather sinister connotation the way the man said them. She told herself that it wasn't like he was offering her a chance to have a say in the matter, but it didn't sound good for poor old Wyatt. Not that she cared that much.

Mitch Childer straightened his perfectly straight tie. "I'll tell Mr. Hoenig that we need the man here immediately. And as far as the limit on programmers, I'll let Deputy Minister Dola know that he'll have to put up with another American for a time. He won't object."

"Why not give me a chance to fix it first? It could be something very simple. I might find out what's wrong right away."

"Go ahead, but if Rashmi Patel is right, there is something structural you aren't seeing. Still, if you can get it working before he arrives, so much the better. We will send him off again. There will be no harm done by bringing him here unnecessarily."

Peggy let her mind run through the possibilities. Her own module was rather small and insignificant. She could mask it. But it didn't seem likely that Wyatt would miss the data-collection and centralization processes Childer had added to the system . . . hell, the code bloat alone would tell him that someone had added things on, but he could overlook her little modification easily enough.

There was a chance that Wyatt would flatly refuse to leave wherever he was. She had no idea what sort of leverage Childer could bring to bear on the guy, but things would be much better if Wyatt refused to come. She could hope he wouldn't want to work there, or that she found the problem before he arrived. That option was the only one she had any control over, unfortunately.

"Fine. You do what you need to and I'll get to work on finding the problem."

"Let me know of any progress."

"Sure." When he left, Peggy gave herself permission to feel like shit for a while. She was so close. Childer was right that Wyatt could probably sort it out in a heartbeat, but that was the last thing she wanted. The very last thing.

She backed up the latest version of the code and copied the source onto her laptop to take back to the hotel. If she worked in her room, without all these morons around her . . . she'd get room service to send up food and some booze. Maybe the waiter would be a hot guy, like in Switzerland. She'd gotten lucky with Franz.

She licked her lips, remembering their nights together. "First, fix the goddamn code, Dory," she told herself.

CHAPTER 21
BITPATS

"The mark of the immature man is that he wants to
die nobly for a cause, while the mark of the mature
man is that he wants to live humbly for one."

—WILHELM STEKEL
IN J.D. SALINGER'S *THE CATCHER IN THE RYE*

MALECÓN DE PROGRESO
YUCATÁN, MEXICO

With Rebecca by his side again, Wyatt happily spent his mornings after breakfast doing his work for the project and the rest of the day with her. It didn't matter that the work was still tainted; it was easy to get motivated, write the basic crap Peggy demanded, when he knew that as soon as he was done, he'd be with her. She did the same. They would sit together on the balcony banging away on their laptops and sharing a pot of coffee. Just as he'd imagined, the adventure was more fun shared. Life in the Mexican sunshine sparkled for him like diamonds. Time flowed like a tranquil river.

"You seem to know about my project," he said one day. "What are you working on?"

She laughed. "I'm trying to destroy your work," she said.

She wouldn't explain more. It sounded strange, but he believed her. Given how he felt about the project, he didn't care if it was true. But he did want to know more about her. And, although he ached for her to tell him whether she would stay with him, or even how long she would be there, he refused to ask. She'd tell him what she wanted to. In the meantime, he worked to learn who this wonderful woman was.

That evening they walked down the beach, just taking pleasure in being together. For the first time Wyatt understood what people meant when they said they enjoyed just being alive. Beside Rebecca he could feel that, but she was a huge factor in that sense of being alive.

"What's your story?" he asked her.

"My story?" she asked. She stopped and faced him. The sand was hot under his feet. "What makes you think I have a story?" she asked. "Why bring this up? Why here and now?"

"Curiosity." Said out loud, it just sounded snippy. "I think everyone has one. Some are dramatic, some aren't, but we all have them. I was thinking about you, about us being here together, and it occurred to me that I don't know your story." He caught the glimmer of something in her eyes. Concern? Fear? Alarm? He didn't know. "Not that I need to know everything about you. It's not like I'm a cop."

"What would you guess?" Now he saw that she had been teasing. Her eyes sparkled with delight at having made him backpedal.

He'd already given it some thought and there was no reason not to tell her. "I think you are trying hard to act as if you don't care about things. I think you are hanging around on tropical beaches to stay uninvolved."

"Uninvolved? I'm not sure where you are going with that."

"You aren't a typical backpacker and you're too old to be a gap-year kid out to see the world. You are poised and confident."

"I can see why that makes you suspicious."

"Not suspicious . . . just curious because I like you. You're bright and well educated, yet you seem to be unconcerned with the world."

"I was trying to be on vacation." She made a sour face. "And now you seem to be trying to mess it all up for me."

"I'm in a thoughtful mood," he said.

"Are you?"

"Yeah." She turned her head and looked out over the water, putting a hand over her eyes to shade them. "Buy me a beer and I'll tell you all about it."

"Extortionist."

The wind caught strands of her ashen blonde, shoulder-length hair and sunlight flashed through it like highlights. She flashed a delighted smile. "Hey, ideas aren't free, you know. Not good ones anyway. Not mine. Nor is intelligent company."

"I have to pay for the company?"

"By being good company. But the thoughts will cost you a beer. Two if we really get into things."

"Into things?"

"I'm feeling serious. If you really want to hear my story, it'll cost a beer."

"Maybe two?"

"Right."

So they sat at a table, under a thatched roof, and ordered two cold bottles of beer. The air was warm, even in the shade, but something about Rebecca's intense look gave him a chill. Suddenly hearing her story, teasing it out of her, didn't seem to be much of a lark. Things had gotten serious.

She waited until they'd each had a long drink of the cold Coronas. "You're absolutely right that I'm not a typical digital nomad or backpacker. I'm not a backpacker at all."

"And not an expat, either. You said you were a bitpat."

She smiled. "That's right. And I told you I was a freedom fighter too."

"I remember. In the context of the conference, I thought that was a curious thing but nothing more."

"That might be the defining thing. This digital age is changing things. Our innovations are changing things for better or worse. Some things that we don't understand now seemed terrible. Later on, when we get a handle on them, they might be our saving grace. Other things that seem convenient and wonderful can become a nightmare. The tools of freedom can be used for oppression. They suit any goal."

"But you aren't part of some revolutionary cell?"

"We aren't revolutionaries at all. We are implementing the tech in the cause of freedom. They put up walls and we take them down. They try to track us and we use their efforts against them. But staying still would let them find us. So, by choice, by my calling, if you will, I'm a perpetual traveler who works in cyberspace. What the travel blogger Andy Graham thinks of as the modern version of a hobo traveler. More importantly, for me, I can work for people who deserve my best efforts."

"Sounds ideal."

She let out a long breath. "Let's backtrack a bit because I came here to tell you the whole truth and I didn't start out well."

"The truth? That does sound serious."

"My real name is the best starting point. It's Megan Philips."

"That sounds familiar."

"I was working for the Department of Homeland Security when I decided to do a walkabout."

"I remember. You disappeared. But that wasn't you."

Her eyes laughed. "No? I was sure it was me."

"I saw the pictures they posted of that woman . . . there was even some CCTV footage. She looks nothing like you."

She smiled a thin smile. "Funny how that works and it isn't magic. I was writing code for the biometric identification system. The government collects all that cool data on every person they can so they can track them. But it's all stored in databases. They pretend its decentralized when 'scattered' is a more accurate term. And that's only physical. I found out that it isn't all that hard to basically reassign a data set to a new identity. Once it's in Homeland Security's database, it ripples around the world. So they are looking for a woman who died a year before I walked away."

"Why? Why leave like that?"

"Because I, and people like me, was giving them power over everyone else. They didn't deserve my assistance, so I removed it. I had developed some code and was testing it. I woke up one morning and learned that I didn't want them to have it."

"Learned?"

"I made a new friend. I woke up on a Saturday morning and she knocked on my door. Seems she'd been monitoring my work and she wanted me to understand what I was giving them—the ones who would oppress all of us for our own good. The fuckers."

"What did she want you to do?"

"To follow my own conscience and do what I thought was right. She took me to breakfast and we talked. She talked about how creative people like me, like you, enable the ones who are petty tyrants and thieves . . . nothing more. We talked all day and late into the night. We bought wine and sat around my apartment while she laid it all out for me, how there were unseen powers that manipulated the visible governments for their own ends. She let me see that they couldn't do it on their own. She explained how the code I was writing would be a giant step for those forces."

"So this woman talked you into leaving your old life entirely? And you took your code with you?"

She shook her head. "No, she didn't talk me into anything—she told me how the world really worked. She told me that I had choices and one of them was to become a bitpat—a free person. As a group that owes its allegiance to no one, they help each other. Like a human blockchain, we are distributed. We have no agenda but freedom."

"And you chose to leave."

"I knew they'd come after me."

"Why? They can't make you write code for them if you don't want to."

"They could take the code and then make an example of me. Treason charges aren't unusual in a case like that."

"Because you joined bitpats?"

"I didn't join them . . . I was told the truth and decided to become one."

"That's amazing. People like you disappearing and it doesn't even make the news."

"That's because they don't want the world to know how many creative, productive people are saying no to them. If they let it out that so many are dropping out, simply falling off the grid, people would be frightened. The idea that the government has the best and brightest on their side is part of their positioning, their brand. If the brightest and best work for them, then whatever they do must be right and good."

"So you changed your identity . . ."

"Eventually I became Rebecca, with an official, legal passport, driver's license, the works. And you are lucky. Rebecca is a much saner person than Megan ever was."

"And no one you worked with noticed it wasn't the woman they'd shared a cubicle with?"

"I wasn't there, but think about it. They built the system. Do you think they were going to point out such a fatal system flaw? Not for all the money in the world. No, much better to let law enforcement chase a phantom. Besides, even if they did report it, all they'd know is that the picture, the biometrics they have, aren't mine. They wouldn't know whose they were. And I've changed my identity twice since then."

Wyatt felt his world tumbling. All his misgivings about the work he was doing for the IMF, the way people were using his code, perverting it . . . he understood exactly what she'd felt. "You said you came here to tell me the truth? How did you know I was here? Why me?"

My friend, her name is Boone by the way, came across your paper. It took her awhile to track you down but she did. Your sister was no damn help at all, just so you know. Then I hacked the airline reservation systems and traced you here."

"Why?"

She waved at the waitress and held up two fingers. "Beside the warm sun and cold beer, I came here to tell you all this. To remind you that you are worth more than the power brokers but you are enabling them. I know you started to break away, to create some distance, but the bad taste lingers, doesn't it? The way they are using ideas. . . . Satoshi's blockchain work, your benign regulator . . . and twisting them until they aren't anything but tools of control. They use tech that should properly be disruptive and make it reinforce the existing chains, the lines of power. They can't do it without your help. You want to see the best implementation possible. You tell yourself that if you work on the project it will be as good as possible, and I came here to call bullshit on that. You are holding them up. You need to let them fall."

"It isn't just that . . . making the system work right," Wyatt said.

"And what's that?"

He felt foolish. "I gave my word."

"To whom?"

"Claude Hoenig. He's my boss. When this started, I told him I would see it through. I know that sounds stupid, but . . ."

She reached over and touched his hand, her gentle caress reassured him. "Not at all. That makes more sense than anything. Our word has to mean something. But think about this . . . what if something unforeseen happened and keeping your word would unexpectedly mean that you had to do something horrendous, say kill someone. Would you do that?"

Wyatt felt a noose tighten around his neck. "No."

"After you got involved, after you made the promise, you learned the true nature of the work, right?"

"Yes, although I should've guessed from the start."

"Fine. But at some point, you are absolved from that promise. When the circumstances are such that you can't continue, consider doing what I did. Walk away."

He laughed. "If I could push a button and get a new identity . . ."

"Bitpats," she said. "If you decide you want to become a bitpat, or even talk more about what that would mean, send an email to Boone at bitpats dot com. Once I've told her about you, that you really are the kind of person she suspected you were, she will be glad to help."

"I get the impression that you are saying goodbye," he said. A sadness crept over him.

"I have things to do and places to be. Bitpats don't just sit around all day drinking beer and talking political philosophy with hot guys, you know. I need to get my ass back to work on a project."

"Will I see you again?"

"The bitpat community isn't that large. If you decide to become one, we could arrange to meet."

The waitress came with the beer and Wyatt took one, feeling the damp cold bottle in his hand. The sun was shining, the salty breeze blew strands of Rebecca's ash-blonde hair, and life was beautiful. "I have to keep my promise . . . for now," he said. "Don't hate me."

Her laugh wafted over him. "I couldn't hate you, Wyatt. You are an honest person. From my perspective, your loyalty is misplaced, but that's not a transgression against me. It goes against your own beliefs, if anything. I think you'll come to see that."

"Maybe." He pushed the beer bottle around on the table. "Now that you've said your piece, is that it? You'll leave?"

"Yes, Mr. Osgood, that is the end of my lecture," she said. "I'm content to let my radical ideas and suggestion ferment, boil in the back of your head, and trust they'll bear fruit. And I'm not leaving immediately," she said. "We have today and tonight. I'll leave tomorrow."

"You are a lousy true believer, you know."

"Thank you for that compliment," she said. "Now pay for the beer and let's go back to the room. All this theoretical talk turned me on."

"That suggestion was worth sitting through the lecture for, professor."

He made a joke of it, but he had to admit that what she said was already gnawing at him. It was all stuff he knew was true. Most of what she said had been nagging at him for some time, was an inherent part of his malaise. It was something to talk to Claude about. Later.

CHAPTER 22

THE LONG ARM OF THE LAW

"We have seen already, that if one man has power over others placed in his hands, he will make use of it for an evil purpose; for the purpose of rendering those other men the abject instruments of his will."

—JAMES MILL
ENCYCLOPEDIA BRITANNICA

CERCLE DE LORRAINE
BRUSSELS, BELGIUM

Osk Barstad generally didn't think much of her job. It paid okay and her title sounded important but Interpol was a fairly toothless organization. They were supposed to fight crime, but they needed local police to make arrests. Then, once she'd gotten the perpetrator, there was a ton of paperwork involved in getting them deported or extradited . . . whatever was appropriate to get them back to the jurisdiction where the crime was considered to have been committed.

With computer crime, especially international banking fraud, it could be a challenge to figure out the proper jurisdiction. Sometimes, especially in high-profile cases, several countries wanted to be involved, other times no one wanted the headache of dealing with it.

It didn't feel much like being in law enforcement.

And computers, as useful as they were, annoyed her. Osk wasn't a programmer. She'd written code during her years at university, but that was it. She'd taken police training, but because she had some classes in finance, she got put on the Economic Crime Team of the Oslo police force. She'd done well and had been loaned out to Scotland

Yard for a year. That was supposed to foster interagency cooperation and let her learn how the Yard did things. She had an affair with the detective she was training with and wound up being recruited by Interpol's financial crimes group.

Although it sounded like she was joining an elite group, she learned that the work was the same. But Interpol did have better resources and training, and she also had a chance to rub shoulders with top economic and financial people. The prestige of it was novel for a time. She did good work and got promoted.

When she gave a talk on Interpol's efforts to detect money laundering at the World Economic Forum in Davos, she got an unexpected invitation to dinner. It was from some major players . . . department heads at the IMF and World Bank. It turned into a dream date. She was wined and dined in lavish style, and courted—they were recruiting her.

"We have our own task force," Mitch Childer told her. "It's an informal group that works together to meet common goals. It functions in ways that our own organizations are unable or unwilling to cooperate."

"I don't understand."

"Of course not. Are you aware of the Bilderberg Group?"

"Just that it was formed to strengthen the US alliance with Europe and prevent another world war."

Childer nodded. "And it is based on free-market capitalism . . . globally. That group continues, but a number of its key members grew unhappy with the tepid efforts and, ultimately, its mundane goals. As a response, they created the Retinger Oculistica, named after Józef Retinger, a Polish politician. Today the Oculistica represents the real effort to create a global, supra-governmental effort to help the world, to provide for worldwide financial and physical safety and security. Naturally, law enforcement is an important part of that."

She was both flattered and curious. "Why are you talking to me? I run a department, not the agency."

"Because it would be useful to have someone well placed in Interpol," a dark-haired woman told her. "Someone who is focused on financial and economic crimes. You don't run the agency, but you run that department. And we understand you do it well."

It had amused her that they had researched her so thoroughly, but her ego was stroked by being the center of their attention. It was a heady business. At dinner they agreed to stay in touch, to pursue her potential involvement. And so they carried on this whirlwind affair, getting to know each other, for a few months before she was officially offered a place among them. Even before they made the offer, she knew they would and she knew what her answer would be.

Ultimately, the money and the allure of working with them, being part of an incredibly powerful and secret group, were irresistible.

On a day-to-day basis, they asked little of her. They wanted to know in advance of any major cases Interpol was investigating and often asked her to nudge things in a direction they preferred. Mostly she just did the job Interpol paid her well to do; only now she made far more. It was more interesting when she was called on to do some consulting. The group would bring together a few of the members and have them answer questions, create scenarios, and sometimes, as she was now, evaluate potential risks and damage control options.

She had been summoned to Belgium and a car brought her to a meeting at the Cercle de Lorraine. It was a high-end private club in Brussels, where heads of industries, royalty, and Europe's most powerful economic influencers met to network. Just walking in made her tremble with delight. The air was thin at this altitude.

The staff knew her on sight and escorted her to a private meeting room. As she went through the dining area, she saw Johnny Depp with a small party eating lunch. In the room, two people, two members of the top ranks of the Retinger Oculistica, waited for her.

As she sat, a waiter brought her a glass of a chilled white wine and then backed away. As he vanished, the meeting started without ceremony. "From what we've heard, the system, this Tanzanian project, has become a mess," the man with green eyes said.

"I've just seen the reports. They've hit some problems, but it is a complex system and this was just a first test."

"A functional test. It didn't do anything."

She shrugged. "It is in its early days."

"We are thinking of pulling the plug on it," he said, turning to the dark-haired woman beside him. "She doesn't agree, but my sense of the status of the project right now suggests that we are in serious trouble." Then he focused on Osk. "Before we make a decision, I'd like your opinion."

Osk didn't know the man's name or whether he was a businessman, politician, or what. She did know that he commanded the respect of everyone in the group. She'd learned early on that many of the private members didn't offer their names. Both of them stared at her, waiting. She knew they expected her unvarnished opinion and she steeled herself to give it.

"I think it would be wise to let the program play out exactly the way Childer has established it," she told them. She saw a flicker of emotion cross the face of the woman. In an instant it was gone, leaving Osk certain that she'd struck a nerve of some kind. Whether that was good or bad, only time would tell. As with the green-eyed man, she'd never been told the woman's name, or who she represented, but it was made clear that she was another one of the inner circle—the directors of the secret group.

The woman sniffed. "Really? Not everyone thinks it's safe to do let it go on. It certainly looks like the project might fail spectacularly. That could call attention to . . . other things."

"What would they find in bad code?" Osk asked.

"The danger isn't with the code or what's in it," the man said. "I don't think it's wise to do something that might end up with nosy reporters digging in and looking for some scrap of a story."

Osk considered that. "I think you'd have more interest from the media if the project was aborted. They'd smell a cover-up or a botched attempt at something. If it fails . . . well projects and programs far less ambitious than this fail all the time. And the IMF would be seen as the fools behind it, not the group."

"Still . . ."

"With this project, you are isolated from blame or even association. Naturally, the conspiracy buffs, the ones who see your invisible hand at work in every election, every international event, will continue to claim that you were involved. They'll see your handiwork in dozens of places where you haven't even operated. There is no more credible evidence of your existence in this project than in those imagined places. The IMF and World Bank are peripherally involved, but it would be suspicious if they weren't. Most people will see that it doesn't take a powerful, secret group operating behind the scenes to create this project or to cause it to fail. Look at Venezuela . . . these countries making half-assed attempts to reap the benefits of crypto and trying to regulate it at the same time are so numerous. Most of them, like so many initial coin offerings, are garbage. Other than the IMF and World Bank involvement in this one, there is no reason to think it will stand out from all the others."

"You make a powerful case," the woman said.

"You asked me to supervise, to investigate this, to construct scenarios . . . I'm damn good at what I do."

The green-eyed man stood up. "Very well, Barstad. We rely on you alerting us immediately if that analysis were to change for any reason whatsoever."

She nodded. "Of course."

The man started toward the door, then stopped and turned back. "I assume you are keeping track of everyone involved in the project? All the people who will know details?"

She nodded. "Yes. Once you assigned the security to me, I began immediately. I've been accumulating names of everyone involved, including the locals and expats working on the project, or anyone who might otherwise be exposed to information about it. I've had my staff doing research into them beyond what we know already."

"Mostly we'll need to know where to find them if there is any need to debrief them."

Osk smiled. Even not knowing a damn thing about this man, she was fairly certain she knew how he would debrief people. It was in those eyes, the set of his chin. He wasn't one to leave loose ends. On one level, that bothered her. Most of the people involved were innocents, but then she'd understood that this group was willing to go to extremes when she'd joined them. This wasn't the time to take the high moral ground. "We know where everyone is."

"Even this programmer who is working off-site?"

She nodded. "We can reach out to him at any time. The company, Hoenig Fintech, paid for his tickets when he left Zurich. That's all in the system. I've sent an agent to keep eyes on him. I've instructed my agent to keep tabs on his exact whereabouts."

The man looked like he might smile, then the moment passed.

"Keep on top of it," he thought. "I'll send you my private, encrypted number. Anything strange or upsetting should be reported directly to me immediately. This Dory woman strikes me as unconventional. Childer thinks he has her covered, but I don't believe it."

"I'll do that."

"And keep an eye on Mr. Childer."

"You think he might do something? What am I watching for?"

"I think he's trying to prove something with this project. He's a lot more emotionally invested in it than he should be."

"It's more or less his life's work."

"And while dedication and loyalty are fine qualities, obsession is not. Reaching our goals means being adaptable and not insisting on a particular path. I worry about him."

"I see."

"While the project is important to us, retaining our invisibility is far more important than the success of this project."

"That's good to understand."

"That's why we haven't troubled him with the possibility that we might shut him down. I think he might object and things could get messy. So we are going to send you to Dar es Salaam so that you can keep a close eye on. . . .everything."

"If you send me there to look over the project, won't Childer suspect something?"

"Actually, we are taking advantage of a convenience. Mitch Childer just requested that we ask you to be there. He thinks you can help him with his little game. The players need a little prodding and reassurance now and again."

"So he will be happy I am there." A thin smile curled her lips. She'd never liked Childer, not even a little. It was good to know that he wasn't loved or even totally trusted by the upper echelon. "I need to write up a report for Interpol justifying my absence to cover the work. That way everyone will have been told the same story. I can be in Tanzania in two days."

"Perfect."

Then the man left.

The dark-haired woman raised her glass. "You did that well."

"What did I do?"

"You managed him. You disagreed with him in a way that didn't confront him. Well played. I think you are going to be an increasingly important asset to the group." She stood. "I'll send the waiter over on my way out. Order another wine and take your time drinking it. I'll leave through the back. Being seen together, or leaving together, is never a good idea."

Osk nodded. Spending a little time in a luxury hotel was certainly no hardship. She would get herself an elegant suite in a nice hotel in Dar es Salaam. She remembered hearing good things about the Serena Hotel. She'd look it up. And then, while she was doing everything this group asked of her, she could also make some connections with the law enforcement people there—personal connections. She considered the rather delicious possibility that some politicians would want to curry her favor. There would be men and women on the take who were made nervous by a visible Interpol presence. She'd offer them her protection for a price and make the best possible use of her time.

In the meantime, she'd live on per diem and invest her salary and additional income in the cryptocurrency coin called Monero. The geeks in Scotland Yard had been talking a lot about how anonymous it was—complaining about it actually—because it frustrated their efforts. That appealed to her, as it would to appeal to any reasonable person who might need to disguise their real wealth and where it was stored.

Osk Barstad was building her own little cocoon, her own reserves, and her own power base. Then, even if this group didn't survive, she would. And she'd have the means to keep living in the style she was rapidly becoming accustomed to. Life would continue to be good even if the political thing was bust. If the group failed, she would persist and that made her feel good.

CHAPTER 23

WITH POLICE SUPPORT

"My deepest thanks to the US government, Senator McCain and Senator Lieberman for pushing Visa, MasterCard, PayPal, AmEx, Mooneybookers, et al, into erecting an illegal banking blockade against @WikiLeaks starting in 2010. It caused us to invest in Bitcoin—with > 50000% return."

—JULIAN ASSANGE
TWITTER @JULIANASSANGE, 10/14/2017

GOLDEN TULIP DAR ES SALAAM CITY CENTER HOTEL
CITY PLAZA, JAMHURI STREET
DAR ES SALAAM, TANZANIA

Sundays were slow. On Sundays, shit-all happened. On Sunday, Peggy Anne Dory decided to go to the hotel's fancy fitness center and work out. She needed to get the crap out of her system, flush it out with sweat. She was spending too much time sitting and eating garbage food and she was losing energy. Besides, a hard workout would let her think and evaluate where she was.

This evaluation, the stuff she needed to think through and get her head around, primarily revolved around some recent changes. She needed to know how they affected her and her plans. Changes like the arrival of Osk Barstad, policewoman extraordinaire, had to alter things. The woman was snooping around and it wasn't clear what she was looking for.

On the other hand, Peggy had to admit that while her instincts told her to be careful around Osk, or any other cop, under the circumstances it was working out. She worked with Childer and she was happily confirming almost anything Peggy said about the code. That made her life, hiding the work she was doing for Childer, easier. The fool woman didn't seem to care what sort of bullshit she fed the Tanzanian government, or anyone else; she would just nod.

She scarcely paid the code any attention at all. She didn't have any interest in it and spent most of her time schmoozing with the bankers and financial types who came in to be reassured that the system would be the Godsend they'd been told it would be. Whatever else she was up to, and Peggy was sure she had her own agenda, she was good at that.

Unhappy at being kept in the cold, one bank wanted Peggy to include one of their programmers in the project, make him part of the team. "We'd like to have him involved. Having him there, safe-guarding our data, will reassure our board of directors," the bank president said.

Barstad was firm. "No. That would create an absolute mess. We'd need to get him a clearance, and then we'd have to authorize every bank, every brokerage firm, every chain store with proprietary data in the system to do the same. You know how that would go. It would result in so much petty squabbling that the project would never be completed."

The banker tried going over her head, taking the grievance to Andwele Kassain and then Deputy Minister Dola, but he got nowhere. Finally, Mitch Childer flew in to take the nervous bankers in hand. One by one, he took all the financial people involved out to dinner and gave them pep talks, or whatever the fuck people like that did in order to twist arms and get shit done.

Not that he'd done it for her, but Peggy was grateful. Mitch Childer, as much as he was one stuck-up prig who had to have a corn cob up his ass, sure knew how to handle people like that.

She knew why he was so eager to help too. She'd noticed a lot about the system changes Childer had asked for that didn't even make much sense to Peggy, who was developing the code. Some of it was counterintuitive. The premise was that a distributed, decentralized system would be faster, more cost-effective, and all that. But this sys-tem centralized all the data on people, companies, and organizations. And although it was a financial system, most of the data was rather meaningless from a financial point of view.

At one point, Andwele had taken a glance at the flowchart Peggy was creating and scratched his head. If that sanitized overview puzzled him, she figured he'd really be flummoxed by learning that the national crime database, all of the country's court records, including those that were suppressed, were scooped up in that mass of information. Everything from traffic tickets to fraud was recorded.

While data of that nature struck her as a curious thing for the IMF to be interested in, she could see why Osk would like it—it gave Interpol, her group at least, access to data that would normally take special requests and time spent working diplomatic back channels to get. When this system was operating, they could see it in a heartbeat—without anyone ever knowing.

None of that did a damn thing to speed financial transactions or provide financial information—the monitoring Childer claimed they were doing, the reason for building the system. Of course, it didn't slow it either; it just added to the cost of building the system. That meant it had to be something that Interpol, or Osk at least, wanted. Who knew if she spoke for the organization?

The question was why the IMF wanted to throw Interpol that lovely bone?

Peggy wasn't about to ask. No matter what extra little tricks they put in the system, with her module installed, her goal was just to see it up and running smoothly. And the sooner the better. In the meantime, when Childer or Osk told her to jump, she would ask how high.

Hoenig hadn't been surprised when Peggy told him that Interpol was on site. "The world is changing."

"That isn't news," she chuckled. "In this case, I think Interpol is getting its fingers into the pie." Then she explained about the access.

"Everything is about big data," Claude Hoenig said. "They are going to scrape everything even though they probably can't handle it all. I wouldn't be surprised if their analysts aren't already overwhelmed by the amount of crap generated by the new world of CCTV cameras running constantly and the ability to pick up chatter of all sorts. Still, Interpol isn't going to pass on a chance to tap into more. I'd assume they intend to do that with every country they help. It's modern spy craft. They use financial data to track criminals."

Peggy didn't care. "I just thought you ought to know," she said.

"I appreciate that. Knowing it could prove useful. In fact, send me some information on how they might access that data."

Peggy laughed. "Dealing yourself in?"

"Something like that. Why not? And how is the project going otherwise?"

"It's coming together. There's going to be a lot more coding than we anticipated in order to do everything that needs doing. That's a lot of data to fuck around with."

"And Wyatt?"

"He's fine. He's bitching about being kept in the dark, but he's delivering on time."

"Kept in the dark?"

"He wants to see the entire spec instead of just working on modules."

"Why don't you give him the spec? The more he knows, the better job he does."

"I'm not allowed to share it. That's the protocol that Childer established here, and once they brought Interpol into the game, they doubled down on the security. They don't want anyone off-site knowing the entire system. They think that even the information someone could get from block diagram or a complete flow chart is sharing too much. They won't even let me take the stuff to my hotel room to work on it."

Hoenig looked puzzled. "I know the information in this system will be useful to Interpol, but it's just a financial transaction system. Why treat it like it contains military secrets? Or is there something I don't know that I should know?"

Having Hoenig prying into the system's details was the last thing Peggy needed. "Because it's a test bed. Childer says that the IMF expects to use this to see how certain features work, so they can network the systems from lots of countries. It gives them useful data. But that means it is a prime target for hackers or anyone else who wanted to disrupt things. So he's cautious."

"We will want a complete set of specs for our files when it's complete," Hoenig said. "That's part of the deal."

"Then you better talk to Mitch Childer and this Barstad woman and make sure that's still on the table."

"Who?"

"The lady from Interpol. She's as nuts about keeping a lid on things as Childer is."

"Maybe because of what's at stake for her."

"Well, at my pay grade, all I can do is speculate. The details are locked down tight. So, in terms of working with Wyatt, the best I can do is describe the new modules to him and let him make them. And not just Wyatt. We've broken the code monkeys here into isolated groups."

"That's not a good approach. I can see why Wyatt is complaining."

"Well, I'm afraid that it's the best I can do, the best anyone can do. All that this crew will let me do is explain their functions and provide timing charts for the interfaces they connect to. Not only am I not allowed to tell anyone what the complete system does and how it does it, in some cases, it isn't clear to me. This crime data is a case in point. From my perspective, it does nothing."

"That's crap," Hoenig said.

Peggy almost laughed. The man was right, it was total crap, but there was enough truth in it that anyone he called would agree with what she'd told him. "They are being cautious. In fact, each of those factions is making their own efforts to control information flow— we've got competitive security. It feels like a peacekeeping mission for the UN, where the troops all have different orders. Childer and the Interpol lady are both doing their thing to keep anyone from knowing anything. I think they even keep the ministry in the dark. I'm pretty sure they review all the emails I send out. Andwele, who is actually seriously out of the loop, seems too well informed about some things I've only mentioned in emails to you or Wyatt."

"Well, the email is on their server. Self-interest on steroids I suppose, but I've worked with intelligence agencies that weren't that paranoid. So is this why you called me using an encryption program?"

"Yes, and it's why I'm calling from my hotel room using my cell. Anything in the office is subject to prying ears of one sort or another."

"They haven't welcomed you with open arms?"

"The presence of the American contingent is tolerated, as a necessity, but that's about it. Andwele wants the project under him, so he resents me running it. Childer resents the fact that I have to know anything at all. The Interpol lady is just fucking bored, I think. But she does look for leaks, and I'm not about to test what I can get away with without having my hand slapped. I think she'd smack hard. She strikes me as a ruthless bitch."

Hoenig sighed. "They really don't like letting the new kids in on the entire game, do they?"

"They?"

"Childer and his crowd."

"You mean the IMF and World Bank."

"To a degree, yes, but not entirely."

"Hoenig, am I supposed to know what you're talking about?"

"Not really. It's just that there is obviously more to this than meets the eye. Some conflicting agendas. I'll call Childer and explain the facts of life. If he expects us to gain much benefit from having Wyatt working with us, we need to be able to bring him up to speed."

"I'll leave that to you," Peggy told him. "Keep me out of it."

"I can do that. You don't like him, do you?"

"Childer? He's a cold fish. Doesn't give a fig about much that's human."

"I meant Wyatt."

She thought about it. "I don't dislike him. He and I are just totally different flavors of geek. He's all idealism and shit."

"And you are all cynicism?"

"Not all. But I'm pragmatic. I just want to get this job done and get out. Wyatt wants the code to be all piss-elegant. He takes it personally if a module doesn't run."

"That makes him a valuable person."

"It makes him a pain in the ass when he won't settle for knowing that the code works. He always wants to know more."

"Like I said, that's one thing I respect about him. And that his analysis of code is usually right on."

"He's a good coder, but his heart sure isn't in this project and that isn't totally because he's kept in the dark, either. You heard him spouting off when we were in Zurich. Even though the core idea is his, I think he'd rather do almost any other project than this one. That's not pragmatic."

"It's a bad situation. I thought the distance would let him relax when it came to his political opinions. I know he won't accept the need for a government to be a trust figure for the cryptocurrency."

"The very idea of setting it up that way makes him ill."

"But you say he's doing good work?"

Peggy hated to admit it. "He grins and bears it. The project would be way behind without him. And now . . . well, there are some problems. I think they are timing related, but I'm not sure. I'm debugging, sorting it out, but I could use his take on it. But given the protocols, the fucking secrecy, he'd have to come here to do the work."

"You know that's a nonstarter."

"Just for a few days," Peggy said. "A couple of weeks at most. We'd wrap this thing up so easily."

"His contract says he doesn't have to," Hoenig said. "We made a deal."

Peggy shook her head. "But he could if he chose to. And he is your friend. Somehow. I have no idea how you two manage not to kill each other, but you are friends. If you asked nicely."

Hoenig was quiet. "Childer talked to me about that too."

"Yeah," Peggy said. "He's big on bringing Wyatt in from the warm."

"I talked to him."

"And?"

"He said no. No way. That is a step further than he's willing to go."

Peggy sighed. "Fuck. Childer is really adamant."

"Maybe if you called him."

"Me?"

"You are the project head. If you asked nicely . . ."

"I'd have to beg."

Hoenig coughed. "You said you wanted it wrapped up. You said if he was there it would take a couple of weeks."'

"Fuck it. Fine. I'll beg."

"Good girl. There will be a bonus in this for you when the project is going along."

Damn right, there will be, Peggy thought. A bigger bonus than anyone imagined. The world was a place of free money if you had the chance to tap into it. And this was her chance.

So, if begging was what it took to wrap this sucker up, she'd beg Wyatt to come bail them out. Give him a chance to play the rescuing hero.

She'd do worse than that if she had to. She was so close that she tasted success, and it was sweet.

CHAPTER 24

COMPULSORY ATTENDANCE

"One good thing about music, when it hits you, you feel no pain."

—Bob Marley

Malecón de Progreso
Yucatán, Mexico

Wyatt Osgood sat at a table on the beach sipping a cold beer and taking in the view. He was alone again. Rebecca had left for Asia. Indonesia, she'd said, although he wasn't sure how much credence to give that story. Not after all he'd learned about her. If she was smart, she would lie about that. It didn't matter . . . regardless of where she'd gone, she was gone.

She was gone, but the beautiful Caribbean Sea was there in front of him, glowing in the late morning light. Of even greater interest, two lean, bikini-clad, or almost clad, girls that had probably gotten off the cruise ship walked past him. They wore their hair pulled back in ponytails and sunglasses masked their eyes as they walked side by side at the edge of the water. When they were directly in front of him, one glanced at him and smiled.

He smiled back and let his eyes feast on their lovely tanned legs and run up over their asses and breasts. They were both lean, but not super skinny. He liked that. Wyatt thought women should have curves.

They continued walking away and when they had gone far enough down the beach that he couldn't see their ass muscles moving anymore, he sighed and turned his attention back to the screen of the laptop sitting on the table in front of him.

After Rebecca left, he'd gotten two calls. First Hoenig and then Peggy called to ask him to go to Tanzania. The project was in trouble. "I'm doing my part, Claude," he'd told Hoenig. "Don't go trying to change the deal on me now."

"I'm not," Claude said. "I was asking a favor."

"That works out the same."

When they hung up, he thought the air had been cleared. Hoenig said he understood. Then Peggy called, telling him how much she needed his help. "It's your code," she said. "I know you want it implemented correctly."

"That's emotional blackmail," he said. "I'm not playing that game. I can either go on the way I am, or you can finish it without me. Those are the only choices."

She hung up sounding bitter, unhappy, but he didn't care. He wasn't going to worry about a project that really shouldn't have been started without more upfront design and more practical parameters. If they were in trouble now, even if he went there, the most he could hope for was to kludge things together. The time pressure, the constraints of the project, most of which he didn't even like, wouldn't allow a good solution to the problems Peggy mentioned.

Finally, she gave up and he let all thoughts of Tanzania aside and focused on the problem at hand. He was working on an idea he'd had that morning, just as he watched Rebecca climb into a taxi and head for the airport. He'd thought of a little tweak to his code that just might mean he could simplify transaction processing, eliminating one more level of overhead. If it worked. In a distributed network, the benefits of that would be multiplied several times over, so it was worth exploring. It might not be timely for the Tanzanian project, but it might help him understand the interactions better and would be useful in the future.

He pictured it working, playing it out in his head. This thread leads to that one, passing parameters, and then waiting to either time out or continue depending on input from . . . suddenly, he realized he'd created another problem for himself. This was a timing problem and solving it would require another tweak. Since Peggy wouldn't let him see the module he was thinking of, he'd just have to write his own. It didn't matter how hers worked.

As usual, once he got his head into what he was doing, the process of coding sucked him in, making him unaware of his surroundings. Now nothing would make him look up . . . not until he got hungry or was interrupted by some external event. The external events could be a bothersome hawker or someone sitting at his table. In this case, the event that broke his concentration was the realization that someone had just put a hand firmly on his shoulder.

"Hello, Wyatt."

The voice was a man's. The accent was German and his English was clearly articulated, almost stilted. When he turned, the man opened the linen coat he wore, showing him a gun. While Wyatt wasn't familiar with guns to any great extent, it was clearly a real automatic pistol. Of even more concern was that the person with the gun knew his name. Whatever was going on, that was not a good sign. This wasn't a random robbery.

He froze in place. "My wallet is in my back pocket."

"I have no use for your wallet," the man said. "I was well paid to come here—to talk to you."

"For me? Are you sure . . ."

"Yes, Wyatt Osgood."

"You don't need a gun to talk."

"But having it ensures you will listen."

The man had a point. Something about him seemed oddly famil-iar yet out of place. He knew this man from somewhere. "So talk and I'll listen."

"It's about your itinerary. I was informed that you are not sup-posed to be here," he said.

"I'm not? Why not?"

"I can't say for certain, but I assume your skills are needed some-where else. I was given to understand that you know where you are supposed to be."

"Dar es Salaam?"

"Possibly. You'd know better than I. At any rate, your presence there is rather important to my current employer."

"Who is that?"

He laughed. "The person who wants you to be wherever it is you were told to go."

"You don't intend to kill me?"

The man came around to face him. He was young, thin, fit, and dressed like some young executive on vacation, with khaki slacks, loafers with no socks, a polo shirt, and a windbreaker. Wyatt caught his eyes and saw a hardness there, a coldness. He had the eyes of a killer. He wasn't joking around.

The man stared back as he put the gun in his belt, letting his windbreaker cover it, and sat down. Wyatt looked at him. "Of course, I'm not going to kill you. That would make it impossible for you to go to wherever you were asked to go and do whatever it is you are supposed to do."

"So pointing the gun at my head was your way of making a point?"

He smiled. "Actually, it was. I find it is quite the icebreaker. See how I have your attention?"

Wyatt shook his head. "Tell Hoenig to fuck off. Remind him that me going on site isn't what we agreed on."

The man smiled. "I would be glad to; unfortunately, I have no idea who this Hoenig person is. Better if you tell him yourself."

"Clyde Hoenig didn't send you?"

The man shook his head. "I can honestly say I have never heard of him." Then he raised a hand, summoning a girl who had wandered over from a restaurant and was cleaning another table. "*Senorita, mi amor, dos cervezas, por favor.*" Then he turned back to Wyatt. "Given the way things work in this wide and wonderful world, and the fact that I don't know who he is, doesn't mean he didn't send me. That's an awkward statement, isn't it? I mean to say that the person who sent me could be your president or the Italian or Russian mobs." He shrugged. "I wouldn't know."

"You don't even know who sent you?"

"That's the wrong question to ask. It's certainly not one I'd ever ask my employers. That would annoy them. Besides, who sent me is really the least important thing about my trip here," he said.

The girl brought the beer and the German paid her in crisp pesos.

"It's important to me," Wyatt said.

"No." The man took a long sip of his beer. "That is satisfying beer. But as I was saying, who I work for is not important at all. What is important is that you be on a plane to wherever it is you are supposed to be in three days. I was told to inform you that your attendance is compulsory."

"Compulsory. That means there is an 'if you don't' attached."

"There most definitely is."

"What is that?"

"I'm glad you asked. I had to go to the trouble to memorize that scenario. What a waste of my time and effort it would've been if you docilely agreed to do what you are asked after all this. At any rate, the scenario is this—if you don't show up at the appointed place within three days, ready to work, then you'll learn that I was forced to make a trip to Colorado."

"Colorado?"

"Yes. And that would make me irritable as I don't like Colorado. I can't really say why, though. It's undoubtedly some irrational prejudice. After all, there is some lovely country there. It's probably a wonderland for camping and that dreary stuff. I'm told that your sister's farm is charming."

"My sister?" Wyatt felt a chill. This man knew too much.

"Ellen, I believe."

"She isn't involved in this."

"I'm afraid she is. My instructions were to explain the choices to you and to be convincing. I'll see if I can do that. Here is the reality: If you don't get on a plane immediately and go do your work, then I will kill your sister. My employer has no need of her and suspects that threat will motivate you."

Wyatt's brain raced. "You can't hurt her." It sounded stupid even as he said it.

The man laughed. "I can't tell you how often people say things like that. They have no idea. I think it comes from bad writing on television. You tell someone you have a terminal illness and they say, 'everything will be all right.' How absurd is that? Of course, things won't be all right. This is the same. You are telling me I can't hurt your sister when we both know that there is no reason at all that I can't hurt her a great deal. I'm good at what I do."

"If you . . ."

"Is Ellen pretty? If she is, and there is no rush about it, then I'll entertain myself with her for a few days before actually finishing the job."

"You son of a bitch!"

"Don't you think a person should take pleasure in their work? I'll confess that a job like mine offers no private life, so I have to grab pleasure where and when I can find it." He drained his beer. "Well, I've said my piece and that's all I came for."

Wyatt considered grabbing him, but the man looked like he knew how to fight and his hand hovered near the pocket holding the gun. "Leave my sister alone."

"That's pathetic, Wyatt. It comes down to this: if you get on a plane and do what it was you were asked to do, then I'd have no reason whatsoever to even go to Colorado, much less bother your sister."

"If anything happens to her, I'll bring the fucking system down."

He shook his head. "Telling me that is a rather empty threat, Wyatt. You see, I have the pleasure of having no idea what you're talking about. Whatever system you mean. . . . I certainly don't care about it one way or the other." The German stood. "Two bits of advice: Don't let your beer get warm and don't make me go to Colorado."

And then he walked away from the beach, leaving Wyatt wondering who, besides Hoenig, would want him on site in Dar es Salaam so badly? He had no doubt at all that if he didn't show up that man would kill Ellen. He also had no doubt that warning her would do no good at all.

But sending someone else to threaten him wasn't the way Claude Hoenig operated. Wyatt knew his past. If he was that desperate, he would've tried harder to convince him to go to Africa. But he hadn't. He could've just said that if Wyatt refused, his people would hurt Ellen. Wyatt would believe him. Claude would never joke about something like that, even with a gun to his own head.

And if he did send someone, some bloodthirsty messenger, it wouldn't be a German. No, even if Claude sent someone, he'd be a clean-cut American. American jobs for Americans was one of his mantras. There had to be plenty of nasty killers with US passports available.

He picked up his phone and called Hoenig. As he waited for him to pick up, he wondered if that was how he had been tracked, through his cell phone. Actually, Rebecca had followed the most obvious path. Any of the parties involved in this clusterfuck of a project was capable of hacking an airline reservation system, or just checking flight manifests out of Zurich. The question was why did he interest them so much? Whoever it was had an interest in getting this system done, and now he was sure that Peggy must've fucked it up badly.

For the first time, Wyatt realized there were more players in the game than he knew about. In that context, some of what he suspected they were doing made sense.

For the time being, he needed to do what he'd been told. Then, when the job was done, he'd confront Claude, get him to admit that he'd had him threatened, or get him to find out who had done it. The guy was a fucking spook after all—he shouldn't have any trouble doing that. But that would wait. For now, he just needed to protect Ellen.

"Wyatt," Clyde said when he answered.

"I'm coming to the site," he said. "I'll fly first class and expect total reimbursement."

"No problem. But I thought . . ."

"I had a change of heart."

"I'm glad to hear that. I'll give Peggy a heads-up. She'll be glad to see you."

"Explain this whole thing to me, Claude. What the hell were you thinking with this project? Why have a hacker running a bunch of coders in the first place? She's smart and she knows code, but mostly in terms of how to pick it apart."

"She's a doer and aggressive. Leaders need that more than coding skills."

"Really? How's that working out for you?"

"Not so good at the moment. Childer is beside himself. The system was all over the place. The modules don't seem to want to play well together."

Wyatt sighed. Hoenig thought all techs were created equal, interchangeable, and unfathomable. "Fine, I'll show up in frigging Africa and figure out what she screwed up. As soon as it's implemented, I'll leave again, right?"

"Of course. We will put you up in a lovely suite at the Serena Hotel. Take a taxi there and your room will be waiting."

Something seemed familiar about the name of the hotel, but he couldn't place it.

Next, he called Ellen. "Wow," she said. "Calling me on an unsecured line?"

"I was in a rush and wanted to see that you were all right."

"I'm fine. Harold's fine. The crops are so-so and the rest of the country is bonkers. Nice of you to ask. Why are you asking?"

"Anyone been nosing around?"

"Not that we've seen. Why?"

"No more of those strange phone calls?"

"Nope. But I remembered the name of the woman. Boone, she said."

"Boone?"

"As in Richard Boone, the actor. Remember watching *Paladin*?"

"Of course." Beyond that, Wyatt thought the name Boone had a familiar ring to it. What was it with these places and people with names that echoed something? Wyatt felt as if something was tightening around him . . . a net? If it was, who was doing the fishing? "Keep an eye out," he said.

"For anything in particular?"

"For anyone who doesn't belong."

She laughed. "No one belongs around here. Not even us."

"It isn't funny. Be careful of strangers."

"You're serious. Are we in danger?"

"I have no idea," he said. "It's possible."

"That's not helpful."

"Something is going on. As you pointed out, this isn't a secure line so I don't feel good about saying more. I don't know anything that would be useful to you anyway."

"Naturally. Okay, I'll give Harold a heads-up for . . . anything strange, I guess."

"That's as clear as I can be."

"You be careful too."

"I'll try. It's tricky."

After they ended the call, Wyatt took the German's advice and drank the beer. While he drank it, he saved the file he'd been working on, clicked on his browser, and booked a flight to Dar es Salaam. He'd leave Progreso for Mexico City that afternoon.

He ordered another beer and opened a document file. When you needed help, support, and you made a request, the best thing you could do was tell them as much as you could about the problem and its background. So he stared at the screen and racked his brain for details, forcing them into chronological order. Then he put the beer down and began composing a history of the project that included everything he knew about it. He explained how he'd heard about it, his involvement, his agreement, and then described the visit from the German and his concern for his sister's welfare. When he'd reread it a few times, he attached it to an email and addressed it to Boone@ bitpats.com and in the subject field, he wrote simply: HELP.

After he hit send, he picked up his beer again and stared at the screen. As a way of fighting back, it didn't seem like a hell of a lot, but his options were limited. He believed every word the German had said and he couldn't think of anyone else to reach out to.

Feeling helpless, he went to his room to pack, wondering about the climate in Tanzania. Whatever the dress code was in the office, they were going to have to put up with shorts and tee shirts. Fuck 'em if they couldn't take a joke.

PART THREE

SOFTWARE PATCHES AND THREADS

1 0 1 0 1 0 1 0 1 0 1 0 1 0 1 0 1 0 1 0 1 0 1 0 1 0 1 0 1 0 1 0 1 0 1 0 1 0 1 0 1 0 1

"Authorities hate those who learn to think, because
they then cannot be trained to hate."

—STEFAN MOLYNEUX
IRISH-BORN CANADIAN PODCASTER WHO SPEAKS ON
TOPICS, INCLUDING ANARCHO-CAPITALISM (ANCAP)

CHAPTER 25

TROUBLESHOOTER IN THE BUILDING

"The difference between a bad electronic cash system
and well-developed digital cash will determine whether
we will have a dictatorship or a real democracy."

—DAVID CHAUM
AMERICAN COMPUTER SCIENTIST AND CRYPTOGRAPHER WHO DEVELOPED ECASH

ARRIVAL
DAR ES SALAAM, TANZANIA

When Wyatt landed at Julius Nyerere International Airport in Dar es Salaam, he found a uniformed driver waiting for him. The man stood outside the baggage claim area holding a sign with his name on it.

He smiled, knowing that Hoenig was pulling out all the stops in order to make him feel like royalty. It was working too. He liked being pampered, treated like the heavy hitter being called in to pinch hit in the last inning of a baseball game. Even better, it suggested Claude wasn't behind the threat on Ellen's life. The person who wielded that stick didn't need to make him happy. He or she knew that Wyatt wouldn't need any additional coaxing, so maybe Claude didn't know about the threat. He wanted to believe that. It would be awful to think that he'd misjudged Hoenig so completely. The man could be cold, but he was human. Whoever threatened his sister, whoever sent the German, wasn't.

The driver took Wyatt's bag and led him to a limo. After a thirty minute drive toward the ocean, they arrived at the Serena Hotel. "There is a suite booked for you," the driver said as he handed Wyatt's one bag to a uniformed bellman. "They are expecting you at the office, but you have time to freshen up. I will wait for you here."

The desk clerk greeted him by name and he was escorted to a lavish suite overlooking the city. He almost felt guilty having the driver cooling his heels in front while he showered and changed. A tall, cool drink from a bottle of single malt whiskey that had a tag on it saying: "Welcome to Dar es Salaam . . . Claude," took off the edge.

Downstairs, he got into the waiting limo that took him to the office where the project was being coded. Driving through the streets, he didn't really see the streets, the buildings, any detail. All his thoughts were internal, a combination of his concerns for Ellen and thoughts on what might be wrong with the program. After all, this was just another city. And this was a fucking business trip.

It was a rude awakening. Despite being sure he was finished with having to go where other people wanted him to be, working under their rules, he was still on the leash. Someone with power and money had other ideas for his future.

Then he discovered a note tucked into the map pocket of the seat in front of him. He gingerly took it out. This wouldn't be from Claude. The note he'd left on the booze told his story. He unfolded it. As he'd expected, this one was less pleasant.

"You are being smart now. This car will take care of your commute. You will focus on nothing but getting the system running. Simply do that and rest assured that everything, and everyone you care about, will be all right."

It wasn't signed, but the language, the tone of it, made him certain that it had come from someone other than Claude Hoenig.

In fact, when had he called to tell Claude that he would be going to Africa, he seemed honestly surprised, as well as pleased. "You, on site? That is more than I could ask for."

"And I will disappear again as soon as this is fixed," Wyatt had said.

"Of course. I'm happy to take what you are willing to give. The contract we have is clear."

He meant what he said, but that didn't mean much. If Hoenig wasn't the person threatening Ellen, Wyatt had even less faith in that promise. If it wasn't Claude, then he was being pressured by someone else. Without knowing who it was, or what they intended, he couldn't know for certain that the threat would be over when the project was done.

He considered telling Hoenig what was going on, why he'd come. That seemed premature. Better to get a sense of things first, find out who was on what side, because it was clear that this project, like most, had people aligned in various camps. At this point, he didn't even really know the players.

But the mystery person behind the threat bothered him. For all he knew, this was just the start of a series of jobs. A clever and sinister person could easily insist on him doing other work for them. It could be endless. If things didn't change, he'd have to do whatever they demanded. It sucked.

The threat to Ellen wasn't something he could eliminate or mitigate easily. In the meantime, he'd do what he was told to keep her safe. He vowed to figure out who was behind the threat. He couldn't deal with the German, but if he cut off the head of the beast, or convinced whoever it was to leave him alone, that wouldn't matter. It wasn't something personal to that killer.

The car stopped in front of a modern, multi story, glass and steel office building. "This is your office. The building houses the Ministry of Finance and Planning, sir," the driver said as he opened the door and held it for him. If he was being held prisoner, they were doing it in style. Whoever had threatened him might not want others to know that Wyatt wasn't there of his own free will, just a happy coder.

He went in through the electronic doors, passing by a uniformed guard with an UZI. A receptionist behind a marble desk greeted him with a bright smile. She handed him a laminated identity card with his picture on it but no name. "It contains a radio-frequency identification (RFID) chip that operates the elevator and will give you access to all the spaces your work requires," she said.

He thanked her, more for her cheerfulness than the information, and walked to the bank of elevators. He stepped into a sterile, stainless steel box. Waving his card over the sensor activated it, and the elevator took him to the sixth floor—obviously, the office where Peggy, and now he, worked. When the door opened, he stepped into a large office that was humming with the sound of people typing, printers and copiers running, the low murmur of telephone conversations.

It was a well lit pale blue-gray room. One wall had floor to ceiling windows. The open space was divided into cubicles with familiar pale blue-gray partitions. He sighed.

After all that had happened, Wyatt found it impossibly weird to be back in a cubicle again. The distance from the cubicle to the beach was far too small to be comfortable.

Granted, these cubicles were in an office in downtown Dar es Salaam, and he was living in a suite in a hotel he'd seen in Sindi's video, but he would still be working in a cubicle. That the cubicle was in Africa might sound exotic, but it didn't make it a better place to be. And it sure as hell wasn't a beach where a wave of his hand caused lovely chicas to bring him cold beer. He'd gotten used to coding with his bare toes wiggling in the warm sand.

"Welcome to deepest, darkest Africa," Peggy said cheerfully. "I'm glad to see you."

Idly, he wondered if she might know who had threatened Ellen. It didn't seem all that likely. In fact, as far as he knew, Peggy knew nothing of his personal life at all. Still, she was a player; she had wanted him there. The only thing that was unreasonable was that Peggy Anne Dory would have access to assassins to send out on assignment. Not that she was too ethical for that. . . . no, she just didn't operate through organizations.

Still, he wasn't going to play games and pretend. "I can't say I'm glad to be here at all."

She gave him an odd look. "No? Then why are you here?"

"I didn't really have as much choice in the matter as I thought."

"Why not?" Peggy asked. "From what I hear, you bought Bitcoin early on. I can't imagine you are doing this for the money."

"No. The money means little."

"And you don't like the project. So I officially don't get what leverage anyone would have over you."

That cleared the air. Now he was certain he could eliminate her from the list. "Never mind. My reasons don't matter. I came to work."

"I've cleared a space for you," she said.

His stomach tightened as he followed her to the cubicle she'd assigned to him—his new cell. It looked exactly like the one in Virginia, lacking only his beach picture. He'd print out one of Progreso and put it up. It would be some small solace to be a picture of a place he'd enjoyed.

"I've had the guys print out copies of the system documentation," she said. "Hoenig said you like to stare at printouts when you work."

"Yeah, the code looks different on paper."

She shrugged and pointed to a box of files. "Well, I imagine the stuff is a little disorganized."

He resisted groaning. It was too theatrical. "Then I guess I better get to work. The sooner we get started, the sooner it gets running and we can leave."

"That's the spirit," she laughed.

There was a ton of paper to sort through. He knew, from experience, that some would be redundant, but he'd have to go through it all. So, without any real enthusiasm, he began the task of sorting through the papers, putting them into stacks that he considered useful to the way he approached a coding problem. When he found flowcharts, he tacked them to the walls with pushpins he found on the desk.

When they were up there, he sat down and flipped through the test results that Rashmi had collected. They made little sense to him. Although it appeared that she'd been thorough with her testing, the results didn't seem to be right at all. The only thing that was clear was that the system had suffered some serious glitches. Well, presumably, that was why he was there.

When he turned to the actual code, initially just scrolling through the lines of code and trying to get a sense of things, what he saw turned his stomach. It was a nightmare—much worse than he'd expected. Peggy was brilliant, but not well organized. She planned cleverly and probably did fine working solo, but she wasn't giving the people writing modules good information or holding them to a standard for writing it. And even at a glance, he could see that, in some cases, the information seemed to change in midstream—a register was being used by two, probably more modules. No one was tracking that. Many of the problems arose from changes that were being made on the fly. She hadn't instituted a comprehensive system for tracking changes. There was a revision log, but it was a mess too.

The deeper he dug, the worse it got. The way it was structured, a lot of the functions routed through a part of the code that he couldn't even find. "What the fuck?" he said. The man in the next cubicle looked over at him. "What's wrong?"

"Everything. Nearly everything. Where are the bank transaction modules?"

The man tipped his head toward the cubicle where Peggy was working. "Ask the boss lady."

The tone of the man's voice spoke volumes. Peggy's leadership hadn't inspired him. Wyatt didn't have a good feeling about it either. He got up and walked over to Peggy's desk. She was the leader, but she toiled away in a boring fucking cubicle identical to his.

She looked up at him. "I'm missing the bank transaction modules," he said.

"You don't need those. They work fine."

"I don't think they do. I'm getting the feeling that they are at the heart of this disaster."

"I disagree and it's my call."

"Sure, I can spend a week ensuring that the other code is flawless, but that won't mean some simple error in the transactions modules won't keep the system from working."

"Start with what you have," Peggy said. "I know this project, Wyatt. I've been running it while you were off wherever you've been."

"If I can work top down, troubleshooting from a macro level first, things will go faster. I'll be able to see that certain things aren't even necessary. I won't waste time fixing them when they need to be eliminated. Other things might need to be approached differently."

"It would take me even more time to explain the overall vision."

"That damn vision idea has been the death of more than one project, Peggy."

"There are still some things I can't tell you."

A look at her stern face told him that she was unhappy about the state of affairs. If that was true, the fact that she wanted to share information but wasn't allowed to sure didn't help things any. "Look, I'm trying to help. These idiots insisted I come here and do my part."

"I didn't really want you here either," she said pointedly. "Other people decided we needed you here to make this happen on time."

Wyatt had guessed that much but wondered who the 'other people' might be, someone besides Claude, apparently. "Can you at least give me a list of the system variables they process and the way you pass them among the procedures that need them?"

She picked up a coffee mug with a black handle and held it in front of her face. In big, cartoonish letters, it said: "God wants you to know she's black." It was amusing, but rather pointless, he thought. He was sure she'd bought it just to piss off Claude Hoenig. It was a way of getting to him without saying a word. But maybe it meant more to her than that, some tenuous link to a religious past perhaps. He found it curious that so many coders were not religious in any conventional sense, but many were superstitious. They turned their coding efforts into grand mythological quests in which they faced down all manner of demons. Either that was because so many of them were also gamers, or perhaps so many of them were gamers because they were intrigued by the fantasy worlds and the metaphors they provided to real life.

"Why do you want those?"

Her question pulled him back from wondering about gods and mythologies . . . speculations of all types. He laughed. "Because one thing I do know about your system is that within that domain all is chaos. Your programmers are each grabbing and using the locations they are stored in. It's a free for all . . . first come first served. I've already found two modules that are quite happily overwriting the data used by the other modules."

"That's just stupid," she said. "Why did they do that?"

"Because of your mushroom management technique, which seems to be simply to keep them in the dark and feed them bullshit. How are they supposed to know? It isn't their fault if you aren't controlling the passing of system parameters. It's a goddamn rookie mistake not to post an updated list of something that basic to system operation."

She considered it. "Fine. Give me an hour. I'll post a master list and send it to everyone."

"I can't believe you didn't start with that."

"Fine, Wyatt. Yeah, I made a mistake. I thought the coders wouldn't just grab registers and assume they were available. I expected a little incentive on their part in trying to work together."

The admission almost floored Wyatt. Peggy had no clue. "I think the addresses of some of the registers might even be in null space . . . invalid addresses. That's one tiny reason the program doesn't run. You send important data to nowhere."

She shrugged. "Your sarcasm aside, how nice that you spotted that. Keep being the clever guy who finds the shit and we can wrap this up. Then you can go back to whatever hole you crawled into sooner, rather than later."

He stared at her. "You called and asked for my help."

"Yes, but not because I wanted to. I'm running the project, but there are other people involved and they decided we needed you."

"But why me? Why was it so important that I be the one to come here and fix your mess? It isn't specialized . . . not really. And you don't like working with me . . . you never have. You could hire some hotshot coders who wanted to be here and they'd do as much for you as I can do. They might be even better because they wouldn't come in hating what the system does."

She pouted. "Look, Wyatt, yes I called you and I asked Hoenig to charm you into coming here, but it was because the big kids involved in this project think you are a special dude. For whatever reason, they think that only a smart ass who publishes open-source papers is smart enough to make this happen. They also thought you were up to speed on the project. They are in a rush and in a panic, which isn't a brilliant combination. And, of course, with the government, IMF, World Bank, and Interpol involved, it's management by committee."

"But I'm not up to speed," he said. "You haven't kept anyone totally informed."

She grinned. "Because the powers that be informed me that spreading the details to the troops, which includes you, was not entirely necessary or desirable."

"Fine," he said. "Then we will do this in spite of them. I want to get it fixed, and quickly. My beach is calling me."

As Wyatt walked back to his desk, he wondered what was going on. The big kids, she called them. That meant the deputy minister of finance, or his minion Kassain, at least. As far as he could tell, the minister of finance himself didn't even know he existed. The short list should also include Hoenig and maybe that IMF guy he'd met in Zurich. Childer, that was his name. And there would be others he hadn't met yet. She'd mentioned Interpol and the World Bank. They were question marks.

Childer was another unlikeable cipher in the mix. When they'd met briefly in Zurich, Wyatt had been put off by the way the man seemed to attach far too much importance to that fucking white paper. That didn't mean he'd be willing to threaten Wyatt to get his cooperation, but it did keep him on the list of suspects.

The project was governmental, even global, and that meant it was inherently political. Besides the ones riding the coattails of the people doing the work, jerks like Andwele Kassain and Haki Dola, there were some other levels of political intrigue that Wyatt didn't even to want to know about. Yet, he sensed they were affecting the work, maybe even the cause of its problems.

Increasingly, he was learning that he never should've published his paper at all. It was doing harm and no good at all, that he knew of. It was a firsthand experience in the truth behind the adage that no good deed goes unpunished. Wanting to share what he knew had all gotten sorts of people thinking he knew a lot more than he was telling, or had some magic bullet he'd withheld. And they used what creativity they possessed in trying to find a way to use it for things it wasn't designed for.

The idea of publishing to make yourself important hadn't occurred to him. Maybe that's what they would've done. As far as he could tell, they spent a great deal of time and effort making themselves more powerful, or at least more marketable. It didn't matter that his motives had been simply to pass along some insights and generate a dialog. No one cared. It wouldn't be surprising to learn that his claim that he had no ulterior motive made him more suspect in their minds. And they all wanted his sweat and tears to be applied to their own ends.

Well, fuck the lot of them.

He wasn't any closer to learning who had threatened Ellen and that seemed to be the necessary precursor to finding a way out. Like publishing the whitepaper, making the deal with Claude had been a colossal mistake. From where he sat, the arrangement wasn't working.

Once he had a plan, once he was in the clear, he'd explain that to Claude—assuming he was certain that it wasn't his old friend who was actually pointing a gun at Ellen's head.

When he got back to his workstation, he glanced at his phone. He'd left it sitting on the printouts he'd been reading and now his message app indicated that he'd gotten a text message. He flipped to it.

"So, we read your missive. All manner of things are possible, W. So tell me. . . . where do you want to take this? Love, B."

His pulse raced. His first thought was that it was from Rebecca, but then he realized it must be from Boone. For all he knew, Rebecca was Boone. She was good at changing identities and appreciated the value of being part chameleon. Whoever sent it, this was an answer to his message, a reply from the bitpats group that Rebecca had told him about.

He entered a brief reply: "In the office now. Will respond in a few hours." He didn't want to go into detail while he was here, surrounded by potential enemies. Besides, he needed time to think. This demanded a thoughtful reply.

Despite it being a place marker, when he hit send he felt a sense of relief. It took a moment for it to sink in that the relief came from the knowledge that there was a chance that he had someone who was on his side. Rebecca had told him that Boone was a smart coder and the smartest people she'd ever met were associating with bitpats. The message held out a thread of hope that they might help him. And he certainly needed help. He wasn't even sure of his answer to that first question. Where did he want to take this? The truth was, he wanted to make good on the threat he'd made to the German, to bring the system down. The trick was to do it without endangering Ellen and Harold. That wasn't something he knew how to do alone.

This network, bitpats, was an unknown, but if there were more like Rebecca, they were a force to be reckoned with. But from what Rebecca had told him, they were an all or nothing group. Ultimately, if he didn't want to deal with this situation alone, he'd have to throw his lot in with Boone's crew. He'd taken the first step down that path by telling them what was going on. He was certain they'd expect him to make a choice before they acted.

He drew a long breath, let it out slowly, and sat down to wait for Peggy's list of locations and system variables. He had no hope it would be complete, but it would start things on the road to recovery—back to working.

CHAPTER 26

RASHMI DEBUGS

"Bitcoin won't be adopted like the iPhone because it's cool. It will be adopted like gunpowder: if you don't own it, you'll be its victim."

—SAIFEDEAN AMMOUS
AUTHOR OF THE BITCOIN STANDARD:THE DECENTRALIZED
ALTERNATIVE TO CENTRAL BANKING

IT DEPARTMENT
MINISTRY OF FINANCE
DAR ES SALAAM, TANZANIA

Rashmi Patel looked away from her terminal, let out a short, frustrated, puff of air, and closed her eyes. Resting her elbows on the desk, she dropped her head into her hands, listening to it buzz as if it was filled with a swarm of angry bees. The long day of scrutinizing code, reviewing as much of it and evaluating it to the extent she could with limited information, was taking a toll.

After unraveling a substantial part of it, she'd reached that limbo state where she wasn't sure what she didn't know. It was maddening. A program like this one should be logical, understandable. If some things were obscure, well, it still had to follow a path, use patterns that someone with reasonable intelligence and the right training should be able to figure out. She knew she was smart and she had the right skill set, but she was stumped. Too many things were going on that made no sense. They clearly had a purpose, but what those purposes were . . . that was the problem. She knew the banking system, the old one, as well as anyone. The processes, the steps that had to take place for the system to function, were familiar to her. Certainly, different banks had variations on the processes. They might handle transactions differently, yet at the core level, they were similar. How these particular processes fit into the system were a mystery to her. It was as if there was the transaction system, which she understood, and someone had threaded another system into it, like a subplot in a novel.

Peggy had told Rashmi rather firmly that she didn't want her help finding the problems. In fact, she'd told her not to mess with it, to mind her own business. Now she wondered if her reluctance to explain things, to show the overall specifications, had some sinister reason behind it. Was there some sort of hack built into the system? Or was this something that the IMF or World Bank had asked for but didn't want to be made public? Or was her own government behind it? Since coming back to pay her debt, she'd found that some elected officials were willing to abuse their power for their own ends. It was possible that Deputy Minister Dola was working with someone. Maybe it was a combination of forces at work. Certainly that Interpol lady didn't seem to want anyone prying into the code.

She ignored the instructions to leave the code alone. That was too much to ask of her. Especially now. The system didn't work as planned and did work in some ways that, as far as she knew, it shouldn't. That bothered her and she had to see what was going on.

Her investigation had gotten stuck. The problem was the transactions, no matter where they took place or how they took place, got routed through a single routine. Obviously, that was part of the problem with the system—there was a bottleneck. Those mysterious lines of code weren't mentioned in any of the documentation.

"Now that is what you call an anomaly."

"Beg your pardon," the coder next to her said.

Rashmi didn't realize he was there; she wasn't aware that she'd spoken out loud. "Sorry," she said. "Just mumbling to myself. I thought everyone else had gone home."

He chuckled. "A coder going home at the end of the day when the project is behind schedule? Hardly."

She clucked her tongue knowing it was true.

"So you found an anomaly? What is this thing? Is that another name for a bug?"

She looked over at him and smiled. "Maybe. It could be a bug or just something odd. An anomaly is simply something that doesn't follow the form or the rules."

"Coding is full of those," the man said. "When you look at the code other people write, you find all sorts of strange things."

"If the code works properly, then there should be no strange things at all."

"Yet, there are often strange things in programs. Most code has anomalies."

She realized that was true, but Rashmi thought that was negligent. "In my experience, in the programs I've written, that only happens only when I didn't take the time to understand completely what the code was doing. If I see it other people's code, it usually means I didn't understand what the programmer intended."

"What they intended is often in the problem," the man said. "I find that what was intended was often just to get the job done so the programmer could go home."

"I suppose so," she said, hoping to let it go. He was right, though. It was troublesome, but true, that most of the coders on the team didn't seem to have a lot of motivation or pride in their work. They were smart but only seemed interested in learning enough to get the job done. She didn't understand the attitude. Why not do it right?

"I do think I can figure it out with some help," she said, hinting. He just stared. He was going to make her ask outright. Fine. "Tell me, did you work on the transaction module?"

His shoulders raised and she saw tension erase his smile. He didn't like defending his work anymore than the others did. "Which transaction module? The system uses a number of them—the escrow transaction module, the bank account module, the . . ."

"But, unless I read this wrong, those all are versions of the same code. You've all just copied the code and modified it for various specific purposes."

He nodded eagerly. "Yes, that's precisely what we did. It helps keep things standardized." As an excuse for being lazy, that was about the best you could hope for; the man's concern was almost amusing. "There isn't something wrong with the underlying code, is there?"

He was frightened that he'd be blamed. That was partly due to uncertainty on his part, but the main component of that fear was the culture of the work environment. So many offices were like this. When a project ran into difficulties, as this one had, the word spread rapidly. The smell of blood in the water attracted the sharks, certainly, but it also put fear into the hearts of the smaller fish in the food chain. His fear was as palpable as it was exaggerated. He wouldn't be fired unless they were all fired. No one blamed the rank and file coders, but they never seemed to understand that. So the hackles raised and the defense was mounted.

If she was to have any help, she needed to put him at ease. "The code is fine as far as I know, Haji. My question isn't about the code, but the operation." Sensing that the question had nothing to do with him directly, he relaxed.

"What about it?"

"I'm just curious about the transaction fee. I was hoping you could tell me what it is about."

She saw the tension go out of the man once he was sure he wasn't being blamed for something. "That's just a percentage that's taken from every transaction."

It surprised her how dense some people could be. "I understand what a transaction fee is . . . I was wondering what this fee is for?"

He blinked. "I don't understand your question. It is a fee for transactions."

"I'm not being clear. I was wondering who is charging this fee?"

He shook his head. "I don't know. The bank maybe. Or maybe it's a government tax. I just followed the spec. It required a routine that executes for every transaction . . . it looks up the current fee rate in a table, calculates the fee, subtracts it from the transaction amount, and sends it to the fee collection account." He twisted his lips. "The code I wrote does all that."

"It does. Like I said, the code seems to be fine. I was curious about why that happened."

The man smiled. "It happens because it's part of the spec."

"Right."

"And what is the collection fee account? Where is it, I mean. It seems to be a variable."

"That's correct. It comes from the daily variables table. I don't know who wrote that . . . I only have the system address." He sighed. "If you have an overall system question, Peggy is the one to ask about that."

"But you never asked her? You weren't curious what the fee was for?"

He shook his head. "I stay as far away from her as possible. She is a scary woman. The last time I asked a question she threatened to cancel my annual holiday if I didn't shut up and finish the code." She could picture Peggy saying that; the man's story was probably true. Peggy wasn't a great leader and preferred that people just did what she said without question. The man glanced at his watch and smiled. "I better get home. I want to see my daughter before she goes to bed."

She laughed, realizing that saying that was a way of asking for her permission—he wanted to be excused so he could go home, like some schoolboy. Well, most of the coders were fresh out of school, so she understood. She was older and they were still adjusting to the idea of women as bosses. "Have a good evening then," she said.

The man nearly jumped out of his seat, making her wonder if he'd been nervous because she was asking questions that he couldn't answer, or simply because he'd been afraid that her questioning might make him late for putting his daughter to bed.

"What are you up to?"

She looked up at Andwele. "Hey there. Up to? Just my job, of course. I was just checking out some function in the code that I don't understand."

"I think you understand everything," he said.

He was trying to be diplomatic. Since their falling out, he'd been distant. Now that she understood him better, knew he was a traditional man, that suited her fine. Still, there was no reason to let that develop into hard feelings between them. They had to work together, and things would always be awkward. Why make them worse. She flashed him a smile and shook her head. "You are a natural flatterer."

"No. It's true. You are the most intuitive person I've ever known when it comes to code and complex systems."

Andwele didn't really understand coding at a meaningful level, but if he was going to be nice, she'd let it pass. "Do you know what the transaction fee is?"

He wrinkled his brow. "What transaction fee?"

"Does the government impose a fee on each transaction?"

He shook his head. "No. That would be counterproductive. We want the costs of the transactions to be minimal. The point is to get investors excited about low-cost transactions. The ministry is even talking about following the lead of what they did in Belarus, where investments in cryptocurrency are free of capital gains tax for five years. We are thinking of a ten-year hiatus if they invest in our cryptocurrency."

"That would certainly help it gain credibility in a world gone crazy with new coin offerings."

"Exactly. I proposed that to Deputy Minister Dola."

She chuckled. "Who will propose it to the minister as his own idea."

Andwele laughed, and for a moment she remembered why she had been attracted to him. It was a fine laugh. "Of course. That's how things work in politics. Naturally, the finance minister, who knows that the deputy minister knows almost nothing about computers, will pretend he believes him and lavish praise on him."

"And give him all the credit if it succeeds," she said. "I hate politics." Rashmi noted his displeasure. Andwele, she realized, enjoyed those wasteful, futile games. "So then, this fee must be something the banks are imposing."

"Perhaps." He didn't sound convinced. "I'm not sure about the specifics of the program," Andwele said. "It's not my place to get into details."

Rashmi's involuntary laugh caught him by surprise. "What's so funny?"

She looked at him, wondering at the fact that she'd once convinced herself that she admired this man. That seemed absurd. Despite being both smart and well educated, he was turning out to be the kind of man unwilling, or unable, to step up to real responsibility. "What's funny is that no one at all is sure about specifics on this project. The ones writing the code don't know what it does. The ones representing the government, who have the task of ensuring it does what it should, don't know what it does."

He stood upright. The reference to him as the one supposedly supervising hit him like a slap in the face. "We have an understanding. . . ."

"But I can't get any real answers about anything. This horse is a camel."

Confusion showed on his face. "Horse? What horse?"

"It's a reference to the old saying that a camel is a horse designed by committee. It's true. Only here, it is probably a zebra, not a horse."

"That's an old joke. And hardly funny."

"What is funny is that we are spending all this time writing a program that will save the country's financial infrastructure, make Tanzania a competitive financial center, and yet no one seems to know how it will do that."

Andwele sank into a chair. "Of course, we know how it will do that."

"From what I understand, the solution is to centralize a decentralized system, base it on some standard, and then let the banks feed us the data that authorizes transactions."

Andwele smiled. "Exactly."

"That's a generalization, not a project description. Even at that, it's a bad one. No one is running this asylum."

"That's not at all true. There are checks and balances . . . and your tests."

"Which are based on more generalizations and hearsay; I can't get anyone to nail down specifics."

"You always have been obsessed with detail. You think you need to understand every nuance of the system. It slows you down, keeps you from seeing the larger picture."

"The larger picture. Well, the picture I see is rather bleak. Given that the numbers aren't coming out right for the dummy data we ran, I obviously don't know enough details. That isn't a problem of too much information, but of almost none."

"What else do you need to know?"

She laughed before seeing he was serious. "This transaction fee might account for some of the error we found. If I had been told about the fee, then my test would have taken that into account."

"And now you know about it. So you can take it into account."

Rashmi couldn't believe he didn't see the problem. "Not at all. First, I need to find out what the rate is based on. Who generates the rate? How is it input into the system?"

Andwele held out open hands. "As I said, I have no idea."

She picked up a pencil and wrote, "transaction fee . . . what is it? Where does it come from?" on a piece of paper and handed it to him. "Then please find out for me. No one talks to me, or if they do, it isn't to tell me anything useful. The bankers won't take a call from me. I'm not important enough."

She saw a flush of pleasure run through him. Her acknowledgment of his importance lifted his shoulders and made her heart sink. The man's self-worth depended so much on what other people thought of him. How could she have misjudged him so completely? "Certainly, Rashmi. I'm sure I can find out what it's all about easily enough."

His false confidence left a bad taste in her mouth. The man wouldn't ask anyone; he wouldn't risk letting anyone know that he wasn't on top of every detail. Even if he didn't understand the importance of a hands-on approach, he'd want to be seen as totally in control. But if there was even a slim chance . . . "Thank you, Andwele. Please let me know anything you find out as soon as possible."

"Of course."

As he stood and walked away, Rashmi wondered what crack that information would fall through. Even if he did ask, she had no reason to think that anyone in the know would tell Andwele anything. She had no reason to think the system was ever going to run properly. How could it with no one truly taking charge?

This failure could ruin her future. Her career was now tied to what had once seemed an exciting and promising project. That didn't bother her as much as knowing that it could've worked, and well. Wyatt had been right about so many things, and mostly he was right that this should've been a simple task. They could've used the existing pieces to create a smooth, efficient financial transaction system, a new currency based on trust in the technology. Instead, it seemed to have devolved into a battleground where competing power bases fought to be the new agents of trust—the banks wanting to retain their stranglehold over the storage and exchange of money and the government retaining its control of the creation and definition of currency.

It was all about power. A technological solution to the country's financial problems was being hamstrung by politics.

Rashmi still had a job to do. Even if Peggy didn't want her getting into the internals of the code, she had a responsibility to her government. Besides, her own sense of pride was at stake. She was part of the project and she would do whatever she could to make it work. She'd use the scraps of information she was tossed and what she could unearth; she would puzzle out the underlying problems that brought the system down and find solutions. For now, that meant ignoring the blustering and turf wars, the posturing of the key players. She had to put her head down and focus on what the hell this code was actually doing, or not doing.

CHAPTER 27

GROUNDWORK

"We don't want change. Every change is a menace to stability."

—Mustapha Mond
Resident World Controller for Western Europe,
In Aldous Huxley's Brave New World

Golden Tulip Dar Es Salaam City Center Hotel
City Plaza, Jamhuri Street
Dar es Salaam, Tanzania

Peggy Anne Dory sat on the balcony of her suite and looked out over the haze that rose from the city. After a hot day, evening finally began shifting into night; the caress of cooler air on her skin refreshed her.

She sat out there, looking out over the city, for some time. She was thinking and worrying. Somehow, in the air-conditioned comfort of her room, ideas and answers wouldn't come. They hadn't exactly blossomed out here either, but she was spending long days inside and it was nice to not look up from your thoughts and not be staring at a desk with a monitor on it.

Unconsciously, she took a sip of the expensive wine in her glass, but it was sour in her mouth. She knew it wasn't the bad wine she tasted—it was her problem that made everything sour. Fear of failure was new to her, at least at this level. Sitting on the edge of her private project being uncovered and the consequences that would entail had her almost in a panic.

But not quite. Although her situation had become so precarious that she could feel the ground shaking under her feet, she trusted herself. She had to regroup, but her ability to control things had gotten complicated. The spectacular system failure, and her inability to manage the team, had effectively undermined her position with the Tanzanian government. She knew Haki Dola had asked that she be replaced. Childer refused but that was because of what she was doing for him. But she thought he might be the one responsible for Wyatt showing up. Without a staunch ally anywhere, other people were getting involved, trying to determine what had gone wrong. Bringing in Wyatt made everything she was doing more difficult.

Looking back at the chain of events that led her here, it was easy enough to see that the system's failure was inevitable. The fundamental mistake she'd made was being a dictator about the whole thing. It seemed smart at the time to just make everyone think she was a control freak. It didn't take long at all for the coders to stop asking for information. But the very secrecy that made it possible to hide her project was the thing that screwed the project's chances of success.

The project itself wasn't that hard. The coding tasks were pretty straightforward and didn't require any particular innovation—at least not the way the government had specified the program. Many of the elements already existed in other systems, and there was no glory in reinventing the wheel. But the job of piecing them together and creating a useful, robust system was a complex task.

Then, of course, she complicated it. She added in the IMF's data-collection modules, a few routines for Interpol, and her own modifications. None of them was an earth-shaking task from a technical standpoint. None of it was innovative or tricky. The real challenge was the vast number of things going on simultaneously. Sales and banking transactions, executing and monitoring loan agreements, contract fulfillment, and tax collection. And everything had to be coordinated.

To make the system run fast enough to do all this (the blockchain itself was slow and cumbersome), Peggy had the coders create multiple side chains for each function. These did most of the heavy lifting. They used them to stack transactions, accumulating batches and verifying them in the separate networks before recording them in the blockchain. That was straightforward enough, but because the side chains had been written by different groups, even though they shared a lot of code, each programmer had introduced a few twists that were needed to accomplish the specifics of the tasks. A real estate transaction differed from the sale of a pack of cigarettes in a small store, or settling a wager—yet the same system was supposed to process all of them. And quickly. That was where it all went wrong.

While she'd found it convenient to keep each group in the dark about what others were doing during the development, that also made it difficult, if not impossible, for them to coordinate things. Instead of having the various coders collaborate, which would lay bare all that she was trying to hide, she'd done all of the interweaving of the modules herself. She'd mapped the variables, the parameters, and thought she'd understood it all, but clearly she hadn't done it well.

It also stung knowing that Wyatt was right—she hadn't seen the obvious and simple solution. If she'd defined the allowable system variables clearly and assigned their addresses from the start and published them, then everyone would have been on the same page, as they said. And yet, that information wouldn't have given anyone an obvious clue about her system modifications. She'd gone overboard with her secretiveness and she damn well knew that. She underestimated how many loose threads her approach would create and overestimated her ability to locate them all and ensure it worked right.

Taking on the entire project might've been a bad idea from the start. And there was a humorous side to it. The idea that Peggy Anne Dory was working in collusion with the IMF, World Bank, and the fucking Interpol lady was a huge joke. If they knew some of the shit she'd done back in the day . . . Thinking back, recalling some of her exploits, she could see that her skills were best suited to hacking systems, not making them. Well, this would be her only system. She would retire from all that shit because she was going to solve her problems, both the coding and the people. This gig still had a window of opportunity, a chance of succeeding. And if she could salvage it, the rewards would be worth it. She'd grab the brass ring and be set for life. There was no way she was letting it slip away without a fight.

She considered her opponents. Wyatt wasn't really an opponent, but he was a threat. He was smart and he'd spot what she'd done in heartbeat if she let him near her code. Otherwise, the man himself was manageable. They got along fine and if he were a different kind of man, seducing him would solve her problem. In Wyatt's case, she couldn't count on lust or love clouding his vision once he sat in front of his monitor. And although he loved to play the radical, he was a Boy Scout, as far as she was concerned. But she was still in charge and he'd accept that, even if he hated it. Best of all, once he did the work he'd come back to do, Wyatt would leave again. He wouldn't be around for the final tweaks to the system. She would've preferred to add her code in after he left; unfortunately, it was integral to the system and adding it later would require a major rewrite. It wasn't a simple addition.

In many ways, Rashmi Patel was the bigger threat. Wyatt was looking for bad coding, but with her financial background, Rashmi would be looking for exactly the kind of thing Peggy had added. She would be examining the actions of the modules, and some of the code didn't have a lot to do with the transactions and she'd see that. Apparently, she had already started down the right path.

Early that day, Peggy overheard two of her coders talking. "Rashmi Patel was asking me who wrote the transaction module," one, whose name was Haji, said.

"That one was yours, right?" the other asked. "Is there something wrong? What's the problem with it?"

"Nothing, as far as I know. Not with my code, anyway."

"Then why is she asking about it? Hasn't she her own work to do?"

"She thought something didn't match the system spec, and it was using my module."

"So you aren't in trouble?"

"No. At least it doesn't seem so. After I showed her my source code and explained how we were reusing it with modifications throughout the system, she said that was fine and that the code was correct. I have no idea what she was worried about. I explained that it was just a basic, fundamental module."

Peggy had been relieved to hear that Rashmi had been satisfied, but she doubted that would last long. She was definitely on the scent and it wouldn't take her long to unravel what was going on. That would not be a good thing—not for Peggy and her plan for early and lavish retirement.

As she finished her wine, she realized she had several courses of action. She could, of course, simply disappear. She could go to her suite, pack a bag, and go to the airport. All she had to do was accelerate her plan. The boat was already in Trinidad, already waiting for her. But that would mean throwing away all her work and having nothing to show for it. She'd be living on the run and without the money to sustain it for long. No, she needed to find the problems and fix them all before Wyatt and Rashmi did. Unfortunately, she didn't think that was possible. She needed another idea.

The last possibility was to hack the system. Put something in it that would explain why it hadn't worked. Something that wasn't supposed to be there.

"Yes!" she said as the implications of that idea reverberated through her.

She went into the room, heading for her monitor, her sluggishness was gone now. Who better to discover some code that had been buried in the system, code that compromised the project, than the hacker-in-chief? She would ensure it was something a villain had added that wasn't in any of the specs, but not in her modifications either. Then a brilliant idea dawned on her. She would 'find' the hack in the transaction module. She'd write a new version with flaws and replace her code. Once the hack was exposed, she'd be expected to rewrite the module with increased security. And all she had to do was reinstall the code she'd written while taking credit for a monumental effort. Hell, if you were going to run a scam, it paid to make it big.

And she'd get to point the finger at the culprit of her choice.

That made her smile. There was no question as to who she'd choose—blaming Rashmi would be fairly simple and obvious. The woman wasn't supposed to be messing with the system, just troubleshooting it. Yet everyone knew she was doing exactly that, which meant that Rashmi was in an indefensible position. She was already breaking the rules and was a prime suspect.

Peggy licked her lips over the prospect. Picking Rashmi to be the one who'd screwed them all over would accomplish several things, and the most intriguing one was that it would be satisfying. She had never liked the bitch. She resented her, with her economics training and formal programming experience. She hadn't had to scramble to make it in life. So, for once, maybe she would learn what it's like to look up from under a pile of dog shit.

The second thing was that letting her take the fall removed her as a threat. If Rashmi was under suspicion, even if they didn't arrest her, or prosecute her, at the very least they'd take her off the project. And then, with someone in the hot seat for messing with the system, Peggy would be able to stall for more time to fix it. She could say that if there was one hack, she needed the time to find any other hacks that might've been missed. No one could fault her for wanting to be thorough, not when a country's entire financial future was at stake.

She'd need to burn that other programmer too. Haji would be able to say that Rashmi was asking about the code, trying to find out what was going wrong. Without him to back her up, she was toast.

She sat back, imagining that outcome and feeling good. First she needed to do something about Haji, get him out of the way. Then, she could "find" the code and get rid of Rashmi. That would mean Wyatt Osgood was the only one of consequence left to deal with. Even though his talent and training meant he was more likely to spot what she'd done in the system, he was a programmer, not an investigator. And he liked people—he wasn't naturally suspicious of anyone who wasn't the employee of a government. For other programmers, the poor chump had a blind spot a mile wide. Handling him would be child's play, especially given that he'd be devastated to learn Rashmi was sabotaging their work. A little sleight of hand would be a simple task. Diverting him, maybe even finding a way to get him to help her while worrying about Rashmi, would speed her task. If she could convince him that helping her might rescue Rashmi . . . well, all sorts of things were possible. And, if push came to shove, he was still a man, and she was a seductive woman. That gave her options.

She grabbed her cell phone and called Childer. "I need an assist," she said.

"What now?" he asked.

"Don't get your nose out of joint. The code will be fine, but I have a problem with one of the coders. He is working out your little routines."

"How?"

"He's smart and curious. That makes him a good coder, but it means he looks at things that are interesting, not only the stuff I want him to see."

"Is he important?"

"Not any more. At the stage we are at, he's expendable. So, if you could get him transferred or something . . ."

"And you can meet our deadlines?"

"No sweat, Mitch." She tried not to chuckle as she imagined him wincing.

"Then it will be done immediately."

"Then I'll get back to work."

"An excellent idea, Ms. Dory," he said, emphasizing his civilized use of her last name.

Then came the next step—one that suited Peggy. Instead of putting her attention and efforts on finding the flaws in the code, Peggy did what she did best—she wrote the hacker code. The remote desktop application she had secretly installed let her access the main system in the office; now she used it to copy her transaction module and then she removed it from the system, storing it safely away. Then she copied the generic transaction module that, as Haji had said, was used everywhere. It would be the basis for her modifications. Having done it so often, it wasn't hard to imagine the code that the evil Rashmi was envisioning she would write, the code she would add to the basic module to give her a backdoor, a way to bypass security and get into the system.

Next, she went to the history files that tracked all the system changes. As the only system administrator, it was easy for her to make it appear that Rashmi had modified the code. Then, wincing only slightly, she introduced a flaw into the code—a change that would cause it to introduce problems similar to those they'd seen in the test.

When she was done writing the evil code she wanted to find, she sat back and let out a long breath. "Fucking beautiful," she said. And it was. She'd managed to produce an elegant programmer's solution to her concerns—it was simple, neat, and had everything tucked neatly into everything else, like nested subroutines.

She stood up and walked to the balcony again, pouring another glass of wine. She let herself bask in the glow of accomplishment. Tomorrow she would go to the office and, when Andwele was hovering around her desk as he would, she would 'find' the code and trace its origins to Rashmi's computer. Having Andwele witness her discovery would make the evidence even more compelling.

And then they would contact the Interpol lady and sick her on the bitch to determine who Rashmi was working for and why she was hacking the system. Obviously, the deluded woman was some kind of terrorist. In the end, the authorities would be grateful to Peggy Anne Dory for thwarting her assault on the system and happily admit that she was just too smart for Rashmi.

"Fucking cool," she said.

She glanced at the time. It was midnight. The hotel bar was open and it might be worth getting dressed again to see if any hot guys staying at the hotel were lingering there, maybe looking for a little fun. A little help passing the time would be a good thing.

CHAPTER 28
ARRESTED DEVELOPER

"If you want total security, go to prison. There you're fed, clothed, given medical care and so on. The only thing lacking. . . . is freedom."

—Dwight D. Eisenhower

IT Department
Ministry of Finance
Dar es Salaam, Tanzania

Wyatt walked over to Rashmi's desk and leaned against it. "I hear there are mysteries abounding in our code," he said. "Code and mystery are a bad combination."

"Well, there are things that are mysterious to me . . . not so much the coding of them, but the question of why they are coded in the first place." She tapped on a manila folder that sat next to her terminal.

Wyatt smiled. The folder was neat, aligned with the desk, and the only thing besides the keyboard and monitor that was visible. That said a lot about the woman. She was organized and methodical. Being around her a lot would probably drive him nuts, but he liked her. She had a good attitude, a dedication to the work, and she was sharp. Under other circumstances, they'd make a great work team, but she wasn't the kind of person he'd ask out for a beer after work.

On the other hand, those big eyes were certainly dreamy. Still, she was a serious person, not a flirt, and quite likely not someone interested in a fling. . And more was the pity. He could enjoy a fling with this lady. The way things were, he was happy to have her around for her insights, even more than her charming smile.

"So the mysteries of which you speak lie in the realm of 'whys' and 'wherefores', rather than the 'how' of the thing?"

"Precisely. The failure of the system to run is one thing—the thing I set out to figure out. But running across things that don't seem justified at all caught my attention. I'm supposed to ensure that the system does what is intended, and certainly all the required functions, the specific modules, are there. The problem is these undocumented things, such as the transaction fee. It's integral to the system, and yet I don't know who authorized it or what the fee is for."

"Beyond collecting money, you mean?"

"Yes, beyond that. But you are making fun of me."

"Not at all. I'm curious too. In fact, I ran into that pervasive, nearly ubiquitous module and wondered about it myself. From the sound of things, you haven't had any better luck getting answers than I have."

"There is a lot of finger-pointing going on," she said. "No one wants to give actual answers. The banks say to talk to the government, and the only people who know anything say I need to talk to the programmer, who is Peggy. But Peggy won't talk to me. At least, she doesn't willingly offer any useful insights."

"Welcome to the exciting world of system program politics," Wyatt laughed. "Most of them are probably scared shitless because they don't have a clue what you are asking about."

"So how do we resolve this? How do I find out what it is?"

Wyatt considered the question, rubbing his chin. "Say, is that goateed idiot in an expensive suit from the IMF still hanging around? It's likely he'd know the answer. He comes on like he's some tough guy, but I bet I could bully him into telling us what it's about. Maybe I can make him realize that his precious system depends on us getting some information."

"He's in and out. I think I saw him yesterday. There seems to be some important meeting happening. Mr. Hoenig flew in last night."

"Really? Claude is here? Well, that's good. That means that he is taking the system problems seriously."

"This morning I tried to talk to Andwele and see if he would help, but he was rushing off to a meeting with Hoenig, the Interpol woman, and Deputy Minister Dola. I assume Childer would be there as well. He shows up for all the meetings."

Wyatt snorted. "But we aren't invited. They want to analyze the problems and propose solutions free of any real contact with the system or anyone who has a remote idea of what might be going on."

She raised her eyebrows. "You don't like any of them?"

"They are all parasites. They pronounce things and then force people like us to make them a reality."

"Forced? I was hired but not forced. Aren't you being dramatic?"

"No, I'm not. On this farm, not all animals are created equal," Wyatt said. "And not all animals are treated equally."

"Are you quoting from *Animal Farm*?" she laughed.

"Absolutely. Always steal from the best; that's one of my mottos. Not the most important one, but still. So help me understand, explain this to me—why is it always the pigs that are running the show in these morality plays, as well as in life?"

"It's iconic."

"Rubbish. That's not an explanation. It's iconic because people use it, not the other way around. Has anyone ever explained why they choose pigs? Why not giraffes? Or zebras?"

Rashmi picked up a pencil and tapped on his hand with it. "In Orwell's case, the story is about farm animals. No giraffes allowed. No giraffes need apply." She winked. "It's not an African thing."

"So evidence of yet another sleazy prejudice. Even so, why not give the cows a shot at being on top?"

"Cows are stupid and not ambitious. That's why 'bovine' is an insult. Pigs are actually smart."

Wyatt held up a finger. "So the pigs tell us. Whatever the reasons, the pigs are in their little sty hatching out the next world view, and soon they will descend on us and tell us how we are to save the world, regardless of whether it can be done—the way they want, or any other way."

"I've never heard you speak so politically before, except about the politics of technology abuse in Zurich."

"Sorry. My long-held beliefs are finally bubbling to the surface. I'm sick of the posturing, the self-serving crap they dish out while keeping us from using the technology for good. All this crap about a national crypto . . . it isn't about smoothing financial transactions or even making the country attractive for investors."

"Then what is it about?"

"They fear the decentralized nature of crypto. They want to co-opt it before the idea of a national currency of any kind is shown to be the crap it is. National currencies force the people to put their trust in a government—this one, another one, they can pick and choose, but ultimately they have to trust someone. The technology promises to eliminate the need for the blessing of politicians. You can choose a currency based on what you think of the technology underpinning it. That would also mean it becomes impossible to control the populace. How do you collect income taxes without currency controls that force banks to be police? How do you collect sales tax when the transactions are not physically processed within a country or even necessarily recorded in the country? And that's just the tip of the iceberg. If property ownership is recorded in blockchains, securely, untouchable, the government can't pass laws about that ownership. As people are empowered to exchange goods and services, and there are no institutions in the way, no institutions subject to national regulation, the governments become irrelevant, except in a more libertarian context."

"Like what?"

"Like being hired to provide courts and police forces and even military, not being able to coerce money from people and then providing the kind of services they want to provide."

She shook her head. "That's a big jump."

"It's coming. You and I are, unfortunately, in the trenches on the wrong side of the future."

"Why are you here if you feel that way?"

"Because I'm forced to be."

"Again, that word."

Wyatt looked at her. He saw her sincerity, her desire to understand. "Do you really want to hear my sad story?"

She nodded. "I really do."

With a long breath, he explained, starting with his revelations about his own malaise, his decisions to quit, his hope that he could make this project better, and then the threat to his sister.

Rashmi sat silently for a time. He thought he saw her quiver. "They would do that?"

"In a heartbeat." He remembered the note he'd been given and showed it to her. "In case I forgot why I left the beach and came here, they gave me this."

"Do you know who did this?"

"Sadly, no. And that makes it worse. I don't think it's my boss, but he has the connections. Peggy would do it without much of a qualm—she's that cold. But I don't think she has the connections with cold killers. That leaves your boyfriend and his boss and the wonderful folks from the World Bank and IMF, represented by the charming Mr. Childer. They are my first choice as the heavies. And that's a shame because I don't know how to fight them. Fortunately, I have friends."

"Friends."

"Bitpat friends."

"That's a term I've never heard."

"People who travel the world freely, working and living through technology."

"Digital nomads?"

"Toss in a strong libertarian to anarchistic streak and that's a fair comparison," he said. "At least from what I've seen so far."

"I've always believed in the need for government," she said.

"That's natural. We are brought up that way, taught that we need them. Years ago the industrial revolution produced massive changes in the world—unleashed disruptive forces of mass production. Leisure time itself was unsettling society. What to do with it? The ones in charge pushed us into consumerism. That sucked up the energy and the new resources and left us with little time to consider that we were slaves. Debt is a form of slavery and we were taught to embrace it."

"That's certainly true."

"They went overboard, but it worked. Now technology is emancipating people—at least the ones who see that potential. If you aren't bound to live out your life working for a company, because the tech lets you work where you want to be, the government loses control, so they respond in a knee-jerk way, with more countries following the US example of taxing you even if you are outside the country. It's a grasping, desperate measure that only works if there is a global effort to control it. And there is. That's why the IMF is involved in this project—not because your country is a debtor nation that needs help. I think this is a test bed for more controls. That's what I see in the code."

"The transaction tax?"

"Exactly." Wyatt pointed at her folder. "What if someone wants to track every transaction? The way to do that is to make them all pass through some trust agent. If not the banks, then a computer program—the very program that was intended to decentralize the process to make if fast and keep the trust independent of meddling humans, who don't tend to be so trustworthy. For who watches the watchers? It's an old, unanswered question. Not satisfactorily anyway. Checks and balances are slow and unreliable when they are implemented in institutions. Proof of work or proof of stake in blockchains is, by comparison, an elegant, automatic, and rapid way to do things."

"So someone deliberately sabotaged this system?"

"The opposite. They want it to succeed but various entities have added their own little tweaks, controls, trust systems that bog it down, and Peggy has been ordered to keep these components secret. There might be several different forces at work here. Failure was inevitable."

"A camel," she said.

Wyatt nodded. "Exactly, only without even the benefit of some intelligent committee. Things were added without any regard for what they did to the overall system performance."

"The medicine prescribed with no thought to the side effects or other medicines the patient might be taking," Rashmi said.

Wyatt laughed. "A perfect analogy."

"So now what? Is class warfare on the horizon?"

He shook his head. "It is already here, but it's a low-level guerrilla action, not open warfare. So far, at least."

"So back to the question of fixing this system. When the people at the top don't give us the information we need, what do we do?"

She slid her chair back. "Frankly, I was about to give up."

"Bullshit," Wyatt said. "You don't give up. I admire that about you. Even if I disagree on the validity of the project, I've worked hard to make it work. You're the same way. You gave your word that you'd see it through. I felt the same until someone decided to change the rules of the game. They broke the contract; now there will be hell to pay."

"Hell to pay? What sort?"

"I still want the project to succeed, but not necessarily the way they want it to . . . you understand."

She nodded. "Now I do."

"But as you were saying, we can't do that without knowing what it is they're trying to do now. So, I took some initiative. I put in a code stub that will track down the addresses the transaction fees are sent to. That will tell us if it is a single fee, and it will let us know where in the code to look for what happens to it after that."

"Are you authorized to do that?"

That amused him. "On this project, I don't think I'm actually authorized to do anything at all. I have no status here that I know of. I don't even have a work permit, as far as I know. I am an emergency measure, and we emergency measures have to take extraordinary steps to do our jobs at times. Besides, I'm a 'take action, ask permission later' sort of guy."

"You, Wyatt? I never would've guessed." The friendliness that filled her smile took the sting out of the sarcasm in her voice.

"And more to the point, I no longer care what is allowed, authorized, or whatever. I have to make the system work, whatever that means, to keep my sister safe."

"How can I help?"

He stopped. The woman was sincere. "You want to?"

She touched her hand to her face. It struck him as a curious and very feminine gesture. Charming. "I got involved with this to do some good. Like other projects I've been involved with, it seems the people who initiated it are the biggest obstacles to success. I don't want to be one of the architects of a new form of oppression, Wyatt. That isn't what this is supposed to be about. And while I don't share your political ideology, while I think that there can be good government, I'll admit that in this skirmish there are only two sides—they own the middle, muddled ground because that works for them."

"Exactly."

"So tell me what we can do."

He turned the chair to face her. "This is a big and dangerous step."

"I understand."

For a time neither of them spoke. Wyatt weighed what he could and should tell her. But as much as he'd shot off his mouth already, nothing but the complete truth would do. She deserved to hear it.

"There is a group," he began, "a collection of misfits like us, people who want freedom and dignity, and they are called bitpats."

Rashmi listened as he told her about the site, about Rebecca, about the mysterious Boone. She took it all in. "And other than Rebecca, you've met none of them?"

"No."

"Yet you trust them?"

"Implicitly. I've told Boone what happened, about Ellen and me coming back. She's been in touch. I told her about the code."

"Despite your nondisclosure? You gave your word."

"And that went out the window when they issued a threat."

She nodded. "Fair enough."

"Boone has resources, but needed me to see what I could discover."

"Can I help?"

He handed her a piece of paper. "The results of my code will be sent to this URL. If anything happens to me, then contact Boone."

"Why would anything happen to you?"

"Because I took out some essential code when I put mine in. Peggy is doing a lot of testing, trying to save her cute little ass, and she or one of the others might find what I did. I'd be surprised if they didn't, but I'm hoping I get the results and can put together an idea of what's really going on before it's noticed. Then, I can take it to them and show who did what to whom. That's why they brought me here, after all. Obviously, there are people with an interest in making sure I only fix the system, not figure out all its ramifications."

"And Boone can help?"

"She has analysts, computational power, available to her. She can help but will need hands here to do some of the work."

"And what's the goal of that work?"

Wyatt rolled his head back and looked at the perforations in the acoustic tiles covering the ceiling. "I'm not sure. Partly it's to keep this system from working the way we think they want it to work. But to do that, we need information. And beyond that . . . it depends on how much time we have."

"How would I contact this Boone?" He handed her a business card. "This is from your hotel," she said.

"Read the other side," he said.

She looked. "Bitpats dot com?"

"Boone at bitpats dot com. Tell her you are my ally."

"All right. That's in case of an emergency. In the meantime, what can we do?"

The sound of footsteps coming their way hurriedly interrupted them. "I think we just ran out of meantime," he said.

Turning, he saw Childer and Osk Barstad headed toward them flanked by six armed security guards. The stern faces of the guards and Osk Barstad, and the smug look on Childer's face, told the whole story, or at least enough of it. They were on a serious mission.

"My guess is that you are their target," Wyatt whispered. "But I've got it. Just follow my lead."

He saw her confusion and put his trust in his estimate of her innate intelligence and strong, if misguided, ethical standard.

Childer came up to them. "What are you doing here, Osgood?"

"Discussing the system problems with an expert . . . someone who cares about the project."

"You've made a mistake," Childer said. "She cares about other things."

"Rashmi Patel," Barstad said, stepping forward, "I am placing you under arrest."

Wyatt jumped from his seat. "Arrest? What for?" He hoped he sounded adequately shocked.

"For sabotage," Childer said. "She's the reason the system is behind schedule; we are charging her with that as well as possible terrorist activities."

"As well as fraud," Barstad said. "We haven't finished analyzing her little additions to the code yet."

"Her what?"

"Her code. She replaced some system code."

"Which part?"

"She inserted code into the system that collects data and reroutes transactions, and probably does much more than that."

Wyatt stood toe-to-toe with Childer and stared down at him. "You mean the transaction routine that was modified?"

"How did you know about that?"

"Well, it so happens that the transaction routine was exactly what we were just talking about."

"What about it?" Suddenly, Childer seemed unsure of himself.

"The fact that she didn't replace that code," Wyatt said firmly.

Childer grinned. "Yes, Wyatt. I'm afraid she did."

"She did not."

His calmness seemed to unsettle Childer's renewed confidence. "How can you be so sure?"

Wyatt smiled. "The easiest, most obvious way. I knew she didn't do it because I put that code there."

"The system logs . . ."

"Are useless. I used her monitor. Peggy didn't have one set up for me that accessed the sections of the system I needed access to, so I usedhers. You know how impatient I am. And I have no regard for protocol at all. Rashmi had a simple password, and the system security sucks big time. Here is a free heads-up. I could make it look like anyone wrote that code." He held out his hands. "But the truth is that it is mine. So, if you need to arrest the author of that code, take me away. I mean, heaven forbid the person who is supposed to fix the system should rewrite bogus code."

A look a fury crossed Childer's face. "Don't cover for her."

"I'm not." He glared at the man. "I wrote that code for my own reasons. No one wants to tell us what the fucking piece of software is supposed to do. I wanted to know. I came in and Rashmi was on the same track, but she spotted my code. I think she was going to take it to Peggy."

"That code is not just analyzing."

"I wanted to find out everything," Wyatt said. "I decided I'd figure out exactly what the system is doing. Then I could make it do what it was supposed to do."

"That isn't your call," Childer said.

The look on the man's face was a mix of anger and confusion. Suddenly, Wyatt realized that the last thing Childer wanted was to lock him up, but he'd committed this stupid play. Now Wyatt had been handed a way he could actually protect Ellen. In jail, he was worthless to Childer or whoever was behind the threat. He'd be helpless, but that would be his strength. He would be unable to do their bidding.

"Well no one ever said what I was supposed to do and what I wasn't, so I decided to make the system work the way I wanted to."

"And steal money while you are at it," Barstad said.

Wyatt considered this revelation, that money was being stolen. Apparently, there was more code involved in this than what he'd put in it. That was interesting, but at least they were talking to him now. "Why work for free?" he said flippantly.

"Then you admit it?"

"I admit everything and nothing," he said. "I admit that there is some shitty code in this system and a lot of it is my fault. I admit to replacing the transaction module with something that would let me know what's going on. Everything else is guesswork. And with Peggy left to her own, I'll be interested to see how this comes out."

"Then you are the one going to jail," Barstad said, glaring up at him.

Behind her, Childer wasn't as pleased as he'd been. Things weren't going according to his plan. "I don't know . . ."

"We will arrest him and get to the bottom of this mess," Barstad said. "This is my case, Childer."

"Very well," the man said.

Wyatt didn't think jail was going to be as nice as a walk on a beach in Mexico, but right now it felt a damn sight better than cowering in front of a terminal being spineless. It was a relief to have a lot of it out in the open. Maybe that would pop the infection, burst it all out.

"Handcuff him," she said. "We will sort this out in interrogation."

An uncertain security guard stepped forward with his cuffs. Wyatt smiled at him. "Either do your job or be prepared to take up arms against a sea of troubles," he said cheerfully. Then he looked at Rashmi. "I apologize for implicating you in my nefarious schemes," he said. "It's helped me to talk to you. You might say it can be a boon to get things off your chest."

"What did he tell you?" Childer demanded of Rashmi.

She flushed. "We talked about the mysterious code and then he went off on some strange political ramblings," she said. "The rights of the people and the coercive power of government. He thinks a national currency is a bad thing. I was going to tell you tomorrow."

"Damn right national currency is a bad joke," Wyatt said. "Freedom is a boon, Rashmi," he said. "Remember that."

"Oh I certainly will," she said. "There is a bit about your ranting that is just too pat for my taste, however, Wyatt."

Wyatt smiled. The woman used inflection to emphasize the words 'bit' and 'pat' to let him know she'd gotten the message. Damn, but he liked smart women. Now if she was only just a little less conventional he could see . . .

"Take him away," Barstad said. She turned to Rashmi. "You are to stay away from the project until I sort this out. You are still under suspicion."

"And do what?" she asked. "I have a job to do."

"That isn't my problem. I'll inform your superiors of your status, and if I find you even looking at the code before I give you permission, I'll arrest you as well."

Wyatt chuckled and turned back to look at her. "See, Rashmi. The pigs don't want our help when it gets down to it."

The guard pushed him through the door and led him to an elevator. "And now I'm going down another rabbit hole," he thought. At least this time it was on purpose.

CHAPTER 29

A CALL TO ACTION

"The future has already arrived. It's just not evenly distributed yet."

—WILLIAM GIBSON
PIONEER OF THE CYBERPUNK SCIENCE FICTION SUBGENRE

IT DEPARTMENT
MINISTRY OF FINANCE
DAR ES SALAAM, TANZANIA

Wyatt's arrest shocked Rashmi to her core. Even though he smiled as they handcuffed him, almost as if he didn't care, her skin was clammy and her hands trembled. Once he'd been taken away, she felt alone in the world—isolated. She hadn't felt outside of the system this much since her first insane, crazy days in London. Then she'd been disoriented, sure that she was the only one who didn't know what to do, where to go. It was distressing to feel that way, to be such an outsider, but naturally, as she learned her way around, the feelings passed. The unfamiliar became comfortable, even home.

This was different. Now this was supposed to be her home, familiar turf, but the world had been turned upside down. Unspeakable things were happening and no one cared. In the chaos of pinning blame on someone, it seemed anyone would do, and the truth was irrelevant. Get someone securely locked away, and everyone could rest peacefully.

She'd always been aware that people and governments abused their powers, but before this moment, before it had almost happened to her, before Wyatt's noble rescue, it had always been distant, theoretical. Now it had intruded into her world in a cruel way.

No one, she believed, truly thought Wyatt was guilty of anything beyond seeing through the charade of what they were, collectively, doing. Yet that crime frightened them more than the actual crimes. Someone other than Wyatt had deliberately undermined the project, but pretending that Wyatt would work to bring the system down, using his political opinions to justify blaming him, resolved things nicely.

It was the morning after the arrest and she wanted to get her bearings. She had to act, but the path to take wasn't clear. An outright confrontation would be both noble and stupid, yet anything less struck her as cowardly. The truth was that the outcome, the result of her actions, was more important than how it made her look or feel about herself. She needed to put things as right as they could be put.

As she mulled over the recent events and considered her options, Andwele came in. It was early, much earlier than he usually appeared. Clearly, he had come to see her while the office was still nearly empty.

"How are you?" he asked, sounding cheerful.

She glared at him. "So what happens now?" she asked. Not that she trusted him to speak honestly, but she had few options. He knew what was going on and might give her a sense of what the people running this circus wanted to happen. That could be useful.

"With the culprit under arrest, the system can move forward," Andwele said. His smugness surprised her.

"He didn't sabotage the system," she told him. "I think you know that. The problem we had was just bad programming, not sabotage."

"But he confessed. And the code that Peggy found . . . it replaced things that had been in the system and added functions that shouldn't be there."

Rashmi almost choked. "Of course. And isn't that convenient for Peggy."

"He didn't have authority to rewrite the code."

"First of all, it's common practice to put in dummy code to figure out what's working and what isn't. No matter what you think he was authorized to do, everyone here insisted that he come to Tanzania and fix the code. So, yes, that was his code we found. But the code it replaced was the problem, Andwele. The code we found wasn't even written until after he got here, and the other code is what brought the system down."

"That's what he says."

"And I believe him."

"He is an anarchist," Andwele said, as if that in itself was a condemnation.

There wasn't much point in denying that. Trying would just undermine whatever leverage she had left. "Maybe, but there is no denying he is a brilliant coder."

Andwele shrugged. "So he can be a brilliant coder in jail."

The arguments made no sense. "Andwele, this project needs him and he was working to put things right. This cryptosystem was going to be wonderful and exciting."

"No one wants that, Rashmi. We want something functional, not exceptional. The point is getting our financial basis established, not innovating."

"And he and I were working together to find out what was going on. We were trying to make it more than simply functional."

Andwele grabbed her arm tightly. "Don't say that, Rashmi," he said. "Never tell anyone else you were working with him. Say that you were chatting about the work and let them decide that he was pumping you for information. Or it's fine to say he asked you many questions, that you talked about the way the system should operate, but never tell anyone you were working together."

"And why not? We are colleagues."

"Because he isn't a colleague. He is a terrorist who was trying to wreck the system or hack it. He is going to pay the price for his actions. If you associate yourself with him, then you will be prosecuted too."

"I didn't do anything wrong."

He snorted. "And you think this is about innocence or guilt? Silly girl."

"Then you agree he was framed. Who would do that?"

"This is about success and failure. Now that we have a culprit, Peggy has some time to make the system work. If she succeeds, then no one will bat an eye if Wyatt is found guilty of his crime. It will be obvious. So you don't want to be one of his associates."

"Why do you need a culprit?" Rashmi asked.

Andwele laughed. "Girl, this is all about appearances. If we can show that we foiled an attempt by terrorists, anarchists, to subvert our national currency, then the world will see how diligent and effective we are. Any little glitches in the startup will be overlooked, or considered inconsequential compared with what might have happened had they succeeded."

"And it doesn't matter that Wyatt is innocent?"

"He has no allies, other than Hoenig, and he is not in a position of strength. He has worked in absentia, after all. Childer likes the idea of blaming Wyatt Osgood for the crime; throwing one admitted anarchist to the wolves for a good cause is a small price to pay."

"So he is to be found guilty for what he believes and not what he did?"

Andwele let go of her arm. "Naturally. And when did you become such an idealistic little girl? I thought that the London School of Economics would have taught you some real-world things, but I suppose not." He sighed. "Someone needs to be the cause of the system delays and it's better to have a villain than have incompetence be the cause. Looking around at the possibilities, who better for that role than a misfit? He is expendable."

"So this was your idea?"

"Not at all. Peggy Dory found the modified code and raised an alarm—someone was tampering with the system. She was certain it was you. Childer and Osk Barstad weren't so certain, but once we had evidence of a malevolent force at work, our path was clear. Fortunately, Wyatt confirmed their suspicions publicly.

"But if we had Wyatt working with us, finishing the work would go faster. Peggy is smart, but I think Wyatt has it all in his head in a way she never could manage. Turn him loose and the system will run beautifully." She took his hands. "Andwele, the man is innocent."

Andwele sighed. "Rashmi, those things are no longer important. As long as the system comes together and does what it should, we are all covered. When we launch the system, the government will be pleased to tell the world that we succeeded despite the attempts of outside forces to stop us. The world will give us time to work out any bugs and forgive the fact that the system isn't the most elegant. After all, it will be one of the first national cryptocurrencies, and one that was created despite the efforts of a physical opponent who tried to thwart it. If the system isn't very good, that doesn't matter—we can have it rewritten later. In the meantime, the government basks in the glory and money pours into the country. Everyone in Tanzania will benefit from that."

Rashmi doubted that. There was little evidence that anyone but the government and the banks would benefit, but clearly, the government, her government, was happy to accept Wyatt as the villain. A foreigner prevented it all from happening sooner and more completely. Interpol, in the form of Osk Barstad, was satisfied that she had the proper person in custody, and she would certainly make a grand press announcement.

She already knew that Childer was smugly pleased that Wyatt Osgood had been exposed as the anti-globalist agent he had suspected him to be. "You cannot trust people who don't see the need for a global authority," he said when they led the man away. "Someone has to lead so that the rest can follow to prosperity and safety."

That was a proposition that the government, almost any government, was delighted to support and knowing that began to make Wyatt's dislike of government, his mistrust of it, clear to her.

Now she saw that even Wyatt's fellow coders deserted him. In their case, she suspected that their enthusiasm for his role as a scapegoat was rooted more in relief than actually thinking he was evil. With someone on the hook for the bad code, many errors, omissions, and plain fuckups were explained away. Anything at all that was not perfect was part of Wyatt Osgood's nefarious plan. It was too good an opportunity to pass up.

Banned from working on the project, Rashmi tried to find out what her own status was. No one wanted to say that she was off the project for the simple reason that then her duties and responsibilities would fall on other shoulders. "Just do your job," Andwele told her. "Keep your nose clean and don't mention Wyatt Osgood."

"How do I do my job when I'm not allowed to look at the code, much less test modules?"

"I don't know," Andwele said. "But you are the one who says that it is up to you to get things done despite the obstacles."

"Not being allowed to do the work and still being held accountable for the results are not an obstacle, Andwele. You can overcome obstacles. This is an impossible task, one worthy of Sisyphus."

"Who?"

"An ancient king of Corinth who was punished for betraying the secrets of Zeus. He had to roll a huge boulder up a steep hill. But the boulder was enchanted so that it would roll away from him. It would head back down before he reached the top and he'd have to start over. So he never accomplished his goal and faced an eternity of useless effort and unending frustration."

"This is no eternity . . . the system will be done soon."

"And I will be the one held responsible for all its faults even though I am not allowed to test it. You see the unending frustration I face. My career is effectively over."

"Perhaps so, but without the fact of Wyatt's guilt, all our careers are over. And I'll talk to Childer. I'll tell him you can be of help. But you'll need to reassure him that you think Wyatt is a terrorist and all you want to do is find any hacks he put in the system."

She looked at him, not believing what he was asking. "That would be a lie, Andwele. I know he isn't a terrorist. You know, once I thought you were an honest man."

"A man must first survive. We can do good things, but you need to join the chorus and throw this American to the wolves. He asked for his fate. Don't pity him. Use his fall from grace to save yourself. You don't get many chances like that."

"And be impoverished by thriving from the unjust punishment of an innocent?"

"Is he really innocent? He hates our system."

"He hates the way you are misusing a technology, applying it to control people when it could be freeing them."

"Ah, you women, always talking about freedom as if it were some grand thing. Wealth, success, those things matter. Freedom is an illusion. We aren't free of death or aging, so why should the fact that we are controlled by people with more wealth and success matter?"

Rashmi couldn't believe her ears. "So you think men should control women, and other men should control them, simply because they can?"

"It's the natural order of things. Just as we can't ensure this project is perfect, all we can do it try and please the ones paying for it. Then things will move along as they should."

"Regardless of the consequences?"

"The consequences of cooperating are that we thrive." He shook his head. "You are so childish. Think about what I've said. All you have to do is denounce Wyatt Osgood to get back in the good graces of everyone. And he is already doomed."

"Without a trial?"

"He will never be tried. We will talk about one, but he is a terrorist, and, unfortunately, he is also an anarchist."

"Unfortunately?"

"If he belonged to ISIS or some other radical group, a public trial would reassure the people and show that we are capable of fighting them. Admitting that we allowed a lone man to infiltrate the project, that we were putting him up in a fancy suite at a five-star hotel . . . that would embarrass the government. Without a trial, we can release information about a terrorist and a foiled attack. We can say who he was and that the investigation is ongoing. Eventually, he will be forgotten." He stood up. "I'll leave you to consider your options, to either be responsible for a project you can't control or denounce the criminal and help us get this done. We might not have a future together, Rashmi, but you do have a bright future in the government. Make the right choice and you will find yourself heading bigger, grander projects than this one."

"Why is that?"

"Because when this succeeds, the minister of finance will undoubtedly retire. His deputy, Haki Dola, will be slotted to take his place and I will become deputy minister. When that happens, I want you by my side—if I can't have you as my dutiful wife, then at least I can have you as my right hand in creating effective economic policy."

She saw him, assessed his look, and understood. The man was willing to let a trophy wife escape, especially when she threatened to be so much trouble. But in that case, he intended to hold onto the economist and programmer who might make him look good. Hidden within that promise was the implied threat of what would happen if she failed to denounce Wyatt. He needed that to demonstrate to the bosses that he was in control and to ensure his place in their plans.

Sadly, Andwele was right about that and a lot of things. The one thing Rashmi was certain he was wrong about, the point he counted on that wasn't true at all, was Wyatt being forgotten. That wasn't going to happen.

"I'll think about what you've said," she told him. "You've never argued your case so clearly before and it deserves thought." And contempt. But that would wait.

"Please do."

Then she stopped. "You know . . . Haji would confirm a lot of what Wyatt and I are saying. He'd tell you that I talked to him about the module, not Wyatt. I was the one exploring the strange things it was doing."

Andwele shook his head. "You didn't hear?"

"Hear what?"

"There was an accident. This morning when Haji parked his car . . . he seemed to have stepped out into the street. He was hit by a car and killed. I'm afraid he can't confirm anything."

A cold chill shot through Rashmi. "I was just talking to him . . ."

"And the driver? What did he say?"

"It was hit and run. There were no witnesses."

Rashmi could barely breathe. "That is . . ."

Andwele put his hands on her arms. "Rashmi, listen to me. It was an unfortunate accident."

"Just as Wyatt was unfortunately arrested," she said, enjoying the way he scowled at the sarcasm in her voice.

"That is totally different."

She had to believe that he was deliberately keeping his eyes closed. "Andwele, the truth is that someone is behind this. There must be. It is absurd to think that Haji was suddenly hit by a car, and that it was hit and run, just when he could supply important information."

"Don't be a hysterical woman," Andwele said. Then he stopped, perhaps realizing how she'd take that. "Think of this, Rashmi . . . Suppose you are right. Then, if someone is willing to kill over the fate of a financial computer system, looking too closely at what is going on will put you in danger too. If that is true, then you need to protect yourself. Peggy tried to make you out as the one who sabotaged the system. Wyatt's confession saved you. He can't save you a second time, and if you persist, then whoever is doing this might decide you must be stopped. If Haji was deliberately killed—and I cannot believe he was—but if he was, then they would have no compunctions about killing you."

She stared at him, trying to determine if he was threatening her. But what she saw was a mixture of concern and fear. In his own, misogynist way, he cared. And, coward that he was, he was frightened for himself as well. If there was a plot against Haji, Wyatt, and her, then, thankfully, Andwele wasn't in on it.

"Perhaps that's true," she said. "I'll think about what that means."

"Excellent," he said, with a smugness that made her think that he was sure she would see reason. "Now I must report to the deputy minister."

He left, leaving her to wonder how she'd ever confused a lapdog with a real man. As much as she disliked Wyatt's attitudes and irreverence, at least he was a man of ethics.

Rashmi shut down her terminal, locked her desk drawer, and left for home. If they wouldn't let her work, they couldn't complain if she wasn't in the office. In fact, until she recanted her beliefs of Wyatt's innocence, her being absent would make the rest of the crew more comfortable. No one likes having a disbeliever in the group. It's a thorn in the side, a reminder that your universe was being questioned.

Besides, she had important work to do that she couldn't do in the office, work that mattered far more than making sure Tanzania had a functional cryptocurrency.

She drove home, changed into jeans and a sweatshirt, got a beer, and sat at her own computer. She didn't need coding tools right now. The best tool for the current job was her word processor. When the splash screen displayed, she began a new document. She stared at the screen for a moment, collecting her thoughts, trying to put things in order. Then she began writing out a history of everything she knew about the project from the first moment she heard about it. She put every detail in chronological order, including the names of the people and their roles, as best as she knew them.

By the time she got to writing about the meeting in Zurich, where she first met the Americans, she was starving. She microwaved some leftover spaghetti, devoured it, grabbed another beer, and went back to work. She wrote about the evolution of the team, the way Peggy had kept the programmers separated, giving them the minimum information. She wrote about how the woman had covered up the failure of the system, adding her own observations as well as the confusing, if sparse, explanations that Childer and Peggy Anne Dory offered.

She paused and then looked around. It was dark. She took a walk out onto the balcony, into the warm night air. Her mind cleared and she focused on remembering. With the memories vivid, she went back to the terminal and wrote about Wyatt's arrival. She wrote a section about what he'd told her about the threat to his sister—the reason he'd come to Tanzania—and his guesses, fears, and conclusions. To all that, she added her own observations. And then, finally, she wrote about their conversation, the apparent intent to frame her and arrest her, Wyatt's confession, and his arrest. She included the little she knew about Haji's death as a sidebar.

She even mentioned Andwele's advice, how he had encouraged her to abandon the truth and Wyatt for her own future, her own life.

"I don't know what to do next," she wrote.

She was tired and hungry again. Turning on the printer, she sent the document to it. When she heard the familiar hum of the laser printer feeding pages into it, she went into the kitchen and made a tuna sandwich and a glass of tea. By then, the printer was done and she collected the document. It was thirty pages long. She hefted the pages and took them to a comfortable chair where she read every word carefully while she ate the sandwich. She marked the text up, remembering new details, or making corrections. This editing excited her, brought some clarity to what she was doing. Grabbing her tea, she went back to the computer to make the changes and found herself expanding sections, elaborating, making things crystalline, both in the document and her own mind.

Finally, she was done. The document contained everything she knew and thought about the project. Again, she started printing a copy. In the morning, she would mail this hard copy to her roommate from college. She was still in London and Rashmi would ask her to hold it, sealed, in case something happened to her.

While it printed, she made a PDF copy of the document, then wrote an email, addressing it to Boone@bitpats.com. "Wyatt Osgood is in trouble," she wrote. "The attached document tells you everything I know." When it was attached, she took a deep breath and hit send.

"And so it begins," she said to herself. "Rashmi Patel, the unlikely revolutionary, has joined the class war."

In her head, Wyatt corrected her: "It isn't a war about class, but freedom."

Even so, Rashmi couldn't imagine a more unlikely freedom fighter than a half Tanzanian, half Indian economist. Yet, there it was.

She was tired and all she could do was wait for an answer and hope. Unfortunately, waiting was a hell of thing to ask of a freedom fighter. Even a newly-hatched one.

CHAPTER 30

MAKING IT WORK

"Bitcoin is a tool for freeing humanity from oligarchs and
tyrants, dressed up as a get-rich-quick scheme."

—NAVAL RAVIKANT
CEO AND CO-FOUNDER OF ANGELLIST

IT DEPARTMENT
MINISTRY OF FINANCE
DAR ES SALAAM, TANZANIA

When she detached herself from thinking about the urgency of the situation, its precariousness, Peggy could calm her breathing and see things clearly. The answer to her problem was nothing more than a lack of information. A program worked when you understood it. Finding a problem was always a matter of moving through the code methodically. Unfortunately, that process took time, which was the one thing she didn't have.

She'd hoped to have Wyatt as a resource. He was quick and saw things at a glance that other people had to study. Giving him components piecemeal would let her pick his brain without tipping her hand. With the botched attempt to take out Rashmi, she'd bitched that up good. No one would be talking to him.

But he'd already been working on it and had probably gotten a lot further than she imagined. And she'd noted that he often took notes at meetings and as he worked. He constantly scribbled down ideas, thoughts, whatever, in a small leather notebook. If he'd found something useful, the notebook could be a goldmine of information.

She thought back to the last time she'd seen that notebook. They'd been talking in his cubicle, and just before she left, he put it in his desk drawer. It was most likely still there.

She walked into the cubicle. Naturally, none of the programmers paid the least attention to her—she was always going into cubicles. And they were intimidated. They didn't want to know what she was up to. They didn't want her focusing her attention on them.

She held her breath as she opened the drawer and looked into it. "Yes!" she said. There it was lying in plain sight. She sighed. The only things she saw in the drawer made her smile. The most important item was his notebook—a Rite in the Rain all-weather spiral notebook. Next to it was a black pen, which she recognized as a tactical pen—a survivalist's tool that doubled as a weapon. She picked it up and weighed it in her hand, amused that Wyatt the anarchist was also a nascent prepper who carried one of these self-defense tools. A tactical pen was a real, functional pen, but it had a metal tip and body. She'd seen the ads for them—you could break glass with the damn things. She pushed a button near the top and a high-intensity LED light came on. This sucker was the Swiss Army Knife of self-defense.

She stuck it in the pocket of her jeans. Wyatt wouldn't need it anymore, and it could come in handy.

She went back to her desk, sat in her chair, and opened the notebook. Many of the barely legible notes were gibberish . . . things he jotted down after their discussions. She flipped through the pages and found the most recent notes. She gasped. This was manna from heaven. Even at a glance, she could see the wealth of ideas he'd left her—this was her inheritance.

As Peggy went through the notes, reading them and putting them in context, her heart pounded with excitement. It was all there—every nuance of it. The man had mapped out some of the system conflicts and his thoughts as to their causes. He'd seen problems in the system that Rashmi's tests hadn't even pointed to and things she hadn't thought of at all.

She dropped the notebook on the desk and went to refill her coffee mug. It was time to get to work. With these notes showing the way, she began to understand some of the problems—problems she had to admit she'd created. Best of all, she saw the solutions.

It dawned on her that it was a damn good thing Wyatt had been the one arrested. Based on what she saw in his notebook, if he hadn't been arrested and had managed to talk to Childer about what he'd found, she soon would've been in jail herself.

Some of the more rambling notes sketched out possible solutions. One thing that made Wyatt a good programmer was that his solutions tended to be simple. He disliked complex code. "A complex problem deserves a simple solution," he told her once. Well, he was consistent.

The things he'd speculated on would've been easy for any of the other programmers to implement. Naturally, there were a few wrong-headed ideas, but most of them were only wrong because he had to make assumptions about parts of the system that Peggy kept hidden. Wyatt was aware of the difference between what he assumed and what he knew.

"Talk to the bitch and check your premises," he had written to himself.

Yes, he'd gotten some things wrong, but that wasn't a problem for Peggy. She knew precisely how all of the pieces of the system fit together—or how they were supposed to. And now, reading Wyatt's notes, she learned exactly why some things didn't work the way she intended them to. She could visualize the rewrites, the changes that needed to be made, and she licked her lips in anticipation.

She made her own notes as she read, jotting down the salient points, correcting his misconceptions as she went. She'd break some of the work into modules and give it to her programmers. That would save her a lot of work and time. She'd do just the critical portions herself. This time, however, she'd carefully check over the code the clowns working for her wrote. Not that she cared about how well the system ultimately worked, but she believed Childer when he said failure was not an option. He wanted it to run flawlessly and she had no interest in finding out what he had in mind for her if it didn't.

In the meantime, she was able to give him some good news for a change. The idea of delivering a cheerful report sounded good.

She took out a cell phone that Childer had given her on his last visit. "For your reports to me," he'd said. The phone was encrypted and programmed to call only one number—his. She assumed it was encrypted.

"I can fix it," she said when he answered. She hated the breathlessness, the relief she heard in her own voice.

"Are you positive?"

She calmed herself, wanting to sound confident, not excited or flighty. "Absolutely. Wyatt was on the right track, but so was I. I've got his notes. I can make the changes myself. I can assign a couple of the bigger coding jobs to the team."

"Rashmi?"

"I don't need her. In fact, I want her kept far away from the project until it's done."

"Her testing . . ."

"Is bullshit. I've got it worked out—the damn thing will work, I tell you."

"Excellent. And you can do it by the deadline?"

Peggy paused. That only gave her two days. She'd have to put in some long days, but then it would be done. That was a small sacrifice. "Yes. No problem."

"You understand . . ."

"Yes, you've said it before, that there's no excuse for failure. They want the system up and running. Well, the truth is that I want it done too. I'll be fucking glad to see the ass end of this project, of this entire town." She almost giggled. She could sense the man wince at her language.

"Very good. I'll be holding you to that."

"Of course, you will," she said.

When she hung up, she still felt a churning in her gut. She didn't trust that man at all. If she didn't need Childer . . . well, there wasn't much she could do about him, no matter what she wanted to do. He was a fact of life. It was a good thing she was working on her early retirement program.

Her own phone rang. A man's voice intoned her name: "Peggy?"

He sounded familiar. That wasn't necessarily a good thing. "Who is this?" she snapped.

"It's Franz. Remember me from Zurich? Your waiter?"

She did remember and she relaxed. She didn't like surprises, especially under the circumstances, but Franz had given her a wonderful time. They'd had an uncomplicated relationship that was nothing but incredible sex. He'd been fantastic and totally focused on her. Both times she'd been in Zurich he'd made an otherwise dreary time come alive. So, of course, she'd thought of him; she missed the fun and games. Still, the timing of his called bothered her. Why was he suddenly calling now? And how did he get her number? "I remember you well," she said. "But how in the world did you get this number?"

He laughed. "You forgot?" he said. "I'm heartbroken." He sounded amused. "You gave it to me."

"No. I don't remember doing that."

"Before you left Zurich the second time, you gave it to me. You said you were going to Africa, to Tanzania."

She didn't remember that at all, but then it had been an exciting time and she'd been on the cusp of this project. It was all possible. She'd hadn't paid any attention to the man's life story—what little he might've told her. It was his body that had interested her. "Sure. But why . . ."

"I'm in the country—Tanzania. As I told you, my cousin is the head waiter at the Serena Hotel and he said that if I came here he could get me a job, so I decided I would try it."

"Everyone should see the world," she said.

"I was thinking more of seeing you," he said. "After all, since you gave me your number in case I got here before you left, I have to think that was an invitation. It's one I'd love to accept."

She let that sit for a moment before responding to him. Something about this entire conversation didn't sound right. She might've done that, told him where she was going and how to contact her, but she thought she would've remembered doing it. Forgetting such things wasn't like her at all. "That might be nice. I'm very busy, but . . ."

"And I'm not busy at all." He laughed. "The job didn't pan out, so I am free as a bird. While I decide what I will do next, I can enjoy a small vacation. That gives me the opportunity to see you whenever you are available and want to play some games."

She thought of the games they had played in Zurich. Franz was a creative person and the memories made her shiver with delight. That was worth taking some time off for. Tomorrow she'd have to hit the work hard but she'd work better if she weren't so damn tense, and Franz had magical ways of getting rid of her tension. "Are you free tonight?"

"As I said, for you, I am free always."

She gave him her room number. "I'll call the desk and tell them to give you a key. I'll meet you there in two hours. I still need to wrap up some things here."

"Your wish . . ." he managed to say before she cut him off. Before she indulged herself, she wanted to map out the tasks that needed doing to make the system work. She would write emails, assign the coding that she could offload to the drones. Her emails would have all the details and would let them know that she expected them to stay all night, if necessary, to get it done. They might bitch, but they knew the project was coming to an end. Soon they could have time off if they wanted it. If the system worked well, she fully expected that most of them would be laid off. The government would keep a small crew to do maintenance and updates. Unless they had other IT needs, the rest would be redundant.

She prioritized the emails so the recipients had to acknowledge them when they read them. She waited, ensuring that the three group leaders read the emails. One responded with a question about overtime, which was a natural enough question. She replied to all of them, authorizing any overtime needed and she even said the government would pay if they sent out for meals. Anything to keep them working.

With that done, with her team at work implementing her system fixes and the solution to the most crucial bits in her head, she could happily put herself in Franz's amazing hands and let him do the things to her that he did so well. It was a night to look forward to.

Tomorrow, refreshed and relaxed, she would come in early, write her piece of the code, and then see how the system came together. She was sure it would work now. And when it did . . . well, that would give her another kind of orgasm, knowing that the system would soon be online and make Peggy Anne Dory a rich early retiree.

CHAPTER 31

A GOOD LAUNCH

"The impulse of power is to turn every variable into a constant, and give to commands the inexorableness and relentlessness of laws of nature. Hence absolute power corrupts even when exercised for humane purposes. The benevolent despot who sees himself as a shepherd of the people still demands from others the submissiveness of sheep. The taint inherent in absolute power is not its inhumanity but its anti-humanity."

—ERIC HOFFER
THE ORDEAL OF CHANGE

DAR ES SALAAM SERENA HOTEL
DAR ES SALAAM, TANZANIA

Mitch Childer intensely disliked the fact that the top people he worked with never used any names. It seemed a small complaint, but to his way of thinking, not being given a name, a way of addressing a person, was uncivilized, a social loose end, almost boorish. After all, they could easily use aliases. It wouldn't bother him in the least if the names they gave were bogus. After all, it wasn't a matter of identifying them, but of courtesy and politeness. Names were a convention and, in Childer's world, it was accepted that conventions came about for a reason. Usually, conventions had something to do with civility or convenience and were therefore reassuring and useful. Conventions were important because they went hand in glove with protocol, and that was nothing more than a commonly accepted way of dealing with things.

With these people, there were no protocols except deference to them. The man with green eyes, the dark-haired lady, the old man . . . the three who truly ran things never offered him a suggestion as to how he was to address them. He had to assume they called each other something . . . didn't people do that? He had no clue what they expected.

That they refused such minor, yet important nuances of social interaction was another reminder, as if he needed one, that despite his stature and his insights into the inner workings of important events, to this group Mitch Childer remained an outsider. Well, not exactly an outsider, but he was new to the inner circle, a recent addition to the group that made the important decisions about the future, decisions, and judgments that would, and should, in his opinion, set the path for the world to follow.

He contributed to the decision-making process. He was at the meetings and his opinions normally solicited. Because he shared their worldview, his opinions were usually simply confirmations of their opinions—his additions didn't amount to a significant influence. Sometimes they seemed to be testing him—it seemed they asked what he thought only to reassure themselves that he was actually one of them, or perhaps to remind him that he still had much to prove along that line.

It had surprised him to learn that being one of the elite didn't automatically confer much real power. He wasn't a true mover and shaker in the way that he saw himself in the future. A true mover and shaker held sway over other elites, and he was far from that pinnacle. That was the truth of the matter. Although Mitch Childer might dine with heads of state, of national banks, of global corporations, and lead them in a direction and convince them to do this or that, in the course of events that shaped the world, such things were trivial. That wasn't power. Not real power. Real power didn't simply influence—it decided and led.

And the reality was that while Childer might dine with heads of state and heads of national banks, while he might cajole known world leaders and guide them in a certain direction, convince them to do what he wanted, those weren't the things that shaped the world— these things were trivial. For those leaders, people who commanded armies, also faced enormous constraints. Behind them were other, less visible men and women, power brokers who made sure that the visible leaders were kept aware of the limits of their power. Primary among these was the nameless trio he worked with, or for, depending on how he felt that day, were the ones who held real power.

It galled him that he knew nothing about those important people personally. Their unknowable names were the tip of the social iceberg that he had no access to. He accepted without a doubt that they held the power of life and death over individuals and even nation states. He'd seen that for himself—it had been demonstrated to him on occasion—not for his education or because it had anything to do with him. The power had simply been wielded in his presence. He recalled when the green-eyed man had been enraged over decisions made by the ruler of a small country and pronounced him unfit to serve. His heart attack occurred within a day.

That heart attack, Childer was certain, was not the stuff of coincidence but a manifestation of the green-eyed man's wish, his personal own power. A quick study, the lesson wasn't lost on Mitch Childer; he took note and surreptitiously began building his own power base. You didn't ascend to the ranks and acquire power—you created a power base that moved you up, made your enemies suffer, and kept you safe.

"You are not a real leader unless you are able to control your people," the old man told him when he'd reported the problems to him and the green-eyed man. "At a minimum, we expect you to do that effectively. Ultimately, you are as responsible for their actions as for your own."

The charge had been unnerving at first, but he began learning what that meant, finding out the various ways of controlling people. Power came in many flavors, all of them tasting delicious to Childer's palate. From then on, things began to flow, and his ability to assert his will had taken a meaningful shape. And the sense of that power was deliciously sensual. It was an addictive feeling, a glorious one.

Yet, he knew his power was still limited. He could apply powerful carrots and sticks to get them to do his bidding, but even then, controlling his people was not the same as controlling other people, much less controlling the events he had been made responsible for. "My people are doing what they should."

"Is that so?" The green-eyed man seemed to be considering that idea. "Then what's the matter? What is going wrong? You see, we expected a certain outcome and I'm not seeing that outcome. If this is what you told your people to do, then I'm concerned."

So, Mitch Childer was unsettled by much more than the fact that he didn't know the man's name or the mere fact that he was powerful. What had him nervous now was the appearance of the green-eyed man, completely unannounced, in his suite at the Serena Hotel. When Mitch Childer had returned from having dinner with Haki Dola and his flunky that evening, he'd found the green-eyed man there, sitting in a plush leather chair. When Childer came in, he looked up as if the arrival was unexpected. The green-eyed man looked relaxed and right at home, casually drinking a fine glass of what looked like whiskey.

He wasn't alone either. Childer wondered if the man was ever alone. There were always people lurking around him, now that he thought about it. Typically, the lurkers were exactly like these, the men in Mitch Childer's room. It was an affront. Deliberate. The men were large, muscular, and faceless. They wore anonymous dark, off-the-rack suits, white shirts, and red ties; they stood silently, unmoving, with their backs to the wall. Each wore an earpiece and stood with their hands crossed casually over their crotches. Statue-like, they appeared not to listen, to be oblivious to his presence.

These things were unnerving. That the man had intruded into Mitch Childer's private space, that he was speaking, talking to him in a rather critical tone of voice, and that he was flanked by those two automatons—those were the things that made Childer perspire uncharacteristically. Even when the man indicated he should take a seat in a straight-backed chair facing him, Childer's discomfort made him fidget. Mitch Childer never fidgeted, not since he was ten.

All these things, but mostly his own unease, put him on the defensive. He knew that was the man's intention and it irked him more that it worked. Normally, Mitch Childer manipulated other people. Being on this end of things was unnatural. "My people are doing what they are supposed to do. They are getting the system working."

"Their efforts have been, at best, crude and inadequate," the green-eyed man said. "We elevated you to do much more than put your puppets through motions. I don't care what you told your people, or even what they did or didn't do. I want the system operational."

"It will be."

The green-eyed man ignored him. "You are here, we authorized this, to get very specific results. Your entire value to us is based on your ability to provide the outcome we've indicated, that we wish to achieve. What else happens, how well you control your people, is irrelevant and unimportant unless we get what we want." The man looked Childer up and down as if he hadn't seen him before. Then he snorted.

"It's coming together. I just talked to Peggy Dory . . ."

The man waved a hand. "The performance of your minions, their attempts to placate you, is less important to me than how well you dress." He scowled. "And the truth is that I don't give a shit about that at all. What they've done is not an issue you should be raising with me. It's a dangerous path, Childer."

"What then? You told me the system needed to do certain things. The code I had them write, the code that will do that, is working. The rest is being fixed now."

The man laughed, then sipped his scotch. Mitch Childer was thirsty but he'd be damned if he'd ask for a drink in his own room. He cast a longing glance at the bar and the bottle sitting there and gasped. It was a Glenfarclas 1955—a fifty-year-old single malt, bottled in 2005. Childer had only read about it—and dreamed of such a thing. Only one hundred bottles were made and they sold out immediately at over $10,000 US dollars a bottle. The green-eyed man saw him looking at the bottle. He raised his glass and downed the contents in one gulp, rubbing it in. Immediately, the guard came over to take the glass from him, walked to the bar, refilled it, and brought it back. The man took it without acknowledging the guard.

Mitch Childer momentarily weighed the effect of standing up, walking to the bar, and nonchalantly pouring himself a glass. The thought of it made him tremble. He had no idea how the man would react and wasn't sure he wanted to find out.

"But the system is not working, Childer," the green-eyed man said. "It all comes down to that. It was supposed to be up and running, a beacon of truth and light for the unwashed—a summons to join the crypto world the way we envision it."

"It is working."

The green-eyed man made a fist, a menacing fist. "Childer, the system failed the fucking test. All that's happened since then, as far as I can tell, is that your people started pointing fingers at each other, and now you have one in jail—the smartest one, Hoenig says, and another kicked off the project. How do you call that working? How can we confidently come here tomorrow and expect to stand next to the government officials and see the system perform?"

"We've made inroads since then. Besides, in the short time span of the test run, we collected an amazing amount of data from the banks on their customers. And the customers who logged on and used social media to create an account . . . well, we have all their information too. To use the system, they gave us permission and don't even realize it. Even if they figure that out, the benefits to them are impossible to ignore—they will happily sacrifice their privacy to be able to use the currency right from their telephones, to do everything that way. And once that door is open, it can't be closed again. We will use that same code in every system in every country. The potential—"

"Unless the system works, there is no potential, man. That's only useful if our prototype is the one they adopt, and there is competition. There are dozens of fintech firms clamoring to make systems like this one that doesn't have our code in them. And some of them know what the fuck they are doing." He sipped his scotch again. "Tomorrow is supposed to be the launch, and you've arrested the key developer."

"He was going to discover what was going on. The people we have will make it run."

They'd better." The green-eyed man stood. "We will be watching the launch and I want you to understand how important this is to us, to the ones who control you."

"New technology always has teething problems," Childer said. "Don't expect it to be a flawless implementation."

"You underestimate us, Childer, or at least me. I'm smart enough to realize that it's a complex system and there could be a few glitches. That's fine. But I'll tell you this much—by the end of the day I better be seeing smiles on the faces of the bankers and the finance ministry people. I better hear a consensus that the system does what we want, that it's robust enough. They'll bitch about this and that, the way it does something, and that's fine. Fuck them. They need to find something to complain about to justify their existences, but ultimately, I don't want anyone suggesting that it isn't the moment to switch over to the new system entirely."

Childer nodded. "It will happen."

"One other thing . . ."

"Yes."

"I assume you have done what is necessary to ensure there will be no loose ends."

"Loose ends? What sort of loose ends?"

"Once we know that the system works, we have no desire for anyone to know about the other . . . features the system provides. It's another way in which you are responsible for your people. Any that you aren't certain of, or need to use again, are expendable."

This time Childer was able to summon a confident smile. "Yes, I have the cleanup plan in place. The programmer, Osgood, will be useful to the government politically for a time. Of course, no one will hear his side of the story."

"I assume there will be no trial."

"No. We will see how we might use him. In talking to Haki Dola, we expect that eventually it will be best if he were to attempt an escape and be killed."

The green-eyed man looked toward the window. "That's a shame. From what I've seen, sacrificing him is a waste of talent."

"He's an anarchist."

"Still. But keep in mind that the one thing we never worry about is political leanings. I don't give a rat's ass about that. If someone is willing to work toward our goals, we can use them."

"I agree, but it's out of our hands now."

He nodded. "Too late to change that situation, I suppose. And what about that girl?"

"The girl?"

"The one your person thought was closing in on what she was doing?"

"Rashmi Patel." Childer licked his lips thoughtfully. In his opinion, killing her would be far more of a waste. He found her a lovely thing. She was far too independent and headstrong, but a woman could be broken of such things if a man was patient and consistent. Unfortunately, the group wouldn't let him risk that. They probably wouldn't even understand the pleasure he might get from breaking her. "She will have an accident."

"Don't overuse the hit and run bit. Be creative."

"She wants to visit London," he said. "We have already introduced the idea that terrorists are trying to stop the implementation of block-chain-based financial systems. So what if the finance ministry sent her to London as a reward. They give her vacation time, put her on Haki Dola's private plane, and then it is shot down?"

"Too high profile," the green-eyed man said. "It would attract attention. I want something mundane, barely noticeable in the news cycle."

Childer shrugged. He'd been looking forward to something dramatic. "Then she can have a heart attack."

"Fine. Or an overdose sleeping pills works just as well. Suit yourself, but make sure it isn't newsworthy. Too many unexplained deaths wouldn't be desirable."

"Of course."

"And what about this key person of yours, this Peggy Dory?"

"Totally expendable and unreliable. But never fear, I'll take care of that disgusting little greedy slut myself."

"You?" The man looked honestly surprised.

Childer caught himself. "I meant that I'll give specific directions concerning her demise, of course."

The man sneered. "As I thought. You don't have any real courage, do you? You're afraid to get your hands bloody."

"That's not my job, not my role."

The green-eyed man considered the statement. "No, it isn't. Better you don't even think along those lines." He nodded at the silent men standing by the wall. "That sort of work is easy enough once you get over your squeamishness. Luckily for you, we need your skills in other areas, in politics, diplomacy, and policy."

Childer let out his breath, relieved to hear the green-eyed man acknowledge his usefulness.

The green-eyed man started toward the door, then stopped and turned back. "Just keep in mind that a failure of the system, or a failure to execute this cleanup program thoroughly, isn't an option. You have important skills and contacts, but you're not irreplaceable."

Then, as if his departure were choreographed, one of his men moved to the door of the suite and opened it; he stepped out into the hallway, looked in both directions, and then stepped back in the doorway. "All clear." The green-eyed man nodded and followed his bodyguard out the door. The other man grabbed the bottle of scotch and followed them out, closing the door behind him.

Alone in his suite, relishing the emptiness that rushed over him, Childer acknowledged that there were many anomalies about that man and one of them was his bodyguards. He struck Childer as the last man in the world he would expect to want or need bodyguards. He himself was formidable, deadly. The dark threats he issued resonated on a far more personal level—they didn't sound like things he would have minions take care of for him. The bodyguards were muscle, but the green-eyed man was frightening.

After the feeling of intimidation that the evil man brought into the room finally evaporated, Childer went to his bar and got out the best scotch he had, a mere 18-year-old single malt. He poured a tall one and drank it down.

He'd been right to reassure the green-eyed man that everything was in place. Now he had to reassure himself that it really was on track. He'd call his people, talk to that bitch Peggy Dory, and make certain, absolutely positive, that she would do her part, that she could do it.

The worst part of his job, of trying to carry out decent policy and make things happen correctly in this technical world, Childer decided, was that the sophistication and specialized knowledge the work required forced him to rely on people like Peggy. He didn't trust her as a person. She'd been a criminal and he knew firsthand that she was corruptible. If he didn't need her, he wouldn't have gone anywhere near her, but he couldn't seem to find a person who was both technically competent at that level and reliable. It was bothersome that he had no independent way to verify what she said, that she could fulfill her promises. She could lie to him, or deceive herself until the final moment. Then, of course, it would be far too late to fix things.

How the hell did you manage people like that? All he had been able to do toward that end was offer large juicy carrots and threaten with a big stick. Then he had to hope it worked. In the long term, that needed to be fixed. When this was over, he needed to find the right technical people, techs who would be loyal to him. He had to increase his personal team—they were his real power base. If he was going to prove himself to those unnamed people, if he ever hoped to lead the world to the globalist vision that he knew it needed to reach, then he would have to find someone like Wyatt Osgood, but a version of him who hadn't been corrupted by strange, archaic ideas of personal freedom. He needed someone with those skills who would understand that giving their loyalty to a man of vision was better than throwing in with the disruptive forces of chaos.

Even the idea of this blockchain technology, that it could operate free of trust agents like the IMF . . . why they saw that as a good thing, escaped him entirely. It destroyed any hope of trusted systems, of predictability—the things that the future of the world depended on. Even individual governments were a source of fragmentation, and from Childer's point of view, they couldn't be done away with soon enough.

Eventually, people would understand. But for these crazy technologists on this project, it was too late. When the project was over, so were they. Regardless of how other things came out, that, at least, would be satisfying.

CHAPTER 32
A SAILING ADVENTURE

"There is nothing more enticing, disenchanting,
and enslaving than the life at sea."

—JOSEPH CONRAD

PORT OF SPAIN
TRINIDAD AND TOBAGO

The 45-foot ketch, *Last Laugh*, shot through the Bocas del Dragón on a northerly heading leaving the Gulf of Paria and then turning to the west as she sailed into the Caribbean Sea. She was flying, running under full genoa on a beam reach that propelled her over the water at 6 knots. The strong equatorial current meant she was doing even better over the ground.

So close to the shore of Venezuela, the winds tended to be a little flukey, so Peggy worked with Frieda, the two of them trimming the sheets to accommodate the changes in wind speed and direction while Billy stayed at the helm.

As they rounded the headland and settled onto a westerly course, Billy put on the autopilot. "Time for a sunriser," he joked. "If we wait until sundowners, we'll have a long, dry day."

"I'll squeeze some oranges," Frieda said, ducking through the hatch and down into the galley.

"I'll be there in a minute," Peggy said. She stood, one hand on the forward mast, and stared out at the sea, loving the feeling of power as the wind pushed the bow through the waves. The water hissed as it ran along the sleek hull, and the boat rose and fell in the swells.

The tropical sun shone brightly and Peggy felt good. It had been too long since she'd last been sailing, since she'd last been among her old friends.

And now, before she joined them in a drink, she wanted a moment to reflect on the path she'd taken, the way she'd come back to this, if only briefly.

Back in Tanzania, as the project drew to a close, Peggy had packed two small bags and hidden them in the closet. Not being big on trust, she wasn't certain what the gang of crooks who were running the show had in store for any of them once the project was running, and she had no intention of hanging around to find out.

Peggy had plans. Big plans. Even a small delay in starting out wasn't acceptable.

But first, she needed to make certain that the system was going to work. In the celebratory aura of success, she would have many chances to slip out unnoticed. If it failed, fingers would be looking for her to point to—and they would be ominous fingers.

The morning of the launch she woke early from a night of fitful sleep. Franz snored softly beside her as she slipped out of bed, intent on being the first one in the office that morning. She dressed in the dark and went down to the lobby and caught a taxi to the office. There was coffee on in the break room, which was a good sign. She filled her mug and went over to stare at the monitor that had been running diagnostics all night.

"How is it?"

She turned to see Mitch Childer standing there, shifting his weight from one foot to the next. He looked as uneasy as she felt and she realized that his fate depended on the system working as much as hers did, and he couldn't do a damn thing to ensure it would work. For a brief moment, she felt a twinge of sympathy for the shitty elitist prick, but it didn't last.

"It passed every test during the overnight run," she told him. Watching the results displaying on the screen, she felt a surge of pride. She'd done this. The code she'd written, based on Wyatt's notes, was running as smooth as silk. "We've been running transactions down every conceivable path nonstop; I threw in some totally bogus ones to see if they would fuck things up, but the system caught those and rejected them like it should. The data is returned to the sender to be corrected. And the tokens, your little e-Shilingis, are ready to send to the addresses the investors gave us at launch time."

"So we are good?"

"We are good." I'm good, you stupid son of a bitch. She bit her tongue. Let him be relieved. Let him enjoy the moment of fame and glory the day would give him.

"You should've taken some pay in e-Shilingis," he said. "They will be worth a lot more soon."

"I'm good," she said. "I don't mind taking risks, but that isn't my cup of soup."

"You mean tea?"

She wrinkled her nose. "I don't like tea."

Childer looked at her as if he still couldn't make up his mind about what he thought of her. He probably thought several things and none of them were any good. "Well, I better get ready. I have to make a speech."

"Oh fuck, there will be speeches?"

"The President of Tanzania will be here. He'll give one, the minister of finance will give one, and then I will congratulate them on their brave foray into the future."

"What a fucking joke," Peggy said.

A thin smile surprised her. "Yes. It is. And a rather silly joke at that, isn't it?" Then he walked away, leaving Peggy wondering if he saw the same joke she did. Ultimately, it didn't matter in the least. What mattered was making sure she was able to make her exit. She called Franz.

"You snuck out on me," he said. "I woke up with the most evil of intentions only to find that you weren't here. That was very frustrating."

"Sorry. I needed to get into to the office early and didn't see a need to wake you. It's a big day here."

"Oh right. This is the day of that big launch of the thing you're working on, right?"

"It is. And once the system shows its stuff to the officials who have gathered to pretend for the cameras that they understand that it is actually doing anything, I'm going to want to celebrate," she told Franz.

"What do you have in mind?" he asked.

She had no desire to tell him what she intended. In fact, she didn't want to waste time on any explanations. Franz was a pastime, not an important cog in things. A clean break, a simple desertion, seemed her best bet. She doubted he'd be heartbroken to find she'd split. Disappointed for a while, at best. "I don't know how soon I'll get away, but the official crap, where the president pushes some bogus button, is set for noon. So how about meeting me for a late lunch at some nice place?"

"Nice place. Like upmarket?"

"Is there anything kinky and crazy in this city? I feel like I've been cloistered and need to break out."

He laughed. "There is a club, a rather exotic place that I've heard about. It's called the Savannah Lounge. By the time we finish eating, the dancing should be warming up. I've heard it's expensive, though."

"Not a problem, my sweet. If this system walks and talks like it's supposed to, then I'll be collecting a lovely bonus," she said. The amount meant that given her plans, it wasn't worth hanging around to collect, but she was sticking more or less to the truth in talking to Franz. "So make a reservation, dress nice, and then you can pick me up in the lobby of the Finance Ministry."

"I'll do that."

So Franz had his assignment, going off on a wild goose chase. She was certain he'd do what he said. She wasn't sure if he was just enjoying hustling an American woman, living off her, or if he had other motives, but he was pretending he wanted to please her, and she was going to use that. Peggy wasn't about to leave anything to chance that she could control, and she didn't want him hanging around the hotel room when she went back to grab her things.

When she disconnected from the call, she checked the remote connection on her laptop again. She'd given it a number of tough benchmarks to run, and everything was running like clockwork. She let out a sigh of relief and stopped the program; then she reset the system and rebooted. That would delete all the test data and reset the registers to their initial values. She manually loaded the address of her wallet into the transaction module, then saved the program again.

It was ready to go. Her money machine was primed.

As people filtered in and began setting up the conference room for the show, she chatted with the programmers, being nicer than usual. They'd write it off to relief that the job was done and on schedule. She knew they all planned a party for later and she wasn't invited. That suited her perfectly.

When things began, a little power struggle simplified her plans immeasurably. She thought she'd have to be in the room in case reporters had questions, but it seemed that being seen by the press was above her pay grade. "You don't need to be in there, Peggy," was the way Childer put it, saying it like he was doing her a favor. He was, but he didn't know it.

As things got underway, Peggy caught a taxi to her hotel, got the duffle bag she'd packed earlier with just her casual clothes—the rest she would leave hanging in the closets. The maids could have them. She had no use for them and wanted to travel light.

Carrying the duffle downstairs, she left without checking out, catching a taxi to the airport. She walked to a status board and looked for the first flight leaving for any major city where she could make connections and found that she was in time to catch one to Barcelona, via Dubai.

In Barcelona, she bought a ticket on a flight that took her to Bridgetown, Barbados. She stayed there long enough to catch her breath and badly needed sleep before buying a ticket on Liat, a Caribbean airline that would take her to Port of Spain, Trinidad, and Tobago.

Sitting in the plane on the last leg, looking down at the blue Caribbean, Peggy thought about the trip that still lay ahead of her. She was looking forward to this segment, the part where she disappeared. If they cared to, Mitch Childer or Osk Barstad, or any of them, could easily track her movements to Trinidad. So far during her escape, she'd used her own credit cards, her own passport. Once she was in Trinidad, that's when she'd really start to disappear.

She was heading to meet up with Billy and Freida; she'd known them for years. In fact, Billy was her first lover. When she moved on, Frieda took him over and they'd stuck together. They'd all sailed together in high school, but after graduation, they parted ways. While she'd gone into the tech world, Billy and Frieda married and took over her father's construction company. They ran it for a few years but they were fed up with all the regulations and the way they changed rapidly. So they sold the company and moved onto a sail-boat. They called her the *Last Laugh*.

Keeping the boat going, not having an income, was eating seriously into their nest egg. Sailing wasn't exactly a sustainable lifestyle unless you had a way to earn money afloat.

About the time Hoenig started talking about the job in Tanzania, when she first started making her initial plans, she'd gotten a call from Frieda called. "We have to replace the engine in the damn thing," Frieda said. "Ours is toast—unrepairable. I don't know where the money for doing that will come from. We've been worried about the cost of just hauling out for new antifouling paint."

That gave Peggy her idea—their distress was an opportunity for her. There was a way to solve their problem and hers too. "I can help," she said.

"Who do we have to kill?" Frieda asked, laughing. "Engines are expensive, Peggy."

"If I fronted the money, would it be possible for you to hang around Trinidad for a little while after the haul out?"

"More or less indefinitely," Frieda laughed. "It's a great place, and the bar at the yacht club is a lot of fun. The anchorage in Chaguaramas, Trinidad, is great."

"Then I'll wire you the money. Send me the info . . . the amount, the bank routing information, and all that. Then you two get your boat in tip-top shape. When that is done, just hang out and party until I call you," Peggy told her. "Deal?"

"You'll buy a new engine?"

"I'll pay for the entire haul out and to restock the galley."

"What do you get out of this?"

"I need you standing by, hanging out, and ready to set sail when I call."

"Any idea . . ."

"In a few months."

"We can be ready in two."

"Then when I do call, you can pay me back by giving me a ride."

"A ride?"

"I want to stow away on your boat."

"Stowaway?"

"I need to be an undocumented passenger. I'll get on in Trinidad and have you drop me off where I tell you."

"I see. And do you need to go somewhere in particular?"

Peggy debated telling her a lie, but opted for the truth. She needed them to be ready for the right voyage. "I want to go to Cartagena, Colombia."

Frieda laughed. "I've heard that it's nice a nice sail there from here this time of year. You have a deal, Peg. You do know it'll take more than a week to make that trip, right?"

She did know. And it would be fine; the trip would mean a week when she was entirely off the grid. There were no facial recognition systems along the Spanish Main to spot a person of interest. They might see a boat or two, maybe a coast guard cutter, but nothing more.

So they made the deal, and when the project came close to its end, she'd called them from Tanzania to give them a heads-up. The boat was ready and Billy would be at the airport to meet her.

It was good to see old friends again. Billy had borrowed a rattling hulk of a truck and took her out to the yacht club, which was far less elegant than it sounded. It was a yacht club but primarily a boatyard with a bar/restaurant that went out over the water, near a fuel dock.

The anchorage was brimming with sailboats, mostly white fiberglass boats ranging from 30 feet up to 45 feet long. Bigger boats needed to anchor elsewhere.

Frieda was waiting at the bar, and they hugged. "Billy will take your bags to the boat. You and I can chat and have a drink. We'll eat ashore tonight. I want to catch up on what you've been up to, not cook."

That was fine with Peggy. "But we can leave in the morning?" Peggy asked.

"As you requested. While Billy picked you up, I went to immigration and the Port Captain and got us checked out of the country. We have to leave in the morning now, but they are nice about letting you check out the night before and avoid the after-hours check in and check out fees. So we leave at first light."

She remembered that Frieda was the skipper on the *Last Laugh*. Billy was a handy mate. "The tide's right then?"

She smiled. "You know it. At dawn, the Guiana current will dominate and sweep us north, through the Boca and North of Venezuela."

"And we'll make a run direct to Colombia?"

"As direct as the wind and tide allow," Frieda said. "And we should have a favorable wind and a following sea. That's a good thing too. We won't be in Colombia until around 950 nautical miles have passed under the keel."

"I'm in no rush, but I do love a good sail," Peggy said.

After a better meal than she expected at the outdoor bar at the marina, they went back to the boat for drinks and to continue their catching up, which wound up, as it sometimes had back in the day, with the three of them together in the large bed in the master cabin.

As they cast off from the mooring just before light and motored out of the anchorage, Peggy realized she hadn't felt so relaxed in a long time.

And then they were at sea, where things were peaceful. With the engine off, making their 6 knots to the West, the warm sun caressed her. Peggy took off the shorts and halter top she was wearing and stretched out on the hatch.

"Enjoy it," Billy said. He was standing there watching her, his eyes shining. "We'll be out here for almost nine days."

"I intend to, Billy. I really intend to."

They shared the watches, with one person always at the helm, although under such favorable conditions, the autohelm did the majority of the work. That meant the other two were free to do the cooking, sleep, take care of chores, and frolic in the master cabin.

The days blurred together and flew by. "There it is," Billy said.

Peggy looked and saw buildings on shore. "Where are we?"

"We are at 10.23.386N, 075.34.244W—the very spot that you requested that we head for." He pointed. "That's Boca Grande ahead, just off the port bow. If you still want us to, we will be dropping the sails and turning on the stinkpot in about five minutes."

She stared at the shoreline. It was all happening. Things were never what you imagined, but this was amazingly close. "Then I'll be going ashore."

"Frieda is breaking out the extra dinghy you had us get." He rubbed his jaw. "You sure about this? You're sure welcome to stay with us."

"That wouldn't be a good idea, Billy. It's been great, but now I'll row in and abandon the dinghy. I've made some arrangements ashore."

"That we don't need to know about," Billy said.

"That you are better off not knowing about."

"Billy, Peggy left a wad of money lying on the counter in the galley," Frieda said, as she unrolled the dinghy and started the pump to inflate it. "What's that about, Peggy?"

"You'll need it."

"Why?"

"You guys wanted to circumnavigate but couldn't afford to, right?"

"Right."

"So you stay in Cartagena for a few days and provision the shit out of your boat. You already got her in Bristol condition, so then off you go—around the world with you."

Frieda giggled. "And then we are kind of hard to reach if anyone were curious about someone who disappeared from Trinidad about the time we left."

"Smart woman," Billy said, admiringly. "Sexy as shit and smart too."

"I like to think so," Freida said as she grabbed one side of the dinghy and helped Peggy toss it over the side. They trailed the painter back to the stern as Billy turned on the boat's diesel.

"I'll go ashore and you two motor on into Cartagena." Peggy kissed them both. She'd put her two bags in plastic garbage bags, tossed them into the rubber dinghy, and jumped in after them. Two plastic oars were wired in on the sides.

"Those oars aren't much to work with," Billy said.

"True, but the prevailing wind and current are onshore. They'll do the work, right skipper?"

Frieda laughed. "Most of it." She grabbed the painter and undid it, then tossed it into the dinghy. The two boats drifted apart quickly. Billy and Frieda stood in the stern and waved, then Billy went to the helm, engaged the engine, and they motored away, heading through the raft channel entering the harbor in Cartagena, Colombia.

CHAPTER 33

VIEW FROM THE WINDWARDS

"You must live in the present, launch yourself on every
wave, find your eternity in each moment. Fools stand on
their island opportunities and look toward another land.
There is no other land; there is no other life but this."

—Henry David Thoreau

St. George's
Grenada, West Indies
Lesser Antilles

St. George's is the capital of Grenada, a Caribbean nation consisting
of six islands. It lies northwest of Trinidad and Tobago, northeast
of Venezuela, and southwest of Saint Vincent and the Grenadines.
Grenada, which is also the name of the main island, is also called the
Island of Spice, as it is one of the world's largest exporters of nutmeg
and mace.

The capital is the country's largest port and its picturesque horse-
shoe-shaped bay, called the Carenage, was once where whalers hauled
out their boats. Today, it's the landing place for tourists disgorged by
cruise ships.

The Carenage is ringed by Wharf Road, which is home to a variety of restaurants and shops. On the western side, toward the mouth,
Young Street rises quickly from Wharf Road and is home to numerous shops. Go up the hill a few blocks to Granby Street and you
will find that Young Street morphs into Halifax. There you'll find
Market Square. As the name implies, this is where the locals sell

spices, vegetables, and souvenirs. Naturally, many vendors offer nutmeg, some packaged with a small shredder. "Spice from the Island of Spice," is the hawker's cry as tourists pass. "Take some home to your friends."

A petite black woman carrying a large holdall bag walked through the Market Square, talking to vendors, asking about the spices, the unfamiliar vegetables, and life on the island. She was an attractive woman with a bright smile, and her interest in the things going on around her made her welcome. She was the center of things, the obvious star. She was followed by another woman, a Filipina, who carried a video camera. The camerawoman panned the market, but always came back to the bright smile of the black woman, then again moving to capture the sights, the noisy market ambiance, and the conversations. Occasionally as they approached, a vendor would shake her head (they were mostly women, wearing brightly colored headscarves) and the duo would respect that, passing her by, but most were eager to be videoed and possibly make a sale.

The woman doing the talking was named Sindi, and the woman behind the camera, was named Anchara.

"Which colors of chili are the hottest ones?" she asked the stout woman who sat next to a large, rather rickety looking wooden table covered with chilies in red, yellow, and green. "I like hot chilies."

The woman laughed. "Well, darling, some of them are flavoring chilies and some are what be giving it heat. You don't go by no coloring."

A good salesperson, she was already putting an assortment of the chilies into a red plastic bag. "You take some of each of them and taste them, darling. Then you see what I be talking 'bout."

Sindi held up the bag for the camera. "My first purchase on the island," she said, then she paid the woman. "A little nutmeg and we will have everything we need."

Another vendor reached over to her, holding out a small cloth bag. "Here you be, darling."

Sindi laughed and paid her too, then opened the bag and let Anchara take a close up of the nutmeg and the small grater. "Now I can have freshly ground nutmeg," she said happily. Then she nodded at Anchara, who shut down the camera.

"I can do some lovely things with fresh nutmeg," she said.

"I'll bet you can. I think we have enough footage of the market," she said, leading her away from the tumult.

Anchara nodded. "If I get a shot of the tourists arriving at the Carenage, that will be enough local color. After all, the focus of this segment is the True Blue Boutique Resort anyway."

"Yes, it is."

"We are going to want to put up a couple of pretty fine videos about that place. I mean, they did give you that amazing villa for the week."

That was true, Sindi knew. The villa was lavish and the resort spectacular. It was situated on the south side of the island, which really was a location that shouted tropical paradise. The Fieldens had done magical things with the resort. "We'll get them some great videos," Sindi said. "It's incredibly photogenic, and after the terrible hurricane season they've had, any boost we give them will be welcome."

"They'll be effective too. Our viewer numbers are way up lately," Anchara said. One of her jobs was marketing the video blog, and she was pleased with herself. "We picked up a lot of new subscribers after you got featured in that rap video."

"That worked out well, I think."

Anchara made a face. "The site did get such a nice bump, but that video was a totally sexist piece of shit. It embarrassed me. He made you look like just a pretty piece of meat. You are a pretty piece of meat, but you are so much more than that."

"And what are we selling in the videos, Anchara? Sindi is an easily influenced high-end pretty party girl. She goes to high-end places and promotes them. You have to forgive anyone who thinks I'm a frivolous airhead. Besides, the moron thought he was flattering me with his lewd insinuations. I have to take that as an intended compliment."

"I suppose."

"And while I'm delighted the numbers are up, what's the word from Tanzania? I know you've been monitoring the situation while I've been making nice with people and making exploitive videos."

Anchara laughed. "Well, their government, in the form of the finance and planning minister, is loudly proclaiming victory and enjoying what your alter ego always calls subjective success. They did the launch, and when the system didn't overheat and blow up in their faces within ten minutes, they quickly declared it a stellar success unequaled in the annals of African history."

As they walked, they continued uphill, reaching a spot where they could look down at the bay. A catamaran was coming in under sail. Sindi watched idly. "As my alter ego also says, whenever things appear to work, the delusional fall prey to believing they've accomplished their goals. They get in a rush to celebrate because second-handers know in their hearts that their time in the limelight is undeserved and won't last."

"And if they don't know it, you, or Boone actually, do your level best to help them see the light and understand their copious failings."

Sindi looked at her friend. "I do enjoy doing that. I admit it. What about the help Rashmi asked us for? Are we going to be able to pull that off? Are things in place?"

"Need you ask?"

"No, and I shouldn't have to but I always will."

"I know. You can rest assured that everything is already in the works." Anchara turned on the camera again and took some shots as the catamaran slowed and dropped its sails. At the mouth of the bay it turned East, heading into the lagoon, where the marina was. "Beautiful," she said. "Buy me one."

"The boat or the bay?"

"Both. How about the island?"

"Maybe I will. First, tell me what you've set up."

"Spoilsport. I contacted some bitpats local to the problem—we have an amazing network there. One woman works with the air control system, and there is a guy who consulted on the original IT work in Dar es Salaam. They assure me that everything we've asked for is doable and they are happy to, in the woman's words, 'fuck things up nicely.' And just before we left the villa, I got a report that everything is in place. I sent Rashmi all of the details and very specific instructions on what she needs to do and when. So we've done our part. The rest is up to her. If she moves on schedule, there shouldn't be any problems."

"You've done well," Sindi said.

"I did what you asked. You always know what to do."

"Are you angry with me?" Sindi asked.

Anchara stopped filming. "Why would I be angry?"

"I'm not sure, but you sound troubled. I thought you didn't seem pleased when I told you what I planned for Rashmi."

Anchara shrugged. "Maybe not. But the way I see things these days . . . that was Boone's decision. Boone's take is Rashmi wouldn't do well floating free. Not yet. She decided that she could use the woman's help."

"You don't agree with me?"

"That's all Boone, not you. It has nothing to do with Sindi and me."

"Yet . . . I'm both Boone and Sindi. Can you be mad at only one of us?"

Anchara turned away. "That's hard for me sometimes. And I'm not angry, not really. See, Boone does a lot of things that I don't care for. Boone can be a ruthless person, but for the right reasons. Boone saved my life." She turned back to face her. "I owe her everything, but she makes me uncomfortable at times. I'll do whatever she asks and help her however I can. But I love you, Sindi. I love working with you, being with you. Rashmi will work for Boone and that has nothing to do with Sindi, right?"

The woman laughed. "That is so wrong, so schizophrenic, that I can't even take it seriously. What sort of objectivist are you, my dear friend, my lover?"

"A fair-weather objectivist, perhaps. A novice objectivist."

Sindi took her hand. "Very well, then. You are also a very efficient assistant, fortunately, and in that capacity worth your weight in gold—to both Sindi and Boone."

"It never confuses you, does it?"

Sindi kissed her cheek. "Sindi is a product of Boone's fertile imagination. Sindi is a reason and an excuse to travel and earn money. Eventually, you'll understand how that works for me, for us."

"And until then?"

"Well, you are very real, and until whatever happens next . . . there is a large, very comfortable bed waiting for us back at the villa."

Anchara giggled. "You might want to make love, but I know you also want to be near the encrypted computer so you can monitor the events in Tanzania."

"They both get me hot," she said.

Anchara blushed. "In that case, we'd better get going."

"So say we all."

"I did put out a general alert to all bitpats. There might be a number of people shorting the new Tanzanian currency."

"It will be great fun to see how that plays out," Sindi said, now thinking as Boone.

"Boone has a strange idea of fun," Anchara said.

Boone tucked her arm in Anchara's and put her head against her bare arm, enjoying the touch of the woman's warm flesh. "You damn well know you enjoy upsetting the apple cart every bit as much as I do, Anchara. Admit it."

The woman gave her a stern look that melted into a smile. "Okay, I'll admit it. It's fun watching you kick ass."

"You like being part of it. It tickles you that you made some of it happen."

She giggled. "Okay, maybe I'm evil too."

"Great. Let's go to the villa and get absolutely wicked."

"Oh yes," Anchara said, beaming.

CHAPTER 34

JAIL HACK

"People should either be caressed or crushed. If you do them
minor damage they will get their revenge; but if you cripple them
there is nothing they can do. If you need to injure someone, do
it in such a way that you do not have to fear their vengeance."

—Niccolò Machiavelli

Rashmi's Apartment
Dar es Salaam, Tanzania

Rashmi woke feeling sick. Sick at heart over Wyatt rotting in a jail cell
and sick over the way various people and forces seemed to be hijacking
the government's financial transaction system. A system that could've
done so much good was being compromised, and she didn't even have a
way to determine who was actually doing it, or what the end goal was.

She suspected Peggy was involved, if not the main culprit, but
the International Monetary Fund, in the form of Mitch Childer, was
certainly complicit. And even Interpol had no interest in learning
the truth. She'd tried to get Osk Barstad to listen to her, but it hadn't
been productive.

"You don't have all the facts, Ms. Patel," the woman told her. "Your
view is biased."

"I have more facts than you do," she said it flatly, keeping out the
emotion.

"The man is an admitted terrorist."

"He's an admitted anarchist with a vested interest in making the
system work properly. I can show you the logs. Unlike some . . ."

"He is responsible for the hack. We have other evidence that shows him to be the prime mover in this. Please leave the investigating to professionals."

That had been her one attempt to alter the course of events. The rebuff was more than a dismissal, it was a warning. Stay away. Childer, Barstad, even Andwele, had their minds made up . . . not that they thought Wyatt was guilty, but that he should pay the price.

So, much of the sickness she felt was the kind that fills a competent person who suddenly finds themselves helpless in the face of injustice and incompetence. It made her stomach churn, her body ache. She had no other inroads into power. Without Andwele willing to back her, Haki Dola wouldn't listen to her. Even if he did, even if he wanted to help, Wyatt was in the hands of the judicial system, such as it was, and his influence there was questionable.

She dragged herself into the kitchen, made breakfast, and let her morning coffee help her start to think clearly. She needed a plan. Doing nothing was not an option for her. If she let them railroad Wyatt, bury him in the judicial system, then she'd never be able to forgive herself. There was a lot she didn't know, but she did know that he was innocent. That meant she had to act.

To Rashmi, an action of that sort was something that happened online. You contacted people, sent up alerts and calls to action. But first you needed to research things, find out who might be an ally against such formidable foes.

She smiled at herself at the way she was thinking of the situation, stating it in such grandiose terms. But how else could it be framed? A lot of the chaos swirling around them was likely political. She knew little or nothing about politics and had avoided it since her first contact with the polluting effects of political agendas. That was one thing Wyatt was right about . . . another thing he was right about. The way the government, the IMF, and the World Bank were so eager to take something wonderfully distributed, centralize it, and call that an improvement, claiming they'd safeguarded it, was mind-boggling.

On the subject of allies, Rashmi drew a blank. She knew of only one possibility. Wyatt told her to send that message to this Boone at a site called bitpats. She refilled her coffee and went to her computer, booting it and going to the site.

"Welcome to bitpats.com," a flashy splash banner said. Underneath was a login box and below that a quotation: "'In the system of debt, one of the two parties is always the slave.' —Andreas Antonopoulos." The rest of the page was black. There were no tabs, no other information.

She wondered who was this Greek they quoted. He sounded like a contemporary of Archimedes, but why would a radical group be citing him?

Unable to log in, she left the site and entered "bitpats" into the search engine. Moments later, she had a page of references but they weren't what she was looking for. A message at the top said: "Including results for bit parts. Search only for 'bitpats'?" Looking through the results, she laughed. Almost all of the results referenced "bit parts" or "bit pays," but there was a site called Nomadic Giant, which seemed to belong to some sort of high-tech gypsy fiction publisher. Nothing useful at all.

She took a breath and decided to check her email. Perhaps Boone had responded to the email she'd sent right after Wyatt was arrested. She didn't hold out much hope for help from some entity she didn't know, whose site was almost a stealth site. Wyatt thought a cry for assistance in their direction would produce results, but he was such an incurable optimist. She recalled the incongruity of the smile on his face when they hauled him off in handcuffs. He beamed with pride as if he'd managed to accomplish something good simply by admitting to the hack. She still didn't understand any of that.

Her inbox was empty except for a single, entirely odd message. It was flagged as high priority, which meant that when it was opened, the sender would receive a message letting them know it had been read. A die-hard techie, this puzzled her, mostly because the email had no sender information—how could someone send a high-priority message, one that would let the sender know it was received, and manage to suppress the sender information? It wasn't so much that they had done it, but the mystery of how.

Intrigued, she opened it. From both the message and context, it was immediately clear to her that it was from Boone. For reasons of secrecy, the sender's information wasn't available. Of course, that didn't explain how these bitpats managed that.

The opening was stark: "Here is what you need to know and what you must do," it said. The entire message was terse, clear, and precisely to the point. "Your lives, yours and Wyatt Osgood's, are in peril and you must follow these directions without deviation. A small window of opportunity is being created for you, but any hesitation will result in failure."

Her heart pounded. This wasn't an offer to help; it was help being put into action. She read it over slowly and carefully. Then she read it again. Finally, she hit reply and typed "thank you," and hit send, having no idea if the message would go anywhere. After all, she was replying to no one.

"Message sent," the email account said, and she sighed again. Things, however bizarre they might be, were happening. Steps were being taken. The message made it clear that things were in motion— the escape, the rescue they had planned, consisted of a moving conveyor belt of activities. This complex plan left her but two choices: either she stepped on the belt and went for what promised to be a wild ride, trusting that everything in the email was true, that these things would happen, or she ignored it completely. There was no room in between those options, no alternative steps.

The end result, even if it worked, would save Wyatt, but it would also end her career. The email made no bones about that. If she took up the cudgel, regardless of the outcome, the person Rashmi Patel would have to cease to exist. Her unknown, faceless saviors would make provisions for her, but for now . . . Rashmi was going to have to trust in forces that she couldn't examine. She would have to abdicate her judgment of them in favor of Wyatt's assessment.

It hadn't occurred to her that when the project was complete she might be considered a threat, but when she'd read it, she knew it was true. The assessment was spot on—the stakes were far too high to leave the doubters, the investigators, behind. Even if she didn't know the plan, the plot, whatever it was, she knew pieces of it, pieces that could be stuck together to create a picture that the plotters wouldn't want shown around.

Yet, staying wasn't an option. Life would not go on. She wouldn't be transferred to some dull maintenance job. No, she would disappear. They had to make her disappear.

And Wyatt would disappear as well. What he didn't already know about what they'd done, he could figure out. They wouldn't want him talking in open court. They couldn't afford to have the alleged terrorist denouncing the IMF and the government for crimes against the people they were supposed to be helping. She smiled. There wasn't a doubt in her mind that, given the opportunity, Wyatt would sacrifice the possibility of a not guilty verdict for a chance to make his case about the evils of centralizing authority, of usurping freedom, for no reason but to control the people.

He was a regular Don Quixote tilting at governments.

For that, he would be silenced sooner or later.

That meant that Rashmi had no choice but to put her faith in the mysterious Boone. It went against the grain to trust in the unknown, the unprovable, the mysterious. She was a woman of science, not a person of faith.

And yet . . . At some point, you have to trust in other things, even if it was possible that an act of desperation would seem logical and necessary in hindsight. In college, she read a book by Nathaniel Branden who wrote that your instincts evolved and developed; a person acted on them and evaluated the results and this process refined those instincts. This was a survival technique—acting on instinct let you move faster than when you relied on logic. She had time, but not the resources, to act logically, and so, logically, she had to act on instinct and hope like hell that she trained her instincts well. And she had to hope like hell that Branden knew what he was talking about.

She looked at the schedule of events Boone had included in the email. "10 am today: A car will pick you up in front of your apartment," it said. She wondered how they got her address. How did they get most of the information they seemed to have? "Be ready with a bag packed with anything important to you. The car will take you to meet Wyatt at the jail; follow the instructions. You won't be returning."

Meet Wyatt? If the instructions were correct, something would happen that would allow him to leave the jail. But there was a catch. "You must move quickly. This ruse will be discovered and there is no guarantee that the attempt will succeed."

That wasn't reassuring, but now that she'd committed herself to following this path wherever it led, she found that didn't matter to her. If she was caught, her humiliation made public, that wasn't important. What was important was to thwart this . . . whatever it was.

She looked around her apartment and laughed. There was little there that she would miss. She had made little impression on her furnished apartment; she just moved in and lived lightly. Any thoughts of nesting, of making a place her own, had been reserved for after she was married to Andwele. When that fell apart, her interest in such things died too.

She would take her laptop, some clothing, and her notes on the project, and nothing more.

Reviewing the instructions and the timeline, she saw that there was time to get a shower and then eat something before the car came. She'd just had breakfast, but the message didn't say anything about meals or how long they'd be traveling. That information would come later. Better to travel on a full stomach just in case.

When she'd showered and dressed, Rashmi felt good. That feeling was dizzying; it dawned on her that it had been a long, long time since she actually felt good—about herself and what she was doing. That sense hadn't excited her since college, but now that she was taking a risk for a reason, she was alive and filled with energy. It was the fact of taking action, of doing something important. She could fail terribly, but at least she wouldn't perish from inaction. She never understood how people could just let things happen to them without trying to fight back. It made no sense.

She looked at herself in the mirror and the smile on her face startled her. It was the same one she'd seen on Wyatt's face when he was arrested. Now it made sense. He had stepped up—declared himself for the cause he believed in. He finished compromising with the second-handers around him and stood there, tall and proud, letting them know that while he was free, they should be sorely afraid. Even when they handcuffed him, he stood taller, straighter, than any of them.

And now, just maybe, if things went right he would be free again. And if not, well they'd go down fighting.

As she cleaned her dishes and put them away, she decided to take a sandwich for Wyatt. There was no telling when his last meal had been.

CHAPTER 35

BUY HIGH, SELL HIGHER

"The people of all countries agree that the present state of
monetary affairs is unsatisfactory and that a change is highly
desirable . . . The destruction of the monetary order was the result
of deliberate actions on the part of various governments. The
government-controlled central banks and, in the United States, the
government-controlled Federal Reserve System were the instruments
applied in this process of disorganization and demolition."

—Ludwig von Mises
The Theory of Money and Credit

Bob & Edith's Diner
539 S 23rd St
Crystal City, Arlington, VA

The two men sat facing each other in the blue plastic seats of the diner's booth. Around them, patrons and waitresses hustled about in a swarm of lunchtime activity. Cocooned in their booth, with their meals served, Claude Hoenig smiled as he watched the other man tuck into his club sandwich. "So this diner isn't too down-market a place for you, I guess?"

The man chewed for a moment, then picked up a napkin to wipe mayonnaise from the corner of his mouth before answering. Then he pointed at his plate. "This is what I've always imagined American food to be like. I love it."

"You've never had this kind of food before?" Hoenig asked. "I know you've been here a lot of times."

The man shook his head. "Every time I visit the US, the morons I meet with seem to think they can impress me by taking me to fucking French or Italian restaurants. Given that I eat in Paris and Milan a few times every month, that's kind of stupid. I don't mean to say the food is bad—those places are usually top drawer and have excellent chefs, but the entire exercise is a meaningless and expensive waste. But you . . . I like you. I like that you brought me to a regular American place."

"Lunch is for eating. Fancy dinners are for making a big impression."

"So if this was dinner . . . ?"

Hoenig laughed. "Sorry. I'd take you to a pizza place I know. And let me tell you—Italians don't know shit about pizza. Once you've eaten one of these . . ."

The man laughed. "Well, you've made a good impression on me. It doesn't hurt that this sandwich is excellent."

"I wasn't trying to impress you," Claude said softly.

"I know." The man grinned. "And that, my friend, impresses me."

With that, they turned their attention to their food. When they were done and the other man had tasted some real apple pie and American coffee (which impressed him less than the rest of the meal), Claude asked the question he'd been waiting to ask: "Since you've come all this way, mind telling me why?"

"The crypto," he said. "We're allocating it now. It's pre-mined, as you know, and the Finance Ministry will control the allocation via the national banks."

"A limited supply, then."

The man arched an eyebrow. "In theory. In practice, fixed, but it all depends on the government showing some restraint."

"Not a safe bet, in my experience," Hoenig said sullenly. "Governments . . ."

"True. So those of us who bought into the project, the initial investors, should be looking for a spike. The first big one will be a sell sign in spades."

That seemed obvious to Claude Hoenig. His company was in line for some of the crypto as partial payment for its services. He'd planned to do exactly that, although more because of cash flow. He'd owe Peggy a bonus for her work. Even if she'd made the job harder than it had to be, he'd promised a completion bonus. And there were other expenses as well. "The initial price was set rather high."

"The speculators will drive it much higher as soon as the Ministry of Finance releases the reserve crypto, which will be at launch time. They want investors coming in right away, and it will be the time for them to do it."

"So we use it as a buy high, sell high, proposition."

The man smiled. "That's a way of looking at it. There's no telling what it will do in the future, as the hedge funds tell you, but you'll want to get your cash out, or at least sell off most of it before the realities of running a national currency become apparent."

"The realities?"

"There will be costs that aren't apparent, and if the government doesn't stick to its announced inflation targets, all bets are off."

"I'm curious . . . Why you are telling me this . . . your concerns are almost insider information," he said. There was more to say, but he wanted to see how the man responded to just that gentle observation.

He saw a flicker in the green eyes. This man caught every nuance. "Because I do like you. Because I think we should continue to work together."

"If the project is successful, why wouldn't we continue to do that?"

The man folded his hands. A young waiter came over to clear their dishes. "More coffee?" he asked. They shook their heads and waited until he melted into the now fading lunch rush.

"I don't want to continue to use your company as an outside resource," he said. "And some things will happen when the project is complete that, if you don't know, if you aren't warned, might scare you off. I hope to cement our relationship by letting you know how things will go and then see where we take that."

"You certainly know how to get my attention," Hoenig said. "I assumed the end of the project would be an anticlimax."

"You'd be forgiven for seeing it that way," the man said. "But this isn't actually the project. It is a precursor to the real project—a test of the ideas and the people who implement it."

Hoenig let a thin, pleased smile sneak across his face. "Trial by fire."

"Exactly. And there will be a variety of winners and losers."

"And collateral damage."

"You're thinking of your programmer, Osgood. He made the mistake of alienating Childer and trying too hard to understand things above his pay grade. It was, unfortunately, a fatal mistake."

"Yet, he could be invaluable for future work."

"He is certainly replaceable. There are other good, even excellent programmers and you've already recruited them. You were, I believe, going to lose Osgood eventually anyway."

Hoenig nodded. "True enough. He deserves better than this, however."

The man sighed. "We cannot right all of life's wrongs. The hordes of refugees from Somali and Libya and Syria deserve better than they get. The Jews in the Holocaust deserved better. Life isn't fair. And, like those poor devils, Osgood's fate is sealed, I'm afraid."

"You could rescue him."

The green eyes focused on him. "Yes, I could. The price, however, is far too high."

"You aren't one to bullshit people, are you?"

"I have no need for that, nor any time for it. Neither do you."

"So tell me, what else don't I know?"

"There are things in the system that Childer put there—for us. He had some excellent ideas that will further our goal."

"Which is?"

The man smiled. "You can't guess? I've wondered who you think I am or who I represent."

"I don't think you represent anyone; and this group? You strike me as globalists," he said.

"And what does that mean to you? Is it bad or good?"

"I'm not sure what form your group takes, but that's what it smells like. You use the IMF and World Bank to diminish the power of nations, replacing them with global initiatives. You strengthen the UN, for instance, but take power from nations."

"We do that and more. But you are not correct in thinking we use the IMF and World Bank or the UN."

"No? It sure looks like it."

"No. We don't use them. We are those groups. They are our creations and we have nurtured them. They are the way we implement policy."

"And who, might I ask, is we?"

"The Retinger Oculistica."

"Retinger? The one who called for what became the Bilderberg conference during the fifties?"

"An evolution, a distillation, if you will, where the elite from the group that came about during the conference in 1954 created a more effective branch. They remain a part of the visible entity but move beyond it. A stealth supergroup."

Hoenig didn't care for the sound of that. "Heady, self-important stuff."

"Spoken like a true believer in democracy."

"I've fought for it all my life."

"And it is withering. Your democracy is blinded by nationalism and paralyzed by its own bureaucracy. It no longer functions smoothly. It was a means of protecting the rights of people, but it oppresses its own people to accomplish that, making it oxymoronic, if not actually traitorous. But I think you know those things. I think you mourn the loss of your democracy far more than you support what has replaced it. Our goals are the same but without such mind-boggling regulations and restrictions. The new technologies hold an amazing promise— that we, a global group of the best minds, can give the people what they want, in terms of a guaranteed state of well-being and security, without the need for rallying them around some flag or false god."

"You think so?"

The man smiled. "And so do you."

"I do?"

"You moved into this technology because you see its strengths and dangers. Technology is disruptive. That sounds bad, but it just means it churns things, tosses out the old simply for being old and inefficient. It used to be information that was the key to the gold— now it's the tools."

"And you want to be there, using your tools to move things in the direction you want."

"Yes. The opportunities it offers the future and the dangers inherent in it both lie in what it's replaced with. Random selection, one country doing one thing with another doing the opposite, will produce chaos. The world is going to be global—it's been going that way for some time now, and blockchain technology is accelerating it. In a technological world, with digital money, nations are no more valid than tribes, and their politics are wasteful and dehumanizing."

"I'll give you no argument on the last point. Partisanship sucks."

"Exactly. We want things that work, and political systems designed in the nineteenth century, or even before, aren't equipped to provide that."

"But you are?"

"Not yet. We are accumulating the people, building the tools, to create a world."

"And crypto is part of it?"

"A cryptocurrency that we control can be the basis for all of it. It will hold up everything else, and the blockchain and lightning networks we implement will simplify economics."

Hoenig considered what the man was telling him. There was a lot in what he said. He started this company with the idea that it would align him with the future. He'd always assumed that the future would mean working with governments, but the man was right. They had the agility of supertankers—they took miles to stop or turn. The current raft of changes required fast alterations, modifications, and even new ways of thinking.

Once upon a time, a Luddite was someone who hated machinery. Now, in a technology age, anyone who didn't embrace emerging tech enough to understand it was one—even if they were computer literate. The dynamic had changed.

Hoenig thought of himself as a patriot, but he was also a pragmatist. Countries were Luddite controlled. Standing up for his values no longer meant saluting a confused and muddled national identity; it meant aligning yourself with the new superpowers in order to ensure that the things you valued were protected.

"And what are you expecting from me?"

"Alternatives, options, and your support."

Hoenig saw what he meant. "You expect the system to fail."

"The currency, not the system. We don't want the country damaged, and we can use your help doing that."

Hoenig turned and looked out the window at the traffic. It looked like America out there, but what did that mean anymore? With the biggest chains worldwide, with companies like Amazon and Alphabet making more money than the GDP of most countries, the world had gotten complex. Someone needed to be in the driver's seat. "Wyatt said it's going to fail, but he was talking about the system itself."

"What?"

"The goodies your pal Childer put into it will slow it down, he said. Plus, apparently Peggy made some changes that may or may not have anything to do with that stuff, and he thinks they are going to trash it all." He looked back at the man. "Wyatt expected to have a chance to fix things."

"If he's right . . . what can we do? The country will have invested everything in that system. There's no way to back up."

Hoenig stared at him. "I've already done it. My people are rewriting the entire system to do exactly what it was supposed to do initially—and no more. If the system crashes, we can reboot with the new code. From the outside, it will look like we made a couple of fixes, rebooted, and voila, it's working."

"But without the crypto?"

"That's totally up to you. The system is still a blockchain—we aren't changing that. That means there will be tokens, but they don't have to be traded unless you want them to be. The system is just a distributed financial network."

"So we could say that we were freezing sales to determine why the currency failed."

"The currency won't fail, just the system."

"I know, I know, but the public doesn't see things that clearly."

Hoenig shook his head. "And here I thought you were against bullshit."

The man sat back. "You're right. More importantly, you are man enough to call me on it."

"Even if you conned the public, the people in the business would call you out on that."

"So what do we do?"

"How critical is this success or fail issue?"

"We want the system to work, but if the crypto succeeds, it will slow down our progress and make it harder to convince countries to work with us toward something bigger."

Hoenig considered the problem. "They'll want to try their own regardless. They see currency as their turf. They'll give up a lot, but giving you control over their currency is throwing in the towel. Rather than try to discourage them from trying, help them, but ensure they only sort of work. Then you need to build a stunningly effective universal cryptocurrency and make it a shining beacon."

"Lure them in."

"With a solid system, rather than promises or threats."

"And you can help us do that?"

"Yes. Instead of fighting them, we do it right and we do it in a way that meets this group's goals and needs. Building it from the ground up, we can put in all sorts of incentives to get people worldwide to adopt it, to clamor for it. Then, no matter how good the national currencies are, why would anyone use them? They'd have to pay a fee to convert to other currencies. No matter how small that fee is, a universal currency will be attractive, especially when supported and endorsed by the IMF and World Bank."

"That's the right direction."

"So, in the meantime, let this currency do whatever it does."

"But your man Wyatt thinks the system will crash?"

"And I agree, based on what little I really know. Too many people have stuck in too much crap. Apparently, according to Wyatt, even Interpol has its hands in there."

The man looked embarrassed. "We need their cooperation for the time being."

"Fine. So let it crash and burn. Then we reboot it after we replace the code with our new system."

"The IMF and Interpol will be pissed."

"It's their own fault for approaching this in such a ham-fisted way." He chuckled.

"That's funny?"

"I was just thinking that Mitch Childer would hate that expression."

"He would. I'll have to use it at the next opportunity."

"So that gets the system back online and the country functional. And if, as you think, the government screws with the currency, well, that's a separate problem. It means that you won't have to make a case for a national currency being a stupid and useless thing—they will do it for you."

The man nodded. "Fair enough. That's actually a better plan as it doesn't involve us having to work at some devious scheme. Devious schemes can fail and leave you publicly embarrassed. The more I think about this, the better I like it. If anyone ever looks at the code, they'll see an elegant, well-written system, and they can scratch their heads about why it went belly-up after the launch." He sipped his water. "Fluoride," he said. "I can taste it."

"That's why I don't drink tap water," Hoenig agreed.

"We still have the matter of tidying up after the launch. The code will be clean, but far too many people will be around who know what actually happened. One case in point: Your Peggy Dory has been a giant pain in the ass."

"That she has. For us all. And, as I said, Wyatt thinks she is up to more things that are off the books."

"Therefore, she won't be available for future tasks." Claude Hoenig heard the undercurrent in the man's voice; it was one he'd heard too many times not to understand exactly what he meant. The man intended for these people to be terminated.

"Collateral damage," he said. "Do I need to . . ."

"No, I have already taken steps to deal with her and that Patel woman once they aren't needed. I could take care of the Patel woman now, but there's no rush and no point in risking the possibility of alerting anyone."

"Fine." Hoenig didn't care much for that part of his work.

"You can be of help after the system is rebooted. There is another loose end that I would prefer to keep my distance from."

Hoenig sensed the opportunity. The man wanted a favor. Doing it would secure his position. He couldn't be sure who really ran things within the group and he'd have to be cautious about offending other powerful people, but getting into the group meant taking some risks, and this man's steadiness, his cautious and measured manner, gave Hoenig confidence. "How can I help?"

When the man told him what he wanted, Hoenig had to smile. He could see why the man didn't want to do that one himself. Such things were always unpleasant, but in this case, he was certain he wouldn't lose any sleep over the job he'd been asked to do. "You've come to the right person for that," he said.

The man nodded. "I know." He grinned. "Well, since we've finished our business over this lovely lunch, is there some local bar where I can buy you a drink?"

"I think we can find one," Hoenig said. "After all, we pride ourselves on being resourceful men."

"So we do. Ruthlessly at times."

Ruthless was the operative word, Claude Hoenig thought. He was sad for Wyatt. He liked Wyatt, but the man was a victim of his own idealistic crap. If he'd only shown a pragmatic streak, then maybe Claude would've tried a little harder to save him. But the green-eyed man was right that for all his brilliance, Wyatt was a liability.

"God, forgive us for what we are about to do," he muttered to himself. Yet, he was sure that God would understand. Claude Hoenig wasn't casting his lot in with the devil. This group might not be angels, but they had a better chance to save the wretches of humanity than the people in his government—and they had the desire to do it.

He could go along for the ride for a time, at least, and see how it all played out.

CHAPTER 36

THE SKY IS FALLING

"Up to 2008, sovereignty created currency. We now live
in a world where currency creates sovereignty."

—ANDREAS ANTONOPOULOS

MINISTRY OF FINANCE
DAR ES SALAAM, TANZANIA

The clear morning sky promised a brilliant day in Tanzania when
Andwele Kassain drove to his office. He felt light, upbeat. The rush
of success permeated everything around him. His morning tea tasted
better; his entire life was brighter.

Even the looks he got from people in the office, from the security guards in the lobby, to the secretarial staff, were better now that
the news of the successful launch had reverberated through the government offices. People who hadn't even known there was going to
be a new currency, a new financial system, knew that his team had
recently done something amazing.

And he had money. Soon he'd have more, much more. With coaxing from Haki Dola, Andwele had invested his savings in the new
currency. Such investing was probably technically illegal, but everyone involved had been given the opportunity to purchase e-Shilingi
before the launch. The value of his savings had doubled and looked
to go much, much higher. The stock market was booming. The entire
financial sector was riding high—and Andwele was known as one of
the architects of that boom.

His future was far different than he had imagined it would be.

From a slow rise through the ranks, he had been catapulted into a starring role. Of course, he hadn't done the work; he really didn't understand a lot of what the system even did. But he had been there at the beginning, and he helped make the case for adopting it. In government circles, sticking your neck out like that meant more than actually doing the work. After all, the technical people, people like Rashmi Patel and Peggy Dory and Wyatt Osgood, were simply employees. Andwele was an administrator, and it was the administrators who made things happen, who cajoled, did budgets, called in favors . . . that was the real work.

As he settled into his desk, his new secretary, a curvaceous and demure woman, brought him tea and a smile. There was an intoxicating quality to her smile. She was not a beautiful woman, but she was respectful and might make a good wife—a dutiful one. He had a close call in getting engaged to Rashmi. He should've realized that an educated woman would not be the kind of wife he expected her to be. That was one of the dangers of these changing times—Rashmi, with her education and her experience living abroad, had intrigued him. She was worldly, and dating her had been a heady experience. She was like no other woman he'd ever dated before—modern and alive. Although it had been exhilarating, he fortunately realized in time that she wasn't suited to be his wife. He was still rooted in more traditional values. For the world to work as it should, to function correctly, women needed to know their place.

Now that he had influence and position, Andwele could and should insist on a wife who would fulfill that role. For excitement and adventure, a modern man could always have a mistress, which was a role Rashmi would never willingly play.

And now she was a pariah. She had no future with the government, or likely with industry either. He was well rid of her, and as he ran his eyes over his secretary's legs, he was happy to be free.

"You got a call from the National Bank," she told him. "Just before you came in." She handed him a note from a Vaun Krueger, who was the assistant to the head of the bank. It asked Andwele to return his call as soon as he got in. "This is an urgent matter," it said.

That they called him was flattering but also annoying. Now that his name was associated with the system, he got lots of 'urgent' inquiries from people who were smart enough to know that Haki Dola wouldn't know anything useful and wouldn't be inclined to find out what they needed to know. That gave Andwele increased influence, but it also made his work harder.

With mixed feelings, he had his secretary return the call.

Right from the beginning, he knew something was wrong, very wrong. "What the hell is going on?" Krueger said.

"What do you mean?"

"Transactions are slowing down."

"There are peak times when they take longer, and if the blockchain isn't able to confirm a transaction . . ."

"I know how the system works, Kassain," he said. "I mean that simple sales transactions that were taking seconds to process are now taking several minutes and longer all the time. And the crypto processing, the conversion from the fiat currencies when investors try to buy it, has serious problems. Not only are the conversions taking forever, we are getting complaints that the transaction fee is growing. It's big enough now to make a joke of the official exchange rate."

"What transaction fee?"

"That's what I'm asking you. You're the one who made the system—you have been the project supervisor. Tell me why a transaction fee is being charged. We need to know what it's for and why it is getting bigger."

Andwele fought to recall any mention of such a thing and came up empty. "I don't know anything about a transaction fee. There shouldn't be one." He struggled to keep the panic out of his voice.

"Then the invoices I've seen are all wrong." Krueger shook his head. "That, I'm afraid, is a scarier thought than a mistake in the fee, because it means we are going to have to start manually auditing everything the system has done. Everything the system does is incurring a fee, and the merchants are complaining about that. It was there from the beginning, but it was so small that no one cared. But it's gone from a fraction of a percentage point to over 6 percent." He coughed. "Excuse me; I just noticed that it's at 8 percent now. And, probably more significant, the transactions are even slower. Mr. Kassain, you need to do something immediately."

As Andwele listened, his secretary began bringing in a stream of notes telling him of a variety of people who wanted to hear from him. The head of the securities exchange, the chairman of the real estate regulation board, and Haki Dola. Beads of perspiration dotted his forehead. "I'll investigate this matter immediately," he said.

He took the message to call his boss with a damp, trembling hand. "Call Deputy Minister Dola's office and leave the message that I am aware of the situation and investigating it," he said as he hung up the telephone. He grabbed his cell phone as he got out of his chair and moved toward the door and called the programming office. The phone rang. No one seemed to be picking up. He tore down the hallway in long strides, wondering what could possibly be going wrong. Nothing should've changed since the day before when the system was working wonderfully.

If the system was truly failing, he had an even more serious question: Who to ask? Peggy Dory had left . . . disappeared. Childer was upset about that for some reason but, for his part, Andwele was glad to see the abrasive woman gone. The main programmer after her was Haji, but was killed in that terrible accident. That left . . . well, most of the ones left were drones, workers with no vision. If he knew what to have them do, they'd do it well enough, but they needed direction. Now there was none.

As he entered the IT center, he saw the staff sitting around. They all looked at him, wondering. "What's wrong with the system?" he demanded.

"What do you mean?" one asked, blinking at him through thick glasses.

"The system is slowing down. Transactions are backing up."

"Possibly," the man said. "But there is no specification for how fast it should run."

"What?"

"No one ever wrote out a specification for how long a transaction should take, so the system is actually operating within specifications."

"But it's too slow. Things are backing up."

The man took out a pen. "If you'll tell me where it is slowing down and authorize a change order, we can start writing the code."

"The entire system is slowing down. It shouldn't do that."

"But there is nothing in the system specification that says it shouldn't. We can only write to specifications."

Andwele wanted to punch the man, but he knew it would do no good. "Then just tell me what the transaction fee is," he said.

The man shook his head. "We don't know."

"How can you not know? You wrote the system."

"We weren't ever told. Ms. Dory said we didn't need to know its purpose, just that it was to be collected."

"I don't think they found out either," a young woman with white eyeliner said. Andwele did a double take looking at her.

"Who? What didn't they find out?"

"Rashmi Patel and Haji. She wanted to know about the transaction fee as well."

"Why?"

"Because she didn't know why it was there. She couldn't thoroughly test the system without knowing where that money was going. Haji wrote the original module, but he didn't know the answer. He got curious too, then he was killed."

"Killed?"

She wrinkled her nose. "In that hit and run accident. So if he found out . . ."

"And Ms. Patel was taken off the system because of her involvement with the terrorist," the man with glasses said. "She never had a chance to learn more." He tapped at the monitor. "You are right about the system slowing down more. Something funny is going on."

"Can you fix it?"

"Of course," he said brightly. "That's what we do."

"Then do it."

"Do what, exactly?"

"Fix it."

He smiled. "If you show me what you want to be fixed, I'll do it as fast as possible. It is going to be break time soon, however."

Andwele's frustration mounted. "After Rashmi was suspended, who did the validating tests on the system?"

"Ms. Dory," the two said. "She said it was all perfect."

"But I don't think she was correct," the young woman said.

"The tokens aren't functioning correctly. That's why the system is slowing."

"Can you tell what is wrong?" he asked.

She shook her head. "I'm not an analyst, just a coder."

"You fools," he screamed.

Neither one seemed to care. The man handed him a form. "If you want us to do something, please fill out a change order. There's a place where you can refer to the lines of code that are incorrect."

Andwele took out his phone. Her number was still in his contacts, but Rashmi didn't answer.

He headed for the door and nearly ran into Haki Dola. "Get it fixed now!" the man screamed, his face flush.

"We don't know what is wrong," Andwele said. "None of these idiots knows anything."

"Then you fix it."

"I'm not a programmer and I didn't design the system, except in theory."

Dola sneered. "You say that now. Until this happened, you've been plenty happy to take credit for it."

"Well, I never claimed to design it, and the people who know anything are all gone, except for the one in jail."

"I doubt he'll be inclined to help us," the deputy minister said. "Childer set him up."

Andwele was surprised to see that his boss knew that it was a frame-up. He was paying a little more attention than he'd thought. "Maybe if we agreed to drop the charges in return for . . ."

"What about yourfiancé? She's smart. She was testing the system for you."

"Until they suspended her. I haven't seen her since then and now she isn't answering her phone."

"Well, if she is your only hope, then I suggest you go find her and do it quickly. The finance minister wants answers—he needs them. He is being overwhelmed with questions from the press, from all sections of the financial community, and the president himself. If we don't have answers quickly, heads will roll, and yours will be among the first, Kassain."

Somehow, seeing the fright in Dola's eyes calmed Andwele, made him think more clearly. "Don't be so upset, sir. Things are slowing down, and yes, there is a mystery about a fee, deputy minister, but those are simply technical glitches."

"Glitches that have caused the price of e-Shilingis to plummet, Kassain."

And there was the nub of the matter. Dola had obviously followed his own advice and invested in the crypto. He might've even borrowed money to invest, and he might have gotten his friends to invest as well. They would all be after him if the currency was crashing. While it would definitely hurt Andwele, he had been conservative and only invested the money he'd gotten cashing in other investments, so he could be patient.

Deputy Minister Dola was threatened on several fronts, it seemed, and Andwele felt a glimmer, a slight tingle of compassion for him. For a man who knew nothing about technology, it had to appear that the sky was falling. He was panicking. Surrounded by chaos, he had no idea what to do to ensure his own survival—his finances and career were at stake. All he could do was shout for someone to take action. And, without a clear idea that there was a solution, he began laying the groundwork to happily sacrifice Andwele, or anyone else, when it came time to lay the blame. The man was terrified and would do anything that kept him from losing his own head.

Andwele was sure that the sky wasn't falling. Certainly, this was most definitely a mess, but it was just a program—it could be fixed. Not that it was something he could even begin to fix—not without help. But Rashmi would help. He was sure of that. She wouldn't let the country suffer just because she was angry with him, or with the people who'd thrown Wyatt Osgood in jail. As he tore down the stairs, heading for the lobby where he'd catch a taxi to her apartment, he weighed his options. She had to help. Then he smiled. If she did try to refuse, he could always threaten to make Wyatt Osgood suffer. Rashmi would hold out hope that he'd be cleared, and he could tell her that the jailers would do him harm before his trial, unless she helped them, of course.

Once he had her on the job finding out what had gone wrong, he could start looking at a way to spin things more favorably. His political instincts told him that, if he kept his head, there was an opportunity to gain a great deal from this disaster. At the moment, he was one of the villains, but if he was the one who fixed the system, who put things right, then he might come out of this unscathed.

And if he could point to another villain, one without any political clout, all the better.

He smiled at the realization that Peggy Dory's sudden departure would suit her perfectly for that role. She had done something to the system and left, without even collecting her bonus, Hoenig told him. She disappeared without a trace. But if he asked Interpol to find her, he had no doubt they'd succeed. They could find her and have her brought back to stand trial.

He sighed at the magic, the brilliance, of his own ideas. It was a wonderful plan and as he gave a taxi driver Rashmi's address, Andwele began mapping out his strategy. He'd keep Deputy Minister Haki Dola out of the loop as much as possible to ensure that he got maximum credit. That wouldn't be hard as long as that fool thought the sky was falling. He'd been thinking only of avoiding blame. But the sky wasn't falling at all. It was just a hiccup in the system. Rashmi would find the problem and fix it, and Andwele would be the one they talked about when the stories were told.

"The brilliant leadership of Andwele Kassain, until then a little-known deputy in the Ministry of Finance, saved our entire country from financial collapse," teachers would tell students one day. "Not long after that, he was overwhelmingly elected president and had an illustrious career."

Yes, it was all within reach, if he was daring. If he played things well, this terrible situation was his ticket to the top.

PART FOUR

EVERYTHING
COMES APART

1010101010101010101010101010101010101010101010101

"'Well!' thought Alice to herself, 'after such a fall as this, I shall
think nothing of tumbling down stairs! How brave they'll all
think me at home! Why, I wouldn't say anything about it, even
if I fell off the top of the house!' (Which was very likely true.)"

—LEWIS CARROLL
ALICE'S ADVENTURES IN WONDERLAND

CHAPTER 37

THE ESCAPE

"The partisan wants to change the law, the criminal break
it; the anarch wants neither. He is not for or against the law.
While not acknowledging the law, he does try to recognize
it like the laws of nature, and he adjusts accordingly."

—Ernst Jünger
Eumeswil (The Eridanos Library)

A dark and dingy jail cell
Dar es Salaam, Tanzania

Wyatt sat in the tiny, dark cell wondering, rather idly under the circumstances, if his arrest had made the news. The thought sprang out of simple curiosity; it wasn't vanity that made him wonder. The answer would tell him something about his future—as in whether he had one or not.

Clearly, the ones who'd set him up, whoever it actually had been, could play it two different ways, depending on what they wanted—assuming the dumb fucks actually knew what they wanted. Either he would be excoriated in the press, shown to be the devil himself, who had descended on the project to wreak unspeakable damage, or they could simply deny he ever existed, much less had come to Tanzania. Little but a tourist entry logged into a computer would ever suggest he was there. At worst, he'd be someone who overstayed his visa—not an unusual occurrence at all.

He expected the first option—they needed someone to parade in front of cameras as the font of all trouble, the person responsible for ruining an otherwise brilliant government project. His best guess was that this is what they were doing. The guards didn't say much to him, but one had shoved a meal tray at him, telling him that a terrorist should be grateful that he was being fed.

While Wyatt didn't particularly care how his captors portrayed him, within reason, he acknowledged that he was slightly uncomfortable being viewed as a terrorist. Being associated with the violent aspects of terrorism didn't sit easily with him. He'd managed to get to this point in his life without ever being involved in anything like a real fight. But even he was willing to admit that it was, after all, only a small step from despising a system to getting pissed off to the point of deciding to overthrow it. And he made no bones about his intense dislike of the authorities hovering over him. It was another small step from attacking the institutions to actually physically attacking the leaders who perpetuated—and now the idea, the possibility of advocating the use of physical violence, had entered his head for the first time. In all fairness to those who painted him a villain, he was at the very least a subversive. And while he had a history of being a rather cowardly subversive, ideologically, they weren't far wrong in casting him as hoping their little bastardized blockchain went totally tits up.

Whatever they did was out of his control now, and it surprised him that somehow he was comfortable with that, or at least at peace with it. He wondered how Rashmi was faring. She was but an emerging rebel. She lived in a middle ground where she still tried to reconcile a strong belief in the goodness of human nature, of the intentions of governing officials, with the reality she was confronting on a daily basis. While that transition stage was important, it wasn't a good place to be when you were threatened. It courted indecision and inaction, which could be fatal.

For himself, however, now that he'd confronted his demon, he actually felt freer in this prison cell than he had on the beach. Here, at least, he couldn't be coerced into doing something he was beginning to see was not only an aggravation but morally wrong.

It had taken him a long time to get to that point, and he saw that it was part of what Rebecca had tried to tell him. It was an odd, off-kilter way, to see things, and yet, the only sensible way to look at the world. The idea that making something work right, something that created jobs and did good things and was in itself wrong when put into the wrong hands, was not an easy place to get to, but it was true. Blockchain, for instance, could make so much possible; perverted, it could become a weapon of mass destruction—at least of freedom and liberty.

"Osgood," a jailer called out and Wyatt raised his head.

"That's still me," he said. "No one offered to change places with me."

"Stand up," the man said as he unlocked the door.

He'd been moved from one cell to another before and noticed that this time the jailer didn't have any backup. The times before, there had always been a man with a shotgun lurking in the background, just in case, he supposed, Wyatt was to make a break for it, perhaps strangle the other officer or slap him with a pocket protector. "What's going on?" he asked.

"I don't know," the man said. "The order is to set you free."

"What happened? What changed their minds?"

"I told you, I don't know." The man was impatient now. "We had an order to keep you isolated and not allow you to talk to anyone."

Not even a lawyer, Wyatt thought. "Yeah."

"And now we have an order to let you go."

"I don't suppose an apology comes with it?"

The man held the door opened and grinned. "If I were you, I'd just be thankful for the part about letting you go."

"Good point." He walked out of the cell wondering if there could be some elaborate trap. Was it a pretense? Was he being told he was set free so he could be killed in a fake escape attempt? There was only one way to find out, and staying in his cell wouldn't protect him if they'd decided to kill him. This way he might be able to see the sun and breathe fresh air for a bit.

At the front desk, he signed a document that affirmed his possessions had been returned to him. All he'd had on him when they arrested him was his wallet, belt, a notebook, and a few coins. It was all there, scrupulously recorded and now counted out. He stuffed them in his pockets and was pointed to the front door. "That's the way out," the man said.

"Just like that?" he asked.

The man scowled. "You expected a parade?"

It wasn't that at all. He expected a summons to some office at least. He expected to be lectured, warned, something. Instead, as he went through the office and walked to the front door, he was studiously ignored. It seemed as if no one wanted to be able to say they'd seen him leave.

Unmolested, unwatched, he stepped through the heavy front door and out onto the street. People walked by paying him no attention. Cars went back and forth. And Wyatt realized that he had no idea where he was. He had no idea if his room at the hotel was still available for him.

The thought struck him that going to the airport would be a smart idea, but his passport and some cash were still in the hotel safe—he hoped they were. He'd need them to get a ticket. He'd seen his credit card among the things returned to him, so he could buy a ticket and get the fuck out of town before someone decided to reverse whatever decision had been made that let him escape being the poster boy for the system failure.

Which raised other questions . . . had they found a new patsy? Did the system actually get fixed? What was going on?

A limo pulled up, black, official looking, with darkly tinted windows. The liveried driver got out and came around to open the back door and hold it. She was a tall, slender black woman, with an elegant bearing. "Wyatt, get in," a voice said from inside the car.

At the sound of his name, he bent over and peered into the dark interior. There sat Rashmi. "What's going on?"

"Get in. I'll explain on the way," she said. "We don't have much time. Boone said it's a narrow window of opportunity."

Hearing Boone's name made some things clearer. The message for help had been sent and received and, as Rebecca had suggested they would, the bitpats had gone into action. He moved toward the door. "Shit's happening," he said.

The driver closed the door behind him and went around to her own seat. "It certainly is," Rashmi said. "Shit is happening, and I have no idea about the big plan."

The driver pulled away from the curb. "The big plan, the important part at the moment, is to get you two the hell out of here," she said. "We need to get to the airport."

"My passport . . ."

The driver passed a large envelope back through the window that separated the front from the back seat. "Everything is here."

"My passport?" he asked as Rashmi took the envelope and opened it.

"Your new one. Wyatt Osgood has to disappear. You won't need his passport anymore."

"Wow," Rashmi said as she dumped the contents into her lap. There were two passports from St. Kitts with their photos in them, but with different names. The envelope also held a stack of US dollars and credit cards with the same names.

"The passports are legitimate," the driver said as she wove expertly through traffic. Boone made investments in those names to get you citizenship. She managed to expedite what can be a lengthy and complicated process, but it was done by the book."

"Who are you?" Rashmi asked.

"I'm your limo driver, of course. Just an anonymous driver hired to pick you two up and take you to the airport."

"I don't see any tickets for flights," Wyatt said. "We won't have a lot of time to catch a flight. I mean, I appreciate all this excellent service, but I get the feeling Boone expedited my release, as well as the passports. When my release gets to the attention of the people at the top, they'll be looking for us."

"Yes, they will, but you don't need tickets. A private jet is waiting for you."

"To go where?"

"Kenya, first. When you land, you'll be given tickets on a commercial flight."

"To where?"

"That's all I know," she said. "For security reasons, I don't need to know more than that. You will learn more once you are out of Tanzanian airspace."

And that was how it went. No one paid any attention as they boarded the small jet. A charming flight attendant served them drinks. "Please be seated. We will be leaving soon."

"Can we make it all the way to Kenya in one hop?" Rashmi asked.

The woman smiled indulgently. "This is a Bombardier Learjet 35 and it has a range of almost 3,000 miles. The distance from the

Julius Nyerere International Airport to Jomo Kenyatta International Airport is only 413 miles, so no stop is needed."

Rashmi's sigh was of relief. "Thank you."

"I was asked to give you this," the woman said, handing her a small box. "You aren't supposed to open it until the captain makes an announcement."

"An announcement?"

She grinned. "It's all rather mysterious, isn't it? I'm enjoying it. Usually, these hops are so boring."

"Why is this going so smoothly?" Wyatt asked.

Rashmi giggled. "Didn't you see the emblem on the tail?"

He hadn't. "I was busy watching for angry people with guns."

The woman gave them an odd look. "Why would there be guns? This is the Ministry of Finance's jet."

"The Ministry of Finance has a jet?" Wyatt asked. "I mean, a country so in debt. . . ."

"They lease it to keep up appearances," she said. "We do a lot of business with smaller governments. They all like to have jets, even if they only use them to fly to other countries to beg for money. It pays my salary." Then she turned and went forward, leaving them alone.

"So you hacked the leasing agency computer? Smart. The fact that it was leased made the job easier."

"Boone did it," she said. "I wish I'd thought of it. It's way too daring for me to think of."

"Boone," he laughed. "I need to meet this person."

"Paladin," Rashmi said. "The knight errant."

"And why are you here?"

"I'm told I needed rescuing as well."

"I thought they'd slap your hand and make you sit in the back of the room for a week."

"That's what I would've thought, but according to Boone, things are far more sinister. I am a loose end to be neatly eliminated at their earliest convenience. The message suggested that I might enjoy an alternative. I agreed. Even if I stayed, my career, such as it was, is over."

"And now?"

"It will be interesting to see what this Boone person has in mind for us."

"That it will."

They sat back and Wyatt tried to take it all in, something he found a lot easier to do in the plush seat of a private jet. Idly he stared out the window, not really seeing anything until his reverie was broken by an announcement. "This is the captain. I've been asked to let you know that we are at a point where you should open the box you were given. Please use the key in the seat pocket in front of you."

Rashmi looked at the box and smiled. "We get to unravel another mystery."

She found the key and opened the box. Inside was an odd looking phone. It rang as she stared at it.

"Better answer it," Wyatt said. "It might be for you."

"Hello, Rashmi," a woman said. The phone was on speaker. "This is Boone. We are on a satellite link so I can talk you through what's going on. I assume everything is going all right?"

"To the best of my knowledge," she said. "Since we don't know the plan, it's hard to say, but we are comfortable for the moment."

"Fine. In the pocket in front of Wyatt's seat, there should be another mysterious envelope. Forgive me, but I do enjoy a little theater, and my assistant likes it even more than I do . . . I like to indulge her." Wyatt listened closely to the voice, realizing he'd heard it before. "Inside you will find two tickets to Rome in the same names of the passports we've provided. I apologize for not consulting you on the names, but there was a bit of a rush in getting the paperwork through. I hope the names are acceptable."

Wyatt laughed. "I am ambivalent about 'Roger' he said."

"I hadn't even looked at mine," Rashmi said. "I'm hoping it isn't Trudy. I hated the only Trudy I've ever known. But what happens in Rome?"

"You use your new credit cards to buy tickets. Rashmi, I want you to fly straight to Singapore. Get a tourist visa on arrival, and you will be met at the airport. A driver will have a placard with your new name on it. I've got some work for you to do . . . I assume you want to work?"

"Of course. If it's interesting work, that is."

"I think you'll find it is that and more. And it pays well. You can settle here for a bit and see if you like it. If not, well, you have a passport and you'll have money."

"That's marvelous."

"What about me, do I stay in Rome?" Wyatt asked.

Boone chuckled and suddenly Wyatt knew where he'd heard the voice. "Wyatt, you can go wherever you damn well please. You will anyway, or so I am reliably informed. Still, I'd like to know where you'd like to try next. We need to stay in touch for any number of reasons."

That sounded promising and interesting. And suddenly Wyatt knew why the voice was familiar. "Sindi?"

"Boone," she said firmly.

"I know that voice."

"Sindi is a frivolous party girl, not the kind of person who arranged international escapes for wanted fugitives."

He was being chastened. "Okay then, Boone . . . I'm not certain. Progreso was nice, but that place is burned for me now."

"That's true enough. And moving to another beach in Mexico wouldn't fool anyone for long. You have to assume they will be looking for you as long as you pose a threat. The thing is, I think you will always pose a threat."

"Me?"

She laughed again. "You. Your very existence is a threat to them because you can't stop meddling and you are smarter than they are. Bad combination."

"I've heard that the Celebes Islands are nice," he said.

"They are, only they call it Sulawesi these days. So start there. When you arrive in Rome, I'll leave a package for you with the FedEx desk in the arrival terminal. It will have information on flights. I think your best bet will be Etihad Airways going to Jakarta via Abu Dhabi and onward, but I'll check. I'll have a bank account there that will be in your new name, and I'll see that you have a hotel room for your first night in Makassar as well."

"Wow. But where is Makassar?"

"It's the capital of Sulawesi, Wyatt."

"Oh."

"I think this will be quite an adventure for you. You don't know anything about the place."

"That's what makes it an adventure," he said happily.

"And that's what makes you such a danger to the ones after you, friend."

"How can we thank you?" Rashmi asked.

"Well, you will work your ass off for me. That and seeing you slip through their fingers is rewarding enough. And Wyatt, we will need your help from time to time."

"Writing code?"

"It's what you do best, right? Rescuing you two was a joint venture, the work of a lot of individuals unwilling to let you die because you wanted to think for yourselves. This isn't the first job like this we've done, and it won't be the last. And there are many other important jobs that need doing—high-tech interventions that are essential. We have made it a goal to do what we can to stop whoever tries to take away our freedom to enjoy the beaches of Mexico or Sulawesi. I thought you might want in on that now that you've tasted blood."

"Have we stopped this bunch?" he asked. "It seems like we left things half finished."

"Not really. Rashmi added some code for us based on work you did and the information you provided. It won't make the system what we want it to be, but we've put a thorn in their side and made sure they know there is an opposition party that is competent. The system won't be what they wanted. It will work the way Rashmi wanted it to in the first place; it will be a clean little financial transaction system that lacks the bells and whistles that the IMF and other people were adding to it."

"How will it get there?"

"The one they've got will crash. And then your pal Hoenig will provide the system we want."

"Claude will do that? I don't get it. Is he working with you too?"

"He is for the moment, but he doesn't know it. We, all of us, managed to push things in a direction where a clever man like that is going to see that he can be a hero by doing what we want. Of course, he doesn't know we want it, but putting up a clean system will strengthen his hand."

"I'm unsure where he stands in all this," Wyatt said.

"Nor am I. But that's the easiest way to resolve the Tanzanian situation, trash the Retinger Oculistica's plan without bringing down the government in the process. That part suits all sides."

"Who?"

"I forget you wouldn't know. Józef Retinger was a Polish politician who was exiled by the communists after the Second World War. He was a founder of the European Movement and the Council of Europe. He initiated meetings that led to the founding of the Bilderberg Group in 1954. The Retinger Oculistica is a secret group within the Bilderberg Group—dangerous, powerful people who are hell-bent on seeing their globalist vision played out."

"Secret?"

"That's the Oculistica part. They are unknown to most governments. Each person belongs to various international agencies, both openly and covertly, and wields amazing power. They use existing agencies to push the world in the direction they want."

"And we are fighting them?"

"We are. How this little skirmish plays out in the long run remains to be seen. There will be a power struggle within the group as this unravels. Losers do not prosper there. Hoenig can only benefit."

"He's a good guy," Wyatt said.

"But a true believer. I can imagine that with his background, Hoenig is a formidable enemy when he wants to be, and he did let them throw Wyatt to the wolves, although he didn't have anything to say about."

"Speaking of being thrown to the wolves, I'm worried about my sister," Wyatt said.

"She's fine. Rebecca explained the situation and we've had her watched. You can call her on this phone when you get to Rome. Use the Paladin App. It's our own little encryption scheme. She can download it to her phone from bitpats.com; the site will recognize her phone and yours."

"Sweet," Wyatt said.

"And now, I need to go on camera and tell the world that the Sandals Resort here in wherever I am is the best place on the face of the earth for a vacation."

"I'll want to see that one."

"You know where to find them," she said.

"I'm going to Sulawesi," he said, letting it sink in.

"I've got a job in Singapore," Rashmi said.

Wyatt gave her a broad smile. "Look at the two of us . . . a couple of frigging terrorists traveling in the finance minister's plane, even if it is leased, heading off to the ends of the earth. Who woulda thunk it?"

Rashmi closed the box. "Boone, apparently." She trembled slightly.

"Where's that flight attendant?" Wyatt said. "We need a stiff drink to toast the fight that lies ahead and bitpats everywhere."

"Yes," she said, closing her eyes and leaving Wyatt to wonder what was going on inside that beautiful head. Even under other circumstances, Rashmi was not the kind of woman he was drawn to. They were far too different. But as a friend or someone on your team, he thought she was incredible.

And Boone seemed to be that way too.

Rashmi opened her eyes again and smiled at him. "Being associated with these people is a heady experience," she said.

She was right. Suddenly Wyatt was getting new perspectives. "Is that good?"

"It means that life is strange and good, and suddenly, rather promising again. It reminds me of my first days in London when things were clear."

"Clear is good," he agreed. So was strange.

CHAPTER 38
THE PRICE OF SUCCESS

"For the powerful, crimes are those that others commit."

—NOAM CHOMSKY
IMPERIAL AMBITIONS: CONVERSATIONS ON THE POST-
9/11 WORLD (AMERICAN EMPIRE PROJECT)

CARTAGENA APARTMENTS
BOCA GRANDE
CARTAGENA, COLOMBIA

Long before she went to Dar es Salaam on Claude Hoenig's dime, as soon as she made the deal with Mitch Childer and was certain that Hoenig's company had the job, Peggy began arranging her escape. Even if she was able to pull her stunt off perfectly, eventually they'd figure it out. Then they would come after her. So, as soon as the system was launched, she needed to be out of there, to be somewhere they couldn't find her. Naturally, the act of disappearing would make them suspect she'd done something, but it was worth tipping them off to make certain she was well underground before they decided to hunt her down.

They wouldn't be pleased. None of them.

The lovely time sailing from Trinidad to Cartagena with Billy and Frieda had not only helped shake off any tail she might've picked up, it had done a lot to help her unwind. As a bonus, she'd been able to monitor the situation in Tanzania by listening to the BBC business news on the shortwave radio. All seemed to be going well. With luck, she hadn't even been missed.

As part of her preparations, she'd leased this lovely apartment in Cartagena. It was in a high-rise building in Boca Grande, situated south of the old walled city, well away from the charming winding streets and throngs of partiers. Boca Grande was a peninsula famed for its beaches, and the apartment had a grand view of the Caribbean. It was owned by a man she'd met in her hacking days. The man owned many places like this and kept them as investments that also had other uses. He bought them with money he'd embezzled from the corporation he worked for. When he was found out, they made great places to hide, and now he was delighted to let Miss X, as he knew her, rent the place for a few months. After that, well, part of what she needed to do in Colombia was make some dark web contacts that would establish her somewhere else, as someone else.

The plan had been put on hold. There was no rush to move, and no dangers in doing so. They'd be looking for her—she knew that because a few days after arriving, the news of the problems with Tanzania's financial system had started showing up.

At first, it had been all peaches and cream. People were signing up to use the system in droves; banks were putting more of their resources into it and adding services through the system; the price of the cryptocurrency, the e-Shilingi, soared from its launch price, which was in parity with the Tanzanian shilingi. The government officially declared their system a success.

As Peggy's e-Shilingi wallet filled with money collected in transaction fees, she converted much of it to Euros. The rate at which the cryptocurrency flowed into her wallet was small at first, but she was soon amazed at how fast it came. She had intended to keep much of it, but now, sensing that there was something wrong, she rushed to convert more. It wasn't working as she planned. The percentage she had programmed the system to steal for her was tiny, so the volume of transactions had to be enormous, and it couldn't be that big. She had no way to check that. She hadn't thought to create any tools that would let her monitor the system—she hadn't given a damn about the system beyond wanting it to last long enough to give her a substantial amount of money.

It had done that and more—enough more to make her nervous. And then, this sunny and humid morning when she plugged her hardware wallet into her laptop and checked it, she found her worst-case scenario had come to pass—the money had stopped flowing completely. She'd been found out, or at least the money had been redirected for some reason.

She'd thought her approach, making the percentage small, would keep her under the radar. The idea came from reading about the fabled "salami technique," a technique that was used by crooked accountants back when accounting first went online. The computers of that time were programmed to only handle amounts down to the penny. Anything less was ignored—the data entry 'rounded down' to the nearest penny. Some accountants realized that this was a golden opportunity. If they captured those thousandths of a cent being lost in data entry and deposited them in an account for a large company with a high volume of transactions, the money quickly added up into substantial amounts that, happily, would never be missed. They stole the money in tiny, thin slices, like salami at a deli.

Peggy's salami, however, had quickly turned into a huge monster of a sausage and, although she had no idea how or why, she was sure that her transaction module was what was slowing the system and increasing the processing time. She'd screwed up and something wasn't working right—a tiny error was increasing over time, consuming large amounts of processing time and resources.

As she paced her apartment, sipping a fine chardonnay, she mulled over the risks, the possibilities, her options. The thing protecting her was that no one could trace the location the money was being sent to—a hardware wallet that she owned. They might guess, but they couldn't prove a link between her and that wallet. Not without getting the hardware in their hands, along with her private key, that is.

The way she'd structured things, the worst case or what seemed to have happened, was that someone had figured out what was going on and changed the address the money was sent to—now they were stealing the money. That was a simple thing if you knew what to look for, but, of course, that wouldn't have fixed the problem. According to the reports, the system had serious problems. The news media were, rather gleefully it seemed, reporting massive slowdowns in transaction processing times. This was international news because the failure of the system was threatening the country's standing within the Society for Worldwide Interbank Financial Telecommunication (SWIFT) cooperative—essential for being able to conduct worldwide business. The price of the e-Shilingi was falling rapidly and taking the country's fiat currency with it. It was all collapsing.

Hungry to know more, she turned her television on to a business channel that was monitoring the situation as live, breaking news. "The Finance Minister of Tanzania has announced that the system was compromised by a terrorist who managed to infiltrate the coding team. He had been captured and was awaiting trial."

"Poor Wyatt," she thought. They'd held back the news of his arrest for a moment just like this one. That was clever of them and bad for Wyatt. She felt bad about him taking the fall, but better him than her. She would've preferred that it was Rashmi Patel, but you didn't always control the outcome of the plans you set in motion.

As she watched, the minister himself, not just that stupid flunky Haki Dola, came on screen. "With this revelation," he said, "that someone compromised the system in a feeble attempt to cripple the government, we have determined the best course of action. This afternoon, the system will be taken down for an hour; later it will be rebooted using a completely new program that our consultants wrote independently from the one currently in use. This backup program has been thoroughly tested. Due to the attempted manipulation of our economy, however, I am suspending trading in the e-Shilingi until further notice. The fluctuating price of our novel cryptocurrency is adding unnecessary chaos when the focus should be on obtaining the smooth, rapid, stable, and inexpensive financial transactions the people and institutions of Tanzania were promised."

"Jesus," she swore darkly as she began to understand what was happening. "The bastards have already rebooted the system with new code." That's what ended her income stream. They didn't want to announce the event and have the world watching if the reboot didn't work. So they'd done it in secret and now they could play out a successful relaunch. "Maybe getting a bigger early payout was the way to go after all," she said to the finance minister who was then abruptly replaced by a svelte blonde talking about her new book on positive thinking for investors.

Despite all the madness in Tanzania, and the twists and turns her code had created, Peggy was pleased. Things had worked out all right for her. She already had enough money socked away in a Cayman Island bank to see her through several self-indulgent lifetimes. And now she was out of it completely. She'd keep the worthless crypto that was still in her hardware wallet just in case it made a comeback, but she'd delete all other references to her work on the system from her laptop.

That afternoon the government of Tanzania made the anticlimactic announcement that the system was rebooted and working successfully. The price of the already purchased e-Shilingi cryptocurrency now sat at a fraction of a US penny, but that didn't matter. Not to the government anyway, although Peggy was aware of a number of stakeholders who would be less than pleased, including Hoenig. He mentioned that they were getting part of their payment in the new crypto as an incentive to make it work. If any of them ever found her, they'd blame her, and there would be hell to pay.

Over the next few days, Peggy filled the time out as best she could. She went to the beach a few times, drank too much, and watched as the story faded from the news. Something that had been broken but was now fixed was hardly worth covering. The success of the system had been tarnished, but that wasn't news either. The real news was that the failure had been due to a terrorist attack, and the government had rapidly responded with transparency. The money lost by investors in the cryptocurrency was hardly a blip that rated only a mention alongside that of a new bear market in US government bonds.

During those days, Peggy became increasingly bored and restless. Despite planning to stay in hiding, the idleness of the life, especially when she had all the money she'd ever need sitting in the bank, was something she hadn't counted on. The reality was that hiding out as a rich woman wasn't the least bit exciting. The truth was she'd envisioned herself surrounded by, and partying with, dashing young people. She imagined that with her money, she'd have her pick of lovely, sexy men and women. Unfortunately, being out in public, especially in high-profile places, before she arranged some plastic surgery to alter her appearance, wasn't a good idea—it wouldn't be safe.

Much to her dismay, all the top plastic surgeons turned out to have long waiting lists. She hadn't counted on a stupid waiting list. Reluctantly, unable to think of alternatives, she was now on several waiting lists. And waiting. And fidgeting. The risk was enormous. Those international creeps would be after her blood, and facial recognition software and closed-circuit monitoring was used everywhere. Even if Interpol didn't have a warrant for her arrest, plenty of the people upset with her would have access to their resources. Hell, Hoenig probably had access to NSA resources. She needed to lay low.

But she also had to keep from going crazy.

Meeting people was hard to do when you were afraid to go out. Without an airtight identity, she had to limit the places she went and the people she met. She wondered if she should've stayed on the boat and gone around the world with Billy and Frieda. At least she'd get laid that way. But now she had no idea where they were.

The bitch of her situation was hiding out without knowing if it was necessary, being cautious, and looking over your shoulder when you didn't even know for sure if anyone was even looking for you. For all she knew, she hadn't even been missed.

That, she thought, would be good.

At some point, slightly drunk and lonely, she called Franz. It was a whim, a crazy impulse rooted in frustration and desperation. He'd sounded glad to hear from her. When she called, it was to hear the sound of his voice, but as they talked, she found she ached for him. "Come see me," she said.

And why not? No one knew Franz. Some of the people had met him, but he was a fucking waiter from Zurich. No one but a really good mindless fuck, she thought, and then she laughed at herself. She was so lonely, so horny, that she wanted to import the fucking waiter.

"I could do that," he said. "I have no money, though."

His reply startled her. She hadn't expected that. She reminded herself that the guy thought she had money. He'd thought that all along, based on the fancy rooms she had, and she'd let him think it. Now it was true. "I'll buy you a ticket," she said. She felt reckless doing that, and it felt so damn good to be doing something that she let herself enjoy the feeling. She was an outlaw, after all, a thief, not a cloistered monk. Outlaws did wild shit.

So after they hung up, she bought him a ticket for that day and sent him the e-ticket. Then she arranged for an Uber ride for him from the airport on his arrival.

She took another drink and laughed, happy. After all, this is the kind of crazy shit she wanted the money for, so she could do things like this.

What better use of the money than to fly a stud halfway around the world so he could screw her senseless. That was what she needed and wanted.

The day he was to arrive she arranged for a catered meal, had the liquor store deliver a case of wine and several bottles of bourbon that she knew Franz liked, and then, just before he was to arrive, she bathed and put on a lacy nightie, wanting to set the tone for their reunion.

Then she waited impatiently. The knock that finally came got her heart pounding. She opened it and saw him there, smiling, looking as eager as she felt.

Their greeting was wordless and passionate. He dropped his bag inside the door, grabbed her in a hug, kissing her; then he then scooped her off her feet and carried her to her bedroom. He put her on the bed, tearing the nightie off her, then he undressed her and took her with an exciting violence. His touch, those magic caresses, the way his lovemaking focused on her, sent her into a delirium of pleasure that left her limp. She'd always wondered what it meant to be ravished . . . now she knew.

After a short time, he got up and got them each a drink. Bringing them back, he sat beside her and they looked into each other's eyes, sipping the bourbon, and she felt arousal welling up again. "Now something special," he said.

She lay there, tingling, wondering as he went out of the room and came back with his bag. He opened it and took out some soft ropes. She watched, unresisting as he tied her wrists to the headboard, then tied her ankles to her wrists. This, she thought, would be exciting. She'd never been bound before.

And it was. He took her that way—with her feeling an unaccustomed helpless. She wouldn't like it that way all the time, but the novelty of it, especially after the long period of boredom, made it erotic.

When he came, he left her that way. She tugged at the bonds. "Undo me."

"I need you to tell me where it is," he said.

"What?"

"The wallet. The place you sent all that crypto. And the location of the fiat currency you converted it to."

Her heart pounded again, but this time from fear. Franz the waiter shouldn't know about any of this. "What are you talking about?"

"Childer told me about your little scheme," he said.

"You know Mitch Childer?"

"I work for him."

Knowing she'd been played, Peggy began to feel fear. "What do you want?"

"Osk Barstad confirmed that it had to be you who stole the crypto-currency, diverting it to a wallet. They want the wallet."

"That crypto is worthless. I saw that on the news."

"Yes. I know that. But I'm certain you didn't leave it in crypto. You aren't trusting enough to do that, and you knew the system would ultimately fail. After all, Peggy looks out for Peggy, doesn't she?"

"I don't know what you are talking about," she said, but her gut ached. He knew everything.

"You are going to give up the crypto wallet and the money. I'll take some of the cash, of course, and pass the rest along to them."

"No. It's mine."

He sighed. "Peggy, I am a professional and I have a few tools in my bag that will help you understand that you are, sooner or later, going to tell me what I want to know," he said. "The only problem with using them is that they will cripple you and certainly destroy your looks—no man will want you. Of course, Childer wants you dead so you can't talk."

"Please, Franz. We can . . ."

"I don't care if you live or die, to be honest. But I do want the money you have tucked away. That's why I'm here, no matter what Childer thinks. You are going to tell me where the wallet is and you will help me transfer that money to my account. You'll do it. It's just a question of how much pain you have to endure before you give it to me."

"But Franz . . ."

He reached into the bag and took out a laptop. "I even brought my own computer so I wouldn't have to depend on you having one. You aren't the most reliable person."

Peggy thought she might pass out. Franz was a brute—that had been part of his appeal. Now he terrified her. "If I give you the money, will you leave me alone?"

"Of course," he said. "If there is enough money, I'll let buy your freedom. For enough money, pretty Peggy, I'll keep you here for a time while I make certain that the money transfer is complete. I'll use the time to make arrangements for my own disappearance. Then I'll leave you in peace."

He sounded so calm, so sincere, that she was certain he was lying. "You are going to kill me." She said it flatly.

He sighed again. "That's true. I'm afraid I must. The people in charge will come after me if I let you live. If you are killed and I send them the hardware wallet, along with a substantial amount of money, they won't care if I disappear. But consider this, you still get a choice: you can die peacefully or painfully. But you do have to choose. In a moment or two, and until I get what I want, you will begin to experience great pain. If you resist with all the stubbornness that I know is in you, then you will be in pain for a long time. You will suffer. And for what? In the end, you will still die."

"I thought you cared about me." The plea sounded weak, even to her.

He laughed. "You were wrong. You were an assignment. Childer sent me to you in Zurich. You were a bitch to bed and then keep track of."

"Franz, let me live. We will have money, and I'll do anything you want."

He shook his head. "You sound out of character begging like that, Peggy. Besides, I'm going to have the money; you are easily replaced with someone of my own choosing."

He reached into the bag and took out a long knife. "I could start by skinning you, but you might not survive the shock of that, and besides, there are so many other interesting options to explore that are just as painful."

She heard a sound, then realized that it was her own scream of terror.

"These new high-rise apartments are wonderfully soundproofed," he said. "And I brought smelling salts, just in case you faint. I don't want you to miss a thing."

The look on his face made her entire body turn ice cold. The bastard would enjoy every moment of torturing the information out of her. Peggy didn't want to die, but she had done her share of suffering already. "You son of a bitch, untie me and give me the fucking computer," she said. "The hardware wallet is in the desk drawer."

He went into the living room and came back with the wallet. "This one?" She nodded.

As he untied her, she weighed her options, looked for an opportunity, some kind of opening, but she could sense his awareness. The man was skilled in just this sort of thing. "Who do you really work for?" she asked. "If you are going to kill me . . ."

"At the end of the day, I work for myself," he said. "Childer paid me to do certain jobs. He had me seduce you, intimidate your friend Wyatt . . . and now he requires my help cleaning up his mess, which includes you and your colleagues."

And that told the story of this entire project, Peggy thought as she took the laptop and went to her bank's website. Everyone involved was working for themselves. No wonder it was all turning to shit, including her dream, her goddamn plan. It wasn't fair.

CHAPTER 39
WRAPPING THINGS UP

"If you lose a big fight, it will worry you all of your life. It
will plague you—until you get your revenge."

—MUHAMMAD ALI

GOETHE
SECHSELÄUTENPLATZ 10
ZURICH, SWITZERLAND

Claude Hoenig sat in the plush chair in Goethe, a fancy bar situated
on the ground floor of the *Neue Zürcher Zeitung* newspaper offices.
He watched Mitch Childer sip his drink, noting how Childer's eyes
drifted, how his gaze seemed to wander around the bar. The man's
lack of focus made Hoenig uneasy. Normally, the man focused his
attention on him like a laser. This should have been a relief, but it was
creepy. He wondered if that was the purpose.

It was time to take the edge back. "Why are we here, Mitch?"

Seeing Childer flinch was his reward. The familiarity of using his
first name unsettled him. It was almost too easy.

"Why? To discuss this disaster—of your making."

"My making? How can that be, Mitch? I understood that the
disaster was caused by a terrorist attack. I mean, that's what's on the
news on every channel. It must be true."

The sarcasm made Childer's scowl tighten. "The Tanzanian government wasn't inclined to tell the truth about what happened, that's
all. They grabbed onto having Wyatt in custody as a convenient
explanation that exonerates them entirely. But we need to talk about
what really happened."

"Which is?"

"Your employee, Ms. Dory, added code to the system . . . a function that didn't work correctly and brought the system down."

"Gee, I'm confused, Mitch. I thought Wyatt Osgood was supposed to be the one who tampered with the code. Now it's Peggy? How convenient that it wasn't one of the locals we were forced to use."

"It was her. Mr. Osgood had nothing to do with that. Peggy Dory completely redid the code after his arrest. She told us she found out what he did and stripped it out. She said the system was functional. At first, it seemed to be exactly what it was supposed to be, but either she screwed up or deliberately booby-trapped the system. Of course, you already know all about the failure of the system. And you know what happened next. You provided the clean code for the reboot. You were amazingly well prepared."

He smiled. "I did as I was told to do. I wrote a new system from the original specifications and eliminated the speculative sales of the cryptocurrency."

"You were told to do this? By whom? Why wasn't I told of these preparations?"

"I got the impression that you had become part of the problem." Claude had no intention of telling Childer who had told him to do it. "That might be why you weren't told."

"I was running the project and I gave no such instructions."

"And so now, you instructed me to come here so you could complain and get in my face. This is one of those command performances where you drag me across the ocean to remind me of who is in charge. I suppose you also think that gives you a lovely chance to dump all the blame on me, on my team, and move along as if nothing happened."

"Management always involves elements that are simply there to remind people of the pecking order," Childer said. "Other elements are for training. When you teach a dog a trick, it's important to be clear what is expected. That can require having him do things that are not necessarily relevant to the desired outcome."

Hoenig smiled at the attempt to insult him by comparing him to a dog. Childer couldn't know the advantage Hoenig had—he didn't give a shit what the man thought of him. Besides, he liked dogs. "The dog usually does things to please the master and because he is given a treat afterward. Where's my treat?"

"If he follows the instructions, he gets a treat. But not if he bites the hand that feeds him. You see, this terrorist story would've been fine for public consumption. Throwing Osgood to the wolves to be torn apart would serve the purpose. But we didn't want him seen publicly. We didn't want him talking."

"He might tell the world about some things you'd rather be kept quiet."

"And he wouldn't be the only one. It's come to my attention that you have been passing information on our activities along to your friends in your government."

Hoenig had to smile at this clever twist that painted him as less than committed to the project and possibly a spy. "My friends in government? No, I didn't tell my friends, but yes, I did talk to people in government. I filed the forms that I'm required to send in because I was employed as an agent of the Tanzanian government. That's US law and you know it. You knew it when you hired my firm. I won't risk having my government come after me for hiding anything. So I filed the forms, and when they came around asking, I told the CIA what I'm doing . . . because they asked. They knew we were meeting . . . you are an influential person, and they wanted to know why an ex-spy was spending so much time chatting with you. I told them about the project because I had to."

"You told them what we were doing despite a nondisclosure. Very disturbing."

"I gave them an outline of what we were doing. I didn't tell them anything they couldn't get from public documents from the IMF, your people, and the World Bank. As it turns out, I didn't even have the entire picture to give them. I didn't know about the little chores you asked Peggy to perform. At the time, I didn't realize that you had her working directly for you."

Childer's eyes twitched. "She was just adding some features."

"That you kept secret."

"And I suppose you told your government about those."

He laughed. "No, but only because I didn't know about them at the time."

"Your loyalty to your government is touching but misplaced."

"It's not only my government; they are also a big client."

"For the moment. You need to see what's happening, Hoenig. This is the beginning of a huge change. National governments, and nationalism itself, have had their day. They are anachronisms in this global world. The multinational corporation was the beginning of the end of their reign. As they've grown in prominence, they've fought the current of conflicting, often contradictory regulations. They've come to see that you can't have nations squabbling over their own interests. They are interfering with international progress like spoiled children fighting over toys."

"That's one reason those corporations hire lobbyists—to try and get the laws and regulations standard from country to country. That approach is probably inefficient, but even companies are still typically rooted in one country, both culturally and legally. New regulations, new attitudes by consensus, need to evolve."

"They only play that game because they're forced to be rooted that way. It's another stupid touch of nationalism that, like people, corporations that sprawl across the world, and are intimately involved in many countries, must declare whose primary jurisdiction they will be under. They need that appearance of nationality, even it it's bogus, but squabbling nations interfere with commerce and growth. They destroy what could be effective programs for ensuring peace and prosperity. They are impediments to public health. Think of the times governments have rejected outside help because their enemies might receive help, or simply because it might make them appear weak."

"You might be right," Claude said. The conversation tired him. Politics tired him. Ninety percent of political rhetoric never went beyond hot air. "That might be true enough, but I still have to operate under US law. My business, my life, my freedom are protected that way. Without the government, I don't have a future."

Childer clucked. "Such a narrow and limited perspective when the future is so promising. Or it was promising. As far as you are concerned, there isn't much future working with me. This project was not well run."

"The limitation, saying only one of my people could be on site, certainly tied my hands."

"True, but then there is whatever Peggy Dory was doing . . . her unauthorized alterations to the system. That doesn't reflect well on you."

"No, it doesn't. I shouldn't have trusted her, but given that I had to manage her and the entire project remotely because of your rules . . . so I wouldn't know what you intended, well, the point is that I didn't know she was altering the specifications. I certainly didn't, and I still don't think that she was stupid enough to do something that would deliberately bring the system down. If she was the cause, then she screwed up. And where were your people during the launch?"

"My people?"

"When we established the working protocol, you had people who were expected to test it before it was launched. That was their entire job, as I recall. The system seems to have passed the testing. So why not blame them?"

Childer rubbed his chin. "Yes, that's true. However, as it happened, Rashmi Patel had to be suspended from the project when Wyatt was arrested. There was a suspicion that she was involved in what he was doing. Peggy did the testing herself."

"And then disappeared before I even gave her a bonus. Suspicious, assuming she is alive."

"The problem is. . . . well, this isn't in the press, but Rashmi has disappeared. As has Wyatt Osgood."

He gave Hoenig a meaningful look. "Wyatt escaped from jail?" That was a surprise.

"So it seems. Apparently, he had high-tech help to do it. While he was in his cell, someone hacked into the jail system computers and issued a bogus release order. Someone also hacked the system that schedules the finance minister's plane. A rented limo took two people to the airport and the finance minister's jet flew them to Kenya. The crew identified Mr. Osgood and Ms. Patel as the passengers."

"So you think that Rashmi Patel hacked the systems and got Wyatt out?"

Childer arched his eyebrows. "We have no idea who did it. I assume she did, but it doesn't really matter now. We'll find them both, and the truth will come out."

Suddenly Childer's angle dawned on him. "You think I did it?"

"You have the expertise and means."

"And my motive?"

"Sentimental attachment to your employee?"

"Fair enough. Truth be told, it didn't occur to me or I might've done it. Under most circumstances, I'm far too law-abiding for my own good."

"Then you might help us catch them. Then we'd find out who was behind this."

"The real terrorists, you mean?" Hoenig was beginning to wonder what was going on. The day was turning out to be one of quite a few revelations. He suspected that there were more forces at work than he knew about, more than Childer was aware of.

Peggy pulling a double cross wasn't a huge surprise, but he didn't think that Rashmi and Wyatt were capable of such good spy craft. And if he hadn't helped them, someone very resourceful, and who was no friend of the project, had stepped in. "I could look for them if you like. I still have contacts in the world that deal with identity."

"No. That's not necessary. I have my own people and resources. I called you here to tell you that you are fired. I'm not at all happy with your firm, and it won't be working on future projects with us. We, you and I, are done." Childer coughed. "I must tell you that I'm not totally convinced that whatever Ms. Dory was up to was unknown to you. She didn't strike me as a particularly inventive person."

"Then you don't read people well at all, Childer. Her creativity is her finest quality. But I see you've decided to blame this all on Peggy. She's the villain of convenience."

"Not her alone. She couldn't and wouldn't have done this alone. As I said, the disappearance of Ms. Patel and Mr. Osgood make them suitable candidates as accomplices."

"If you do catch up with them and if any of them talk . . ."

Childer looked at him calmly. "They aren't going to have a chance to do any talking. I've already talked to Interpol and other officials who understand the problem with letting them have access to anyone. No, once they are captured everything will be tidied up nicely." He licked his lips. "As a matter of fact, and this is something for you to consider, Mr. Hoenig, I have a lead as to her whereabouts. Shortly, I'll know who she was working with. If there is anything you'd like to tell me. . . ."

"That little tidbit doesn't intimidate me, Mitch. You see, I'm telling the truth. I wasn't involved in her scheme. I was being well paid for the work we were doing and happy with the arrangement, at least financially. The potential to earn more was all I wanted. I had no need to do anything to damage the system. As it is, we all have egg on our faces from what's happened. It was a high-profile failure."

Childer twisted his lips. "It's not pleasant being embarrassed at the failure of something like this, but we can recover from that and we have gained some critical information. We have moved a step closer."

"Toward what?" Hoenig asked. "This was a joke."

Childer caught himself. "A plan to build a system that does work. This one, even the system you finally brought up, was a useful test of a rather minimal system. The banks are happy; although the loss of the cryptocurrency is a shame, this software can be the basis for the next one."

"And there always has to be a next one, and it always has to be bigger, huh?"

"Yes. We don't stand still. In my world, there is always a more comprehensive and overarching plan. That's how things progress, and the IMF and World Bank have lofty goals. To that end, I'll expect you to send me the code from both this version of the system and the one that didn't work. I intend to have it analyzed and then fixed by competent contractors. Not you."

Hoenig knew he was smiling without intending to. A smile would be the last thing Childer expected and being able to surprise him added to his pleasure. "That's fine. You got some valuable things from this project and so did I."

"You did?"

"Actually, yes. I've seen enough, learned enough about this kind of project. As you say, there will be others, even if they aren't with you."

"Any government that wants to have the banking industry on their side will want my people involved."

"Oh well, then."

"You don't seem upset at all. That surprises me."

"Even Americans can sometimes understand being in something for the long haul, Mr. Childer. And that means you don't hit a home run every time at the plate—or score a goal every time you kick the ball, to use a European metaphor. We failed. I've lost some people. Now it is time to lick my wounds and move on. Believe me, there will be other opportunities."

"Well, I can't see how, but perhaps there will." Childer stood and adjusted his suit coat. "And now I must move on as well."

"To Washington or Zurich?"

He smiled. "To the Ukraine, actually. Yet another government thinks that with our help it can lower its transaction costs and position itself on the cutting edge of this blockchain movement." Hoenig was sure the man didn't know he was sneering.

As Childer turned and walked out, Hoenig sighed. Then he picked up his phone and typed "on his way" into WhatsApp and hit send.

"Ready," was the message that came back.

Claude Hoenig couldn't honestly say that he ever liked Peggy, although sometimes she had been fun to work with. He did understand that she was marked now. She'd put herself on an international shitlist— if they caught her, she was doomed. He was sympathetic, but she had put her own neck in the noose by thinking she could pull off a scam at the international level. It was easy to see that she underrated the politicians and bureaucrats she was conning and didn't understand the stakes. As stupid as some of the people were, it must've seemed like a cakewalk.

He doubted that Rashmi Patel or Wyatt Osgood had ever been anything but pawns, if even that. After all, he had no idea whose pawns they would've been. Clearly, Wyatt was set up because he learned something about the system functions that he wasn't supposed to know. He'd learned it at the specific moment that needed someone to blame for the current setback. The most likely scenario was that he discovered what Peggy was doing and Childer was worried about him telling the world what the IMF was up to.

And Rashmi . . . there was a cipher. He didn't really know her. If she had helped Wyatt escape, who knew what her reasons were?

Hoenig liked Wyatt. The cantankerous, anarchistic coder was good people, even if his ideas were unpalatable. And if Rashmi had helped Wyatt out, then Hoenig owed her for that, even if he didn't know her. Childer turning down his offer to help find them spoke volumes—he didn't want them to live and go to trial. That would be an unnecessary waste of good people.

He thought of his best friend Turner who was still in the CIA. He could contact Turner and tell him the story. He could ask him to put out the word that any misleading information about the where-abouts of Rashmi Patel and Wyatt Osgood that was passed along to Interpol would be considered a favor. Maybe he'd be willing to do a little hand-waving that would give them a head start. It was surpris-ing they'd gotten this far and a little, subtle help might just be enough to get them somewhere safe. Even if the Tanzanian government per-sisted in claiming that the system was brought down by terrorists, Interpol wouldn't be expending too many resources, or much time, chasing what was, at worst, essentially a white-collar crime.

It was ironic that Childer, just like Peggy, hadn't considered the stakes carefully enough before getting into the game. He thought he was protected because of his position. Claude Hoenig had seen it before with guys like that—they were like comets that shoot across the heavens and look like something special in the firmament. In the end, they found out that they were still subject to gravity, like the rest of the herd. Childer was certainly a player, but he was about to learn that he was completely replaceable.

He picked up the phone and made a call. A man answered. Hoenig pictured him—those piercing green eyes set in the dark face. He smiled, thinking of the team he'd put on the task of finding a name to go with that fierce visage. "It's in motion now," he said.

"Let me know how it goes."

"It will be on the news tonight. Watch it yourself."

"All right. Are you prepared to get on with the other things we discussed?"

"Yes. I've hired the right people for the task. Ukraine, correct?"

"How did you know?" The man sounded displeased.

"A little bird from the IMF just sang that tune to me."

"Not a bird singing," the man said. "Simply one last gasp from that leak before it is plugged."

"Completely."

When he hung up, Hoenig waved a hand to summon the waiter and ordered a double scotch. His new staff needed to get up to speed fast. They'd be doing a lot of projects for the new management. And all of the jobs he'd be working on would be stuff that Turner would be delighted to hear about. Information was better than gold—it was his personal crypto. It was just as volatile, and he intended to invest it wisely.

He glanced at his phone. A news alert had met his search criteria. An American woman had committed suicide in Cartagena. She'd jumped from the roof of a high-rise apartment building. She'd been identified as Peggy Anne Dory. The motive for her suicide was unknown and she left no note behind; the government had no record of her entering the country. The local government was launching an investigation to see if the building complied with all relevant building and safety codes.

He shook his head and ordered another double scotch and raised his glass. "Here's to you, Peggy, you poor bitch."

CHAPTER 40
COLLATERAL DAMAGE

"If your enemy is secure at all points, be prepared for him. If he is in superior strength, evade him. If your opponent is temperamental, seek to irritate him. Pretend to be weak, that he may grow arrogant. If he is taking his ease, give him no rest. If his forces are united, separate them. If sovereign and subject are in accord, put division between them. Attack him where he is unprepared, appear where you are not expected."

—Sun Tzu
The Art of War

ANDWELE'S OFFICE
MINISTRY OF FINANCE
DAR ES SALAAM, TANZANIA

There was little left to do, Andwele thought. There was nothing at all that he could do to salvage his own situation, and there nothing useful he could contribute that might solve the bigger problems. He was helpless.

That feeling of helplessness began the moment he discovered that the system was crashing. It had increased when he went to Rashmi's apartment and found that she was gone. Since then, it had continued to grow.

Learning that she and Wyatt were both gone, that someone had engineered the programmer's release from jail, made him feel dizzy and totally disconnected.

This was not the right working of things. The world was not supposed to be a place where doing your job got you in such an impossible situation. It wasn't a place where a girl like Rashmi could stand up to the government and walk away with whatever she wanted. Better people than Rashmi, more powerful people, had decided that Wyatt would be punished for the mistakes that had been made. Yet she had defied them. She'd taken their scapegoat out from under their noses.

That left a vacuum—an unmet need for people to take the blame, and a few candidates who were sufficiently powerless. After all, a scapegoat couldn't be someone with the means to fight back, someone who was able to publicly defend themselves. That would never do. So Andwele suspected that he would be high on the list.

Of course, a lot depended on who had the ear of the finance minister. In all fairness, none of the blame was his. He'd been presented with an idea that had been vetted by his own people, as well as the IMF and the World Bank. And the idea, Andwele was convinced, had been a good one. It was the implementation that tore things apart. If they'd simply done it themselves, without fanfare, the system would have been almost exactly what it was now.

Hoenig told him that the minimalist system would save the day and it had. The idea of a cryptocurrency was dead, but the rest of the benefits of the new system were real. Even the banks, who had lost money due to investing in the crypto, were admitting that. Things were basically good.

"What went wrong?" the finance minister asked him in private, with only Haki Dola in attendance.

"We couldn't have known," Haki Dola said plaintively. "The system wasn't what we wanted. It should've worked."

"What went wrong?" the finance minister asked again, looking past Haki Dola and right at Andwele. Oddly, the look was reassuring.

"Too much complexity in the system," he said. "After examining what had gone on, that was the inescapable conclusion. And complex systems tend to fail."

"Why was it so complex? I don't understand that. Did you underestimate the task?"

Andwele shook his head. "Even if the task was more complex than we envisioned, it wasn't anything new or groundbreaking. The problem was that everyone involved with the implementation added things."

"Without permission?"

"Without our knowledge. We had no idea that any functions were being added. Now we know that Mr. Childer apparently asked Ms. Dory to add features that had nothing to do with the transactions. She took notes and left them behind. They compromised the system. She added some things that we don't yet understand."

The finance minister looked at him, making certain that it was clear that he was still addressing Andwele and not Haki Dola. "What sort of things did Mr. Childer add?"

"He collected every bit of data that was available, on the nature of the transactions, histories of the people involved . . . it turns out that when you combine the purchasing records of the populace with their banking information, you can learn a great deal about anyone."

The finance minister smiled. "I believe that Amazon has demonstrated the validity of that as a business model."

"Yes, Minister, that's true. We aren't entirely sure what it was all used for, but a great deal of that information seems to have been channeled into some computers that are used by the World Bank and Interpol."

"And none of you knew a thing about this?"

"We trusted the contractors who were vetted by the IMF," Haki Dola said, sweating profusely.

"The same IMF that caused part of the problem? You didn't question why they wanted hands-on involvement in implementing the system, did you?"

"No, sir," Andwele said. "I believe we were flattered to have them taking such an active role, selecting contractors and so on. It seemed to validate the whole program."

"And what about the programmer that you arrested. The one who escaped with the help of another programmer . . . your fiancé, I believe?"

Andwele shifted uncomfortably. "The story that the programmer, Wyatt Osgood, sabotaged the systems seems to have been a ruse the IMF used to keep him from finding out what they were doing. How the escape was perpetrated, and Ms. Patel's role in it, are mysteries. Interpol has warrants out for them, but I doubt there is actually any evidence against them for any crimes."

"I see," the finance minister said. He looked levelly at Haki Dola for the first time. "And was this actually the IMF, or simply this Mr. Childer, who was doing all this?"

Haki Dola quivered for a moment. "I'm not at all certain."

"Are we pressing charges against him? A trial would be messy, but it might be enlightening."

Dola looked at Andwele who sighed at his boss's distress. "I don't think any law was broken, Minister. If Childer accused the programmer falsely, he could sue personally . . . the changes to the code were breaches of protocol and procedure, but there doesn't seem to be a profit motive. And there is no crime against fouling up a computer system unless you can prove a malicious intent."

The finance minister snorted. "Then we are at the end of this."

"And we have a working system," Haki Dola said.

"At the expense of great political capital. The kindest thing I can say to you, Haki, is that you were a negligent and naive fool. I have to accuse myself of the same thing, of course, for I didn't look over your shoulder. I made the mistake of thinking you understood the importance of the project and would keep tabs on it. That makes me the fool. So now I am going to ask for your resignation."

"But Minister—"

"And I'll give serious thought to tendering my own, assuming the president doesn't ask for it outright." He looked at Andwele. "That leaves you."

Andwele sat up straight. "Sir, I . . ."

"You will continue monitoring the system, Mr. Kassain. I'll need you filling in for Deputy Minister Dola until I, in collaboration with the president and his cabinet, decide what actions to take."

"But we have the terrorists to blame," Haki Dola said. "Why must any of us suffer when we tell the world that it was sabotage?"

The finance minister's smile was thin. "Let's forget, for the moment, that the claim is total bullshit and consider the practical implications. First, your hacker is gone. You have no one to parade in front of the press. Besides, if we admit we were hacked, then how will we get the global financial community to believe that the system is safe now? No, we will plead incompetence and human error and let a few heads roll. We are already announcing that, through the brilliance of our techs, the problems were corrected and the system is now sound. We will say that we asked too much of the system."

"But the cryptocurrency? The world will say Tanzania failed to produce a national cryptocurrency."

The finance minister smiled. "If people ask about that, we will tell them that we tried to do far too much at once. We will explain that there are limits to what a cryptocurrency can do with the existing technology . . . in the face of tasks that the financial system required, plus those that the international agencies wanted to impose . . ." he smiled, "the crypto shrugged."

Haki Dola choked. "It shrugged?"

"Yes. It faltered and was unable to carry the load we'd imposed on it. So we eliminated it as a source of speculation, reduced its workload to that of being effective tokens, free of the distractions of trading, and found that it works marvelously."

"And now?" Andwele asked, not sure he wanted to hear more.

"Go about your tasks. Deputy Minister Dola, you will take care of yours immediately."

"Thank you, Minister," he said, seeing that they had been dismissed. As they left the office, Andwele chuckled.

"What's so funny," Dola demanded.

"The press release," Andwele told him. "Picture it. The communications people will tell the world that we built a system based around distributed ledgers and blockchain; that it was supplemented with lightning networks and worked perfectly, except the crypto shrugged."

"That isn't at all funny." Dola grabbed Andwele's jacket by the lapels. "This can't be the end, Andwele. You need to talk to the finance minister further. He seems to value your opinion. Go back in and insist that they bring back trading in the currency. Tell him the country shouldn't lose face."

"It seems he's already accepted a certain loss of face, and now he wants to move ahead, cutting the losses. Trying again would be a gamble."

"But everything I had is invested in it. I'm penniless."

"Haki, you know as well as I that I have no control over that decision. It was made before we went into that meeting. There won't be a national cryptocurrency anytime soon. The trades are all going to stay in fiat, digital, but in fiat currency. The government won't put its name on an attempt to resurrect the e-Shilingi. It's dead."

"Yes," Haki Dola said sullenly. He released Andwele's jacket and composed himself. "I suppose you are right, Andwele. But it is a bitter pill."

"I lost money too," he said.

"I lost money I don't have," Dola said simply, then he opened the door to his office and went in.

Andwele walked back to his own office where he accepted tea from his secretary and considered his options. They wanted him to stay, the finance minister said, but for how long? And did he have any kind of future with the government, or would the taint of the failure bury him where he was? Certainly, if anything else went wrong, if there was more blame to spread around, with Haki Dola gone it would fall on his shoulders.

It seemed a reasonable thing to simply gather his things from his desk and slink away, but then what? He needed to ride this out. Suddenly, he missed Rashmi. She was a smart woman who understood the nuances of things. For a woman, she understood a great deal. Of course, she was gone . . . somewhere, and even if she was here, she wouldn't help him. Not anymore. That bridge had been burned.

A commotion in the hallway caught his attention—shrieks and screams were heard. "Go see what's going on," he told his secretary. When she returned, she looked almost faint. "What is it?"

"It's the deputy minister," she said.

"What about him, girl?"

"He shot himself. He's lying dead in his office."

Andwele found himself staring at his own hands and resisting the urge to run out into the hallway, to run to Haki Dola's office and see for himself.

Blame was a terrible thing. It was unfeeling and ruthless in its persecution of a person. Haki Dola was something of a fool, and certainly an incompetent boss, but he didn't deserve this terrible fate.

Andwele picked up his phone to call the finance minister. Perhaps, if he faced things squarely, something good could come of this. Perhaps he could escape taking the blame for all that had gone wrong and avoid joining Haki Dola in disgrace. It might all blow over if the system kept working. After all, they weren't the perpetrators, nor were they the intended victims, if there were any. No, Haki Dola was simply collateral damage, although that made a stark and rather sad summary on the end of a life.

CHAPTER 41

SACRIFICIAL BUREAUCRAT

"The fundamental concept in social science is Power, in the same sense in which Energy is the fundamental concept in physics."

—BERTRAND RUSSELL
POWER: A NEW SOCIAL ANALYSIS

SOMEWHERE IN EUROPE

Mitch Childer sat sweating on a cold concrete slab in a warm, dank room. As far as he could tell, he was alone, but then he couldn't tell much. His head was covered with a dark, heavy cloth of some kind that was secured around his neck. It was difficult to breathe, and he couldn't see anything. His wrists were tied together behind his back and his ankles were tied together. It seemed like he'd been tied this way with his head covered for a long time. It felt like an eternity—he couldn't even guess how long it had actually been.

They had left him in this room to wait and worry. With the ropes tight enough to cut off his circulation, at first he had been uncomfortable, then the pain became agonizing. Now his ankles and wrists were numb.

Whoever these men were, they'd grabbed him as he stepped out of the Goethe, after his meeting with Hoenig. Unused to physical conflict, he'd put up no resistance as the two burly men grabbed him by the arms and swept him into a limousine that was waiting for them at the curb.

He was caught totally unprepared. He'd assigned two men to keep an eye on him, but had them wait outside. He had felt safe in the club.

But then he emerged, blinking in the bright sunlight, and was grabbed. The men, his captors, hadn't said a single word to him. As the car pulled away from the curb with him sitting between the two men, they covered his head with this bag, this dark cloth. Then they tied him up like a Christmas goose—rather roughly and totally unnecessarily, he thought. He had no chance of escaping these rough men.

When he was bound and they pushed him back in the seat, he spoke to them, calmly, reasonably. He wanted to learn something, to find out who they were and what they wanted with him. The damage was done; now he wanted to expedite things, get whatever was going to happen moving so that he could get through this and move on. He felt that if he could get them talking, then he could negotiate with them. He was a powerful man, with resources. "I'll pay you to let me go," he told them.

He got no answers. He might've been dealing with deaf-mutes for all his questions, his offers, got him. The men sat back, each one keeping one hand on his arm as if he might make a break for it.

They drove for a long time, not stopping. It was long enough for them to leave Switzerland entirely. They could be in Germany, Italy, or France for all he knew. Despite being familiar with them all, he had no way of knowing which direction they had headed when they left Zurich. Not that knowing what country he was in would help him, but Mitch Childer had spent his adult life using information to gain an advantage. In his world, knowledge was quite literally power. Not knowing where he was, why he'd been taken, what they wanted from him, all those unknowns contributed to his growing sense of helplessness, of being out of control. If he didn't know where he was, how would his people find him? He was a valuable commodity and his disappearance would be noticed sooner or later. Then they would search for him. He was sure that the green-eyed man had ways of finding him, as did Osk Barstad, but it would take time before they were aware that he'd been abducted. Hoenig had stayed behind and would assume that he'd gone to his meeting in Ukraine. So the trail would grow cold quickly. They'd never know when he disappeared, and even if they did, who would remember a limousine passing in the streets of Zurich, or notice where it had gone?

Given all the time he had to think, to dwell on his situation, Mitch Childer was able to come up with few possible scenarios to explain his capture. Wondering why he had been taken made his mind race. He was a powerful man, yes, and reasonably influential in financial and some political circles, but that power and influence would be of little value to a kidnapper. His influence and power required him being at his desk, in circulation. He could understand blackmail; with blackmail for something, they could force him to act in some way that pleased them, but a kidnapping simply compromised his ability to do anything.

So perhaps the point was to remove him from his power base, to neutralize him. But why? Nothing among his current projects suggested any reason to take him out of the way. He wasn't an obstacle to anyone.

That left only one realistic possibility—they thought he had some cash value as the object of ransom. But he wasn't an ideal target for that sort of thing. A kidnapper with the resources that this group had would pick a richer target, one with a family who would raise money for his return; Mitch Childer had no family.

So it had to be political.

Thinking about the possibilities made his heart begin to beat erratically. If his disappearance was politically motivated, it had to be non-Western thugs doing it. The IMF was a multinational effort, and he worked for most Western governments, treating them, he thought, with a reasonable equality. They would band together to protest his abduction. That left only one faction—actual Islamic terrorists.

The Islamic group did, he had to admit, have grievances with both the IMF and with him personally. He had helped the Western powers freeze their assets. If that was who they were, then they knew that taking him wouldn't reverse that. So their motive had to be revenge, or perhaps they wanted to send a warning to others who would consider opposing them.

But why now? And why Zurich? The Swiss would not be pleased, and the Islamists enjoyed the freedom of being able to operate in Swiss territory. This could change that. The Swiss government didn't really care for political extremists of any type and abhorred political statements that were violent. This put their status at risk.

Now, sitting alone, sweating, feeling the numbness spread through his body, Mitch Childer discarded all those thoughts. The truth was that he had no idea who was behind this or why he'd be chosen.

Time was confusing in the darkness under the hood, and the aching of his numbing body was the only reference he had to anything at all. Otherwise, he existed in a void. And so, when he heard footsteps coming down a set of stairs, what should have been apprehension was more a sense of relief. The waiting had been intolerable and now at least something was happening.

People, how many he couldn't tell, moved around him making metallic sounds as if they were assembling something. Then he felt heat. He was aware that a bright light had been turned on, and he was more aware of the heat on his skin than the light it gave off. It was focused on him. "A ransom video?" he asked, and he heard his voice croaking. He had gone a long time without speaking, without a drink of water.

Someone grabbed him by the collar and jerked him into an upright position. Blood tried to rush to his hands and feet and he cried out in pain. He was aware of another man standing on the other side of him and that man began to talk, giving a speech in Arabic. Mitch Childer knew no Arabic, but he could tell this was a speech written in anger. The man's hostile, demanding tone of voice throughout the short and intense speech told Childer that his fate was about to be determined.

When the man finished speaking, someone ripped the hood off his head, jerking Mitch's head. He was dazzled by the brilliant light and tried to focus, tried to get his bearings, to see who these people were. The men beside him were masked and wore uniforms that any terrorist would be proud of—with automatic weapons slung over their shoulders, long knives in their belts. Two others, dressed similarly, stood behind them.

As his vision cleared, as the blurred faces sharpened, Mitch Childer's blood turned cold. He saw the cameraman—a Westerner who could've been a businessman dressed in a suit was holding the camera. Behind him was the shock. Another man, also in a suit, stood watching with his hands in his pockets, exuding calmness. He couldn't see that man clearly, but he knew him and was certain that if he was closer he'd be staring into green eyes.

Mitch Childer suddenly knew that this was all theater—a play being acted out for politicians, and for power. Despite the illusions being created, his predicament was real, and if the man behind the cameraman had written the script, there would be no rescue.

The man who made the speech shouted something, and the man holding him up pushed him down to his knees, bending him forward. One of the men handed the speech maker a long sword that shimmered in the light. Seeing him wave the sword, Mitch knew that he was to be the sacrificial goat, or bureaucrat, in this case. The group, his group, the Retinger Oculistica, wanted the world to know for certain that any failure of their new technological efforts had been due to these heathen, savage, throwbacks, not because of incompetence.

Most likely half of these men were on the CIA's payroll, but for the purpose of this enactment, they were masked terrorists. And who would question their identity when they would have Mitch Childer's dead body as evidence that they were sincere in their conviction to the cause? Ironically, the real terrorists would bask in the glow of international condemnation for his murder, for his execution at the hands of his own people.

In terms of the global agenda, much was hanging in the balance. Mitch Childer saw that, for whatever reason, his death had become inevitable; now it was a way of gaining political points. From the point of view of the Oculistica, anything he might contribute to the cause through his work was more than compensated for by the publicity his death would bring and the focus it would give.

Then, with the camera capturing every moment, another man grabbed Mitch Childer's hair, holding his head down facing the ground. The man who made the speech raised the sword over his head. From his submissive posture, Mitch could see the tension in the man's legs as he prepared for the strike, and he felt a sudden, incomprehensible calmness. *"Allah hu Akbar,"* the man cried, and then he brought the blade down on Childer's neck.

For a brief moment, Mitch Childer felt the cool touch of the metal of the sword on the back of his neck. It was eerily peaceful as that cool line seemed to move slowly, spreading around his neck like a necklace. And then, there was an explosion—pain and emotion blurring, and then . . . Then there was nothing at all as his world spun into blackness.

CHAPTER 42
BOONE'S TAKE

"A good traveler has no fixed plans and is not intent on arriving."

—Lao Tzu

Chinatown
Kuala Lumpur, Malaysia

The video camera panned around the chaotic market, taking in the scene around them. Noisy hawkers shouted out the virtues of their wares in Malay, Chinese, and broken English at tourists who stumbled through.

"We are in the night market in the Chinatown district of Kuala Lumpur," Sindi said.

Anchara moved toward the vendors, getting close-ups of some of the stalls, and of Tibetan merchants sitting cross legged in front of silver snuff boxes, stacks of Kris knives with serpentine ridged blades and a richly decorated bone handles, and assorted leather goods.

"This vibrant market is centered around Petaling Street in a district that is also known as Chee Cheong Kai or Starch Factory Street. That's not a particularly sexy name, I know, but it's a reference to the history of the place—it was once known as a tapioca-producing district. Now, Chinatown is largely a tourist destination, but it is also much more. It comes alive after dark when it transforms into a lively and vibrant night market filled with hundreds of stalls offering all kinds of goods at dirt-cheap prices. And if you like to bargain, well these merchants expect you to haggle over the price and will be disappointed if you don't try to talk them down. It's shopping at its best."

As Anchara stepped back for a longer shot, Sindi waved for her to turn it off. "What's wrong," Anchara asked as she lowered the camera and switched it off.

Sindi grinned. "Nothing is wrong. I'm just hungry."

Anchara stuffed the camera in a leather bag that hung over her shoulder. "Seeing as this is a dire emergency . . . about one block back we passed a hot pot vendor whose food smelled pretty great to me."

Sindi winked. "You get sick of the hotel food, don't you, Anchara?"

"Sometimes. Mostly, it's nice to have something to eat that's closer to the kind of thing I grew up eating. You know me."

"Then a hot pot meal it is. As long as they have cold Singha beer."

Anchara laughed. "My guess is they've got a ton of it, and if they don't, well, we can send someone to buy a couple of large bottles for us. The street vendors won't let you suffer a terrible thirst."

"Have you had your ears on?"

Anchara shook her head. "You are the premier techie off the grid. Why do you talk like you just discovered CB radio last week?"

"Because I just heard the song last week."

"The song?"

"'Convoy' by C.W. McCall, good buddy."

"I've never heard of it, and to be honest, I don't think I need to hear that one."

"It's a cultural experience that can be missed without pain. Now tell me the news."

"I've gotten messages from Singapore telling me that Rashmi is settling in fine. She's tackling a big citizenship project that will be used in Ecuador. Wyatt made it to a village in Sulawesi where it seems he's trying to figure out what he wants to do next—he'll outgrow that place fast, but that's okay. Interpol took them both off their bad guy list, so although he'll want to keep a low profile in case whoever got Peggy Dory is still hunting, he should be good."

"We don't know who did that?"

"Best guess is that the Oculistica were behind it. They have that kind of reach."

"What are they saying about the beheading of the IMF idiot?"

"The gruesome video of him being killed has been popping up all over the place. A couple of different terrorist groups are saying

they did it to show the world what happens when you force governments to eliminate subsidies for their people. That narrows the list
to about five countries that Childer was forcing to eliminate subsidies in return for promises of dubious financial assistance. Given
that he had that many enemies, the terrorists' claims might even
be true."

"And Tanzania is saying that his death had nothing to do with his
work there?"

"That's their story. Even though the terrorists are convincing, I
don't buy the timing. It's suspicious. And I feel bad for that poor guy
getting his head cut off."

"Yeah, but is getting shot or blown up any better?"

"The thing is Childer was a big wheel on their cart, so his death
is our gain, right?"

"According to what Rashmi said, he wasn't really that important.
He was trying to make a name for himself with the project, but he was
hardly hands on. As with many of that sort, he was more of a schemer
than a doer. With him gone, the group will just reorganize."

"Reorganize the IMF?"

"I was thinking of the Retinger Oculistica itself, actually. The
IMF will just bump a bureaucrat up the food chain. But the Oculistica
got their fingers burned by letting the IMF be front and center. They
won't want to play that angle a second time. It was a screwy operation
at best—poorly thought out."

"What should we be looking for? In terms of their reorganization,
I mean?"

"Put out the word to keep tabs on Claude Hoenig. He's the wild card
here. He's got the code and the expertise to move the project forward.
I'll want to know who he hires, where he goes. And he'll be going a lot
of places. He's going to be the centerpiece of their new efforts."

"How so?"

"I think he's just coming into his own. He wanted in the crypto
game and now he's in it big time. He likes being a player, being in the
know, and in this world, that's the way to do it. Now he can replace
Childer. Hoenig might even have been responsible for his death—he
has the resources and isn't squeamish about killing people."

At the hot pot restaurant, rickety round tables were scattered over the sidewalk with plastic chairs around them. They sat down. "It does smell good," Sindi said.

"We can do a video of this place, one of your surprises—Sindi slumming."

"You know, that sounds like a brilliant idea. Contrast the service, the ambiance, and the food with that at the hotel. That would be great fun."

"Without alienating the hotel, please," Anchara said. "Don't make my job harder."

"Spoilsport."

An ancient Chinese woman came over to the table and turned the fire on under their hot pot to heat the water. They ordered large bottles of beer and drank it gratefully as the woman made trips to the kitchen, bringing out colored plastic plates piled high with fresh vegetables, shrimp, meat strips, and tofu. A younger woman brought them small saucers of sauces and two bowls of sticky white rice. When the water was hot, they used their chopsticks to put food in the water, taking it out, dunking it in the sauces, and eating it with rice.

"This is good," Sindi said. "Simple, but fresh and good. A lot of restaurants could learn from this place."

"Damn. I wish I'd had the camera going for that little speech," Anchara said. It would make a good quick take or a wrap up for the night market."

Sindi grinned. "Well, if it means that much to you, I wouldn't mind repeating myself . . . for posterity."

"You are a blatant attention seeker."

"Yes, but that's just my overcompensating for being an unknown underground hero," she laughed.

"Speaking of that, I want you to know that it pisses me off to be the one who keeps waking Boone up on a lovely warm night like this."

"You don't want Boone to enjoy it?"

"Not when I'm enjoying Sindi's company so much . . ."

"You have always liked Sindi best."

"What's our goal now? That of the bitpats, I mean. This little exercise clearly shows that national governments intend to create centralized cryptos and preempt distributed networks. How do you steal their thunder?"

"Ironically, wanting the national currencies to fail puts us on the same side as the damn globalists. They want to replace them with a global, centralized monetary system that they control, whether it's through cryptocurrency or something else, and we don't want that at all."

"So what can you do to keep a global cryptocurrency from getting traction? I mean, if it's going to be centralized, clearly a global system is better than a hodgepodge of local ones. I mean, it's true even of fiat currencies. The Euro worked better than national currencies and that sets the tone for public opinion."

"Maybe we can't stop it. But we can push to get people using decentralized networks for those things. If we can make inroads into getting acceptance of smart contracts, for instance, we show that a centralized trust agent is unnecessary. I think that success, proving the usefulness of blockchain as it was intended, is the best weapon we have. The more people accept and use decentralized networks and avoid banks and governments, the harder it will be for the institutions to suck them back into centralized systems. They know that too, and that's why we are at war."

"And that's all we can do?"

"Hey, freedom is a seductive force. We have to keep reminding people of the situations that take freedom away, and how they are compromising their freedom by using those trust systems. Then we show them that centralization is less efficient and not as safe."

"And you think that's enough?"

"Well, we have to overcome a long history of people relying on government regulations to protect them, so that's a problem. Also, you can't force people to want or even value freedom, Anchara. Your appreciation of freedom was learned the hard way. Now you will fight tooth and nail to keep it. Some people think a compromise is possible. Or they think it's a choice between freedom and security."

"They are wrong."

"And that's why we run bitpats. That's why we help create new systems. This isn't just a collection of people who like each other. Through our efforts, we want to make it clear that you can't compromise with tyranny and show that it isn't even necessary. And, while we are at it, we try to provide options for fighting back, or at least so people can stand their ground."

"And yet, some think that governments will protect them, that it needs to reduce or even eliminate individual privacy to do that."

"They do, but then people think all sorts of things. We aren't a cult and we don't focus on what people ought to do. We are paying more attention to things we can do, practical things. We have to accept the sad reality that you can't do much to set people free if they've been taught to embrace their slavery. As long as they are willing to abdicate decision making to entities they think are superior to themselves, then they will fight to keep their shackles on—they make them feel safe. No, for those people all we can do is set an example. We resist the tyranny of a smothering government and lend assistance to those who think their privacy is something to cherish."

"Cherish is a powerful word, lady."

"Privacy and freedom are powerful subjects, worthy of strong words and strong attachments."

"You do know that you're an idealist, right?"

"Me, Boone, or me, Sindi?"

"Both or one or the other, depending on what the topic is."

"Then probably I'm guilty as charged."

"Good. I like idealists." Anchara grinned. "I will confess that I enjoy Sindi's optimism about the likelihood of a good meal more than Boone's about the future of the world."

"It's easier to enjoy . . . I admit that. But no one said it would be easy, Anchara. I know I've never said that."

"No, you've never said it was easy."

"So, instead of making it easy, I try to make it fun."

"Make defiance fun," Anchara said, turning the words over. "Now there's a motto I can go for."

"And now, as the world as we know it can't be saved, at least not entirely, over this meal, why don't you get out the camera and I'll wax enthusiastic over KL hot pot meals."

"And cold Singha beer," Anchara said. "Never forget the beer."

Sindi grinned. "You know me better than that. I'd never forget the beer."

"No, you wouldn't."

CHAPTER 43

SOLUTIONS

"Power, like a desolating pestilence,
Pollutes whate'er it touches."

—PERCY BYSSHE SHELLEY
"QUEEN MAB"

A PRIVATE VILLA
PRASLIN ISLAND
THE REPUBLIC OF THE SEYCHELLES

"So tell me what we have learned from all of this," the old man said. He addressed the group somberly. "After this fiasco, how should we proceed and why will our efforts be more effective this time? These are my questions." He sat back, folded his hands on the table, and waited.

He was in his customary place, the head of the table, and somehow the man managed to make Claude Hoenig feel like he was singling him out with his gaze, even though he was actually looking at each one of them in turn.

The green-eyed man stood up. "The main thing we learned is what we should've known all along. Having the IMF run the project gave it the wrong focus. It looked like interference from the beginning. It's fine to have the international agencies supporting such a project, but it should look as if it is totally the brainchild of the government . . ." he nodded toward Hoenig, "working in concert with their contractors."

He noticed a scowl on the face of a tall, dark-haired woman. "I'm still not clear on why you staged such a theatrical death for poor Mitch Childer. Of course, he had to go, he fucked up horribly and put our goals at risk, but why not a suicide or something that wouldn't attract so much media attention?"

The green-eyed man considered the question. "There are already suicides associated with the project—the deputy finance minister did himself in. And then the project head was found murdered, or perhaps it was a suicide under suspicious circumstances in Bogota."

"Cartagena," the woman said.

"Yes, Cartagena. We want this to die down; we don't want a death that would be entangled with others. Because we had the resources, it seemed reasonable to have a terrorist group who kidnapped and beheaded Childer for the crime of being with the IMF and interfering with local governments. The group operates in several countries where the IMF has managed to make things worse for the people, and they've executed other bureaucrats to make their point. As it happens, they were delighted to accept the credit for his assassination even though they had nothing to do with it. This way, his death coincides with the end of the project but seems unrelated, especially since it took place in another country."

"The idea, then," the woman said, "is that any news about the Tanzanian system, other than it struggled and now works fine, should be low key and something that fades."

"Which is why," the green-eyed man said, "we've had Interpol withdraw the warrants for the two missing programmers."

"But don't they know too much?"

"Not really. Neither of them seems interested in telling the story. If they turn up and make a fuss, we can deal with that—I will deal with it quietly. Chasing them publicly keeps the story alive and will make people ask what they might have done. We are, after all, claiming that no crimes were committed, that all went reasonably according to plan."

The old man coughed. "Well, whatever the reasons you have, we are on this course now and I'm satisfied. It seems a reasonable path to take. I'm all for keeping attention elsewhere as much as possible. That brings me to my second question: How do we proceed? Are we well positioned to continue, or do we need a new tactic?"

"We are very well positioned, sir. In the aftermath, Mr. Hoenig's firm has been hired to create similar systems for a number of countries.

He's had a chance to review all of the features that Childer was trying, crudely, to implement and had his people make them integral to the system. There won't be any patchwork fixes this time. The system will be a known entity."

"That will be a nice change," the dark-haired woman said. "What about moving forward? We help these countries implement their cryptocurrencies, but ultimately, that isn't what we want."

The green eyes turned on him, and the man nodded. "Following the instructions I was given, my programmers have already incorporated the idea of a universal basic income, a UBI, into the system."

"But will the countries go for it? They've always resisted."

"Things change; positions change. But we've made provisions for it and have begun discussing the idea with the various finance ministers. Naturally, a universal income of any kind is something that will require broad governmental support. Truthfully, many governments are opposed to the idea for a variety of reasons ranging from the pragmatic, such as cost, to a more philosophical one."

"And so?"

"We've made some inroads by pointing out some benefits of the idea to them—contemporary thoughts that haven't been intuitively obvious."

The old man coughed again. "What benefits? We want a global UBI so we can control the populace. How does that help them?"

"Controlling their own people is one of the benefits they can relate to. They've slowly come to see how a universal basic income ties the entire population into their policy decisions. People will tolerate a great deal from whoever generates their income. Furthermore, a UBI almost guarantees the immediate acceptance of their national cryptocurrency. How can it fail if everyone is paid in it and can use it to pay their taxes and make in-country purchases? And, as a follow-on, we've even addressed the idea of an intermediate token."

"What's that?" the old man asked. "Another complication?"

"This token represents the beginning of the end of national cryptocurrencies," the green-eyed man said. "The intermediate token would make the individual national cryptocurrencies we create interchangeable without the regulatory problems of exchanges to do the job. With it all under government control, the people will be able to spend their local crypto to make purchases in another country in the program without having to go through an exchange. Similarly, the IMF and World Bank can buy intermediate tokens to deposit the money being loaned to a country directly into a national bank."

"And why do we want that?" the woman asked. Claude Hoenig was impressed by the focus of all these people. Mitch Childer seemed composed, but clearly he was way out of his league.

"Will you explain, Mr. Hoenig?"

Claude cleared his throat. "When we demonstrate the effectiveness of this international financial coordination, other countries will want to follow suit. Quickly, the intermediate tokens will become the dominant means of foreign exchange, making it the de facto international currency. Sooner or later, we will convince a government to simply adopt these tokens in place of the costly effort to introduce a new national currency and, ultimately, it will become a world currency."

"A major step toward global control," the old man said brightly.

"What we've sought from the beginning," the woman said.

Hoenig was caught up in their excitement. "Yes, and we can make it available to people worldwide, whether their governments want to cooperate or not. We will offer incentives to use the tokens that will make them irresistible. And when we have enough momentum, you can implement the universal basic income and no one will be left outside the system."

The green-eyed man sat down. "With people everywhere signing up to use the system, giving us all their personal information, we will create the universal database we need in order to track everyone. Even if people want to resist, if they don't want us collecting the data, they'll still give it to us because they will be outside the system otherwise, and our system won't just be financial, it will include messaging, social media, and all communications. Without using our system voluntarily, buying into it by giving us access to everything, they won't be able to buy things, to create smart contracts, which will supplant other types entirely."

"Why will that happen?" the old man asked. "The regular contracts work just fine."

"Evolution," the woman said. "They are talking about technical Darwinism. The efficient will drive out the inefficient. And smart contracts eliminate arbitration."

"Actually, arbitration is built in," Claude said.

"Yes, I see what you mean," she said. "The point, my point, being that arbitration is an inherent part of the contract, not an added step. Disputes become a thing of the past."

"Along with national currencies of any type," the old man said, rubbing his hands together. "And your approach will make this happen?"

The green-eyed man nodded. "It will. As the Tanzanian government said, their cryptocurrency shrugged. It couldn't carry the weight demanded of it. When we choose for it to happen, they will all shrug."

"Delightful."

"And no one will care. Our new approach, presenting it this way, will make governments, organizations, and the people beg for a switch to an international cryptocurrency, and we will be there to make it happen. Once it begins, any residual desire to preserve national currencies, or even any enthusiasm for national governments at all, will fade quickly. Soon enough, it will be clear that national laws on trade or finance are obstacles to people getting what they want. They are worse than redundant; they are holding the world back."

"So we simply demonstrate our alternative vision?" the woman asked.

The green-eyed man smiled. "And then we have to be patient for a time. Some, the diehards, the sentimentally patriotic, will need to suffer through attempts to keep nations alive and relevant."

"An effort doomed to fail," the woman said.

"And we will be there, ready to help them make the transition from a failed nation state to a prosperous part of a global future."

Hoenig felt their contentment. They were, after all, visionaries, and they had good reason to believe their vision was coming true in the near future. Such visions, in his experience, seldom played out as intended, and he wondered if these powerful people truly shared the same vision or if there were differences that would undermine the effort.

Whatever the case, however, that played out, he knew that change was happening. Change was the new norm and resisting it was fatal. No, just as he had in the days of the spy games, he would move with the changes, try to anticipate the flow, because this was the game. And just as in the days when he was a covert agent for his government, the stakes were life and death.

"I suppose," the old man said, "that this token, our global cryptocurrency, will have to have some sort of cute name. They all seem to."

The green-eyed man put his hands on the table. "Well, an appropriate name, at least. It's up to this group, of course, but given the history of our project, we were thinking about Phoenixcoin."

That was the moment that Hoenig saw them all smile at once. "Yes, it's time for the Phoenix to rise again," the old man said. "Well done." A thin smile crossed his face. "I think it's the perfect time for the world to see the Phoenix again."

There was a satisfaction in the man's voice that Claude Hoenig found oddly troubling, but then much about the Retinger Oculistica was troubling if he thought too much about them.

It would be an interesting ride to see where aligning himself with these people took him. Interesting for him and for the world.

EPILOGUE

A BUNGALOW
ON STILTS OVER THE WATER
TUMBAK, SULAWESI

It wouldn't have been reasonable to say that Sulawesi was everything Wyatt had hoped it would be, but it was beginning to look like it was everything he wanted for the moment. He'd needed to escape to the middle of nowhere and this village of Tumbak, on the northern coast of Sulawesi, seemed to fit the bill. It was greener than his Mexican paradise had been. It still had beaches and clear water, but they tended to be small places that were quiet, rather than large expanses of white beach.

The village was a Bajo village. The Bajos were the sea gypsies of east Indonesia. He smiled. It seemed a good fit for he was a bitpat, and they were boatpats. Each, in their own way, lived as free as life allows.

Much of the village was built out over the water, and he rented a small cottage on stilts that had a boat dock and a lovely porch with a view of the lagoon. It came with a big, soft hammock. With the installation of a satellite dish, he had adequate Internet access to do his work. In short, he had what he'd asked for, so when Boone asked him to do a few things, he was happy to oblige. He couldn't refuse her after all she had done for him and Rashmi.

And Rashmi, it seemed, had successfully disappeared as well, only she'd been absorbed into the bitpat community. He caught cyber glimpses of her from time to time and she sent an encrypted message telling him that she adored Singapore and the work she was doing. She was meeting people and coming alive.

That pleased him. His only discontent was feeling alone and he considered relocating to some more populated place. Part of him was jealous of Rashmi in Singapore. But he'd made his choice, and the truth was that the villagers were pleasant and welcoming, and from time to time he saw lovely dark-skinned women, who seemed shyer than those he'd met in Progresso, and perhaps more intriguing because of it. That held promise. He had to learn the customs and the language before he could expect much to happen.

The village chief became a regular visitor and began teaching Wyatt Bahasa Indonesia, the local language.

"*Selamat siang,*" the chief said as he arrived. That was the way you said good morning when it was later in the morning. "We go beach?"

Wyatt smiled and turned off his computer. "Yes," he said and then added, "*Ya,*" trying to practice his Indonesian. Going to the beach seemed like an excellent idea.

The chief led the way out onto the dock where a longish boat waited. It was filled with a cooler of beer, an assortment of food, and several villagers. It looked like they had a party in mind. A couple of the girls gave him quick looks of curiosity and that encouraged him.

The chief motored the boat along the coast. Most of the best beaches were remote and this one turned out to be rather special. Wyatt jumped out in shallow water and helped pull the boat onto the sand. They unloaded it and several women started setting out the food while some men dug a pit and started a fire.

The entire thing was a lot more than he'd expected. Instead of a picnic, they intended to have a small feast.

Other boats arrived with more food and more people. Two men sat on mats in the shade of trees above the waterline and began drumming. Everyone was having a grand time, and Wyatt drank beer and did his best to join in the festivities.

He felt a little out of place, awkward. That might change over time, but it made him restless.

At sunset, the food was served and he ate roast pig and some vegetables he couldn't name, washing it down with beer.

Then things were loaded into the boats and they headed back to the village.

Wyatt sat in the evening shadows, acutely aware of the young women in his boat sitting near him. He was unsure of himself. He was living in a new culture and it had its own rules and protocols. He was torn between being forward and left behind. He had no way to know what reasonable behavior was, and while he didn't mind being a little unreasonable at times, it was a small village and he didn't want to upset his hosts.

So, he sat and ached to touch one of the lovely young women. When the chief finally dropped him off on his own dock, Wyatt was disappointed and relieved at the same time. He was also lonely, achingly so.

He walked down the dock toward his porch. Someone was there. The air was still but the hammock rocked. A light shone from inside his cottage, casting shadows. He moved cautiously forward. "Hello?" he called.

The hammock moved again. "Hey, sailor, new in town?" It was Rebecca, lying in the hammock. The wistful light shining out onto the porch bathed her in yellow, and he stared at her; he saw that she was deliciously naked. She smiled at him and gave him a welcoming smile, then held up a bottle of Jameson's. "I come bearing gifts," she said.

"You are a gift," he said, running his eyes over her luscious curves.

"Oh no," she laughed. "I'm no gift, ever, Wyatt. You have to earn me. Again and again."

"If you hang around, then I'll do my best," he said, tearing off his own clothes and walking toward her.

"You were the one who left the last time," she said. "And I understand why. One or the other of us might need to leave from time to time, but as long as what we have is earned, we will always return to each other."

As he moved closer, he realized that he knew what she meant. They owed each other nothing, and they had the opportunity to give each other everything. He took her in his arms, relishing her warmth. He wanted her. He would make love to her and they'd share a great passion. Then, later she'd tell him why she had come. Then they would make decisions about what happened next, for the future was simply constructed out of a series of decisions. You tried to make the best ones you could and hoped that led to another good decision.

But there were no guarantees. He knew her coming here would only partly be because of an attraction for him as a man. Part of it would be because of the rest of who he was and what he had to offer her. Some of that would be personal and some would be work; although for people like them, those things blurred together.

Like him, Rebecca was serious about the work she did. Currently, she worked with Boone and, he supposed, with Rashmi. She wanted to transform the world, make it freer. It was a worthwhile cause.

She'd expect him to get involved in that effort, to commit to being a bitpat. And now he knew that he'd happily join in. He needed an outlet for his anti authoritarian creativity and he shared their values.

Where that would lead them was unknown—it was the beginning of their adventure. They might be able to accomplish a great deal from this little cottage for a time, but at some point, they might need to go somewhere else. Whatever it was, he knew he'd want to do it—with her, it would be exciting. And hell, they were bitpats after all. They were nomads, like the Bajo, but instead of nautical nomads, they were Internet nomads. And they were crusaders too, in their own way. In Tanzania, Wyatt learned that you needed to take up the fight or the people who wanted to steal your individuality, your privacy, would sweep it away. It took a special group to see that and to do something effective to stop it.

Now, as he held Rebecca in his arms, felt her warm body against his, her warm lips on his, he was glad, delighted, that besides being the resistance, they were also hedonists. The combination made the struggle worthwhile.

"I am an outlaw, you know," he told her. "A wanted man. I'm stuck hiding here. That isn't much of a future."

"Not anymore," she said. "They called off the dogs."

"Why?"

She shrugged. "Remember I told you that they don't want the world to know that good, capable people are refusing to play. They certainly don't want the public at large to think we are forming a resistance. Especially if there is a glimmer of truth in it. So they are pretending that it was all a mistake. The system works and all is forgiven.

Officially, that is. I wouldn't drop in at the Ministry of Finance in Dar es Salaam anytime soon for a friendly chat if I were you."

"Damn," he said.

"That upsets you? You're free."

"And while that is a good thing, it means that I've lost my bad boy cachet."

She bit his earlobe. "Then you'll just have to make the effort to show me what a bad boy you can be."

Wyatt felt a tingle and he knew he would do his best.

THE END

A BITPAT'S MANIFESTO

As technology frees people from the drudgery of manual labor, it also hems them in—tying them to a specific identity defined by biometric data, by documentation that is promoted as a way to provide security and protect our freedoms. This is a deliberate deception. The "freedom" the government protects is the freedom to carefully monitor our lives. We are not free, but living at the end of a tether.

Freedom of expression, for instance, is restricted to types of expression that are considered responsible discourse. For our protection, even telling the wrong joke in an airport becomes a federal crime. Advocating an insurrection, the expression of an idea, would be a federal crime. Freedom and secrecy are incompatible, and a free society has no secret acts that can be violated. (Privacy, however, is another thing and it is rooted in individual rights.)

A world of secrecy and monitored behavior is not free. To call it freedom is an Orwellian newspeak version of the idea—the term is co-opted and redefined to describe a life that is not free at all. In the newspeak world, you are free to be a good citizen, free to behave. Although in the US, if you cross the lines set by Homeland Security, even being a good citizen doesn't protect you from having all your rights, including that of what passes for a fair trial, from being suspended.

In the process of implementing such draconian measures, individuals become hobbled by the need for licenses, passports, visas, permits, and other documentation that assists the monitoring. Filling out the forms, collecting these (necessary) documents, moves along the path of labelling each individual without any regard for who and what they are.

The trend is intensifying. In the name of protecting the common good, governments and their agents use the newest technology, follow the digital breadcrumbs it leaves, to watch and control the populace. It's to protect them—often from themselves. But where does it stop? Clearly, the ultimate goal, in the words of songwriter Phil Ochs, is to "put the people in concentration camps; make damn sure they're free."

These modern, high-tech concentration camps are often not physical or even tangible. They are created with the barbed wire of "Know Your Customer" (KYC) and anti-money laundering regulations and are driven by an intense concern to know who goes where and what they do. Some of these things evolve out of controls to prevent illegal immigration and overstaying. Some evolve out of concerns about terrorism, but they are all controls and ultimately they create physical barriers.

The move to protect freedom by diminishing it serves to erode privacy. When everything is public, nothing is personal. When all data is collected, then society begins to see that data as communal property, which can be freely used to expose, exploit, and otherwise control the people who are not interested in controlling others.

There is a group that detests and resists this trend. They are called bitpats. Bitpats are, largely, technologists, or at least people who are not opposed to technology, but they do oppose it being used as a tool of oppression. Bitpats love freedom and they are patriots, in the sense that they have an allegiance to freedom.

Expats choose, or are forced, to live outside their home country. Bitpats see the world as their country. They see their allegiance to freedom as more significant than allegiance to some nation state.

Essentially, bitpats are a dangerous breed. They are free thinkers—interested in the free and unfettered exchange of ideas, of exploring knowledge and understanding what is possible to understand without any prospect of being persecuted for their exploration.

Government secrecy is the enemy of free thought or the free exploration of ideas. That government fears that the dissemination of knowledge is clearly evidenced by the growing numbers of classified documents unavailable to the unanointed. When "traitors" like

Edward Snowden manage to release secret documents to the public, the results tend to be embarrassing to the government and anticlimactic for the rest of us. Largely, the documents prove what we suspect, that the classified, top secret information is primarily concerned with the fact that the government spies on people, including its own citizens.

The passion for secrecy is dangerous for inquisitive minds. Classifying information does not make it inaccessible, but, in an Internet age, digging for the truth leaves a trail that can be interpreted and spun as being treasonous, as if knowing things that are true could ever amount to treason in an age of reason.

Moving the search to a dark web, like fleeing the scene of a crime, is viewed as an admission of some nebulous guilt, or the desire to "hide" something. And dark places are always, eventually, brought into the light. Such efforts at concealment frighten the powers that be. This is so wrong. A desire to hide something—to keep private things private, secrets secret, does not necessarily serve some evil or nefarious scheme, unless, of course, a desire to be a free individual is considered evil or nefarious. Often, as not, attempts to secure one's privacy are simply because it is no one else's business—a right, unfortunately, not secured adequately by any constitution or human rights efforts.

And there is the nub of the problem, the reason that bitpats exist. They reject the notion that information about their lives and thoughts is public property. For the most part, bitpats reject the notion that public property is a good thing in the first place, given that anyone desiring freedom is at the base, a libertarian, if not an anarchist.

In joining together, bitpats can pool their resources to resist the tightening yoke of control. Working together voluntarily masks the contribution of one individual and allows the group to maximize its talents.

Despite the benign intention of bitpats to achieve liberty and freedom (and make no mistake—they are radicals, revolutionaries), they aren't a threat to anything but secrecy and oppression. Their resistance is not violent, but neither is it passive, for bitpats are, by their nature, disruptors. They employ the disruptive nature of technology; they exploit its strengths and weakness to buttress their fortresses. And, thus, they threaten the goals of the intelligence agencies and police forces worldwide.

Bitpats are the very embodiment of the term apolitical. They will not take up arms or demonstrate against governments while making pointless political statements. Instead, they spread across the face of the planet, finding an environment that suits them, and work together using technology to protect themselves. They have no particular meetings, no dues, no secret handshake. Their contributions to any resistance are totally voluntary and welcomed.

As such, they are a threat to a world order that no longer values freedom, but they are a blessing to any world order that sees it as a natural right.

—Boone
www.bitpats.com
Boone@bitpats.com

ACKNOWLEDGMENTS

The authors would like to thank Don and Lynne Gallian, BlueRidge, Gigi Porter and Dagny Sellorin for their help and encouragement as we wrote and produced this book.

ABOUT THE AUTHORS

J. LEE PORTER

J. Lee Porter is a former IT specialist, programmer, and data analyst for banking, security, and government agencies. He left the IT world behind on July 4, 2016, declaring it his personal independence day to travel the world full time in search of inspiration for his writing.

ED TEJA

Ed Teja is a writer, poet, musician, and boat bum. He writes about the places he knows and the people who live in the margins of the world. After being friends with tech giants, pirates, fishermen, and a coterie of strange people for many years, he finds the world an amazing place filled with intriguing, if sometimes crazed, characters.